Stiletto
SISTERHOOD

FALLON DEMORNAY

w by wattpad books

W by **wattpad** books

An imprint of Wattpad WEBTOON Book Group

Published in Canada by Wattpad Books,
a division of Wattpad Corp.
36 Wellington Street E., Toronto, ON M5E 1C7

www.wattpad.com

First W by Wattpad Books edition: April 2022

ISBN 978-1-98936-599-1 (Trade Paper original)
ISBN 978-1-77729-000-9 (eBook edition)

Library and Archives Canada Cataloguing in Publication
information is available upon request.

Printed and bound in Canada
1 3 5 7 9 10 8 6 4 2

Cover design and illustration by Elliot Caroll

To all of my devoted readers on Wattpad:
I hope this inspires you to always chase your dreams and to
embrace your Sisterhood.

Chapter One

Priyanka Seth was always a girl with a plan, and arriving hungover for a life-changing interview—*sans panties!*—was not part of it. Jumping into the backseat of a cab already loitering at the curb, Priya slapped a hand on the Plexiglas divider. "I need to get to Sutton Place then straight back to East Fifty-Third and Park before eight."

The driver lifted heavy-lidded eyes from his phone screen to meet hers in the rearview mirror. "You got a pair of wings in that purse?"

Opening her clutch, Priya frantically dug inside. "I have . . . seventy-seven dollars with your name on it if you can figure it out." She handed over the wad of mixed bills and the cab roared like a waking panther and charged—slamming Priya into her seat with an *oof*. While the car tore down the street, she unlocked her phone and scrolled through her contacts for the one person who could save her in her hour of need.

The line rang twice before Caitlin's bleary face filled the screen, all rumpled violet hair and sleepy dark eyes. "For the love of *Vogue—what!*"

"Cait! Oh thank *God*! Get up, get up right now. I'm on my way to your place. Meet me outside in ten minutes. It's an emergency. A Stiletto Sisterhood Code Red Emergency." If citing their code like a preacher would a passage from the Bible made her a touch melodramatic, so be it. Her life was on the line.

"Wait, slow down. I can't follow *stupidity* this early without coffee." Caitlin vanished in a flash of bedding and the creak of floorboards. "Where's the fire?"

"I'll explain when I see you, but I'm pulling a walk of shame to a last-minute interview, and I need to borrow a suit."

Caitlin's face smushed close to the screen. "You realize there's a height disparity between us? Like six inches? I'm good, but I'm not a wizard."

"No, you're Caitlin Choi-Emerson. Fashion guru. Savant of suits." As a self-taught stylist, Caitlin's brand was menswear made boldly female—with lush fabrics, daring cuts, and all the accessories. "If anyone can save me from this seventh circle of hell, it's you."

"Ah, flattery," she purred. "Well played. I'll see what I can dig up."

"Thank you. And Cait," Priya added with a panicked jolt before disconnecting, "something basic, okay?"

"Boo." Caitlin sighed. "See you in ten."

As the cab sped down the Upper East Side streets, mercifully empty on a Sunday morning, Priya combed through her purse for any other clues to fill in the missing gaps of last night's hazy memory. There was a receipt from the bar for almost three hundred—*holy fuzzknuckles!*—dollars, some spare change, and her lipstick cap but no lipstick. Of course it had to be her favorite *discontinued* shade.

No random numbers or drunken texts appeared on her

phone, and by some miracle, all social media came up clear of damaging posts, but in her gallery there was a *video* . . . and given the thumbnail, it was absolutely NSFW.

Priya hugged the phone to her chest and closed her eyes with a fervent prayer before lowering the volume and hitting Play. Her voice slid out first. All heavy panting and hot gasps. The answering accompaniment of a man's laugh was smooth and wicked as he whispered something that got swallowed up in the start of a killer orgasm and ended abruptly with a partial view of his face. Vague and blurry as her memory, but it stirred a fleeting recollection of quick hands, a hot mouth. And something about an elevator . . .

True to her word, Caitlin stood waiting on the curb, dressed in yellow sweats, orange heels, and oversized sunglasses, a white garment bag hung over one arm.

Priya pushed open the passenger door and Caitlin slid in, draping the garment bag between them. "As requested."

"I could kiss you." Priya drew down the zipper and her joyful smile vanished with a horrified gasp. "It's *teal*."

"And?"

"I said *basic*."

"It's a solid." Caitlin dipped her chin, sunglasses sliding to the tip of her pixie nose. "No pattern. No texture. No *fun*. Basic."

"Didn't you have anything in black?" Priya sputtered as the cab pushed back onto the street, careening toward her certain demise. "Or navy? Charcoal?"

"What makes you think any of those exist in my wardrobe?"

"Oh my God."

"It's June, Priya, and with your complexion? This color is confident. Striking. This commands attention."

"Cait, this isn't a fashion editorial spread. It's an interview." Head in her hands, Priya groaned. "You had one job. One!"

"Okey dokey." Shrugging, Caitlin reached for the zipper. "Then don't wear it."

"No! Give me the pants . . . I'll make do."

Caitlin removed the trousers from the garment bag and handed them over. "Are you going to tell me what this is all about?"

Kicking off her heels, Priya slipped her feet into the pant legs and delicately shimmied the trousers on, careful to keep her skirt over top. "I went to the soft opening of that new Manhattan bar everyone's talking about. The one owned by that hot artist from Toronto."

"Pathos?"

"Yeah."

"Bitch!" Caitlin tossed Priya a glare sharp enough to kill a man at three paces. "We were supposed to go together when they officially open next month."

"Yeah, well, I'm sorry, but I got an invite from that guy from Stikemans I went to dinner with last week."

"Greg?"

"No, Matthew."

"Whatever. Stop talking before I shove you out of this cab."

"We'll go there for their brunch event—all-you-can-drink mimosas. My treat, okay?"

Caitlin's scowl softened. Marginally. "Fine."

"Anyway. After inhaling enough tequila to flatline a frat boy, I got an email notifying me that my Monday morning interview was being shifted to Sunday at eight."

"Who sends out emails after midnight? Or requests an interview on a Sunday morning?"

"I'd call her Satan, but that somehow makes her more perfect." Sucking in a breath, Priya grunted. "Oh *no*. I can't fasten the zipper."

"I tried to warn you."

Twisting in the seat, Priya stretched out as flat as she could manage across Caitlin's lap, but there was nothing. Not even the barest ounce of give. "Why do these pants have no stretch?"

"This isn't off the rack, Priya." Caitlin leveled a baleful glare. "Lycra is tacky, and everything I own is tailored to *me*, therefore I don't need stretch."

Priya whimpered at the memory of her custom suit, the one that cost an obscene amount of money, pressed and waiting in her mom's apartment clear across town. "What am I going to do?"

"Reschedule?"

"This is Marai Nagao. Her calendar is always packed weeks—months out, even. I can't miss this interview." Especially not when there was a yearlong mentorship on the table. Some of New York's most successful lawyers and judges had been molded like raw clay by her hands. All kinds of doors blown open. "Might as well kiss my entire future good-bye."

Priya had already gone through three separate interview stages just to get this far. First with HR and then two more with senior partners. Nothing—nothing—was going to derail Priya from this moment. Not a brutal hangover or lost panties.

Shucking off the trousers, Priya folded them across her lap. "This is a disaster."

"We can salvage this." Caitlin spun a finger at Priya, taking in the train-wreck ensemble with a narrowed gaze. "The skirt's vintage Valentino, yes?"

A smile pushed at the corners of Priya's lips. Trust Caitlin to sniff out a label. "Yes."

"Classic A-line. Tasteful. Not a deal breaker for an interview of this magnitude." With a giddy wiggle of her shoulders, Caitlin plucked the jacket out of the garment bag and shoved it at her. "Put this on. It was meant to be a bit oversized, so it should fit."

Priya slid on the jacket—definitely a size too big—while Caitlin attacked her mane of thick black hair, twisting it up into a tight chignon, somehow taming it into submission with bobby pins and ChapStick, then added a silk scarf tied in a loose knot around Priya's neck for a final flourish.

"*Et voilà!*"

Priya frowned despondently at the picture Caitlin snapped on her phone. "I look like a hungover stewardess for a cheap airline."

"Do not insult my masterpiece." She chef-kissed her fingers. "I call it Tequila-Hoe-Chic."

"Hilarious."

"I thought so."

Priya removed the scarf and handed it back to Caitlin. "Less is more, right?"

"In the words of the great Coco Chanel, absolutely. You could use a bit of mascara to brighten those bloodshot eyes, though."

"Fresh out."

"Lipstick?"

"Lost it along with my panties, apparently."

"I'm sorry." Caitlin pushed her face so close to Priya's that she was all eyes and nose. "Repeat that for me but slower."

Priya hung her head. "I lost my panties in some guy's Fifth Avenue apartment."

Caitlin sputtered, blinked, and then doubled over in rib-cracking hysterics. "Stop," she cackled in a rasp that pushed well beyond laughter into out of breath. "Oh, it hurts. It hurts. I can't!"

Priya tucked her tongue into the pocket of her cheek. "Are you finished?"

"Almost." She straightened, eyes glistening with tears. "Oh wow. That's my workout for the week. Did you at least search the place before jumping into the cab?"

"Of course!" After tumbling ass-first out of bed when the alarm went off, Priya had hunted for her clothes like a deranged maniac, starting with the pale-pink pleated skirt by the foot of the bed and black Louboutin heels near the door with her purse on top and all her remaining cash, cards, and ID tucked inside. Everything was accounted for, except her underwear. Hot-pink lace—hard to miss and even harder to lose. Yet she had done just that.

And now she was minutes away from sitting down in front of her literal idol, bare-assed with tequila fumes wafting from her pores like expired perfume.

"It was a studio. Not like there were many places they could've gone. He—whoever I hooked up with last night— must've taken them."

"Ew." Caitlin's nose scrunched with a scowl. "He's a panty thief?"

"Apparently. But he had the decency to pay for a loaded breakfast before ghosting me while I drooled into the pillow." Not that she'd had time for anything more than finger-brushing her teeth. She'd snatched a pancake on the way out and inhaled it in the elevator, nearly choking on the damn thing. "I don't remember his name, and I'd barely even know what he looked like if it wasn't for the video."

"Stop." Caitlin flagged a hand like an officer halting traffic. Or a criminal. "First, you need to lay off the shots—think of the brain cells. Second, you own those pants now." She nodded toward Priya's lap. "Third, you have a *video*, and you're only just telling me *now*?" Her chin lowered to match her hushed voice. "Is it good?"

"Good enough that I wish my booze-addled brain had left the memory intact."

"Ah, tequila. She's a cruel bitch to us all, yet you gotta love her style."

"Miss." The driver rapped a hairy knuckle against the partition. "Your stop is up ahead. Where'd you want me to drop you?"

"At the corner would be great."

"All right, skank." Caitlin set her hands on Priya's shoulders as the cab jerked to a halt. "Best advice I can offer you is to keep your head high and pull your shoulders back. You are Priyanka Victory *fucking* Seth." She punctuated each syllable of her name with a heaving shake. "Founder of the Stiletto Sisterhood, queen of any room she walks into, a force to reckon with—goddess extraordinaire—even without undies. Shall I continue?"

Now Priya did laugh. "No, that's plenty. Thank you."

"Good. Because if anyone can turn a walk of shame into a stride of pride, it's you."

Caitlin slid out of the backseat first and held the door open as Priya struggled to steer herself across the sticky fake leather, and she felt a lick of sympathy for all those scandalized socialites who'd been caught with a lens up their skirts while exiting a car.

"Careful, Britney. Don't want to give someone a heart attack."

"It's not as easy as it looks." Sighing, Priya smoothed down her skirt, grateful there was no tunneling wind. The last thing she needed right now was an impromptu Marilyn Monroe moment. Torn between a laugh and a groan, she hugged Caitlin tight. "I owe you for this."

"Slay this interview and we'll call it even. Go get 'em, G.I. Jane. See what I did there?" She smacked a hand to Priya's butt. "Because you're commando." Laughing, Caitlin jumped back into the cab, blew a kiss through the open window, and sped off.

Head swimming, heart racing, Priya took a moment to gather herself. This was it. No turning back now. "Chin up," she whispered. "Game face on."

Chapter Two

Isobel Morgan, often the paragon of patience, cast her eyes to the ceiling and prayed for the strength not to shove her fiancé down the stairs.

"I can't believe you're kicking me out of bed before dawn. *Again.*"

"Baby . . ." She sighed, hands clenching and unclenching in impatient fists. "It's nearly eight. You know he'll be up soon."

"Seriously—come on, Tink, we're engaged now. I think we can stop the charade." At the base of the stairway, Kyle Peterson whirled around, and, even with a scowl on his face, she was struck by the beauty of him. Broad shouldered and lean, his face dominated by tempest-gray eyes, sullen full lips, and a chiseled jaw. Even brooding, he was breathtaking. Maybe more so. He could've easily modeled if his heart hadn't been set on soccer.

It was staggering to think in three short months she was going to be his wife.

They'd met as kids at summer camp but had gone separate ways until high school. That first moment she'd seen him again, when he'd smiled at her from across the field, her heart had tumbled right out of her chest and onto the shorn grass at his feet. Every single girl in school, even the seniors, wanted him, but it was Isobel Morgan he'd asked to be his date for the fall dance, and shortly thereafter to be his girlfriend. Kyle "the Pan" Peterson—the fearless boy who flew on the field, and Isobel Morgan, his Tinker Bell.

Because you bring magic to my life. And I bring adventure to yours.

"It's his house. I have to respect it." Isobel looped her arms around his waist and wiggled Kyle back toward the doorway. *Three feet. Just three more feet.*

"Which is why you should come to the condo instead." Kyle planted himself like a tree on the threshold and arched a brow. "You *are* coming over tonight, yes?" Isobel held her breath. "It's your turn, Tink."

Yes, it was. He'd made the effort every day for the past two months, but nights away from home made her anxious and too stressed to sleep. Even in Kyle's arms, which was her favorite place to be, she found no solace from the nagging worry.

Did he take his meds?

Is he throwing up?

In pain?

Did he get dizzy and fall, again?

"Tink?"

Grabbing him by the collar of his shirt, she yanked him in for a pacifying kiss, mainly to stop the storm she saw brewing in his eyes from turning into a full-blown hurricane. "I'll call you later. Also, don't forget about our lunch meeting with the coordinator."

Kyle's frown slid into the pout of a toddler being told he had to eat his dinner if he wanted dessert. "Do I have to?"

"Well . . ." Isobel shuffled, barefoot. "Don't you want to be there to see the venue?" There weren't many locations in Toronto available for a late-summer wedding that matched her stringent, environmentally friendly perspective and vegan lifestyle with Kyle's need for . . . style, as he put it. But the loft space in the Distillery District was *perfect*, and this was her last chance to get in there to see it before signing the paperwork.

Kyle scraped a hand over his head, mussing short brown curls gilded from his recent trip to Miami with his team. "Babe . . . I've really got to rest up for the game tomorrow. Coach says I have to take it easy after stressing my ACL in practice."

"Right. Of course." Isobel's heart twisted, but she masked her disappointment with a smile. After signing with Toronto FC last summer, Kyle had pushed hard to keep up with his team. He wasn't a kid kicking a ball across the field anymore. He was a professional athlete, and that came with expectations. Responsibilities. Demands. He was living his dream; the least she could do was manage a coordinator meeting. "I'll take care of it. Don't worry."

"You're the best, Tink. How'd I get so lucky?" Kyle framed her face with his large, calloused hands and kissed her swiftly. God, she loved kissing him.

Isobel jolted as the sound of her father's alarm clock, loud as a foghorn, blasted overhead. "I'm sorry," she whispered, struggling to withdraw from his embrace. "You've got to go."

"Yeah, yeah." Kyle rocked back, tongue skimming the edge of his perfectly shaped teeth. "Later."

Bruised with guilt, Isobel eased the door shut—gently— and winced at the whine of the hinges. They were overdue for a bit of grease. Once it was shut and locked, the chain latched in place, she gave the foyer a quick whisk before sprinting into the kitchen to start the kettle.

She hated forcing him out. Quiet mornings with Kyle were always her favorite part of her day, to be lost with him in the filmy glow of light running along the crease of the horizon where nothing existed beyond Kyle's arms and the rhythm of his breathing. Those moments brought her the most peace. The most joy. The most love. All before the chaos of the day swooped in and spun her through the gamut of work, chores, bills, and lawyers.

Floorboards shifted and creaked overhead. She'd give her dad five minutes of wrestling on his own before heading up to check. To keep her hands and mind busy while waiting for him to dress and the kettle to boil, she unlocked her iPad and opened her ever growing to-do list.

The wedding was three months away, and though she'd gone to considerable lengths to keep everything simple, Kyle wanted fireworks. More than half of his guests were people she'd never met, but he insisted they were vital. Even with the wedding coordinator and a ruthlessly planned checklist to keep her on task, there was still so much left to do. She'd struck gold with her dress, at least. A vintage 1950s gem found in an online LA thrift store.

Seating plan revisions – 5.0, remind Kyle to email his additions

Track dress shipment to confirm customs clearance

Cake tasting on Tuesday at 4 p.m. Kyle?

Sisters: dresses—final measurements and color preferences

Call Priya re: lawyers/settlement advice, she added.

Isobel smiled as she thought about her sisters. God, it had been so long since she'd made a trip down to New York. Even though she and Priya lived the closest—before Caitlin temporarily relocated last fall for her fashion internship—they'd both been far busier in the last few months than Isobel cared to think about.

Priya and Shayne had been the first to meet just before starting high school, and Eshe the winter thereafter, when Priya had gone to London for one of her mom's speaking engagements, then Caitlin a year later. Isobel had joined the Sisterhood last during one fateful summer when she'd gone to Manhattan with her dad to see relatives visiting from Ireland.

A truly glorious day. The kind that hummed with promises and changed lives.

While she had been in line at a Starbucks, nose in a book as usual, some guy had dumped his iced latte over her head and cackled with his friends. Isobel stood there, locked in a mortified tableau that stuttered in halting frames of movement as the cold, slushy brew slid down her face.

Isobel was no stranger to being bullied, but it never got any easier to swallow every time some jerk thought it would be hilarious to humiliate her because of her huge reading glasses and the wild curls she had no idea how to tame.

Four-eyed mutt!

Three simple words that, when strung together, became something sinister. Dangerous. And that flung her back to when she'd been six and playing with some kids who'd just moved into the area. They'd invited her and two others back to their house a few doors down. Thrilled, Isobel had raced down the street with them, but being smaller, she'd lagged behind and was the last to reach the porch when their mother, wearing a robin's egg–blue dress, glared at Isobel through the mesh screen and snarled, *I don't let mutts into my home,* before shutting the door solidly in her face.

Isobel had stood there for what felt like a year, frozen with a shame she couldn't understand. *Mutt.* A confusing, degrading word. It didn't make sense.

I'm not a dog, she'd wanted to say. *I'm just Isobel.* Just a little girl who wanted to play with the rest of the kids, and for reasons she couldn't understand, was being pushed out. Ostracized. Told *no* when she hadn't done anything wrong. But tears came instead of words, and Isobel raced home to the comfort of her father's arms. She'd cried for weeks after, and those kids never asked her to play again.

Thankfully, more often than not Isobel escaped notice thanks to the white-passing attributes of her fair skin and green eyes, but even then, she'd never forgotten that day. Even now, if she closed her eyes she could remember the slate-colored sky carrying the chill of early fall, the exact shade and texture of the brown, bricked house. Five terrible minutes stamped into her little mind with such alarming clarity that they left a brand.

A scar.

And that moment in Starbucks had, too, but she wouldn't have changed it for anything, because it was when she'd met Shayne. Even back then, barely sixteen, Shayne moved with a kind of swagger that was all attitude and honesty. Though there wasn't a single tattoo or piercing in sight (those didn't start to appear until she hit twenty), she didn't need them to convey her confidence. Or defiance.

It was in the set of her sullen mouth and the gleam of her vivid, burnt-whiskey eyes as she'd stepped forward to defend Isobel when no one else would. A shy little nerd whom Shayne dusted off after breaking the guy's nose with two sharp jabs. Afterward, in the bathroom, she gave Isobel a spare shirt from her bag to wear and introduced Isobel to the other girls who would become the greatest loves of her life. Her sisters.

And for the rest of the summer, Isobel was sucked into a whirlwind of female company unlike anything she had ever experienced before. Every day she wondered when it would end. Would they cast her out as quickly as they had roped her in? Isobel wasn't beautiful like Eshe or smart like Priya; she wasn't popular like Caitlin or confident like Shayne, or even really all that interesting. Or so she'd thought, until these girls showed her different, and the longer she spent in their company, the more she'd started to dream. To hope. And finally, believe.

But as the days of summer grew shorter, it became harder not to lose that newfound sparkle. And perhaps it was sensing Isobel's unease about what would happen when they all parted ways that spurred Shayne into action.

They'd gathered in Priya's apartment in Chelsea on their last afternoon together. Her parents were off vacationing in Dubai but had left Priya with a hired chaperon, Ms. Mills. As Ms. Mills had a penchant for muscle relaxants on a Sunday afternoon, they'd snuck a couple of bottles of rosé upstairs to the master bedroom's massive walk-in closet; the entire space was as large as Isobel's bedroom.

That closet had become their inner sanctum, their place of worship. Even Shayne seemed mesmerized by the beauty of towering heels. There, they'd gorged on greasy pizza, surrounded by hundreds of gorgeous stilettos stacked on shelves, glittering like jewels in the light, and toasted the end of a glorious summer and the forging of new friendships.

That was when Shayne sat up. "Swear," she said, casting her stern gaze to each of them in turn, her Spanish accent thickened with wine, "no matter what happens, we will always be friends. Nay, more than friends—*sisters*. And let nothing sever our vow: not distance or whatever bullshit life throws our way. We will stand together. For each other. We will inspire each other, and together we will take over the world. Own it." Drunk on excitement as much as she was on alcohol, she'd tried to stand but could only manage to stagger to her knees. "We need something to swear on."

"Like a Bible?" Isobel mused.

"Too religious," Eshe answered.

"Too patriarchal," Caitlin corrected.

"Let's use *this*!" Priya plucked a stiletto off the shelf. Black and glossy with a lipstick-red bottom.

"Why a shoe?" Caitlin mused, eyes crossing.

"Because they're powerful and sexy."

"Yes, but they're basically a modern-day corset meant to appease the male gaze."

"Then let's take it back." Priya grinned. "Reclaim it as an icon of strength and resilience. A weapon we will wield in the pursuit of our dreams."

"You know," Isobel chimed in, "the word *stiletto* means slender dagger."

"Stiletto Sisterhood," Eshe mused, letting the name settle and take shape. "Has a ring to it, yeah?"

Drunk and giggling, they stuck their hands in like athletes at a big game and swore a vow of sisterhood and fidelity. Five girls from different walks of life drawn to each other in unexpected ways, but once together, they'd found a love deeper than friendship. They were family.

Friends by chance but sisters by choice.

And true to their vow, even with distance dividing them, their friendship had held strong as they crossed the grueling academic gauntlet and entered the terrifying landscape of adulting. Textbooks were traded for budding careers built on the back of twelve-hour days for crap pay and acquiring things like actual bills in their own names that boomeranged every month—hounding for blood.

Some mornings Isobel lay in bed, gazing at the cracked plaster ceiling in her bedroom, and longed for simpler days of essays and exams. But nothing would ever be simple again. Especially not after the accident. Her stomach still clenched with terror at the memory of the day she'd received the phone call from the hospital.

Your father is in surgery.

Broken spine. Fractured skull.

We're not sure if he's going to pull through.

Prepare for the worst.

Her father, a construction foreman, had plummeted nearly three stories, but not before pushing aside the crewman working beside him when he realized that the faultily assembled scaffolding they were standing on wasn't going to hold—thereby saving the man from joining him on the way down.

It had been touch and go for weeks after, and by the grace

of God and her father's sheer stubborn will, he'd pulled through. But it took nearly a year before he'd managed to walk unassisted, and the war was far from over.

"There's my best girl." Declan Morgan declared as he entered the kitchen, his glowing smile marred by the shadow of a grimace. Deep grooves of chronic pain slashed between his brows, furrowed around his mouth, and hung in bags beneath his eyes, aging him well beyond his fifty-two years, and robbing him of vitality. They'd been faint at first, but with the passing days and countless surgeries, she'd watched those cracks and crevices sink as deep as scar tissue.

In an effort to slow the erosion, Isobel made a concerted effort to be his constant source of happiness and hope, just as he had always endeavored to be hers. Abandoning her iPad, she plucked up her steaming cup of green tea, sweetened with a hint of agave syrup. "Did you sleep well?"

His answering laugh was bone dry. "Like the dead." Always the same answer. The same lie. She knew he slept poorly. The proof was in the weary bend of his back and the heaviness of his steps. Even with the prescribed painkillers her father hadn't had a good night's sleep in almost three years. He pressed a kiss to her cheek. "You're up early."

Isobel gestured guiltily to her screen. "Tweaking my pitch." It wasn't a complete lie. She had been editing it—mentally—all morning while Kyle slept next to her. Now she just needed to plug in the minor changes.

"That today?" His eyes brightened. "And here I thought it had to do with shoving Kyle out the door."

"You heard us?"

"I may be getting old, Bells, but I'm not dead." Reaching

for her hand, he gave it a tender squeeze. "Why do you think I've taken to setting the alarm for eight instead of six thirty?"

Isobel winced. "Dad . . ."

"He's not wrong," her father interrupted. "You're a soon-to-be married young woman. Next time, let the poor lad sleep in." Declan pulled her in for a hug and tucked her head under his chin. "As for your pitch, you'll be wonderful, love. You have a talent with words. I'm sure your boss will be dazzled."

Though Isobel was grateful for the subject change, her stomach twisted into an anxious pretzel. "I hope so." Pushing for recognition or asking for more had never been her strong suit, but after being thoroughly pressed by her sisters, mainly Priya and Shayne, Isobel had relented.

As nervous as she was, Isobel knew it was time to ask for the change. She'd worked for *The Six* for three long years, and adored the local Toronto talk show with all her heart, but asking for a promotion from production assistant to *writer* was a huge step. *The Six* kept assistants on a part-time, hourly basis instead of salaried payroll, and if she was going to continue to support her father, she needed more money. Benefits.

Perhaps it would've been easier to leave and work elsewhere, but she loved *The Six*, and was passionate about storytelling—especially news that mattered. But it wasn't easy breaking into media without having finished university. She'd quit after her first year and gotten a job to cover expenses while her father recovered, but it was growing increasingly apparent her dad would never go back to work, and his settlement claim had been in court for three agonizing years, the finish line nowhere in sight. Even if she wanted to go back to finish her education, they could barely afford it before, with grants tempering some of the financial sting. It would be impossible now, with the weight of all the bills dragging her down like an anchor into a sea of debt.

Online certificates had helped supplement her résumé, but it wasn't nearly enough to make her stand out against someone with an actual degree. So Isobel had decided the only way to move ahead was to *show* them what she was capable of.

And, oh God, she really was going to be sick!

"Do you have time to join me for a bit?" her dad asked, reaching the breakfast nook containing a little half-moon shaped table with two mismatched wooden chairs, where they'd both sat just about every morning as far back as she could remember. A chair scraped and stuttered across the tile in his shaking grip. Even the simplest tasks were a challenge, and Isobel had to stop herself from rushing in to help.

Growing up, he'd seemed invincible. Barrel-chested like a superhero, with strong arms, rough hands, a big heart, and an even bigger laugh. It had been the two of them against the world after *she'd* left them. Isobel swallowed that knot of betrayal and fear. She would not think of her mother, not now, and certainly not in front of him. It was too beautiful a day to be sad, and like a bloodhound, her father would sniff out the cause. She didn't want to upset him either.

"No, I have to rush to set for today's recording, and then meet the wedding coordinator for a late lunch," she said, brightening her voice with the eager anticipation of a bride-to-be.

Declan nodded as he sank into the chair, masking a wince as his weight settled into the uncompromising wooden frame. As she sipped her tea, Isobel's gaze shifted to the living room— to the beat-up leather recliner and the plush hunter-green sectional they used to cuddle on together to watch sports—and she wondered how she was going to steer him there without bruising his ego.

Maybe I should turn on the morning news. Lay out a sudoku puzzle. She'd encouraged him to do them for cognitive therapy. He'd hit his head in the fall, and she'd read somewhere that brain exercises were crucial to helping the rest of the body heal and restore memory and clarity. Fortunately for her, he'd taken a real shine to them.

At his wheezing grunt, her gaze flitted back to see him hunched over and struggling to tie the laces on his left shoe.

"Here." Setting her cup on the counter, she rushed to his side and urged him to ease upright. He'd dressed in jeans and a plaid shirt, the buttons misaligned by two. Her fingers itched to redo them, to smooth out those creases around his shoulders, but instead she busied herself with the task of his laces. "Why didn't you call me to help you?"

He swiped her question aside with a calloused palm. "I can manage well enough on my own. No need to fret over it." Maybe it was the Irish in him, or being a single parent for most of her life, but Declan Morgan had always been a proud man and would sooner yank out his own teeth than ask for help.

She clipped his nails, combed his hair, and on bad days, helped him climb out of bed or shimmy into his clothes. Over time the list of things she did for her father grew, shrinking his independence. Smothering him. So last fall she'd hired a contractor to modify a few areas around the house—installing a second handrail at the stairs, a bar in the shower so he could heft himself about as he needed or hold on to when he felt faint. Though the cost had been a blow to her meager savings, knowing it let him hold on to his dignity had been well worth it.

At least Kyle had shouldered most of the wedding expense, although Isobel had insisted on contributing where she could.

Finished with his laces, Isobel rocked back on her heels. "Can I make you something to eat before I go?"

"I'm fine, love."

"Dad, you need to eat." *You're wasting away.* His arms were pencil thin and his legs near to bone where they had all once been solid, chiseled muscle.

"Why must you always make a fuss?" The creases deepened around his eyes. "You should be out enjoying yourself, not rushing home to fuss over me."

"It's not a fuss to take care of someone you love." She rose and set her hands to her hips. "Besides, it's a gorgeous day out. Maybe we could stretch your legs at the park later this evening. Dr. Gora says you need to get out and walk more. Strengthen your muscles with those gentle exercises the physiotherapist taught you so we can start incorporating yoga into your routine."

Declan scrunched up his nose. "I hate walking almost as much as I hate the idea of yoga."

"We'll make it a short one," she promised, not backing down. Whether he liked it or not, she intended to follow the doctor's instructions to the letter. But she wasn't above bribery when necessary. "If you're good then I'll take you to the pub later for a pint of Guinness. *One.*" That perked him right up. "But only if you do everything I ask without a grumble."

"Where'd you learn to be so tough?" His features slid into a frown but a smile shone in his eyes.

Isobel pressed another noisy kiss to his cheek. "From my dad, of course."

Chapter Three

Nausea was a bitch that wouldn't quit, twisting Priya's tequila-pickled stomach into a mess of nerves. The elevator rocketed up to the thirty-seventh floor, and she raised a hand to her mouth to stifle a booze-soaked burp as the urge to let it all spew out sat at the back of her throat like a finger hovering over the button of a detonator.

Waiting to be pushed.

Oh please, let me get through this nightmare without puking.

The doors pinged open when she reached her floor—so high up she'd swear the building swayed under her feet. Bright lights bounced off white walls, floors, and furniture. Stark as an art gallery without a hint of color or contrast aside from the polished wood receptionist desk and the impeccably dressed young Black woman manning it.

On a Sunday . . . ?

Wincing against the glare, Priya approached the desk, and the receptionist lifted a single halting finger in acknowledgment as her other hand raced across the keyboard. When she was finished typing, she shifted her gaze to Priya, and, to her credit, barely blinked.

"You must be Ms. Seth." A welcoming smile brightened her

luminous skin. "I'll let Ms. Nagao's assistant know you're here." Her fingers flew once more over the keyboard but stalled when her eyes landed on Priya again. "Something wrong?"

"I'm just . . . confused," Priya whispered, like a sinner afraid to be caught in church. "It's *Sunday.*"

"*Defense doesn't rest,*" the receptionist intoned. "More than just our company motto. Marek, Nagao & Silver has a vast, rotational staff to ensure the office can remain open and operational through weekends and holidays, when needed." She removed the headset from her ear. "Heather will be with you shortly. Is there anything I can get for you in the meantime? Water? Cappuccino?"

Spare panties? The weight of dread—and impending vomit—kicked Priya's tonsils, and she did her best to swallow it all back down. "Water would be great."

"Still or sparkling?"

"Sparkling."

"Wonderful. Ice?"

"Sure."

"And would you like a slice of lemon or lime?"

Seriously? "Just the water, please. Thanks."

"Certainly. I'll just be a moment." She was gone in a flash of long legs, high heels, and a soft gray suit that Priya was debating how to bribe her out of when the glass doors beyond the desk opened and a stern, red-lipped blond strode out, looking as sleek as a model.

Brown eyes fell on Priya, and her stride faltered, like she'd skidded on wet flooring, before recovering. Barely. "Ms. *Seth*?"

"That's me." Priya extended a hand. "You must be Heather."

"Are you insane? What on earth possessed you to waltz

26

in here like—?" Heather's gaze raked her from head to toe, scathing with judgment. "No. No. No. I can't accept this." She flapped her hand and set the other to her brow, eyes pinched shut. "Turn around and leave this instant—before *someone* else sees you. I'll tell Ms. Nagao you had an emergency and couldn't make it."

Priya's mouth tumbled open as her dreams popped like a filmy soap bubble before her aching, undoubtedly bloodshot eyes. "What? No. No way. I'm *here*. On time, might I add."

"A clear mark of stupidity. Leave, now, before I call security to escort you from the building. For your own good."

Considering the matter closed, Heather whipped around and Priya scampered as fast as she could to head her off. "I don't think you understand what I've gone through to get here, both personally and professionally. I can't—*won't*—let you send me away. I can't blow this."

"Have you looked at yourself?" Heather scoffed. "You've already blown it."

"Then what else have I got to lose?"

"Dignity? Ms. Seth, I think you fail to understand the scope of what you're up against. If you walk into our boardroom looking like. . . . This is an interview with the managing partner of the firm, *not* casual Friday at IKEA. Marai Nagao will eat you alive."

"That's my problem," Priya said defiantly, crossing her arms. "Show me the way, or step aside, but I'm going through with this interview."

Heather rolled her tongue along the edge of teeth and, after a moment, shook her head. "It's your funeral." She stepped around Priya with a sigh. "This way. And keep up."

"Oh, the receptionist was just—" At the arch of Heather's brow, Priya swallowed the rest and gave her skirt a tug to urge it down as low as she could manage. Pushed almost to a jog by Heather's determined gait, she followed her down a long corridor of glass fronted offices and rows of cubicles.

Mercifully, most were empty.

Turning a corner, Heather opened a heavy set of double doors into a midsized conference room where Marai Nagao sat with her back to them, laptop open. Reality slammed into Priya like an eighteen-wheeler, and a stream of expletives stuttered through her throbbing head, following the staccato rhythm of clicking keys.

Heather cleared a gentle throat. "Ms. Nagao, I have Priyanka Seth here for her interview."

A head turned, sleek in its motion, as if every gesture, no matter how small, was done with the utmost authority, confidence, and purpose. Dark hair slashed down one side of her slender face in a biased bob while the other was razed short in a stylized fade. It gave her a contrasting edge that was all corporate samurai, as a *Forbes* article once called her, and Marai owned the moniker right down to the collection of katanas she kept on display in her office the way most men had signed sports paraphernalia.

Narrow eyes struck Priya first, highlighted by thick, dark lashes and bold brows, and full cheekbones dropped to nude lips with pale skin that shone without makeup or enhancement. Marai might be well into her fifties, but she was *stunning*.

A shiver of admiration trickled down Priya's spine as Marai set a pointed chin on the back of her hand and a subtle flick of fingers was all it took for Heather to spin on her heels and evaporate through the conference room doors. Palms pressed to her thighs, she rose from her seat and stopped before Priya, arms crossed and hip cocked, the lines of her pencil skirt accenting a lithe body with killer calves.

"As one of Harvard's youngest magna cum laudes,"—her eyes slid over Priya, glacial in scrutiny—"I must admit I'm . . . disappointed."

If it was possible, Priya would have folded herself into a series of tight, compact origami squares until she vanished on the spot. "Ms. Nagao—"

"I do not accept meaningless platitudes. Sorry is an excuse for the weak."

"I wasn't—"

"And I do not appreciate interruptions when I'm speaking. I have fired associates for less." The look in her dark eyes held the power to cripple the soul as she punctuated her threat with a moment of scathing silence. "If you can't be bothered to take this interview seriously, I can't be bothered to waste my time on you."

No. Panic flared through Priya's chest as Marai whisked around. In a handful of strides, she was within reach of the door. *No, no, no, no, no. Do something. Fast!*

"Zimmerman v. Wexler!" Priya blurted.

The world eased to a grinding halt of heart-stopping suspense as Marai turned in a single, graceful move. "What did you say?"

"Your art forgery win from 2003." Priya pushed authority into her voice. "You mopped the floor with Wexler's defense team and made yourself into a household name for litigation. All because you deigned to show up to court without a bra."

A fact that would've gone undetected had it not been for the courtroom losing power amid a heatwave in July. Undoubtedly roasting beneath her wool blazer, Marai removed it during her final address to the jury, and the next morning, plastered across the front page of every major paper and newsroom headline was a snap of Marai Nagao's nipples clearly visible through her crimson blouse.

"Wexler's defense team accused you of relying on your feminine wiles to sway the decision of a predominantly male jury, but instead of allowing yourself to be buried by bad press," Priya went on, "you leveraged the scandal—accepting every subsequent interview and media op to redirect the focus toward your client. The case. The groundbreaking win. And because of that you became name partner at twenty-seven. A legend."

It was a bold move. Almost as bold—or idiotic—as Priya's outfit, but now it was time to drive the point home and hopefully, win her own case. Because nothing short of falling on her sword was going to save her from this mess, and she hoped the naked honesty would not go unnoticed or unappreciated.

"I know I look like a mess. I thought about weaving a witty story to make me appear less stupid than I do right now, but the truth?" She resisted the urge to clamp her eyes shut with shame. "Last night I was drunk. *Really* drunk, when I accepted the interview update. This morning I barely had enough time to make it here, let alone sprint all the way home. So I opted for punctuality ahead of presentability. Accountability over apology, because if I can't convince you to look beyond this to see *me*, then I don't deserve to be here. Period."

Smothering silence fell between them before a glint of amusement sparked in Marai's otherwise indescribable gaze. "Clever girl. We're all hands on deck this weekend with an unexpected roadblock in a major case pushing to retrial. The change, though last minute, was necessary, and considering that all the notes from your previous interviewers were glowing in testament to your poise and professionalism, I suppose I can make an allowance this once."

Priya's knees weakened with relief so swift she nearly wobbled. "Thank you."

"As for that media hoopla, I would've been mortified if not for something my mother told me, often: '*If there's ever a day when you're caught with your pants down, do what any straight white man with more privilege than sense would do—show them both cheeks and zero fucks.*'" Crossing her arms, she raised her chin. "Marek, Nagao & Silver has four international offices— London, New York, Toronto, and Tokyo—with over eight hundred of the best lawyers handling the most sensitive and complex commercial litigation, white-collar criminal matters, and regulatory proceedings. We've maintained a ruthless and impeccable reputation for more than thirty years." Marai's brow arched the barest fraction. "And you think you have what it takes to join our ranks?"

"I do." Pulling back her shoulders, Priya imagined herself wearing her pristine suit instead of creased Valentino. "I was the president of Harvard Women's Law Association where I organized campus visits with various female Supreme Court justices, litigators, and activists. I am a prominent and passionate advocate for women's rights and offered aid to victims of rape and domestic violence," she said with a burst of pride. "Pursuant to that, I interned for two semesters as an investigative analyst for the Sex Crimes Unit of the Manhattan District Attorney's Office, and—"

"Your résumé is impressive, Ms. Seth, otherwise, you wouldn't be here," Marai interrupted. "What I'm interested in ascertaining is: Why you?"

Because I deserve this.

Because you are everything I aspire to be.

Because I don't lose.

If the accomplishments and vast references Priya had practically sold a kidney to acquire weren't enough, what was left?

"If you're not interested in hearing about what I've done, I won't waste your time with a rehearsed speech, tears, or an eloquent soliloquy about my life's ambitions," Priya said at last. "I can't tell you *why*. I can only show you."

Marai's gaze remained brutally intense. Impassive as stone. Unreadable. And just when Priya was about to give up all hope, she nodded her head with a faint incline. "I think we're done here."

Relief rushed through her so fast and bright, Priya was dizzy. Every inch of her light and airy with threads of helium-inflated balloons lifting her straight off the ground. "I got the mentorship?"

"A job, yes—contract based, to start—but the mentorship,"— Marai extended a cautionary finger—"must be earned."

The threads of those balloons were cut with a brutal *snip*— and Priya thumped solidly back to reality. "Earned?"

"Everyone at this firm possesses stellar academic credentials, but it remains to be seen if that's *all* you bring to the table. If you want the mentorship, you'll have to prove you're as good as you think you are."

Buzzing sounded between her ears, something like a deep, internal scream of anguished fury. "I didn't realize this was a . . ." *Contest? Competition?* "I thought—"

"If I hear anything other than thank you slip out of your mouth, I'll rescind my offer."

Priya snapped straight. Nodded. "Thank you."

"*Hm.*" Marai nodded, then tilted her head in thought. "Seth . . . any relation to *the* Lakshmi Seth, by chance?"

Priya tried—with every flagging ounce of self-control she still possessed—not to sigh. "She's my mother."

Marai's unreadable expression flickered for the barest moment with surprise. Fascination. "I'm amazed you didn't lead with that little detail."

"Name dropping is lazy. And tacky. If I succeed or fail, I want it to be based on merit."

"*Hm.*" Marai lifted her chin. "Heather will be in touch once HR has the necessary paperwork and the final stages of our background checks are completed, but you will start sometime early next week. When I see you next,"—her gaze crawled over Priya, dissecting every molecule before reaching her eyes and remaining there—"I expect you to be both punctual *and* appropriately attired."

Chapter Four

If time flew when having fun, it grated to an insufferable crawl when hungover. As adrenaline receded, the drumming in Priya's skull reared up with a vicious fury. The kind that demanded hard-core painkillers. Or a shotgun.

Priya punched the elevator call button and bent at the waist, one hand braced on the wall as she sucked in slow, deep breaths while counting to ten. All she wanted now was to get home, crawl into bed, and *die*.

"Well, well, well. Look what the tiger dragged in."

That voice—sinful, deep, and velvety—stroked up her spine and glided across delicate nerve endings like a tongue on her skin. Intimate and bold. Hearing it snapped her senses awake. She recognized it as well as the low, heady rumble of laughter that followed.

Panty Thief leaned casually against the wall at her side, his body doing all kinds of things to a suit that should have been illegal. Priya prided herself on having a keen eye for detail, but her dehydrated brain short-circuited in three short words.

Broad. Tall. Delicious.

Dark, styled hair, skin golden from heritage instead of sun, molten hazel eyes—more green than gold—and full lips framed by the hard edge of his jaw. And that was just his face. This guy was breathtaking while sober, but drunk? It was a wonder she hadn't lost more than her panties.

"I thought I saw you *streaking* down the hall."

Heat flashed in her cheeks at his choice of words. "Hilarious. And I think you meant cat," she said, tugging the flouncy, pleated hem of her skirt down a desperate inch even though it already fell to the knee. "But either way, I take umbrage. I'm not a feline."

"Yes, you are. I have the scratches on my back to prove it." Then his smile flashed, and somewhere in heaven, an angel had a screaming orgasm. "I think these belong to you." He pulled a scrap of hot pink from his pocket and spun it on the end of a capped pen.

Mortified, Priya snatched them before anyone happened to walk by and witness him waving her panties like a flag of truce. Or a call to war.

"So." She tucked them into a tight wad in her first. "You are the guy I slept with last night."

"Alas, to my great dismay, we got as far as my shirt and your panties before you succumbed to an alcohol-induced coma. You slept in the bed; I took the couch and nothing happened once you passed out." He laid a hand over his heart. "My word as a gentleman."

"What kind of gentleman steals a girl's panties after a random hookup?"

He blinked at her, surprised and amused. "You truly don't remember a thing?"

Priya whisked a hand at herself. "Alcohol-induced comas often lead to gaps in memory."

"Fair enough. Allow me to fill in the blanks." He advanced

closer under the pretense of discretion, but the gleam in his eyes said he was enjoying this little game of cat and mouse.

She held her ground, even if it meant letting him into her personal space. Close enough to see the flecks of amber in the dark-green irises and smell the hint of soap on his skin.

"You peeled them off," he whispered, "and stuffed them in my suit jacket before we got on the elevator."

A wave of chills spiked down to her toes in a mix of embarrassment and need. Priya locked her legs beneath her for support against the waves of his easy charisma.

Why, hello, whoremones, we meet again.

"I didn't realize I had them until I was already in the building. Go ahead." He nodded to the short corridor that led to emergency stairs around the corner. "I'll stand watch."

Scowling at him, then forsaking his presence and modesty—because what hadn't he already seen?—Priya rounded the corner and wiggled into her hot-pink underwear. Better than walking around bare assed for another second.

"You're lucky. I considered chucking them in the bin when I got here. They almost fell out during my interview." He laughed brightly. "Christ, wouldn't *that've* made an impression?"

"Interview?" *Ah!* Amazing what a pair of panties could do for a girl's confidence. She stepped out to rejoin him in the corridor. "You had an interview *this* morning?"

"Seven forty-five sharp with George Silver." He rolled his teeth over his bottom lip and shrugged. "Which is why I left so early. Ditching a woman is not my style, I might add. Had I known you were also supposed to be here, I would've tried a little harder to rouse you, or at least stuck around for breakfast and the mutual walk of shame."

Mutual? Nothing remotely mutual about it when he looked like he'd walked straight off a *GQ* cover. By some stroke of luck, or genius, he'd gone out the night before in a full suit, sparing him the humiliation of looking like a hot mess, but the utter sincerity in his voice softened her, and she found it hard to doubt him even if she wanted to.

"So that wasn't your apartment we went to last night?"

He shook his head. "A friend's. He lets me crash there from time to time. He's currently out of town; it was closer than my place and you were . . . impatient." His eyes gleamed wicked as a devil, all charm and heat.

Priya attempted to match his smirk with one of her own, but her face felt tight and warm. If he'd also had an interview this morning, that meant he was one of the many associates she was up against, and while ordinarily it wouldn't bother her, one thing she'd learned at Harvard was to never lose your edge; she'd already done that by losing her panties. She couldn't afford any more surprises.

"I figured I'd leave early and come back after, but ordered breakfast in case you happened to wake before I did."

The elevator chimed as the doors opened, and she strode inside. "Where did we meet?"

"I was outside Pathos finishing a call when you swept out for some air." He pressed the button for the ground floor before she could reach it. "We got to talking and both agreed we'd have a lot more fun elsewhere. The rest—" He shrugged. "I think explains itself."

It did, indeed. "Well, thank you for being so . . . candid. And for the food," she added, grudgingly, arms crossed.

"My pleasure, Priya." Mirth glimmered in his eyes as she

remained silent, her cheeks blazing. "Take it you can't recall my name either?"

Shit. She closed her eyes, hoping now that she'd seen his face, heard his voice, a hint of it would rise through the fog. *The ring of laughter, the tipping of shot glasses, the wild heat of his mouth, his voice hot in her ear, panting something . . .*

Har. . . vey, Har. . . din, Har—dammit!!

"Allow me to formally introduce myself. Hadrian." He thrust out a hand. "Hadrian Marek."

The elevator chime for the ground floor shot through Priya like a bolt of lightning. Any other time she'd have made some glib remark about a man built like a god being named after a wonder of the world—but it was *Marek*, as in Marek, Nagao & Silver, that robbed her of breath. "You're *his* son?"

"Guilty." Holding the elevator door open, he allowed her to step off ahead of him.

Wonderful. Of all the random almost one-night stands, she had to have one with the son of the founding partner of the firm. Swallowing a groan, she closed her eyes. "Did I know this last night?"

His expression flickered for the barest moment from amused to guarded as he fell into step with her. "No. We stuck to first names only."

Not much of a surprise there; Priya was used to withholding to avoid being interrogated about her famous mother. It wasn't often she was in the company of someone who did the same. "Wait a minute." She squinted, a memory jostled loose by her shame. "Shouldn't your first name be Aurelio? After your father?"

"Personally, and professionally, I use my middle name.

I prefer it because people always bastardized Aurelio, and it affords me a sense of individuality—a way to stand apart from his legacy and forge my own."

Priya knew a thing or two about identity, about the importance of carving out your own and escaping the long, dark shadow of a famous parent. As soon as people heard the name Lakshmi Seth, their eyes lit up.

But didn't she—?

Yes.

And you're her daughter?

Yes.

Then once the glow of awe faded, the glimmer of speculation immediately followed. Dissecting and measuring her against her mother's many accomplishments and accolades. And though Priya loved her mother, worshipped her even, being the daughter of a Nobel Prize–winning author demanded nothing less than perfection. It was an exhausting precedent to maintain, but she wasn't about to let understanding soften her resolve. This guy, however hot, was the enemy. An obstacle standing in her path to glory, and the only way to remove him was total annihilation.

Priya pushed through the revolving door and out onto the steps leading to the street, and winced against the muggy glare of late-morning sun. Her head weighed about twenty pounds, and she'd seriously kill for a shower, a gallon of water, and a soft bed in a very dark room.

"Well, guess I'll see you around, tiger." He tossed her a teasing wink as he strode away, and Priya refused—*refused*—to check out his perfect ass.

For more than a second.

* * *

Isobel's phone vibrated wildly in her hands, *SHAYNE* blazed on her screen, but she swiped Decline. Now was not the time for distractions, though she was mildly annoyed it wasn't Kyle. She'd texted him while rushing to work, asking if he'd be okay coming back to the house later. Given the state of her father this morning, spending a night away from home didn't sit well with her. His response was sure to be anything but pleased.

Kyle was impatient lately, and it was getting harder for her to hold it all together. Kyle. Her father. The settlement. The wedding. Her job. *Life.* Something had to give, but Isobel was no stranger to pressure. She could pull through. Three more months and then things would ease. Three months and then everything would be perfect.

By the time she'd arrived on set at *The Six* she almost believed it herself.

"Mercy heavens, you're cutting it to the wire." Sharon, the set manager tossed her brittle length of overprocessed red hair and flashed small, tea-stained teeth in a thin-lipped, relieved smile.

The woman was built like a linebacker—all shoulders, narrow hips, and belly on strong legs—and her physical appearance contrasted with her preference for wearing florals, colorful acrylics, and enough gold jewelry to open a small boutique. She moved with the speed of a charging bull and ruled the set with momma bear protectiveness. Of everyone at *The Six*, Sharon held the longest tenure of fifteen years, and Isobel adored working with her.

"Sorry." Isobel set down a holder with three cups of coffee wedged inside, each one a different brew, depending on which side of the bed her boss had woken up on. "What's the weather report for the day? Hurricane, thunderstorm, or nothing but sunshine?"

"Norman's only shouted fuck three times in the last hour—so all signs point to sunny with scattered clouds. He'll certainly be better with that coffee you're allowing to get cold."

"Right." Good mood meant venti Americano with cream, honey, and a sprinkle of cinnamon. Isobel plucked out the appropriately marked cup. "You take the macchiato this time."

"You're a gem," Sharon called as Isobel approached the set stage.

"Morning," Isobel said, handing her boss his coffee.

"Isobel, I was just about to call for you."

She started at the sight of his mile-wide grin. The kind he usually reserved for affluential guests or Ben Lambert, owner of *The Six*. *Wow. A real good mood.* "I'm sorry, I know I'm a little late."

Norman smoothed his tie, adjusted the knot. "Not a problem. Don't worry about it. Listen, we're flipping to a live segment in about five minutes. When I flag you, I need you to step into frame for me, can you do that?"

Isobel blinked. "Ummm . . ." *I'm not dressed for live TV.*

"Don't stress, it's easy. We just need to catch an honest reaction to a *TMZ* leak. We've already set a marker for you. Wendy,"—he snapped his fingers briskly—"make sure Isobel knows where her marker is. And get her some powder. Too much shine."

Wendy Liu, the on-set camera assistant, a middle-aged woman standing four eleven with a bowl cut, bifocals, and pink buttoned-up cardigan over khakis, rushed in. "Yes, yes, of course."

"Great. Perfect. Now scoot." Norman shooed Isobel away as the makeup team gave him a final dusting with seconds to go before live to air.

Returning to her position at the side of the stage, Isobel could feel her phone continuing to buzz relentlessly. Fishing it from her back pocket, she frowned as the screen exploded with message after message after message. All of them from Shayne.

Isobel—where are you?

Isobel answer your phone!

ISOBEL FOR THE LOVE OF FUCK—pick up!

Isobel—

Brace yourself . . .

Isobel barely had a moment to absorb the messages let alone brace for anything as her name roared across the set. The spotlight punched on, catching her like a deer in high beams.

From behind, Wendy gave her a prodding nudge. "Your marker!"

"Right." Isobel stepped forward into the glare of hot lights. And wow, this was intense.

"Isobel Morgan." Norman held out a hand. "Thank you for joining me this morning."

What? He was talking to her like she was a guest. But that wasn't possible. Today's feature was about a writer who'd started online with a platform—Wattpad—and went on to have her debut break out on the *NYT* Best Sellers list. *Just go with it, Isobel.* God, she hoped her face wasn't showing an ounce of her confusion. "Ummm . . . happy to be here."

"Of course you are." Norman walked across the stage and reached for her hand, leading her back across it. "For those of you just tuning in, Isobel Morgan is our production assistant, and has been an integral part of *The Six* fam for two years now."

"Three . . ."

"And just last fall," he blazed on, "she got engaged to Toronto FC's newest midfielder, Kyle 'the Pan' Peterson. Look at them."

A picture blown up to nearly eight feet flashed onto the large screen over the stage. It had been taken on the day he'd proposed. Kyle stood with his arms around her, an adoring smile on his face while Isobel was caught somewhere between laughter and tears. It was her favorite picture of them. One she'd deliberately kept *off* social media.

"How did you get tha—?"

"Tell me, Isobel, when is the big day?"

A sickening feeling curled in her belly. "September twenty-eighth."

"Less than three months." Norman's brows pushed up. "Fast approaching."

"Yes."

"You must be swamped with all the planning."

"Of course." Her phone vibrated madly in her hand but Isobel was too terrified to look away from Norman's clown-wide grin to answer.

Brace yourself.

"So, tell us, Isobel." He stood in front of her, so close he nearly stepped on her feet. "Did you know Kyle was having an affair?"

Shock. Disbelief. Confusion. All of it mixed in a bubble of nervous laughter that burst from her throat. "What?"

"With Teri Mauve. You've heard of her, haven't you?"

"I . . ." She blinked, struggling to breathe. To focus. "I don't think so. No."

"She's an aspiring singer with a bunch of unsuccessful songs under her belt. She became a viral celebrity after bombing her audition for the *High Note* five years ago, and now she's about to break the internet again—with this."

Cameras panned in Isobel's direction, and then she saw it. The recording streamed across cable television and their network website to hundreds of thousands of live viewers.

"What are we looking at?"

Isobel shifted on her feet. "Umm . . ." *Focus, Bel. Focus.* So she did. On the monitors. On the clip that bounced in a weaving, incoherent loop, almost like a clipped boomerang. Skin. Lots of skin. And then it froze on a mirror reflection of a man and a woman. She recognized him immediately.

Those eyes. That mouth.

Kyle naked.

Kyle naked with another woman.

Kyle having sex with another woman.

"Isobel?"

Isobel groaned. "I can't—" But her legs wouldn't move. Her body wouldn't respond.

"Shocking, isn't that right, folks?" The studio audience roared behind her. "Can't imagine the wedding will take place after something like this. Tell the audience what you're feeling."

Feeling? Nothing made sense. Air rushed out of her lungs, leaving her dizzy. Hot and flushed. *No. No.* She pressed a hand to her belly. The world shook, spun, and—in a whirl of lights and color—she dropped like a stone, and spiraled into black.

Chapter Five

It took Priya twenty minutes, and another dent in her rapidly depleting bank account, to summon an Uber home.

Worth. Every. Penny.

Though her parents sent a quarterly stipend to cover her living expenses, Priya had another two weeks to go before the next installment. Not that she planned to take any more money. As a soon-to-be working woman earning her own paycheck, and the sole occupant of the family apartment in Chelsea, it was time she stood on her own two feet.

Last year her mom and stepdad had decided to move back to Amsterdam and had given her the option to come with them. She'd said no. Priya had been fortunate enough to travel the world with her mother, bouncing across most of Europe and parts of Asia for conferences and engagements, but nowhere had ever felt quite like home. Not like New York.

This was where Priya's heart beat fastest. She loved the rush of the city, the ruthless beauty of it. New York demanded strength. Perseverance. And it was demanding it from her right now.

Unlocking the door, she zombie-shuffled into the kitchen, desperate for something to quench the dry ache in her throat.

Plucking a glass from the dishwasher, she filled it with water from the tap and guzzled it down while inside she *screamed* in frustration.

This wasn't supposed to happen. She was a top student; she'd excelled at every challenge and conquered every adversary. Priyanka Seth did not *lose*.

So why did this feel like a loss?

Because she'd thought having her résumé plucked out of an endless pile by Marai Nagao meant her days of sweat, blood, and effort had finally been recognized? It was galling to think that after years of personal sacrifice and academic hell she now had to compete against a slew of associates, clawing out throats like on some warped reality TV show.

Mom wouldn't have had to prove herself. Lakshmi Seth entered a room and conquered. Dominated. At twenty-four she had already been a world recognized published author. Now she had hundreds of essays, poems, and novels under her belt. Several of her works had been adapted into films, plays, and TV series.

She'd been flown in just last week to do a poetry reading at Barack Obama's birthday, for crying out loud. Priya had watched the livestream and was mesmerized by her mother and, as always, a little intimidated. She spoke with such intensity and conviction, melding her passionate views on gender, sexuality, and racial identity into words that eviscerated the soul. She was utter perfection and always made it look so effortless. So easy. A swan, ever graceful on the surface, you'd never know how fast and hard those legs were churning beneath the water. Unlike her daughter.

Priya pounded her glass against the counter hard enough

to satisfy without breaking it. She'd nearly blown her final interview, and now she had to deal with Hadrian Marek to add a layer of icing to the cake. Priya pressed the heels of her palms over her eyes and groaned. *Bed. Get to bed.* She'd sleep off this misery and then start fresh tomorrow. Work out a game plan. Because the second she entered the doors of MNS, she was going to do so like a freaking amazon. Hadrian Marek—and the other associates—were in for a battle. A war.

Body aching, eyes watering, Priya lumbered into her bedroom with a sigh—*oh yes. Oh yes, finally*—and toppled face first into a downy mountain of heaven. She managed to wriggle up another few inches before strength failed. Whatever. She'd gone far enough to plug in her dead phone—who cared if her feet hung off the edge of the bed? If a demon wanted to drag her below, she'd almost welcome hell at this point. Anything that made the beating behind her eyes stop. The pain had even migrated down to the nerves in her teeth.

Eyes closed, she sighed into sleep, and barely five minutes later her phone wailed like a banshee, raising her from the sweet mercy of oblivion.

Whoever is calling is dead. She would kill them slowly. Agonizingly. Pushing up onto shaking arms, she snatched her phone with fingers hooked into claws, prepared to draw blood, when she saw the name on her screen.

Shayne wasn't one to call. She texted or sent voice notes. Calls were not her thing, and according to the time, what had felt like five minutes was in fact two hours. Priya swiped to answer and was greeted with the chaos of muffled voices and the blare of background music.

"Hey—Priya?"

Shayne's voice rang in her skull like a struck bell. "Where are you? Why's it so noisy?"

"At the gym, ducked into the office to call you, but these walls aren't soundproofed for shit. Listen, Eshe's flying out to LAX tonight and we're catching the next plane to Toronto as soon as she lands."

"What?" Priya jolted upright and was slapped back down by a fresh burst of pain exploding behind her eyes. "Why?"

"Isobel needs us now. Right now. Told Cait to swing by and help you pack; send me your travel info so I can book you and Cait a flight at the same time tomorrow morning."

"What's going on? What's happened?"

"A fucking shitstorm of epic proportions," Shayne answered, "and our sister is caught in the middle of it."

* * *

Isobel woke in a recliner, stretched out with a bit of damp, folded paper towel on her brow and Sharon hunched over her, fanning a hand. Every finger was adorned with rings that caught the fluorescents and sent sparks to dance before her eyes. Bejeweled fireflies.

"Oh—oh she's conscious. Oh thank heaven! Isobel?" She snapped her fingers twice. "Isobel, how's your head? Can you see me?"

"I . . ." Isobel struggled to focus. To stand. Her head was spinning and her stomach twisted in knots, but at the forefront of it was confusion. *Why am I here? What happened?* But then it struck her like a battering ram to the solar plexus.

Kyle.

The video.

Oh God, she'd fainted. Fainted. It wasn't a dream. It happened. And the truth of it caused Isobel to sway into Sharon with a groan.

"Easy, sit back down." Sharon steered her back into the deep leather chair and Isobel pressed her fingers to her eyes, massaging them in slow, careful circles. She would not lose it in the office. Not in front of the people she worked with. They might be a small crew, but the last thing she wanted was anyone else witnessing her mental breakdown after fainting live on-air.

"There, there." Sharon stroked her back with long, rounded circles, knees popping and stressing the joints of her dark-wash jeans. "You've had one hell of a morning."

"How long was I—?"

"Unconscious?" Sharon arched a brow. "A few minutes. Norman had the interns swoop in to carry you into Ben's office and asked me to wait for you to come 'round."

"Ben . . ." It was then she took in the space. Dark-blue walls and white trim, charcoal carpet with boxes piled up the walls and stuffed under or against any available nook they could find. Isobel hated the chaos of clutter, and a workspace like this would suffocate her. Perhaps a strange detail to notice, but her reeling mind desperately latched onto anything it could to hold steady.

She was drowning in the deep side chair made from reclaimed distressed brown leather and studded brass trim that Ben Sawyer, the owner of *The Six*, sat in when taking power naps between meetings. Just then the door swung open, and Ben hastily rushed into the room, all belly on a skinny body. It must've wrought absolute havoc on his spine. Norman charged in behind him.

Seeing her, Ben's pinched face brightened. "There she is. How's the poor dear?"

"Still wobbly as a newborn lamb," Sharon answered, worry etched into a deep furrow between her penciled in brows, one of them half rubbed away. "I don't think she should move just yet."

"I'm sorry." God, her voice sounded like she'd flossed her windpipe with barbed wire.

"Not a worry, dear, not a worry. We're just glad you're all right." Ben nodded, his crown of white hair bobbing like algae caught in a tide. "Sharon, get the girl some water. Perhaps some aspirin too."

"I'm fine, I think. I . . . nothing hurts." *Aside from my heart.* That part of her felt like it had been ripped from her body and tumbled in a dryer with sandpaper and shards of glass.

"Good. Excellent. But you should still get some water into you."

"You heard the man." Norman snapped his fingers irritably at Sharon, then gestured vaguely at the door.

She hooked her tongue over the edge of her teeth. "Sure thing, boss."

As she walked out of the office, Norman cleared a stack of files from the settee and Ben plunked himself down.

"Isobel, dear girl, I know you're not feeling well, and I hate to be indelicate, but I must trouble you for a moment of your time." All anxious, nervous energy, Ben set the points of his elbows atop his knees, hands together as if in plea or prayer. "First, we want to apologize to you, on behalf of *The Six,* for the terrible shock you went through. Isn't that right, Norman?"

"Absolutely," Norman answered, though he didn't appear sorry in the least.

Shock? He made it sound like she'd touched a hot mug or gotten a splinter. A minor inconvenience. *I was ambushed.*

"We needed drama. Impact." Norman scrubbed a hand over the back of his neck, sighed. "The reality is people aren't interested in staged reactions, and very little grips them anymore. They want raw, real content. Unfiltered and authentic. Your truth. And look!" Grabbing the remote off the desk, Norman turned on the flat screen mounted on the wall. "These are the numbers from this morning's airing. Just *look.*"

A graph dominated the screen with a vivid blue line climbing across a harsh white background. The spike was massive, and rising by the second with clicks, shares, comments, and likes.

"It's not what we usually do, I know, but we were given limited notice to act quickly. Do I agree with Norman's brash actions? No. Most certainly not." Ben leveled the other man with a stern glare. "But they've undoubtedly yielded fruit, and our sponsors are *thrilled* by the response we're getting."

Fresh tears seared her eyes. *And that made it okay?* This wasn't just about numbers and ratings. This was her broken dreams splattered across the internet for all to see. She'd always counted on her work to be stable, and safe, and *sane.* Instead, it had ripped her heart from her chest and was now stomping on it. "I'm sorry . . . I'm really not feeling well. I need to go home."

"Of course you do." Sympathy colored Ben's voice but desperation shone in his eyes. "However, before you leave, I'm going to level with you, Isobel. *The Six* has faced a tough year.

A tough few years, if I'm totally blunt. We're a small network. Started out as a family-run paper, then expanded to morning cable, and now we need to go broader if we're going to survive, but it's a challenge, you see, with larger conglomerates beating us to the punch, as it were. CTV. CBC. Global . . . they always get the prime cuts of meat whereas we make do with bones and scraps."

Isobel murmured a soft apology though she wasn't quite sure where this was going or why she was apologizing for anything. Caitlin would claim she was a classic Libra. *Always avoiding conflict.*

"In fact—" Ben sighed. "The news industry as a whole has been hit. Papers are closing and some accomplished journalists are losing their jobs as readership migrates to social media vultures with their flashy celebrity headlines. It's a goddamn crisis forcing many to adapt and change with the times. We've been a little reluctant to follow suit." Slender fingers tugged on the collar of his shirt, revealing the flash of a gold chain with a jade Buddha. A gift from his wife. "Now I've got my back to a wall with little choice. I accept the inevitable or I sink further into irrelevance. It's your generation driving the market, so we need to tap into that vein if we're going to have a pulse for the next year. But today has given us a leg up. One we sorely needed."

"I'm sorry, I don't . . . what exactly does this have to do with me?"

Ben's small brown eyes shifted to her face but had trouble staying there.

Norman, however, had no such compunction. "Picture this." He held his hands before him like an artist framing a scene. "You and Kyle in the room together for the first time since the viral break of the sex tape. Jilted soon-to-be bride confronting her cheating fiancé, giving our viewers an exclusive behind the scenes insight into the scandal. We're offering you the entire morning segment. That's *two hours*." Norman drew his iPhone from his back pocket. "But we need you to call Kyle right now and get him to agree to exclusivity. Once we secure his agreement, I can have the production team put together the media contract within the hour."

"Think about it." Ben leaped in when Isobel's mouth tumbled open. "We could give this real heart and depth . . . *empathy*"—he raised a triumphant fist—"by sharing your side of the story and showing other young adults how an act of a moment can destroy a lifetime."

Isobel swiped her sweating, tingling palms over her thighs. She'd just been humiliated. Devastated. Her entire world had shattered in front of hundreds of thousands of people—soon to be millions—and they wanted *more*?

"I know this is painful." Ben's eyes softened, innocent as a puppy. "And I'm sorry if our proposal is indelicate, but we have a limited window here. Eventually someone will put money on the table—and we'll lose him."

Good. She wanted no part of this whatsoever. "I can't . . ."

"Isobel, please—"

"I said no."

Ben's shoulders slumped and his hands flattened at his side, a restless thumb beating a steady tempo against leather. "You were supposed to sit down with Norman later today, yes? To discuss a proposal for a promotion?"

"Yes?"

"Then as your boss, I'm going to have to ask you to reconsider. More than the future of *The Six* hangs in the balance here."

Isobel stiffened with fresh shock. *If you want the promotion, you'll do the interview. You'll sell us your soul, your heartache and pain.* He didn't say the words, but he didn't have to. The implication hung between them like the filthy laundry he was asking her to air. "Are you . . . threatening me?"

"Ben is just highlighting what's at stake." Norman clapped a hand to Ben's shoulder. "And if you're serious about being in the media you'll need to learn this is what the job demands. Putting yourself in the line of fire for the sake of the story."

"This isn't a story; it's my life."

Norman spread his hands with an easy shrug. "It's always someone's life."

Her heart kicked into a fast, uneasy rhythm and tears stung her eyes, but she blinked them away, holding the fragile threads of herself in place. Preserving what remained of her dignity.

Isobel lurched to her feet, stiff as an old woman. *Say something. Speak up. Defend yourself.* "I—I'm sorry, I have to go home."

Ben's brow furrowed with lines of irritation, but he masked it with a charming smile. "Yes, go and get some rest. We can reconnect tomorrow morning. Here." He handed Isobel the media engagement letter, and then offered his hands for her to clasp, caging her in his grip, clammy and cold. "I trust you'll make the *right* decision. For all of us."

Chapter Six

You complete me—Priya had always hated that saying. It inherently implied you were lacking before this other person came along to magically fill some cavernous void you weren't able to fill yourself. And sure, it might feel that way when the dusty season of a dating drought came to an end, but it was a message she refused to stand behind.

Love should enhance, but never, ever complete.

You should complete yourself. Period.

Which is why she'd crafted the motto for the Sisterhood—chase dreams not drama (aka *relationships!*). They were going to be the generation of women who would learn to save not only each other, but themselves. To take charge of their own happiness and sense of self-worth, to tackle their greatest ambitions and fears. And conquer them together.

And sure, commitment could be a beautiful thing. A powerful thing. It took an individual of unique ability to bind themselves so completely to a cause or a person, for the intricate facets of self and soul to grow alongside another so that all lines ran parallel instead of diverging.

A skill Priya lacked, if she was honest—and certainly what her ex-boyfriend Bhavin would say if ever interrogated.

Isobel, however, was a creature of commitment. Reliable, dependable, and constant as the North Star, she possessed the biggest heart and an unflagging sense of loyalty forged in true selflessness. A beautiful trait that could easily transform from virtue into vice, blinding her with the prettiest shade of rose-colored glasses that obscured the infinite gray of the world. Of people.

Priya pulled up to park at the curb. Isobel's family home sat in a happy residential stretch of Woodbine Corridor, a street lined with stately maples. The house itself was a semidetached red brick, with a faded cedar fence, green siding, and a bright yolk-yellow door.

Her last visit had been at least three years ago, following the accident, and she knew better than most that not all memories contained behind that door, despite its cheerful color, were happy. Isobel was seven when her mother, battling chronic depression, walked out and never came back.

Perhaps that was where it all started for her, Priya mused, throwing her car into Park. Isobel's compulsive need to keep everything in place. The same. Growing up as an only child with no one else but her father for guidance and comfort, she'd latched onto the Sisterhood and become its emotional glue. Its beautiful, beating heart. A heart that had to be carefully and ruthlessly protected, because when broken, it shattered.

"Time to wake the dead." Caitlin swiveled in the passenger seat, lavender hair gelled into a styled faux hawk, and dressed in a glaring neon green off the shoulder top with matching high-waisted pants and chunky black heels—she looked like a megawatt Riddler, but with more flare.

Shayne's snore, muffled beneath the wide brim of the black

panama hat placed over her face to shield her from the sun, ripped from the backseat. The rest of her was curled up as best she could manage considering Eshe's long legs occupied most of the dainty Prius.

"Oi!" Eshe jabbed her in the ribs with a pointed elbow. "Wake up, Shay. We're here."

"Fuck. Me." Groaning, Shayne pushed up the brim and rolled on her cheek to look out the window. "Hey!" she barked when Eshe gave her another persistent shove.

"Well? Hurry up."

Shayne glared over her shoulder. "Y'know there's a door on your side, right?"

"It leads into the road." Eshe flicked her hand. "Now move. Honestly, you're slower than treacle in January."

Opening the door, Shayne shambled out on stiff legs. "I'm jet-lagged."

"Oh, bugger off about *jet lag*. I'm the one who crossed the bleeding pond, yeah?"

In order to synchronize their travel itineraries, Eshe had made the trip from Heathrow with a layover connection through LAX where she and Shayne had met up to travel together to Toronto in first class, which Shayne had insisted on paying for in recompense for the brutal slog. For all her faults, no way would Shayne ever abandon a sister to ride solo in economy.

"If you want to play the who's more exhausted game, get in line." Priya shut her door and hit the lock button on the key fob. "I'm running on fumes."

"Entirely self-inflicted," Caitlin said, rounding the hood. "So, tell it to the jury, 'cause you'll get no sympathy from us."

Shayne popped the trunk and rooted out Cait's large

suitcase first and dropped it to the sidewalk with a heaving grunt. "Jesus fucking Christ. What's in there, a body?" Hands on her knees, she made a show of panting.

"You act surprised," Priya said. "When has Cait ever traveled light?"

"The fuck does she need so many clothes for three days?"

"A lot can happen in three days." Caitlin glared at them both, unimpressed. "And I like to have options."

"Are you done taking the piss or can we go inside?" Eshe raised the paper bag she'd cradled with all the tenderness of a beloved child in the backseat and swung it like a pendulum between them. "The ice cream's melting."

"Cool, but like . . ." Caitlin held up hands with two-inch-long hot-pink nails bedazzled with Swarovski and filed to points. "I don't *do* manual labor."

"Don't look at me." Shayne slung the strap of her black duffel over her shoulder and tipped the brim of her hat off her face. "You're hauling your own shit from here."

"Come on." Priya waved toward the suitcases. "I'll give you a hand." Huffing and puffing, with Priya at one end and Caitlin, the other, they shuffled down the skinny cobbled walkway and up to the front porch, freshly painted the same deep shade of green as the siding.

A black iron bench sat beneath the bay window, joined by a tall blue planter for company. An assortment of greenery poked out the top and swayed with every stroke of wind.

Caitlin set down her first suitcase with a heavy thud. "One more."

Shayne snickered as Caitlin loped back down the walkway. "You're not gonna help her with the rest?"

"She's lucky I managed this far." Priya sighed.

Eshe smirked. "I've got ice-cream duty."

"Fuck, Priya, you look terrible." Shayne frowned at her. "Didn't you sleep at all before the flight?"

"I *never* sleep before I travel. And it doesn't help that I was really hungover yesterday." Priya, dressed in yoga pants and a matching jacket, dropped her brow to Shayne's shoulder with a whimper. "Why does your body suddenly reject alcohol at twenty-five?"

Shayne wrapped an arm around her, stroking her back. "Hear it's worse after thirty."

"Kill me."

"Kyle first."

Fire in her blood, the haze of exhaustion steamed through Priya's pores. *Yes, Kyle first.* She'd devised all manner of cruel torture for him while en route to Toronto. "I can't believe him. Three months until the wedding and he pulls this? Idiot."

"Thank fuck for that. Imagine if this happened *after* Bel got hitched?"

Priya shook her head with a sigh. Shayne had never masked her disdain for Kyle, barely concealing an eye roll or whispered curse every time his name came up in conversation. But when he'd proposed last fall?

Isobel had come down to New York for one of his games, and he'd proposed afterward, while the team celebrated at a posh Manhattan restaurant. The fact that he'd done it without thinking to include any of the people who mattered to Isobel most—the Sisterhood or her father—should've been a huge red flag right there. It had caught all of the Sisterhood by surprise, but Shayne most of all. Isobel had FaceTimed the girls to share the news. Later that night Shayne had broken two fingers venting her anger against a concrete slab.

"There." Caitlin dropped her last bag at their feet, dark-brown skin glowing with effort.

"Bravo." Shayne offered mock applause. "Now you've got two flights of stairs to look forward to."

Caitlin's smile fell. "Boo."

"All right. Let's do this." Shayne wiggled out her shoulders then pushed her chin left and right, cracking her neck like she was about to enter the ring for a fight, before she punched the glowing white button of the doorbell with her thumb, painted in chipped midnight-blue polish that matched the messy waves of her shoulder-length dyed hair.

It wasn't long before the door swung open and Declan Morgan stood in front of them. His ash-blond hair might be tinted with gray, but his brown eyes were bright behind bold, chunky red frames. Even though his injury had robbed him of muscle, he was still Gerard Butler badass with Sean Connery swagger.

A dazzling smile broke across Shayne's face. "Hey, Pops."

His gaze flowed to each of them, mixed with joy and pain. "Girls." He stepped back so they could haul their bags inside—and hugged each of them in turn. "I told her you were coming as soon as I got Shayne's call. She's upstairs waiting for you. Been there since it all happened." Worry colored his cheeks, wavered in his hushed voice. "She won't come down. Won't talk about it."

Priya swept a soothing hand over the narrow back that had once been so broad. Isobel was right, the man was wasting away, and it made her even more ashamed she hadn't taken the time between Harvard and her studies to visit.

"You know Isobel, Pops—too busy tackling everyone else's problems to burden anyone with her own."

"That's what scares me." His eyes moistened. "Go on." Removing his glasses, Declan swept a knuckle across his cheeks. "See if you can crack her stubborn shell. I'm down here if you need me."

Priya's heart twisted at the defeated curve of his shoulders as he ambled to the living room.

"He looks miserable," Eshe whispered. "I've never seen him so sad."

"Heartbroken," Caitlin agreed.

"What did you expect?" Priya sighed. "His only child is grieving, and he can't do anything to help her through it."

"He can't." Shayne pushed up the brim of her hat. "But we can."

* * *

Isobel heard them in the rumble of voices and creaking of steps that rose steadily in a messy mixture of sounds long before the door opened.

Brace yourself.

She swiped at her face and sat up in bed. There wasn't an inch of her that didn't ache, right down to the apples of her cheeks, sore from hours of silent, gasping screams she'd smothered in her pillows so her father wouldn't hear her agony. Though she imagined the pain of her tears seeping through the cotton of her pillows and mattress, down into the floorboards to rain on him like poison.

Grief spread like shadows, shifting and sliding through

any available nook and crack it could find. And Isobel was fractured all over.

Brace yourself.

Inch by inch, she imagined threading herself together, tightening the seams, one at a time, so when the door swung open and Shayne swaggered in, Isobel hoped the smile on her face at least shone sincere, even if it trembled at the edges.

"Hey." Shayne's sly grin didn't hide the concern in her intense dark gold eyes.

The rest of the girls spilled in after her. God, her room was a mess. Her father had converted the attic into a bedroom when she'd turned thirteen, giving Isobel her own walk-in closet and en suite bathroom. As a kid, she'd felt so grown up, having the entire upper level to herself, and had taken considerable pride in decorating it, from the wash of ivory paint on the wood-paneled walls and sloped dormer ceiling to the array of photographs and artwork she'd collected over the years.

Landscapes and whimsical scenery, Isobel surrounded herself with poetry—either in word or in image. Things that sparked the imagination and made it wander beyond the confines of her bedroom.

Handmade curtains swayed in the tender breeze that swept in through her open window, perfuming the air with the scent of jasmine blooming in the garden just below. But all she could see now were the wads of tissues scattered by her bed, stacks of empty mugs, and a few plates with half-eaten slices of toast she'd struggled to choke down. Even she was a miserable sight to behold in an oversized T-shirt, fuzzy socks, and matted curls in desperate need of a wash, tied up a sloppy mess.

God, she really should've taken a minute to shower. Brushed

her teeth at least. Why hadn't she forced herself out of bed once her dad poked his head in to tell her they were coming? That felt like barely a moment ago, but she blinked at the filmy light filtering through the window, and realized, to her horror, it was morning. Barely twenty-four short hours since her life went up in smoke. So why did it feel like she'd aged a year?

"Hiya." Plopping down next to her, Eshe handed over a paper bag stamped with a swirling logo. "We got you some ice cream—vegan, of course, which wasn't bloody easy to come by, let me tell you."

Isobel peeked inside to find a glass jar with a black lid. "Rocky road?"

"Seemed appropriate considering the current state of affairs."

A faint smile strayed across Isobel's dry lips. "Thank you."

"Guys, I know this isn't the best of circumstances, but can we *please* take in this moment?" Removing her hat, Shayne tossed it across the room, aiming for the bedpost but missing the mark by a mile and bouncing it off the windowsill. "All of us. Here. Together!"

"Wow, you're right. It's been . . ." Priya hooked her sunglasses into the neck of her fitted yoga jacket. "Eighteen months?"

"Since my birthday party in San Diego." Caitlin spun in a circle—a haze of eye-watering lime green.

"A fucking eternity!"

"I'm sorry you all rushed out here. You really didn't have to come."

Eshe turned to her, shocked. "Of course we did."

"But—"

"First rule of the Stiletto Sisterhood: sisters above all else.

No way would we leave you to face this alone." Priya sat down on the bed. "So, we're here now. How are you holding up?"

"Not well," she admitted. The four of them gathered around Isobel and listened as she shared every brutal detail, from being blindsided on-set to her confrontation with her boss to arriving at Kyle's. There was little she remembered from that walk. Thirty-seven minutes lost in a fog that only cleared when she entered the still quiet of the condo.

I should be crying. The thought ricocheted inside of her like a pinball as she'd stood in his bedroom, but it wasn't pride that stopped her as much as an aching, hollow emptiness. The bullet of his betrayal had shot her clean through, leaving her shell-shocked in its wake. Numb. Barren. Like she'd slipped out of her body, floating and detached from her skin, stripped from her bones and sinew so all that remained was a dry husk.

Crossing the room, she'd toggled open the blinds—the cheap, white plastic variety that hung in vertical slats, and her brain snapped to the moment they'd argued over curtains at Pottery Barn. Kyle had wanted to spend a ton of money, insisting it was for quality not the brand, but she'd wanted to make them herself with fabric she'd found at a local thrift store.

They'd walked out empty handed.

In hindsight it felt stupid to remember a six-month old argument but as the narrow beams of light furrowed through the somber gray space, she realized there wasn't much, if anything, connecting her to him. To this place. He'd purchased the condo after signing with TFC, using most of the bonus even though she'd made it clear she couldn't move out of her father's home after the wedding. Kyle had insisted on proceeding with the investment.

Only now did she see it for what it was—a way out. All the signs had been there, right beneath her nose, if she'd only pulled her gaze from the horizon long enough to stare down at her feet. But Isobel was always looking ahead, that was her biggest problem. Worried if she pulled her attention away from the carefully mapped out horizon, something would change, fall out of place. And vanish. As it had now. Her delicate, papier-mâché world crushed by clumsy, thoughtless, selfish hands.

Isobel stopped at the foot of the bed where Kyle lay tangled in sheets, face down and snoring into a pillow. Sunlight danced across curls shorn close to his scalp they went from brown to almost golden near his nape. He'd let it grow out when they were younger, and she'd always loved his hair. The soft, springiness of his curls against her fingers. She'd been sad when he'd decided to cut it off after signing with TFC.

She watched the rise and fall of his wide, chiseled back, the warm copper tone of his skin, for a lingering moment. Once, back when they were just little kids at summer camp, they'd sat together and made up little stories about where each unknown feature on their faces had come from. A fun game that had fused them as a couple of kids without moms.

Isobel's hand pressed against the ache in her chest, to where the pendant dangling around her neck, and all the sweet memories attached to it, blazed hot against her skin, shooting her from the present moment straight into the past. It had been his first real gift to her. A gold charm of Tinker Bell midflight with two birthstones dangling from the tips of her wings. An opal for Isobel and a garnet for Kyle. Inseparable. Destined for each other. Soul mates.

Isobel imagined smashing her hand into the walls, breaking

bones and tearing flesh—if only to feel *something* again. She wanted to scream. And to fall into his arms and let him hold her. How could the person responsible for causing so much pain be the same one she craved comfort from? Slipping off her engagement ring, she dropped it on the messy bed and walked away without a word.

Just as she hadn't stood up for herself with her boss, she'd failed to find the strength to confront Kyle, folding like a wilted flower hammered by the rain, and fled home to bury herself in blankets and tears.

"I can't believe your boss tried to extort you after you were blindsided on-air." Priya shook a furious head. "You should sue his ass. I'll help."

"Right after I deck the asshole," Shayne agreed. "I hope you told him to fuck off. Otherwise I'm happy to do it for you."

That teased a laugh out of her but it burned as acrid as her tears. "No, it's fine. It's done, you know? But I can't go back. I can't . . ."

"You won't have to," Priya assured her. "What about Kyle? Has he tried to contact you at all since?"

"No." Isobel hung her head. "I sent an email to my production manager, letting her know I quit, and then shut off my phone, deleted all my social media to cancel out the noise." But there'd been no calls or messages or knocks at her door other than ravenous reporters hounding her for her story.

A resurgence of tears swelled in her eyes, and Isobel couldn't tell what hurt more—the chill of her naked finger or that he let her go without a fight? Or an apology? Tears splattered on the back of her hand. Isobel stared at those broken orbs, mired in a blurred mess she couldn't find her way through. A haze of agony.

This pain. This pain is going to cleave me in two.

She could almost feel the strings in her heart snapping. One by one. Fragile threads plucked under careless fingers. One summer, she'd gone to Mexico with Priya and Shayne, and had bought a gorgeous peasant blouse from a street vendor. She'd loved that shirt. Its hand-beaded detailing and ruffled sleeves, and the way it fell gracefully off her shoulders. But when she got home, she'd discovered the elastic woven into the neckline was coming undone. Ruptured stitches in an unraveling seam. And despite every effort, Isobel couldn't stop the ruin. The decay.

I'm falling apart. Isobel swiped furiously at her eyes. *Just like that shirt, I can't hold myself together.* But she had to. God help her, she had to be strong even if her entire world was gone in the span of a couple of hours.

Job. Fiancé. Future. All of it.

"I was so ready to be married, but I guess apparently he wasn't." Isobel pressed her eyes shut, as if trying to dig through the tangled mess of her thoughts and emotions to find the right words.

Priya brushed a lock of brown hair from Isobel's face. "You did the right thing, babe. Hard as it is, you'll get through this."

"Really, I'm fine. I think I'm . . . empty." Removing the top of the jar, Isobel peeled back the layer of protective film but ventured no closer to digging the wooden spoon into the melting dessert. "I've cried so much—until my head hurt so badly I could scarcely breathe. I thought my brain was going to liquefy in my skull. I didn't sleep because of it. Then it just stopped. So I think that's it. I'm empty."

A lie. She was nowhere near empty. She'd had eight years with Kyle—a lifetime—and the loss of it was going to demand a serious price. Her suffering on the path to healing had only just begun, but she needed to convince them, and herself, that she was strong enough to endure this. *Because if I can't?* Isobel didn't want to let her thoughts continue down that dark path.

"Holy mother of Prada." All eyes turned to Caitlin. "Sorry, I googled Teri Mauve." She gagged over the photo, then flashed it around for them all to see. "She's like forty. Does the guy have no standards?"

"It's a well-documented fact," Priya said with an authoritative lift of her chin, "women sleep with who they want. Men take what they can."

"Well." Eshe picked at her nails with fingers as long and graceful as her legs. "I think even if Kyle had cheated with a goddess like Rihanna, Isobel wouldn't feel any better or worse than she already does."

"True." Caitlin swiped across her screen and flinched in disgust. "Ew, these keep getting worse. But listen to this." She rocked onto her knees, eyes glued to her phone. "Reports say that the release of the video was likely a revenge thing, after Teri Mauve was caught having sex with her best friend's long-time boyfriend. Apparently, she likes them *taken*."

"Okay." Eshe shook a disgusted head. "While I'll never sanction attacking another woman over looks or age, I'm all for dragging one for not honoring girl code."

"And that right there, theydies and gentlethem, is why I made a marriage pact with Earl last month," Caitlin said.

"Your flatmate?" Eshe slid her fingers into her thick, dense, outrageously long curls and gave them a shake from the crown. "The one from Brisbane, yeah?"

"One and the same."

From her perch on the windowsill, Shayne scoffed with feigned disgust. "I thought I was your backup future husband?"

"You're now the backup to my backup. He has a better closet."

"Rude."

"Sorry not sorry." Caitlin blew her a kiss.

"Why not just marry the right guy for love? Or *person*," Isobel quickly amended, as Shayne went in every which direction imaginable. Love, for her, didn't have boundaries, just feelings and connection.

Caitlin shrugged a breezy shoulder. "Because monogamy is a dying, idealistic belief. I'm sorry, sweetie, but it is. We are a culture of excess. More this. More that. So, marrying a platonic friend just makes practical, long-term economic sense. This way we'll live happily ever after, swapping clothes and having hot, illicit sex with *other* people."

"Preach!" Shayne toasted the air with her half-finished lemon lollipop. Her third in the span of an hour, but it kept her hands from reaching for cigarettes.

"I'm sorry, I wish I could be so . . . pragmatic, but I can't. I don't know how."

"*Ma petite chérie*, I know it feels like you're all alone in this dark hole, but we've been there." Caitlin flopped across the foot of the bed. "I was wrecked after Fabian, remember? When he ghosted me after our baecation in Colombia, like a total *dickwad*?"

"And I dropped near a stone after ending things with Charles," Eshe added. "Shay . . . what about you and Gabriella?"

Shayne's lips flattened into a grimace. "We do not speak of those dark days."

"The point is," Caitlin continued, "heartbreak sucks, but it does get better. Eventually."

"Priya's never been cracked." Shayne wagged her sucker. "Heart of granite and steel. Impenetrable as Fort Knox."

"Except to us!" Caitlin amended.

"Bhavin certainly didn't make a dent. Poor bloke."

Caitlin mimed a heart snapping with her fingers. "I don't think Priya shed a single tear."

"She was bed-hopping outside of a week after she dumped him, and hasn't stopped since."

"What exactly is wrong with bed-hopping?" Affronted, Priya crossed her arms. "I'm single and enjoying my freedom, thank you very much."

"And I applaud you for it." Shayne clapped her hands. "But you didn't exactly suffer, did you?"

"Well, between residency and law school, we almost never saw each other." Priya scowled. "Besides, it's easier when you're the one doing the dumping."

"Which is why I now hit it and quit it—respectfully." Shayne swiped a hand over her mess of navy hair. "Can't change what's happened, damage is done, so guess it's time to move on, right, Bel?"

Move on? How? That was the million-dollar question, and one Isobel didn't really have an answer for. "The hardest part of all of this is what do I do now." She looked down at her hands and shrugged. "No job. No wedding to plan. No fiancé . . . if it wasn't for my dad, I'd have nothing to do except drown in this pain."

"*Oooh.*" Caitlin wiggled giddy hands. "I brought my tarot! Want me to pull some cards? Commune with your divine guides and ancestors?"

"Fucking hell." Shayne laughed. "If you say Mercutio is renegade with Pluto cheating on Nirvana type shit, I'll have to slap you."

"It's *Mercury.*" Caitlin rolled her eyes. "And for your information, we do have a full moon in Libra tonight with four planets currently retrograding in Aquarius, which is a lot of air energy, just so you know, and tomorrow another two are stationing—*ow!*" Caitlin swiped at the back of her head.

"I warned you."

"Here's a thought." Beaming, Eshe gave Isobel's shoulders an excited wiggle. "Why don't you come back with me to London? Get away and take your mind off your troubles?"

"I think that's a great idea," Priya agreed. "The distraction will do you some good."

"I can't. I wish I could, but I can't." Isobel hugged her arms around her knees. "Bills are piling up—I can't afford to be unemployed right now."

"If you need funds just tell me how much." Shayne chewed on the stick of her finished lollipop.

"I appreciate it. I do. But we'll be fine. Once Dad's settlement comes through things will be different. Better."

Priya set a comforting hand on Isobel's thigh, but the tightness in her jaw was all frustration and determination. "Any development there?"

"Not much, no. But his new legal aid lawyers are optimistic they can undo the mess from the previous ones."

Ever the eternal pessimist, doubt shone vividly in Priya's eyes, but Isobel knew she wasn't about to pop that filmy soap bubble of hope, no matter how fragile and insubstantial, and as of this moment, Isobel loved her fiercely for it.

"Flip me their emails and whatever settlement paperwork the construction company is proposing. I'll review and give you some notes to take back to your lawyers by the weekend. Okay?"

"Aren't you . . ." Isobel winced. "Terribly busy?"

"Never too busy for my sisters." Leaning in, Priya gave her a noisy kiss on the cheek.

"And if you need a job, I've got lots of connections in the entertainment scene here in Toronto. Club owners, promoters. I could put in a word with a bunch of them, see what turns up?"

"What am I going to do for a nightclub, Shayne? Fetch vodka for bottle service?" Isobel sighed. "*The Six* wasn't much, but I wanted to do something of value before I settled down, started a family. A home. Children. That was my dream. That was always my dream. I feel so lost. Oh God . . . there's *more.*" Her face twisted with a wrenching sob and she folded into Eshe's arms.

"Fuck this." Shayne rose from the windowsill. "I'm canceling the pity party, effective right the fuck now."

"Shayne."

Ignoring Priya's whispered warning, Shayne muscled her way onto the bed, catching Isobel under the chin. "Here's the hard truth, Bel—you're better off without him. You love with all your heart and give with every breath, so that's why I know—we know—everything good and wonderful about your relationship you built. You created. Now it's time for you to fall in love with yourself. All that effort and energy? You get it back, and that's a win. A huge win. Even if it doesn't feel like it right now. But it's up to you to seize this opportunity with both hands and fight like hell for it. Because you deserve to be fought for, Bel. So fight. And come back stronger than ever." Shayne notched Isobel's chin higher when it wanted so desperately to fall. "Kyle broke your heart, but I'll be damned if I let him break your spirit too."

"I love you." Isobel smiled around a watery sniffle. "Like Jack Sparrow loves rum."

"I love you, too, like RuPaul loves drag." Satisfied, Shayne planted a firm kiss against Isobel's lips, still wet with tears. "Time to break you out of your self-imposed prison sentence, hot stuff."

"What's the plan?" Priya asked.

"I'm thinking we go big. Manis, pedis, massages, dinner, drinks, and dancing," Shayne answered. "The works."

"I don't know. I can't leave my dad alone all day *and* night."

"You most certainly can and will!" Declan appeared from the shadows of the corridor where he'd apparently been eavesdropping and stood smiling through tears on the threshold. "I won't hear another word on the matter. You're going." He wagged a determined finger at her. "Even if I have to drag you out myself. Finally get to enjoy a bit of quiet and pizza without interruption."

"Thank you, Pops!"

"I don't know what to wear."

"I'm sure Cait can MacGyver something."

"On it!" Caitlin vaulted from the bed with a squeal and sprinted for the closet.

"Priya, you've got face duty." Shayne clapped her hands like a general commanding her troops. "Eshe, hair."

"What about you?" Priya mused.

Pulling her phone from her back pocket, Shayne gave it a wiggle. "Access to all the hottest spots in the city, and while I do that"—she smirked at Isobel—"get Priya to tell you how she lost her panties."

Chapter Seven

You only had one chance to make a first impression, but Priya woke up early Monday morning, determined to do the impossible and forge a new one. A stronger one.

"Morning, tiger." Hadrian toasted her with his Starbucks as they joined the line waiting for the elevators. His eyes raked over her navy two-piece and lingered on her lacquered black pumps. "You clean up well."

"Are you mocking me?" she demanded, annoyed that in the span of thirty seconds he had her questioning whether her tapered pantsuit and sleeveless white blouse, which she'd considered confident sophistication, would be interpreted as trying too hard.

Or worse, boring.

After her summer internship with the DA, she'd quickly learned the endless frustrations of being an attractive woman in a male dominated industry: you were either quickly dismissed or became the object of male attention. As a result, all her suits came with pants and blouses buttoned high with minimal cleavage to keep her male colleagues' attention drawn to her eyes when they spoke to her, not down at her breasts.

"Did it come out as mockery?" he asked as he steered them

toward the elevator that flashed their floor number on the screen. "Sorry, didn't mean to offend you. Must be the London in me. Makes everything I say sound frustratingly arrogant."

"Whatever. Not like I need corporate fashion advice from someone dressed like a peacock." She spun a finger at him. "You do realize you're a lawyer, yes?"

"Guilty as charged." Hadrian grinned and stroked a hand over the lapel of his quarter-lined summer jacket. Dark blue-green fabric with a discreet tonal grid pattern in a slightly lighter shade for visual richness complemented his vibrant paisley button-down shirt and lavender tie. A shark's tooth dangled from a leather cord around his throat—a pretentious hipster pendant to play off his equally pretentious outfit.

Caitlin wouldn't know whether to jump him or raid his closet.

"Lucky for me MNS isn't quite so rigid," Hadrian continued. "Marai Nagao, herself, is famous for her red power suits and shaved hairline."

He had a valid point. Irritated by that fact, Priya punched the button for the twenty-seventh floor, and tried not to think about the first time she'd ridden in an elevator alone with him, though it was exceedingly difficult. After landing back in New York she'd watched the video more than a few times, and knew enough about her body to gauge that, based on the sounds she was making, whatever Hadrian had done to her was good—*very* good.

"You know." Hadrian leaned in casually at her side as more bodies spilled into the elevator, wedging them tighter into the back corner. "It's customary to follow someone's compliment with one of your own."

Priya swung a glance at him over her shoulder. "My hair looks wonderful this morning."

"Say that again?"

"You complimented my suit; I complimented my hair—as per your suggestion of 'following up with one of my own.'"

"That's not what I meant, and you know it."

She raised a bemused shoulder, her lips itching to curve into a grin. "We're lawyers. Our profession demands specificity; next time you'll know to be more precise."

Smiling, Hadrian slid his tongue along the edge of his teeth and a lick of heat flashed low in her belly. "Duly noted."

The doors pinged open, revealing Heather, hands on her hips and hellfire in her eyes. "There you are! You're *late. Both* of you." She swung her arm in a summoning circle. "Everyone's gathered in the boardroom as of ten minutes ago. I was sent to track you down. *Move.*"

"I don't understand." Priya panted, once again jogging after Heather. "The morning meeting is scheduled for eight thirty?"

"As you'll learn, meetings tend to change frequently. A memo went out late last night with an updated calendar invite, advising everyone to be here for seven forty-five."

The color fled from Priya's cheeks. "*What?*"

Stopping outside the boardroom doors, Heather pierced Priya with a cool gaze over her shoulder. "The details of your incompetence are not *my* problem. Ms. Nagao doesn't tolerate tardiness."

"Easy, tiger," Hadrian whispered, his hand pressed to the small of her back. "What's done is done. Shake it off."

The doors pushed open, leading into a colossal boardroom with a lake-size table flanked with long leather benches against the walls allowing another thirty or more to pack in, while those who couldn't secure a seat were left standing. Heads whipped around as they entered, and Priya's gaze skipped across the seated associates—expressions ranging from amused to predatory—straight down the length of stoic senior partners to a severely unimpressed Marai Nagao waiting at the head of the table. And here she was, one of the last kids to find her desk on the first day of school.

Priya wove around the slew of bodies, finding an empty chair between a stocky Asian guy and a mousy white girl with thick glasses, hands folded in front of her.

"Now that we are *all* in attendance, let's get back to business." Marai uncrossed her arms. "We at MNS hold to a unique tradition. Two percent of our annual caseload is pro bono, and after careful review and selection, we've set aside one file for each of our associates." Raising a remote, Marai flicked on the screen at her back. "As you can see, we've broken you into teams, and each of you will have weekly check-ins with your assigned coach to ensure you don't slide off the rails with your case. This is an important opportunity to provide meaningful support to this firm, and a chance to make a strong impression on the senior team. To sell yourselves. Performances will be graded based on their assessment of your abilities, and the associate with the most impressive score will be mentored by me, personally, for one year."

Marai paused, bracing herself on the table. "Once, a long time ago, I was plucked from the bullpen by a name partner. His guidance shaped me into the woman standing before you today, and I've paid that forward ever since. In twenty years, I have mentored thirteen men and women and of those, more than half have advanced to prestigious roles, including our very own Daniella Morales and Winston Chu—two of our youngest senior partners. This year, however, will be my last."

A collective murmur of surprise broke out around the table, even among the senior team.

"Why?"

Priya's head snapped up at the unexpected gunshot, and for a single, horrified moment she thought she might have voiced the question aloud, but it was, in fact, Ms. Mouse to her left.

"We haven't formally announced it as of yet, but George Silver is retiring at the end of the year, therefore I will stand as sole managing partner until we, as a firm, appoint a successor." Murmurs circled the room, along with Marai's gaze. "Any other questions?"

Priya raised her hand and waited for Marai to reach her before she spoke. "Who decides *what* case we get?"

"They will be handed out by a short list of senior partners up for consideration to replace George following his departure from the firm. As always, we thank them for graciously donating their time to this exercise, so I expect you all to take this very, very seriously because your actions will not only reflect upon you, but on your team coach, as well. Your sessions begin this afternoon, following completion of orientation for our new hires. After that you will have until tomorrow morning to prepare your brief and meet with your coach to discuss." Straightening, Marai dusted her hands. "You all talked the talk in your interviews, or else you wouldn't be here. Now it's time to show me what you're made of." Answering laughter rippled among the senior team.

"Let the games begin."

* * *

Orientation gave Priya an anchor in her storm. The associates were split into smaller groups and whisked from floor to floor, each specializing in its own area of law, from corporate mergers and acquisitions to litigation class action defense, and anchored by a department head, with Marai Nagao and George Silver at the summit.

The last stop was IT, for the new hires to collect their security badges, employee codes, work-assigned laptops, and phones. If Priya so much as sneezed within the walls of the firm IT would know. By the time she'd reached her assigned workstation, Hadrian was already tucked into his cubicle, two over to the left of hers.

"Hi, neighbor." He reclined in his chair, polished shoes propped on the edge of his desk.

Ignoring him, Priya slotted her laptop into its dock and logged in. Of the new associates, she'd sized up three who'd been assigned to her team during the orientation, and with less than an hour before the team meeting, she set to work googling the first.

Jessica Borland—the mouse. Only child of a real estate mogul father and interior designer mother. Brought up in an orthodox Jewish household and a Columbia grad, she'd helped immigrant families navigate social services, the immigration detention system, and voter registration, translating for Yiddish-speaking clients.

Calvin Chan, born in Hong Kong and immigrated to the US at the age of six. According to an interview conducted in his third year at Brown, he overcame a challenging childhood. Abandoned by his gambling addict father, raised by his mother, one of three young boys. They'd lived out of a Buick for several years. After scrolling through his social media, Priya discovered that Calvin was also currently battling retinitis pigmentosa, a slow but progressive loss of vision, starting with peripheral. As of yet, there was no cure.

She'd only just opened a new browser to start digging into the third when her alarm pinged. Three thirty had galloped upon her like the Headless Horseman brandishing his flaming pumpkin and sharp sword, and she was out of time.

Priya made her way to the firm's library, positioned between the second and third boardrooms, across from one of four file rooms. A dozen high bookcases stacked with legal texts in various leather-bound volumes lined every wall, and Priya could almost see herself working late nights with her peers, pouring over briefs, and drowning in research.

A trio of tables was set up at the front, but only one had five chairs on one side with the senior partner coaching Priya's team standing at the other. She waited until they were all seated before swooping thick curls over her shoulder in a rioting mane that reminded Priya of Eshe.

"Welcome. My name is Daniella Morales, but everyone calls me Dani." She smiled wide, revealing a slight gap between her front teeth. "As Marai explained earlier this morning, I will be your coach. Outside of today, these cases"—she perched her fingers on the stack to her right—"will be managed in your own time. As associates for MNS your priority will be the day-to-day responsibilities, after which you can work through your assigned case. I don't expect you'll find many available windows, so a word to the wise: make each minute count. After tomorrow we will meet weekly, and my assistant, Xander, can help with coordinating, but don't delay—my calendar fills up fast. Now, on to the fun part. Taryn Jobin, as you were the first of this group to arrive this morning, you get first dibs. Use this advantage wisely."

Taryn, a poised young blond, smiled like a thoroughbred racehorse being awarded a rose garland. She took her time, flipping through the cover pages, and settled quickly on the third file. Given the incline of Daniella's head, Priya was willing to guess she approved of the selection.

"That leaves four remaining," Daniella continued once Taryn was reseated. "And there's a surprise twist for this portion of the game. Depositions." She wiggled her fingers with a devious grin. "Consider this a fun little icebreaker, and a chance to improve your standing as well as learn a little something about your fellow competition. We'll do two ten-minute rounds with one of you playing the deposing counsel and the other the deponent. The goal is simple—rattle the cage."

It took every ounce of control she had for Priya to resist punching a triumphant fist into the air. This was it—her moment for redemption; to wipe the slate clean and show not only the other associates, but her team coach, just what she could do.

Calvin pushed his glasses up the bridge of his nose. "How can we depose each other? We just met today."

"If you expect me to believe you haven't been sizing each other up all morning," Daniella said with a smirk, "then you either think I'm stupid or you are."

Judging by the thinning of Calvin's lips and his reddening cheeks, he fell in the latter.

"Who gets to be the shark and who the minnow? Priyanka Seth." She gestured at a vacant chair to her immediate left. "If you'd please."

Unbuttoning her blazer, Priya slid into the seat, and for the first time all damn morning, a calmness settled into her bones that presaged going to war. She loved this part the most. Sitting in a courtroom, squaring off with a judge and tearing into a defendant on the stand. She lived for the rush. The thrill. But she could hold the stand just as efficiently.

"Now." Daniella bridged her fingers beneath her chin. "Who should be your opposing counsel?"

One of the associates stood and cast Daniella a disarming smile. "I'd like to volunteer."

"Ah, Mr. Winship." Dani looked at Priya. "Any objections?"

Michael Winship. Unlike the rest of the associates in the room, he wasn't a new hire, and though she'd planned to dig into him last, she'd run out of time. But studying him now, she could see that his suit, though expensive, strained against his arms and legs. He wasn't big, but it was clear he'd packed on some muscle quickly and hadn't taken the time to invest in an updated wardrobe, not because he couldn't afford it but because he wanted people to notice the change and admire him for it.

She'd chewed up a dozen like him at Harvard. Priya sat a little straighter. "None."

"Please state your name for the record."

"I've already been introduced."

Michael slipped his hands into his trouser pockets. "Humor me."

Feet crossed at the ankles, Priya set her hands in her lap

and met his gaze. "Priyanka Victory Seth." A lick of irritation lashed at the way his lips skewed derisively at hearing her middle name.

"And what's your background?"

"American. Born and raised."

"By birth, but not nationality." He flashed an arrogant smile but something else lurked beneath the snark and sarcasm. A meanness she'd come to know rather well growing up in a predominantly white community.

Asshole. But all the better, for her at least, if he played the race card. It was lazy and so utterly predictable she almost sighed in pity. Priya was no stranger to microaggressions or overt racism. She had lost count of the number of times people had spoken to her in slow, exaggerated sentences, assuming she didn't understand English. Or commented on how she was *actually* very pretty for a *brown girl*. A lifetime of it had given her thick skin. No way was she going to let this douche bro rattle her. "I don't see how that's pertinent."

"It's a simple question."

"An irrelevant one."

He advanced, soles whispering over rough carpet. "It's not a big deal. Answer the question."

Yes, it is a big deal. A big deal that I have to explain what I am instead of who I am. "If you're asking about ethnicity, my mother is from India." She spoke coolly, calmly, but didn't hold back the flash of irritation in her eyes; the flames were too high—too hot—for her to contain them completely.

"Lakshmi Seth, am I right? Nobel Prize winner?"

"Yes." She heard a few whispered comments, a couple of soft gasps.

Michael whistled low, gave a soft round of applause. "She's created some big shoes for you to fill; following in them can't be easy."

Where he was going with this line of inquiry? What was his strategy? His plan of attack? Surely he couldn't be stupid enough to target a woman as accomplished as Lakshmi Seth. "I'm very proud of my mom."

"And what about your father, Priyanka?"

"His name is Hernan Suarez. Former CEO of Suarez Communications before he stepped down seven years ago, and now he sits as chairman of the board. He and my mother reside, currently, in Amsterdam, while my mom completes a yearlong teaching engagement."

"Wait, I'm confused. You're referring to your *step*father; I asked about your *father*."

"He *is* my father." Basic deposition tactics: answer the question directly, keep to fact, and minimal emotion. *Calm movements. Soft expression. Don't give him an inch.* "Hernan's been in my life since I was seven and married my mom when I was eighteen. He raised me. Loved me. Provided for me. I don't see how much more I can clarify the subject."

"That's sweet, but I wasn't talking about bedtime stories and backyard barbeques. I'm talking about simple, basic biology." Michael braced himself on the table between them, a predator closing in for the kill. "*Who* is your father?"

Ah. Here we go. "I don't know who he is."

"And that's because approximately twenty-six years ago your mother visited a specialist for artificial insemination with sperm from a carefully screened, anonymous donor."

"It's not a state secret."

"How old were you when your mother told you?"

"I found out when I was thirteen."

"Found out. Interesting choice of words. Did she not tell you?"

Priya skimmed her tongue along the edge of her teeth. "No. There was a file in her study containing all her medical documentation compiled while planning her insemination. She was using it as the basis for a collection of essays she'd decided to write for her next book on creation and identity. I saw it when I came home from school and confronted her later that evening." A startling secret revelation her young mind had struggled to process. To accept. She'd made the mistake of telling a friend at school she'd thought she could trust—needing someone to confide in, to share the burden of discovery, to shoulder her confusion and pain. Instead that friend blabbed to the rest of her class, and before end of day the entire school knew.

Freak!

Alien!

Science experiment!

Priya came home sobbing and begged her mother to enroll her in a new school. *Running away won't fix this, Priyanka. You're going to have to find a way to endure.* And though part of her had resented her mother for not swooping in to save her, Priya walked through those doors for the next three years with her head high, pretending she didn't hear their mean jokes and cruel taunts. She'd weathered the onslaught of ridicule and scorn, and after that, she'd never made the mistake of telling anyone ever again, until her sisters.

"How did it make you feel when you *found out*?" His words pressed on her like a knife to a wound. "Confused? Angry?"

"Sure."

"Is that why three months later you walked into a boutique and tried to steal a four-thousand-dollar calfskin leather jacket?"

Priya's heart stuttered then stopped for a horrible, terrifying second. And all thoughts of deposition strategy escaped her mind.

He knows. He knows. He knows.

Shame and humiliation surged beneath her skin, flashing from head to toe in alternating waves of hot and cold. *Breathe, Priya.* But her lungs collapsed and refused to expand, like the balloons for a wildlife fundraiser that she'd coerced her mother into letting her organize for sixth grade. Fresh out of the packaging, she'd blown and blown and blown until she was red faced and panting, but not a single balloon would inflate.

That was how she felt right now. Limp. Compressed. Defective.

"Answer the question!"

She jolted under the severity of his tone. "Those records were sealed." Remembering that helped stave off the shock. They were sealed. So how did Michael figure it out? Even the *wise and all-knowing Google* wouldn't be able to pull up that ancient skeleton, especially not in such a narrow window of opportunity. But *how* and *why* suddenly became irrelevant as the pain of degradation burned away in wakening flames of rage.

"So you don't deny it? You, Priyanka *Victory* Seth, an

associate for a major law firm—tasked with upholding the law—committed a crime?"

"I was thirteen and angry. It was a childish act of rebellion." Admitting it aloud was like chewing on glass. Painful and bloody. *Don't let him see he's gotten to you.* "I made a mistake."

"Spoken like a true criminal. *I was upset. I made a mistake.*" He mimed tears. "Maybe I'd believe you, if there weren't three other incidents over the span of six months. Hardly a singular lapse of judgment. Earlier you said you were proud of your mother; do you think she'd say the same about you?"

"Yes."

"You say yes, but your tone lacks the conviction I heard in you earlier. Can't imagine she was thrilled when police escorted you home. Makes me wonder how Lakshmi Seth, one of the greats of our time, the voice of movements and inspiration to generations, must feel about having—"

"Stop it."

"—a thief for a daughter? Admit it, Priya, there's a part of you, however small, that wonders to this day: Is my mother secretly disappointed? Embarrassed? Ashamed?"

Her throat seized; the ache too fierce for her to speak. To breathe.

"That's time, Mr. Winship. Well done, you two."

Well done? She'd cracked and now everyone knew the chink in her armor. Before the end of the day this would spread like blood in the water—just as the gossip about her parentage had in school—and the sharks would close in to tear her apart and feed.

"Thank you for graciously completing our first round." Daniella lifted two file folders and held them out for Priya and Michael respectively. "As for the rest of you, let's take an adjournment. Stretch your legs, grab some water, and we'll continue in twenty minutes."

The associates didn't require further prompting, and by the time Priya collected her satchel, the library had emptied out. Shouldering the strap, too angry to think coherently, she stalked off in search of her target, and found Michael at the end of the corridor, surrounded by several of the other associates. His back was to her as he enjoyed some joke—probably at her expense.

Priya tapped a firm hand to his shoulder. "I'd like to speak with you."

"As you can see—" He tipped down his chin, still smiling. "I'm in the middle of a conversation. One you've rudely interrupted."

Fine. If he wanted to do this in front of an audience, so be it. However, the other associates at least had the sense to move on while she squared up with Michael. "What I consider rude is crossing personal boundaries."

"We were asked to rattle the cage, and that's what I did. Don't like it? Tough." He shrugged. "I took aim at the biggest target on the list. You. So now it doesn't matter what anyone else does for the day—no one is going to top that."

"You expect me to believe that was a *bring down the wunderkind* strategy? No. It was personal." She edged in closer. "If you've got something against me, come out and say it with some balls. Unless your parents spayed you like a teacup Chihuahua?"

"Wunderkind. That's cute." His eyes wove around them, assessing the corridor before he continued, voice hushed more for intimidation than discretion. "Crossbreeding aside, you're a fucking science project conceived in a petri dish with a famous mommy who kicked open all kinds of doors for you while the rest of us worked to get where we are. I'm not going to sit back and watch you swoop in on her coattails, leveraging some *woman of color* affirmative action bullshit to push your way to the top when I've devoted nearly two years to this firm. That mentorship is mine by right."

Staggered, Priya locked her knees underneath her for strength. Not only was he a racist and a misogynist, but a purist. A trifecta of trash juice left out in the hot July sun.

"If Marai agreed with that she would've picked you already. Whether I was born via IVF or through good old-fashioned *sex*, I am a human being and deserve to be treated with a modicum of respect."

"You think what I did in that deposition was cruel? Just wait." His eyes bored into her. Through her. "I'm not finished with you. Far from it."

It took every ounce of self-control Priya had left to hold her ground as he walked away, but she was more than shaken. More than bruised.

Not here. She needed somewhere safe to escape. To breathe. Priya set her sights on the ladies' room at the opposite end of the floor. Far away from the general crowd. But she had to cross the bullpen to get there. Hadrian caught sight of her as she blazed down the row, and from the expression that crossed his face at the sight of her, she definitely looked as bad as she felt.

"Tiger?"

"Not now." She barely made it through the doors of the

bathroom before the first sob, a sharp bubble, ruptured in her throat like a bomb. Diving into the first stall—floor to ceiling walls without gaps or crevices—she bolted the door shut and pressed herself against it. Shaking.

Breathe, Priya, breathe. Carefully, she slid, boneless, to the floor, and willed her heartbeat to ease, her thoughts to clear. When she was a kid and life got too heavy, too overwhelming, she'd hole away in her bedroom closet, sit there in the dark and breathe for hours and hours until her mind settled and her anxiety eased. These attacks didn't spring up on her as often anymore, but when they did she had minutes to rein it in or face the dizzying explosion that left her defenseless and unable to do much of anything except ride it out.

But she couldn't hide in here forever.

Priya held her breath, counted to three, then released— slow and easy. Her thumb and forefinger pressed together as she mentally chanted the *deeply relaxed* mantra her therapist had taught her back in her second year of law school. Beneath the wall of her chest her heart still bounced and beat in an unnatural rhythm, but the numbness was easing out of her fingers and the rolling waves of panic slowly smoothed out in the iron grip of her self-control.

She'd faced some truly horrible people in her life, but it never got any easier. Only more exhausting. More draining. And this was next level with the stakes stacked so high she thought everything was going to topple over and crush her.

I'm not finished with you. Far from it.

This was not the time to fall apart. This was the time to pull herself together. To plan, prepare, and return fire. If Michael Winship wanted to take her on, so be it; Priya was never one to lie down and die. He'd won this battle, but the war had just begun.

Chapter Eight

She gave herself one more deep breath to pull on her big girl panties before exiting the bathroom, but instead of returning to the bullpen, Priya wove her way to reception.

"Mr. Harrison is not in at the moment, may I take a message?" The receptionist spoke into her headset, eyes fixed on some distant point beyond Priya's right shoulder. "Yes, I understand, you've mentioned that three times already, but as I've explained several times as well, Mr. Harrison does *not* want any calls sent to his voice mail as he's—" She halted midsentence and rolled her dark eyes at the ceiling. "You can do so, if you'd like, but I'm—*okay* . . . asshat." She ended the call by pressing the tab on her headset and sighed. "I apologize for the foul language. That was inappropriate."

"Sounded perfectly appropriate to me." Priya reached over the polished wood partition of the desk. "I'm Priyanka Seth—Priya."

"Lorraine." She accepted Priya's hand. "I know who you are."

"Of course, you do." Resting her arms on the flat partition ledge, Priya leaned in. "Who organizes the distribution of firm-wide emails?"

"Those would come from the office of the managing partner."

So, Heather, if not Marai, herself. "How are new hires added to this distribution list?"

"Requests are created as a ticket and sent down to IT."

"Anyone can create a ticket?"

"Yes, but certain requests require manager approval." Lorraine arched a brow over coal-black eyes swept with metallic gold liner. "Does this have anything to do with Michael?"

"How did you know?"

"As 'gatekeeper' you learn to have eyes and ears everywhere." Her fingers flew across her keyboard so fast Priya could only watch in envious fascination as she never looked down once. "Nothing gets past me. *Nothing.* Like Michael making a copy of HR's approved résumés for final interviews a few weeks ago."

If that was true, then it certainly accounted for why he was so prepared to shred her in their mock deposition. He'd known about her for weeks and had been plotting nearly as long.

"I have a nose for people, and something about him always rubbed me raw." Lorraine tucked away her keyboard tray and the printer at her side rolled to life, spitting out a single sheet of paper. Grabbing a pen, she looped a gloriously complicated signature, added her personal stamp with employee code, then handed it to Priya. "Take this down to the eighth floor and ask for Andrew Reid specifically. He'll be able to tell you anything you need to know, but if he gives you any guff"—she paused with an eye roll—"tell him I said *yes.*"

"Yes, to what?"

"He'll know. Good luck, Priya, but I doubt you'll need

it." The phone shrilled on the desk, three lines at once, and Lorraine adjusted her headset with a wink. "Anyone with an eye for shoes knows you're not someone to mess with."

After the second round of depositions concluded, Priya waited until near end of day before slipping down to the eighth floor. Unlike the rest of MNS, it hummed in near silence. Servers ran in endless uniform rows, dense black columns with whizzing blue lights tucked behind walls of glass like beloved crown jewels. An older man stood observing them, dressed in a blue collared shirt, his black hair cropped low over large, pushed out ears, and his nose buried in a clipboard.

"Hi." Priya stopped him by blocking his path. "I'm looking for Andrew? Can you show me where to find him?"

"Eight-oh-three." He gestured vaguely to the right before shuffling off, lost in his clipboard and numbers.

It took Priya three passes around the labyrinth before she found the right office. The door was open, and a young Black man sat behind a desk holding three monitors the size of flat-screen TVs. Artwork on the wall depicted fantasy warriors—a few of whom she recognized, including her imaginary husband, Khal Drogo.

"Door to the elevator bank is that way." Andrew punched a finger toward the left wall without looking up. "If you hit the kitchen, you've gone too far."

"Andrew Reid?"

His eyes lifted from the screen and popped wide in surprise. "Okay, you *really* must be lost."

"I don't think so. I'm Priyanka Seth." She smiled her brightest, most winning smile, and he shrank behind his screen, guilt written all over his face. "The firm's distribution lists—I need to know if any recent changes were made, and if so, by whom."

"Can't help you."

She crossed her arms. "Can't or won't?"

"It's against company policy." Andrew pushed back his chair so fast it bounced off the wall behind him, and swiped awkwardly at his narrow tie. "I could lose my job."

"Lorraine said if you agreed to help me, her answer was *yes*."

That perked him up. "Lorraine? She said yes?"

"Yes."

"Lorraine," he enunciated slowly. "*Yes?*"

"Yeah . . ."

"Yes!" Andrew shot up on skinny legs and raced in whooping circles around his desk like a hyper Pomeranian. On his second lap, he flopped back into his chair with a megawatt grin so boyish in its charm she couldn't help but smile too. "I've begged that goddess for *months* to let me worship her over dinner, and she said yes!"

Priya planted her hands to his desk. "It comes with a caveat."

His grin flickered the barest fraction before he straightened with a grumble. "I do not have the words for such treachery."

"How about elvish?" At his confused expression, Priya nodded towards his poster.

"You're a Lord of the Rings fan?"

"More of a Throner."

Slender brows flattened in scrutiny. "Wolf or dragon?"

"Oh, dragon all the way." Andrew's eyes lit up like high beams and Priya barely resisted the urge to smirk. "I need that name."

"It was Junior Associate Michael Winship." Andrew's eyes lowered as he sighed. "He asked me to remove your name so when emails were sent out to the associates or the broader internal organization you'd be out of the loop. He also asked that I rope emails from the firm into spam. He knew it wouldn't hold for long but figured it would put enough of a dent in your reputation to set you back."

Bastard. "Why?"

"Why, what?"

"He's trying to ruin me, and you're helping him. Why?" Priya leaned over his desk, nose inches from his. "I'm sure your instinct is to lie, but I'm warning you right now don't—unless you want me to rip your throat out. Because this isn't just about a job, this is my dream, and I promise you, I'll rain fire on anyone who tries to take that away from me."

Andrew blinked, sharp and fast. "You . . . you have a vein throbbing." He spun a finger in the vicinity of his forehead. "It's freaking me out."

"Then I suggest you answer me."

"He . . . uh . . . it's my grandpa." That stopped her cold. "He's elderly. Lonely. So, he developed a bit of a problem with online gambling and racked up his credit cards. Nearly twenty-two of them before I caught on after getting a pretty angry letter from collections. I managed to convince the loan officer coming after him that he would make good on thirty percent, and I would cover the rest before the year was out. Two weeks after your first interview Michael came to my office and told me that I was to flag if you got hired, and if so, he'd tell me what to do next. If I refused he'd make sure my grandpa was criminally charged. His dad is a senior VP at the bank."

"What a dick!"

"Total Joffrey incarnate."

"Did you tell Michael about my sealed record?"

Andrew scraped a hand over his close-cropped curls, carefully smoothing his waves. "I can't answer that."

"You just did." Arms crossed, Priya worked her tongue along the edge of her teeth. "Was there anything I should know in Michael's background check?"

Andrew shook his head. "He's clean."

"Guys like him never are, they just haven't been caught. Yet." It rankled to think he had the one up, and she was at a loss as to how to even the score.

"You're not going to ask me to fabricate something are you? Threaten me into compliance?" Andrew squinted at her. "Like he did?"

"No. But I won't let him get away with this."

"Please." Andrew shot to his feet. "Please, you can't report him. I'll be fired for sure."

"Don't worry. He went after your family. Far as I'm concerned, you're a victim." Priya planted her hands on her hips. "But you are going to put me back on those lists and fix my incoming emails as well. Immediately."

Andrew bobbed a frantic nod. "Yes, ma'am."

"Stop it. We're basically the same age."

"Sorry ma . . . miss." He swallowed, his fingers wiggling the knot of his tie. "Sorry. You're like Khaleesi-walking-through-fire levels of intimidating when angry."

Priya released a dry laugh. "You have no idea."

* * *

"You know, playing hard to get after a booty call isn't the way to twist a guy's arm into a relationship."

Halfway into her slacks—panties on—Priya jerked to a pause.

Derek Tseng, an investment broker she'd met sometime last December, was a casual friend with benefits whom she hooked up with occasionally for no strings attached sex. She'd come by his place after work, just shy of nine, and jumped his bones. The release of endorphins cleared her head, leaving her sharp and focused, which she sorely needed after Michael had body slammed her during their mock deposition.

Derek had always known what this was between them. Priya took considerable pride in being more than clear on that front, so there was no way something that stupid could have come out of his mouth.

Priya angled her gaze over her shoulder. "What did you say?"

"This thing you're doing." Still beneath the sheets, Derek sat up, chest gleaming with sweat. "The mad dash out the door barely minutes after I come isn't the way to get a guy to want more from you."

Or, apparently, he was.

Pulling her pants on the rest of the way, Priya fastened the waist before sitting on the edge of the bed. "Who said anything about wanting a relationship?" She slid a foot into her pump.

"Every single woman out there." He held up a hand, let it fall. "A guy can't breathe around a chick anymore without her plotting how to get him down the aisle."

She wiggled on her other shoe. "That's bullshit."

99

"Come on. I'm thirty-one, successful, attractive—overall, a desirable catch—and we've been messing around for months. You're telling me a relationship hasn't crossed your mind once?"

It took every ounce of restraint not to roll her eyes. Or laugh. She'd had many variations of this conversation in the past but it never got any less exhausting. What was it about a woman satisfying her own sexual needs that went so far over a guy's head he couldn't grasp it?

Finished with fastening the last few buttons on her blouse, Priya flipped her hair over her collar and let it fall in all its I just got laid glory. Tucking a leg under her, she scooted around to face him. "Not every woman uses sex as leverage. Or a weapon." Smiling gently, she brushed a hand over his cheek. *Poor, stupid, clueless boy.* "I had sex with you tonight because I was in the mood for sex, and I'm leaving right now because I want to leave. That's it."

His gaze skimmed over her, partly unconvinced and partly insulted. "I don't think we should do this anymore."

"I think you're right." Dropping her hand, she pressed her lips to his cheek, then left him scowling in the dark.

By the time Priya got home her humor had burned off to annoyance, but Derek's fragile male ego was the least of her problems. Sitting at the kitchen island, she pulled out the pro bono file from her satchel and opened up her work laptop. The case was a run of the mill dispute between an old tenant refusing to pay her rent as a result of property damage and loss, namely a couple of dead cats and some bubbling paint.

Throw a rock and she'd hit five hundred of these before breakfast. Rent disputes were about as exciting as parking tickets. Even if she won there was nothing here that would set her apart from the pack. It was a total waste of her time and effort, especially given all that was at stake, but any lawyer worth her salt rarely, if ever, accepted the first offer on the table. There were bound to be a thousand other pro bono requests. It all boiled down to whether or not she could convince Daniella to assign her a new one.

Armed with that thought, Priya woke the next morning determined to plead her case.

Daniella, like the rest of the senior partners, was already in the office, and judging by the coffee mug and scattered papers, she'd been in well before seven.

At the gentle rap of Priya's knuckles to the door, Daniella raised her gaze from her monitor. "Is it that time already?"

Priya hesitated on the threshold. "I can come back, if you're busy."

"It's fine." Daniella waved her in. "I don't have a spare moment to breathe between now and next week. Sit. Tell me about your case."

"Well." Priya resisted the urge to squirm. "I'd actually like to be reassigned."

"Really?" Daniella drummed her pen against the edge of her desk. "And what were you hoping for?"

"A wrongful dismissal claim or workplace sexual harassment are well within my wheelhouse."

"Something with gravitas."

"Exactly."

Daniella nodded decidedly. "Why not a shiny grand theft auto? Or how about investment fraud? No wait! I've got it." She clapped her hands. "Attempted murder! And then," she plowed on, saccharine sarcasm dripping from every word, "we can book a mani-pedi and swap ex-boyfriend stories."

Priya closed her eyes with a sigh. "Okay, I get it. You don't need to rub salt in the wound."

"What exactly is the issue with your current case?"

"It's a rent dispute."

"And?"

"A high school student with a B average could win this blindfolded. This won't help me get the mentorship. Not after—" *what Michael did to me.* Priya didn't have the voice to finish the statement, but Daniella seemed to intuit the rest.

Daniella laced her fingers together. "Do you have any idea how fortunate you are? A junior associate, ink barely dry on your law degree, and already you have a case of your very own to run. Maybe instead of whining about it not being *good* enough for you, you should embrace this opportunity and learn from it."

"I'm not trying to be ungrateful."

"You sure as shit sound like it." Rounding her desk, Daniella reclined against the edge. "Is it glamorous? No. But guess what, ninety-eight percent of the cases that walk through our doors aren't, yet we're still expected to toil away and do our job. You want gravitas, watch an episode of *Law & Order*. Otherwise, I want you to suck it up and get it done. Is that understood?"

Priya cleared her throat. "Yes."

"Good." Daniella whisked her hands toward the door as if trying to speed up drying nail polish. "Dismissed."

Thoroughly whipped into submission, Priya left Daniella's office, tail tucked between her legs, but she hadn't made it more than three paces before she was stopped by a shrill woman with steel-gray hair wrapped in an elegant chignon, her pinched nose raised high in the air as if sniffing her out.

"Ah, Priyanka, brilliant." Priya recognized senior partner Karen Hill from the corporate website's partner list. She thrust out a hand and shook Priya's briskly. "Lovely to meet you in person. I was just about to have my assistant get in touch. I received your note and I'm delighted to accept your offer to oversee the briefs for the Portman merger."

"Briefs?"

"Yes." Karen blinked up at her. Even in heels she barely cleared five feet. "Portman is one of my oldest clients. Thank you for stepping up to the plate on this task. I know," she plowed on, oblivious to Priya's utter confusion, "usually, we wouldn't allow a new hire to jump in ahead of more senior associates, but I admire a woman who knows what she wants and isn't afraid to dive in the deep end. Bravo."

"I . . ."

"We'll need the brief ready for Thursday. You can manage that, can't you? Great," she continued without awaiting an answer. "It's a meaty one, so please be thorough and if you need any guidance, my door is open. Oh!" Karen bounced on her toes like she'd been jolted by a shock collar. "I have a call in three minutes. My assistant will email you the brief shortly." She snapped her fingers at Priya. "Again, lovely to meet you. Ta!"

Priya blinked at the smoking trail the woman blazed down the corridor toward her office, impressive considering she was the size of a twelve-year-old. *What just happened?* Portman merger? Briefs? Not that Priya was about to complain. A senior partner had just sought her out directly, but the how and why was the question, and triggered a soft warning to toll inside her head.

Still trying to absorb the absurdity of what just happened, Priya returned to her desk to find another senior partner, Robert Manley, pacing like a furious penguin, wearing a track in the carpet.

"There you are." He rounded on her, his face dominated by droopy eyes, and sparse black hair sprinkled atop his head like pepper on a boiled egg. "I came by your desk three times in the last thirty minutes. Where the hell were you?"

Priya barely smothered her groan. "I was finishing my coaching session with Daniella."

"Why was that meeting not in the associate group calendar?"

"It should be."

"Well, it wasn't. I had Glenda confirm availability before slotting in fifteen minutes for us but now I've got to leave for an external meeting."

No, it most certainly had been in there, she'd seen it earlier this morning before heading over to Daniella's office. Which meant someone had removed it. As all associates had access to the calendar, she didn't have to hazard a guess as to who. "I apologize for the oversight. How can I help you, Robert?"

"How can you *help* me?" Robert scoffed, chunky veneers exposed in a wide, flat-lipped mouth. "You can help me with the Murdoch files, which are ready for assembly in the Specter Conference Room."

"Murdoch files?"

"Yes, the ones we were instructed to hand over to Jarvis Financial ahead of trial next week. Why are you looking at me like I'm speaking Dutch?" he demanded, nose wrinkled like he smelled something especially foul.

Priya certainly did. A skunkish bouquet of bullshit mixed with robust greasy undertones of subterfuge. The associates already on the floor made a show of busying themselves with their emails or phone calls, but she caught enough shifting gazes to know they were enjoying the show. And even though Michael wasn't in the bullpen, she could feel him gloating.

"Of course. I'll see if I can block out time later this afternoon."

Robert cocked his head to the side in a sharp, irritated twitch. "Is there something wrong with right the hell now?"

"Karen asked me to tackle briefs for her client merger."

"Portman?"

Priya nodded.

"Drop it. Murdoch billables are triple what Portman will yield; this takes priority."

Hadrian rose from his seat, withdrawing his earbuds. "I'm happy to take over while Priya completes the brief."

"Why don't you focus on your own responsibilities, Mr. Marek." Robert drummed a fist against the panel dividing Priya's cubicle from the next one. "Instead of swooping in to save Ms. Seth as if she were some damsel in distress when she's perfectly capable of speaking for herself."

Hadrian sank back into his chair. "Yes, sir."

Robert rounded on her again, chest puffed, eyes squinted. "When you're done binding, have them boxed, labeled, and ready in the mail room for collection Thursday morning. Courier pickup is at eight."

"That's in three days."

"You'll need every spare second of that time. So snap to." And snapped fingers on both hands in her face.

"Of course, I'll get it done. Thank you." But she was speaking to his rapidly retreating back at this point. Annoyed, Priya rushed out of the bullpen to the copier room, where a young redheaded intern, identified by the yellow badge worn on a lanyard around his neck, was working. "I'm here to collect the copies of the Murdoch files?"

"You can get started with those." The intern gestured to the row of trollies lining the wall with mounds of printed paper heaped on top, sorted into alternating stacks by a litany of colorful Post-its.

"*All* of these?"

"Yup. And I've got these two copiers dedicated to printing the rest of the materials. Should be done in another thirty minutes or so."

Holy fuzzknuckles. Robert hadn't exaggerated in the least— this was going to demand every spare second she could find from now until Thursday, and even then, she was unlikely to finish the task on top of the rest of her work, let alone even set eyes on the Portman brief.

"Wonderful. Thank you." Gripping the handle of the first trolly, Priya wheeled it down the hall and across to the Spector Conference Room. Seven trips later, she dialed out to reception from the conference phone. "Lorraine, hi, it's Priya. Can you do me a favor and transfer any calls that come to my desk to this extension? I'll be working out of Spector for . . . quite some time."

"Already done."

"Great. Thank you."

A sharp whistle shot from behind her, long and shrill. "Anyone who elected to take this on single handed is either incredibly ambitious or stupid. My vote is for stupid."

Priya ground her teeth at the smug note in Michael's voice. Gently lowering the receiver to the desk, she spun on her heel. "Funny. I don't recall asking to take on this Herculean task."

"Maybe you were too drunk to remember," Michael whispered. "*Again.*"

Her heart froze. *My interview.* Only Marai had been in the boardroom when she'd made that declaration—and no way would the managing partner of the firm have uttered a word of it beyond those closed doors. *So how does he know?*

"But, hey," Michael went on while her thoughts spun, "if you can't hack it, then by all means go straight to Robert and tell him you need an intern, or twelve. I'm sure it won't affect your associate score. *Much.*"

Yeah right. After complaining to Daniella about her case, the last thing she needed was another senior partner lowering her score because she'd dropped the ball, even if she'd been set up to fail by Michael. And now for the next three days she was going to be tied up with a task that should've gone to the firm's interns or paralegals—keeping her far away from the bullpen and any opportunity to place herself in front of the partners for more important work.

"If you think this is enough to break me"—Priya crossed her arms, more to keep herself from slapping the smug grin off his face—"think again."

"We'll see." Michael winked. "I'm just getting warmed up."

Chapter Nine

Isobel sat in the bottom of her shower, pressed into the tight corner, steam billowing around her like a hazy cloud—thick as her despair. This was her one place to escape. To hide. Not that there was any hiding when the pain of loss attacked her at her quietest moments—vivid images of Kyle with that woman shot through her mind like bullets, punching holes in her heart. Her peace. Her sanity. All she could do was press her fingers to her eyes and wait for the images to fade, but they lingered like shadows.

Even asleep she found no peace. When she dreamed, it was of him, of what should have been, and in those tender fantasies her heart soared with so much love, so much happiness. And for an instant, a brief, terrible, torturous second before the film of sleep slipped away like gossamer, she almost believed it all was true until reality set in with a brutal weight that crushed her soul. Breaking her heart all over again.

I miss him.

I hate him.

I want him back.

I want to run until my legs snap off.

I want to scream.

I want him to hold me until every inch of me stops aching.

Groaning, Isobel planted her face in her hands. *This must be what madness feels like . . .* A slow unraveling of sanity and a stealthy numbness that settled into her bones, icing her skin from the inside out. She didn't feel anything anymore. Not even the blazing-hot water streaming down on her like a waterfall.

How was she supposed to unweave a life? Create something new in the wake of this devastation? Starting from a blank page was a daunting pursuit, like deleting an entire manuscript and then glaring at that blinking cursor, stark against the glare of a white background, trying to find the words all over again.

It felt impossible, but she couldn't succumb to the darkness of tears and despair. If not for herself, then for her father. However much she might want to wish away the past, there was no going back. Only forward.

God, give me strength for this, and everything else that comes next.

Isobel stayed in the shower until her skin turned pink and her hands wrinkled, carefully weaving crude stitches into the broken fragments of her heart with fragile threads of determination. It was messy, brutal work, but it did the job, fusing her into some semblance of a person again.

Sweeping a hand across the mirror, she blinked at her reflection. Damp brown hair struggling to curl after years of being straightened into submission with a flat iron, large green eyes a little too big for her face, and pale skin shot with freckles. Every summer more cropped up, and Shayne often teased that by the time Isobel was fifty she'd be a Dalmatian.

Beneath it all she could almost see into herself, to every

suture and staple holding her broken pieces and frayed edges together. Still tender and raw and vulnerable to tearing, but soon enough they would mend into vivid healing tissue, and eventually fade into silver scars. Forever marked by the trauma, even if all the damage was internal, and that simple thought terrified her most.

I'll never be the same again. Isobel pushed the pitying thought aside and, after she was dressed, eased open the door to the guest room only to be met with the heavy rattle of guttural snoring. She'd had a few days with her whole Sisterhood, but Shayne had stayed behind.

"Morning." Shayne groaned into her pillow as Isobel lowered herself to the edge of the bed. "Are you seriously going to keep sleeping? It's after noon."

"DJs don't keep to regular hours."

"You haven't spun a single night since you got here."

One narrowed eye blinked at Isobel through a messy fringe of navy hair. "I'm conditioned."

"Okay, Pavlov." Isobel slapped Shayne's butt through the comforter before rising. "I'll check on you later."

"Where y'going?"

"I've got to see the travel agent today and beg her to cancel the honeymoon." Isobel's heart tightened in her chest, strings drawn so tight she could scarcely breathe, afraid the sutures would refuse to expand and her poorly mended heart would shred again.

"The fuck for? That's Kyle's problem to sort out. Not yours."

"Well . . . not exactly." Isobel rubbed her palms together. God, they were sweating already. "I paid for it with my line of credit."

"Hold on." Shayne stuck a finger in her ear and wiggled it obnoxiously about. "I thought I heard you say you paid for the honeymoon."

Isobel swallowed hard and Shayne, wearing a ripped oversize shirt and nothing underneath it, pushed up in the bed, ominous as a waking storm, and exposing lean arms and legs covered in bold tattoos. Most of them were heavy and bold black, but a few popped with rich red, vibrant blue, and punches of butter yellow.

"Tell me something." She blew a lank piece of dark-blue hair out of her eyes. "If Kyle is the one making bank, why on earth would you do something so stupid?"

"It wasn't stupid. I wanted to . . . well . . . contribute." And not just with the honeymoon. She'd paid for the dresses—hers and the bridesmaids'—and the photographer, while Kyle took on the bigger items like the coordinator, venue, food, and entertainment. Wasn't that the definition of marriage? Two people sharing the load?

Maybe it would've been smarter, easier, to just have allowed him to cover the entire thing, but Isobel had wanted to carry her weight in the relationship. Now that weight had become a noose that was going to strangle her if she didn't cut it off—fast.

"You contributed by planning the damn wedding and acting as his personal assistant."

Isobel flinched. "I wasn't his assistant."

"You handled his bills, his expenses, his laundry, ran his errands, booked his appointments." Shayne listed off on her fingers. "And now this. How much did you spend?"

"I don't think—"

"How much, Bel?"

Isobel hung her head. "Twenty grand."

"Twenty—" Shayne's eyes nearly exploded from her head. "And he let you carry that?"

"Well . . ." Isobel stroked a hand down her arm. "He picked it." And why did that suddenly hurt so much to admit? He'd wanted lavish and exciting, and she'd agreed to make him happy. Anything to make him happy, even if in her heart she'd wished for something smaller, simpler.

"*Sonofa*—" Shayne curled her fingers into fists and bounced them in the air like she was resisting the urge to swing them. "Give me ten."

"Oh, you don't have to get up. I can manage on my own."

Shayne kicked the comforter off the bed and swung onto her feet. "Bel, I love you, but you've got a glass jaw."

"What's that supposed to mean?"

"It means they'll take one look at that sweet face and level you with an uppercut. You need someone who knows how to hit back in your corner." Standing at the foot of the bed, Shayne swiped a thumb across the tip of her nose. "Lucky for you, aside from music, fighting is what I do."

Isobel sighed. Shayne wasn't wrong. Where she shied away from conflict, Shayne actively sought it out, encouraged it even. Maybe having her tag along wouldn't be such a bad thing. "Okay. I'll wait for you downstairs."

Shayne was down in less than eight, dressed in boyfriend jeans and the same ripped graphic T-shirt she'd slept in. "Let's roll." She shoved aviator glasses on, followed by her panama hat, and sauntered out the door with that carefree swagger she'd practically trademarked.

Declan beamed, shaking his head. "Always a character, that one."

Shouldering her purse, Isobel hugged her father. "Will you be okay for a few hours?" She'd heard him shuffling back and forth to the bathroom most of the night. He'd started a new course of drugs for pain management but so far all of them had wrought havoc on his stomach.

"Yes, love." He stroked her arm. "For what it's worth, I'm glad she's here . . . so you don't have to do this all alone."

"Thanks, Daddy. I'll call you when we're done. Maybe we'll grab something for dinner on the way." Along with some fresh ginger and mint so she could make a tea to settle his stomach.

"Fried chicken?"

"Grilled."

Declan grumbled. "Can it at *least* be breaded?"

"I'm willing to negotiate." She kissed him again. "Call if you need me." Rushing out the door, Isobel scanned the street for Shayne, and her heart dropped at the sight of a silver Audi parked at the end of the drive. A man was perched casually against the hood. Sun flashed across his warm brown skin, teased gold from his coppery hair, and added warmth to his smile.

Kyle. Isobel blinked the mirage away. *God, Isobel. It's just the Uber driver.* She mentally slapped herself, annoyed by the way her heart had seized with a moment of panic—or hope?—at the notion of Kyle waiting for her. She couldn't tell if the sharp sting lancing between her ribs was relief or disappointment. Perhaps it was both. Was it possible to want someone so badly and yet wish with every breath that they stayed away at the same time?

"Hey." Shayne frowned. "You good?"

"Yes. I'm fine."

Once inside the car, Shayne slumped into her corner and pulled her hat brim low over her eyes. Isobel was grateful for the quiet moment to collect herself. After this she had paperwork to complete for her new legal team. Again. A never-ending process, cycling over and over, slowly grating her into a nub. But determination made Isobel hold on despite the voice deep inside that begged her to surrender the fight and find a way to make ends meet without the settlement.

She'd done it before, in those early days after the accident, when it rapidly became apparent that her father would be unable to return to work for some time, if ever. Isobel sat at her kitchen table and drafted a budget, laying out all the expenses line by line. Once she sorted out how she could manage the bills and stay in the black, her heart settled. But that was when she had a job. And according to that ruthlessly mapped out budget, which she'd followed faithfully for three long years, she had two weeks before things got murky, and another two weeks from there before she was in real trouble if she didn't start recouping every dime she'd sunk into this wedding—and fast.

Ten minutes later they arrived at the travel agency.

"This it?" Shayne asked, standing outside the massive glass doors. "Bougie spot."

"Yorkville is basically the Manhattan of Toronto."

Shayne snorted and tapped a hand on Isobel's arm. "All right, let's do this." Dragging open the door, she waited for Isobel to enter before swaggering in after her, and whistled low. "Fuck, bro, even the air smells expensive."

Lavender sweetened with honey and peaches—decadent, and soft as the pale coral walls gilded with gold accents and crystal-clear mirrors.

A stunning blond with overfilled lips stood behind a glass reception counter, then floated toward them wearing a crisp black suit that fit like she'd been born in it. Her hair, straightened into a flawless sheet, was bleached to perfection and freshly cut to her jawline. "Hello, Isobel, and welcome back to Eluxe Travel."

"Hello," Shayne purred with a slanted grin that Isobel had personally witness charm far too many men and women into her bed. Everything about Shayne was potent. Addictive. Raw. She could bring you to heaven or drag you to hell, but wherever she was going was exactly where you wanted to be.

The receptionist spared her a lingering, appreciative glance but otherwise held her composure. A remarkable feat. "Is Amelia expecting you today?"

Isobel drew in a bracing breath. "Yes, I called this morning."

"Perfect." The receptionist swept out a hand, drawing her inside to the crisp, ivory on ivory lounge. "Have a seat and I'll let Amelia know you've arrived."

Isobel sat down and Shayne remained standing, thumbs hooked in the belt loop of her jeans as she watched the receptionist return to her desk.

"Goddamn," she whispered. "I may need to visit Yorkville more often."

"Shayne . . ."

"Relax." She smirked. "I'll wait until *after* our appointment before I work my magic."

Barely a minute later, the gold lacquered doors opened and

Amelia strolled out, also wearing a crisp black suit, a polished brass name tag pinned to her lapel. Glossy brown hair parted down the middle of a mature face plumped with a dewy sheen that verged on plastic thanks to fillers and injections. She beamed at Isobel, features barely moving. "Hello, Isobel. It's wonderful to see you again." She shook Isobel's hand first, then turned to Shayne, and what little smile she could manage fell away. "Our pickups are at reception. This area is for guests only."

"Excuse me?"

"This is Shayne," Isobel corrected. "She's with me."

"Ah." Amelia clasped her hands. "Apologies, I thought perhaps you were a courier. Lovely. Well, why don't we head to my office, and we can chat?"

"Yes, thank you." Isobel rose on rubbery legs, grateful that the walk to Amelia's office was a short one. Once inside, Amelia closed the door behind them and gestured to the seating area—a plush set of couches around a gilded coffee table made of gold and glass, topped with several hundred dollars of pristine pink peonies.

"Now." Amelia sat down and crossed a leg. "I think I know why you're here."

Isobel squirmed in her seat while Shayne sat sprawled at her side, legs and arms spread like she owned the place.

"I speak on behalf of the Eluxe team to say we were all devastated by the news." Amelia shook her head, diamonds sparkling at her ears. "Utterly horrible. If there's any way we can assist during this difficult time, we're more than happy to help."

"Thank you. The thing is—" Isobel cleared her throat. "I need to . . . cancel the trip."

Amelia set her clasped hands in her lap with a reserved sigh. "I'd hate to appear indelicate, but we can't do that. Unfortunately, the package you elected for does not allow cancellations or reimbursements this close to the scheduled travel date, and I'm afraid our policy is absolute."

"But . . ." Isobel struggled not to stammer. "You just said you wanted to *help.*" *This is what I need. The only thing I need.*

"Yes, by reworking your package to something more amenable to a solo traveler."

Isobel pinched the bridge of her nose. "I appreciate that there is a policy in place, but please try to imagine my circumstances. This was an expense I could hardly afford to begin with, and now it's even worse. My father is ill, and I've lost my job because of this."

"I'm so sorry, but I'm afraid the best I can do is issue a credit on file for a maximum period of one year until you're ready to rebook. Cancellation is out of the question at this point."

"What about a partial refund?" Isobel blinked away frustrated tears and struggled to find her voice. The words. "As . . . it's . . . just me."

"I'm so sorry, but that's out of the question."

"Why the fuck not?"

Amelia blinked at Shayne before recollecting her composure. "Because she's contractually obligated for the entire quoted amount, or higher. Our policy—"

"Is to be a hard-ass?" Shucking a wrapper off a lollipop, Shayne tossed the wadded bit of plastic film on the coffee table. A dueler throwing down the gauntlet.

Amelia watched it bounce before it rolled to a stop, fingers curling in her lap. "As I said, we're happy to hold a credit and rebook for the same value, but we cannot refund at this time, and we cannot reduce the amount owed." She spread her hands in apology. "Now, as I said before, I'm happy to rework the trip."

Shayne removed the sucker from her mouth with a juicy pop. "How much."

"How much to what?"

"Upgrade."

"I'm sorry, you want to *increase* the package?"

"Yes." Shayne rocked forward, propping her elbows on her knees. "With three more people and push the dates up for the second week of August."

The agent blinked a dozen times, so fast it was like she'd been electrocuted, or was rebooting her motherboard. "I'd have to review flights and availability with the airline and hotel, but I expect if we keep to standard suites and economy flights, we should be able to—"

"Fuck that. First class for all five, and get us a three-bedroom penthouse suite. Make sure it's got one of those jetted soaker tub things and swim-out access to a private pool. You're also gonna refund her." She jerked a thumb at Isobel. "And bill me for all of it."

"What are you doing?" Isobel whispered.

"Hijacking your honeymoon." Shayne winked.

"That will be a—" Amelia cleared her throat. "Significant increase in cost."

"Doesn't matter."

"We're talking *thousands* on top of what was already paid."

"Yeah, and I said it doesn't matter."

Amelia's face softened with a doubtful smile. "I'm sorry, but can someone like you even afford such an expense?"

"Someone like me?" Shayne rolled the stick of her sucker between her teeth, her grin cagey. Isobel knew the look well. It meant the other woman was standing on very dangerous ground. "Lemme guess, you see a young punk covered in piercings and tattoos, dyed hair and ripped jeans, and you think no way does this girl have pockets that deep." Withdrawing her phone from her pocket, Shayne unlocked the device and turned the screen. "This ought to put your concerns to rest."

Her home screen was a picture of herself with her family. It was an old photo but even without the tattoos and piercings, Shayne was unmistakable as she stood shoulder to shoulder with her brother and the queen of England, inside the splendor of Buckingham Palace.

Isobel knew how much Shayne hated revealing her familial heritage to strangers, but right now, given the sharp gleam in her eyes, it was apparent she was enjoying every second watching Amelia, who had nearly stopped breathing, gasp like a dying fish.

"You're—" Her eyes shot back to Shayne, all color fading from her cheeks. "You're—"

"Royalty?" Shayne finished for her, clicked her tongue. "Yeah. So unless you want me to call the owner of this shit stain and cut you out of a pretty fucking sweet commission, I'll give you another opportunity to pull your foot out of your mouth."

"If I offended you, I'm sorry." Amelia smoothed a shaking hand against the wall of her chest. "I'll need a little time to prepare an updated quote for your approval, if that's all right?"

"Cool." Rising from the couch, Shayne plucked a business

card from a plastic holder. "Call when it's ready." And swaggered from the office.

Isobel followed her and made it as far as the sidewalk before her calm fractured. "What was that?"

Shayne spun around, her sunglasses catching the late-afternoon light and reflecting Isobel's scowling face. "What?"

"*That.*" Isobel gestured broadly at the door they'd just exited. "I wanted to get out of this trip, not locked in further. What were you thinking?"

Shayne squinted at Isobel over the rim of her glasses. "There was no getting out, Bel. Not the way you wanted. So." She shrugged once. "We'll go together for our Sisterhood anniversary next month, and I'll foot the bill. Problem solved."

"No. No it's not." Isobel crossed her arms to hide their trembling. "You can't throw money at everything."

"Why not?" Genuinely baffled, Shayne lifted her hat and shoved her fingers in her hair, sending navy waves flouncing into a disorderly mess that somehow was both chaotic and attractive. "What's the point of having it, then, if I can't use it for good shit?"

Pinching the bridge of her nose, Isobel sighed. God, her head ached, and her stomach was a knotted mess of guilt and anger and frustration. "Forget it. I'm sorry. I'm just . . . tired." *Emotional. Broken. Destroyed. A complete and utter mess.*

"Cool." Shayne hooked an arm around her shoulders, roping her into a side-hug. "Now, I'm fucking starved and sure as shit not eating any more of that vegan crap you've got at home. Let's get tacos. My treat."

Chapter Ten

Priya capped the lid on another banker box and stamped it with the label before adding it to the growing wall spreading down the length of the Specter Conference Room.

It was astounding, really, just how much paper went into each one, and after pushing nearly fourteen-hour days, her confidence had given way to exhausted panic.

"How's it going?"

Priya turned at the sound of Hadrian's voice. "What does it look like?"

He turned, taking in the endless stacks lining the length of the conference table. "How many are there?"

"I've finished forty boxes, with at least another seven to go and I've still got half of the Portman brief to complete, also due tomorrow morning." Priya gripped her hair in her hands with an aggrieved snarl. "I haven't had a moment to breathe in days." Ricocheting between meetings and grunt work, she felt like a chew toy caught in a tug-of-war between two pit bulls. "I don't know how Michael did this, but he's screwed me, big time." And since he no longer had Andrew under his thumb, it was even more frustrating.

"Michael went to Karen putting you up for Portman, and as

soon as Robert got wind of it, he pounced on you for Murdoch. Both are gunning for name partner and despise each other. Their rivalry is almost as old as this firm."

And the bastard, with two years of home field advantage under his belt, had leveraged it to set Priya up for failure. She'd been given two complicated tasks at once, and the only way out was to deliver on both. "I can't go down like this," Priya groaned. "I've got hours ahead of me to finish and can barely see straight at this point. It's impossible."

"Well, you're in luck because I've got an open evening and an available set of hands." Removing his blazer, Hadrian cuffed his sleeves to the elbow.

Priya cast him her most cutting side-eye. "Why?"

"You're drowning, and I just want to help."

"Or maybe you just want to hold my head underwater." She snorted. "And take all the credit when we're done."

"I wouldn't do that." Dark brows lowered, but otherwise his gaze remained sincere. "Not when I think we stand to gain more by working together."

"Forget it." She rolled her shoulders, shrugging him and the notion of allyship off. "Tigers are solitary creatures. I work better alone."

"They're counting on it." Hadrian jerked a thumb in the general direction of the bullpen. "A stray dog can take down a tiger if it's in a pack, which they are, and they're gunning for you."

"Why do you care?" she asked, her gaze searching his but for what, Priya wasn't entirely certain.

"When you're dispatched who do you think they'll come for next? The only reason I wasn't first on the hit list, as

Aurelio Marek's son, is because they need to be stealthier to remove me." He tapped a finger on the tabletop. "Maybe you're right and you stand a chance solo. Clearly, you're too proud to turn to anyone for help, but I think the smartest move is for us to work together—we'd be untouchable."

Even if she didn't want to agree with him, Hadrian wasn't wrong. As she'd suspected, word of Michael destroying her in his deposition had quickly made the rounds, but she wasn't about to let Hadrian see her sweat, or anyone else for that matter.

"I'm supposed to trust you won't screw me over too?"

"I don't fight dirty. If I did, I would've played the nepotism card the second I was hired."

"Maybe you still plan to rip the rug out from underneath us. It would be a smart move. Play the wolf in sheep's clothing until it suits you to bare your fangs."

"I could," he agreed without reservation, though his expression was one of surprised disappointment. "But I asked to be considered with the same strict provisos and performance requirements as everyone else. No preferential treatment." His gaze deepened in thought as he toyed with the shark tooth dangling from the leather cord at his throat. An unconscious gesture, perhaps a reflex. "I used to play football—soccer— back in London. Damn near went pro, so maybe that's why I'm competitive, but I want to win but on my own merit. It's sweeter that way."

And how could she argue with that? A man built on a foundation of hard work and integrity was one she could respect and admire, but it would also make beating him a challenge. So why did that thought both excite and terrify her?

"Come on, tiger." He bumped his shoulder companionably to hers. "What do you say?"

Sipping leisurely from her nearly finished water bottle, Priya assessed him. He was charming, almost arrogantly so, and stupidly gorgeous, but all that aside, his eyes shone with a sincerity that laced through the rich baritone of his voice. Hadrian might be many things, but she sensed a liar wasn't one of them, and right now she really needed someone in her corner. The weakness in her armor had been exposed, and though she'd dodged a couple of bullets already, the odds were that the next was bound to take her clean off her feet. Priya needed an ally if she was going to live to fight another day.

"Friends now, enemies later?"

"Has a ring to it, doesn't it?" His smile flashed, full, genuine, and with enough charm to part a nun's thighs. Or hers, if she wasn't careful . . .

"I'll agree on one condition."

"Anything."

"No sex." A laugh nearly burst through her at his crestfallen expression. "We're colleagues, Hadrian, and if we're going to work effectively together there have to be boundaries. No sex. No flirting. No physical contact of any kind. We need to be focused. Professional."

His lips skewed into a playful grimace. "Hard line on that, huh?"

"Firm."

"No room to negotiate terms?"

"None."

"You drive a hard bargain." Hadrian sighed. "But I accept your terms."

"Good." She thrust out a hand. "Then let the best lawyer win."

"Indeed." He shook it once. "Can we at least consummate this alliance with food?"

"Please don't tease me right now." Priya's stomach growled with desperate need. "I'm fragile."

"I'd tease you about many things." He winked. "But never this." Returning to the doorway, Hadrian dragged in a cart bearing a set of takeout containers, a couple of bottles of Perrier, some plates, and cutlery.

She sniffed at the containers. "What is it?"

"Sushi."

"From where?"

"Juno."

Hunger intensified. "I love that place."

"I had a sneaking suspicion since you mentioned it a dozen times the night we met."

Prizing the lid off one of the containers, she nearly wept in gratitude at the array of fresh sashimi. "I could kiss you."

"Alas, rules are rules." Hadrian dropped his chin with a soft laugh. "A simple thanks will suffice."

Priya popped a meaty piece of salmon into her mouth and moaned, succulent fish melting on her tongue. "What would've happened if I said no?"

"Then you'd be eating for two and I'd be at home watching reruns of *MasterChef.* Sit." Hadrian rolled out a chair. "You eat, I'll take over—just point where you want me to go first."

* * *

While Hadrian boxed files, Priya focused on the Portman brief before diving in to help him, exhaustion weighing heavy on her shoulders. It had taken them both the entire night, but they'd gotten it done with seconds to spare.

"All right, tiger." Hadrian yawned, eyes red with fatigue. It wouldn't take much more than a wave of air conditioning pushing through the vents to knock either of them over. "I have more caffeine than blood at this point, but I need another espresso. Want one?"

"Please. A double."

He sighed into a weary shuffle. "Comin' right up."

"Hadrian." He stopped by the doorway. "I don't say this often, but thank you."

"Don't mention it." He winked before exiting.

And barely a minute later Robert entered the conference room, arms pumping and chest puffed like an Olympic speed walker. "Well, well, well." He swung to a sharp stop next to Priya. "You got it done."

"I said I would."

Beady eyes scanned her from head to toe. "Pulled an all-nighter?"

"Two." Priya's gut lurched. Teamwork, Priya. "And Hadrian helped with the last push. He's pretty dead on his feet too."

Robert puckered his lips, nodding swiftly. "We have a dark room on the twelfth floor. Lock yourself in there for a couple of hours, and Hadrian can have the room after you. Ask Lorraine to book it—tell her I don't care who's on the schedule, they're out and you're in."

"Thank you, Robert."

"No, thank *you*." Robert rocked on his heels, his chunky

teeth split in a wide grin. "It's not often we get an associate who doesn't mind getting her hands dirty. Usually, it's all kinds of guff and pushback—*why can't a paralegal this, or an intern that*—but you showed you're a team player, regardless of rank. And not above sharing the praise with a fellow associate, to boot." He tapped the tip of his round nose, winked. "Don't think that kind of integrity will go unnoticed."

Priya smothered a grin as Robert scuttled out of the room. Oh, if Michael could be a fly on the wall, how much would it anger him to know his plan had not only flopped but backfired?

* * *

Arms trembling, Declan rolled into downward dog, sinking deep into the pose.

"There. Deep breaths, Dad. Remember to breathe with each stretch." Guiding his every movement, Isobel helped her father slide into child's pose, opening his back and hips while giving his body an opportunity to relax. To rest.

"Okay, lower to your knees and when you're ready, sit back."

"Christ," Declan grumbled, and sat on his heels, red faced and sweating. "When does this get relaxing?"

"Soon, I promise. Can you manage getting to your chair? I think you've earned a proper breakfast."

"Proper by whose standards?"

Isobel smirked. "There will be bacon. I promise."

Exuberant joy lit his face, and whether it was the promise of greasy pork or the yoga, he sprang to his feet with a bit of a spring to his step.

Leaving him to get comfortable in his worn recliner, Isobel

ventured into the kitchen and opened the fridge. After learning about the reason for her separation from Kyle when the story spread like a rash across the city, her father, docile as a lamb, now woke early every morning for daily yoga. Apparently, emotional blackmail was the card she'd needed, and she was more than happy to exploit it, under the circumstances.

She pushed him to do thirty minutes of yoga in the morning and another thirty before bed. At night he slept like a baby, and in the mornings he seemed more rested. The hard lines under his eyes were no longer carved quite so deep, and already she could see a vast improvement in his balance and flexibility. Every day the small increments of progress gave her hope, and right now hope was something she needed.

A few more weeks of this and then she planned to nudge him into more advanced stretches to strengthen the weak muscles of his back as well as open those that had overcompensated for his injuries. It would be a slow process, but one vital to restoring some measure of mobility to his range of movement, and hopefully afford him some measure of relief over time.

Losing herself in the homey task of boiling eggs and frying thick-cut bacon—a treat for his compliance over the last week—Isobel poured green tea into a couple of mugs and left them to steep as the bacon drained on some paper towel. Finally, she sliced up fresh heirloom tomatoes and cooked them in a clean skillet with some avocado oil, even though her father would have preferred the leftover bacon grease not go to waste.

What he doesn't know won't hurt him.

Setting out a couple of plates, she loaded them up and

carried them out to the living room so they could eat while her father turned on the TV and sank into the hunter-green couch. They'd had it for the whole of her life; the cushions sagged in the middle, the armrests were hard, and the floral print near worn off, but it was wide and deep and smelled of home.

"You going to wake Shayne?" Declan asked when she returned a second time with their tea. He frowned at the mug she set next to him but didn't say a single word of complaint as he brought it to his lips and sipped gingerly.

Claiming the corner of the couch, Isobel cracked into an eggshell with the side of her spoon and shaved off the top to sprinkle salt and pepper over the firm white. "If I try going in there before noon, she'll take my head off."

Declan chuckled warmly, dunking a bit of whole wheat toast into the yolk of his soft-boiled egg. "And what about you? What's on the docket for today, *hm*?"

"Well, with the wedding stuff behind me it's all about finding a job. I've been in touch with a few recruiters, one of whom I'm going to meet with this afternoon."

"Sounds promising."

Isobel only nodded, not wanting to tell him that the few places she'd scoped out thus far had only connected with her in hopes of scoring an interview, and she'd walked away utterly humiliated. This time, she'd decided to put herself in the hands of an agency, and under her mother's maiden name to deflect attention.

Making the change on her résumé had felt like a colossal betrayal, but after she was in the door it would be easy to correct during the interview itself, she reminded herself, finishing the last bite of her egg. But at least this way she could avoid being lured in under false pretenses. Again. She'd have to veer away from the news and media circuit for a while, until the frenzy blew over. As the scandal's hype had escalated quickly beyond the first week and skyrocketed into the start of the second, Isobel wasn't sure when exactly that might be. Things were so bad she'd unplugged the house phone and limited her trips to the crucial and essential.

Mercifully, the refund from the travel agency softened the strain of bills, but she'd sobbed for the rest of the evening, as quietly as possible. Shayne was so pumped about their Sisterversary trip that Isobel didn't have the heart to tell her she had no intention of actually going. How could she? This was supposed to have been the start of her new life. What was she supposed to do in Greece? Celebrate her failure?

"Bells?" Isobel met her father's gaze, concern melded into his features. God, she'd zoned out again. "You all right, love?"

How do I answer that? Truly answer that? Isobel forced a smile. "I'm fine."

The lines between his brows deepened.

"What I did is unfortunate and inexcusable, but my actions are not a reflection of the TFC."

Kyle. His voice from the TV, soft as a summer breeze, but the shock of hearing it after so long struck her with the ferocity of a bullet to the chest. Isobel dropped her fork, and it clattered with a bang at her feet.

"I regret hurting someone I loved deeply, but pain is a process—a part of life—a learning experience from which I have learned and intend to grow." Kyle sat behind a fan of microphones, hands clasped on the table before him and the Toronto Football Club's logo at his back.

Declan moved so quickly he was almost a blur, searching for the remote. Any other time she would've been thrilled to see him moving with such ease and speed, but as of this moment Isobel was stone. Nothing penetrated except for Kyle's voice—his hollow words—ringing inside her head.

"What's done is done. It's time for me to move on. I'm ready for the next phase of my life and my career, and am grateful for the support of my coach, my team . . . during this unfortu—"

The TV snapped off, leaving Isobel's horrified reflection mirrored in its black surface.

Pain is a process—a part of life—a learning experience? That was it? Eight years and a broken heart summed up so feebly, like none of it—the anguish and loss and betrayal—mattered so long as he *learned*. Learned what, exactly? What could he possibly learn from this ordeal that was worth destroying their future?

Her father gripped the remote in both hands and squeezed so tight the plastic shell groaned. "I'm sorry, I should've had more sense than to put on the TV."

"It's fine. I'm fine." Finding purpose in movement, Isobel dropped to her knees to search for the discarded fork that had skittered under the couch, and found it within easy reach, amid balls of fluff and a stray sock.

"Bells—"

My actions are not a reflection of the TFC. "I'm fine, Dad, really." She plunked the fork on the stacked pile of plates. Carrying the dishes into the kitchen, grip unsteady, she dumped them into the sink—ceramic and cutlery clattering— and cranked the faucet before adding far too much dish soap in the basin rapidly filling with scalding water. Bubbles frothed, rising like her temper.

I'm ready for the next phase. Grabbing a plate, Isobel scrubbed until her fingers screamed. *Time to move on.* Of all the arrogant, manipulative, selfish!—Slick with soap, the plate flew from her hands and smashed on the floor at her feet. Isobel pressed her mouth into the crook of her elbow as grief rolled over her in a furious wave.

"Bells?"

"I'm fine." She waved him back with the sodden rag. "Stay there while I clean up the mess."

"Stop. Just stop, love." Declan closed his arms around her.

"Daddy, please. I said I'm fine."

"Lord above, I raised a stubborn child. A fact that pleases and vexes me in equal measure. I might be broken, but dammit, I'm a long way off from useless. Lean on me, love, even if only a little."

And that was it. The final straw that broke her. Isobel sank into his embrace. "I don't know why this is happening." Again. Again! All her carefully knit seams and mending scars ripped apart. Tore open. And the pain. God the pain . . .

"Oh, my darling girl. My brave heart," he whispered as a sob escaped her.

Isobel swiped furiously at her face. "I don't want to cry over him. It's weak. Pathetic."

"It's not weakness; it just shows how deeply you loved, and now it's trapped inside of you. Desperate for a way out." He kissed her forehead. "No one has a heart like my darling girl. So open to love without fear, but the price is the devastation it suffers in the wake of loss. So cry, and cry as much as you need to and don't be ashamed for it. Pain demands to be felt before it can be released. Today or tomorrow, it will keep coming back until you do, so do the work now."

"But I have been, Daddy. I woke up today and felt good. Like I was finally healing, and now I'm here, crying, right back where I started. I haven't moved forward at all."

"Grief isn't a straight line, love. It's a wheel. One day you're on top and the next you're flattened beneath it, but eventually the wheel will stop spinning and you'll rise from this misery stronger for it. Better for it. It feels impossible now, but we'll get through this, love."

She rested her head on his shoulder, careful not to transfer any weight onto his body. God, how she missed being able to wrap her arms around him and squeeze. To pour all her grief and sadness into the firm, fast circle of his arms, knowing he could take it. That he could carry it all. Her shield. Her hero.

Now it was she who had to carry it all for him. To stand for him. But there were days she wanted to crumble under the pressure, and she hated that weakness—did everything she could to push it out of her, but right now it was crushing her instead. Burying her in rubble.

Just then the doorbell rang, and Isobel pressed hands to her eyes, willing the tears to recede. "I'll get it," she said, drying her hands on her thighs and then mopping up the mess of her face. Wondering who it could possibly be, she opened the door to find a woman standing on her porch.

She spun around, a phone set to her ear as a friendly smile flashed across her face. "Larry, she's home. I'll call you back." Hanging up, she slid the phone into her Louis Vuitton purse. "Isobel, hi. My name is Nneka Evans."

"I know who you are," Isobel answered, her voice so small

it was nearly swallowed by the wet roll of tires on pavement as cars whisked down the street. She'd watched Nneka on TV delivering the evening news until she'd transitioned from in front of the camera to behind it as a producer with MTV. There was barely ten years between them, and already Nneka was everything Isobel aspired to be.

God, more press. More reporters hounding for blood. It was never going to end. When the scandal had first broken, reporters called at all hours of the day and night looking for a statement. Then there were random people who phoned her as a prank. Fed up, she'd shut it off all together hoping they'd get the hint, but apparently the natural progression was to now show up on her doorstep.

"You people are *relentless*." Isobel stepped back, retreating into the safety of her home. "*Leave. Me. Alone.*"

"No—no wait!" Nneka braced the door before Isobel could slam it in her face. "Please, hear me out. Five minutes. We can speak on the porch if you don't want me coming inside, and if you don't like what I have to say, I'll leave."

Isobel raised her chin, her grip bone-white on the handle. "If you're not here to interrogate me and exploit my pain, then what do you want?"

"Sharon called me. From *The Six*? We go way back and well . . . what Norman did to you was abhorrent. Obscene." Nneka's hand lowered from the door, and her brown eyes glimmered like a honed sword ready for battle. "So how would you like his job?"

Chapter Eleven

Maybe it was a mark of desperation, but Isobel's curiosity overcame her better judgment, and she ushered Nneka inside, closing the door, and leading her into the living room.

"Dad, it's all right," Isobel said when her father let out a grating curse. "Ms. Evans is here about a job offer."

"Is she now?" Declan struggled out of his seat, eyes blazing with condemnation and warning. Somehow Isobel knew, despite his frail frame and chronic pain, he was prepared to toss Nneka bodily over his shoulder and heave her out the door to protect his daughter.

Tears seared the back of Isobel's eyes at seeing the barest glimmer of the man her father had once been standing before her. "I'll be fine." Kissing his cheek, she gave him a gentle nudge. "The rain has stopped. Why don't you sit in the garden and do some puzzles?"

Declan's gaze flickered to Isobel, and he nodded grudgingly. "I'll be close if you need me," he said, and toddled off. A little stiff in his movements, but otherwise well enough that she could see he wouldn't need her help managing the back steps.

"Would you like some coffee?" she asked when they were alone. The words sounded hollow, but she'd been raised to never be rude to a guest in her home. Even if the guest wasn't exactly welcome.

"No, thank you." Nneka sat down in the center of the couch and crossed a leg, her coral skirt flaring around her calves. "I won't keep you long. I squeezed this trip in between meetings."

Isobel sat down in her father's armchair, keeping the coffee table squarely between them like a border, dividing enemy lines. "You said something about a job."

"Yes. While I can't give you Norman's job at *The Six*, I can offer you one on my team." Nneka cupped both hands around her knee. "I guess it's safe to say you've been avoiding all media platforms lately?" Isobel nodded and Nneka echoed the gesture. "Well, you've become a bit of a rising celebrity, and there has been a tremendous outpouring of support online from women who connected with your story, Isobel. And after scoping out your blog, I was rather impressed."

"My blog?"

"Yes. Especially your bit on the Black Lives Matter movement here in Toronto. *Herspiration* is one of the most elite women's magazines in New York outside of *Vogue* or *Cosmo*. As their new media director, I'm tasked with assembling a team of promising young professionals to launch our digital brand. I want you to become one of our first content curators, connecting to viewers, sharing news you are passionate about, but adding that human touch you bring so well. You'll become the cornerstone of our digital brand, straddling the median between print and on-air by writing articles for our online magazine as well as being the voice in front of the camera, featured in spotlight segments released online anywhere from two to three times a week.

For those you'll sit down with me during our live show to create a highlight reel and boost our digital numbers."

Isobel's heart stuttered, then roared back to life. "*Me?*"

Nneka laughed, pleased at her stunned disbelief. "I know it's not exactly something you're qualified for, but apparently people are really interested in hearing what you have to say. So am I. How does that all sound so far?"

Isobel tucked a lock of hair behind her ear, suddenly wishing she wasn't dressed in old sweatpants and a paint splotched Nirvana T-shirt. "Incredible. I guess I'm just surprised you think *I* can do that?"

"You've got a great look for the camera and a wonderful voice. Frankly, I'm stunned *The Six* didn't give you the opportunity to put it to good use, but I'm grateful they didn't because then I probably wouldn't be sitting across from you right now."

Isobel rubbed her sweating palms on her thighs. Even if this seemed to be everything she'd ever hoped for, when all was said and done, there were particulars that had to be addressed. "Can I ask about the salary?"

"Fifty thousand to start, with a minimum annual bonus of five percent, plus other incentives like a corporate gym membership and four weeks paid vacation."

If Isobel wasn't already sitting down, she'd have toppled right over. That was nearly twice what she made at *The Six* with just the salary alone, and she'd certainly never seen a single bonus with them—not once in three years. With this, and her father's settlement agreement, Isobel wouldn't have to worry from one month to the next if she could afford groceries *and* hydro after being wiped out by the mortgage.

"If you agree to all that, then I can let the studio know you're on board and have my assistant coordinate a walk-through of the set in New York. How's early next week?"

"Wait . . ." The whirling spin of excitement lurched to a sudden, brutal stop. "You want me to commute for work?"

"We're an American company and our hub is in Manhattan, so unless you know how to teleport, yes. But don't worry, it won't be every day. I'm there three times a week for our on-air shoots and in-person interviews. Aside from that I work remotely. You'll only be in one or two days a week, at most, and elsewhere when needed. Is that a problem?"

Isobel's nervous fingers picked at a stubborn dried patch of robin's egg blue paint on her knee from when she'd repainted the living room last spring. "It's just . . . my dad isn't well."

Nneka's eyes softened. "Yes, I read about his accident on your blog, it was especially evocative, but I'm afraid this is crucial to the role. We need someone who can be mobile, often at a moment's notice. We can't *always* report from behind a desk or in front of a green screen. Viewers want a more intimate and human approach. You, in the room, with the subjects. I know it won't be easy, but do you think you can you handle that?"

No. But she swallowed the word. Nneka had emerged from the ether, a glorious manifestation offering Isobel not only a job, but her dream. If she said no, what were the odds she'd ever have another chance? Another opportunity? And as she sat there, desperately trying not to fidget, she could almost hear Priya urging her on.

Say yes now. Worry about the details later.

So why was she hesitating? Because it all sounded too

good to be true? And as the saying went . . . "Let me ask you a question, and I'd appreciate an honest answer."

"Shoot."

"Are you offering me this job because you believe in me . . . in my voice? Or is it to build off the hype wagon?"

"Both," Nneka answered, without pause or hesitation. "But the hype won't last long, so it's up to you if you want to play it to your advantage or not." Uncrossing her legs, Nneka stood and circled around to the front of the coffee table, and given it had a solid oak pedestal, sat down on top of it. "Besides, Kyle Peterson isn't holed up afraid of the world. You shouldn't be either."

God, Kyle. Where she'd avoided the limelight, he'd flocked to it. Basking like a lion in the sun. "I won't . . . I can't—talk about what happened." It wasn't just a point of pride. It was self-preservation.

A gleam of pure empathy softened Nneka's eyes. "Don't worry, there's much bigger news to tell. Unfortunately, you're living in the generation of viral scandals, but soon enough this will blow over. I give thanks to the goddess each morning all of my bar-top dancing days happened before the advent of social media. I prefer to think of my god as a woman," she added with an amused wink. "Who needs another man in charge? Think about it." Rising, Nneka plucked a business card out of her purse. "But I'll need an answer *soon*."

* * *

Too restless and wired for sleep, Priya decided to make better use of her morning of freedom. Standing outside of the crumbling ruin, she checked the address twice to be sure it was the right place and sighed hugely. Boarded windows, graffiti covered walls, and neglected roofline, it wouldn't take more than a severe storm to send the shingles scattering like dead leaves. The string of brownstones would've been a marvel in their former glory, but now they were a dilapidated eyesore in the midst of a haggard block.

The only thing keeping it together was the sheer stubborn will of the woman who lived inside. Priya walked up weathered front steps. Massive divots had been worn into the stone and the front door hadn't seen a decent coat of paint in far too long. Forsaking the broken intercom, she tested the knob, found it unlocked, and entered a dimly lit corridor. She knocked on the first door to her immediate left.

She didn't have to wait long before it was pulled open. An elderly woman with a dense cloud of silver-white curls, shockingly bright against the warmth of her skin, each one bouncy and beautifully coiled, stood in the doorway.

"Yes?" She stood hipshot in an eggplant purple top cut to fall off the shoulder, mom jeans, kitten heels, and a filmy ankle-length kimono that matched the violet shadow swept over shrewd brown eyes beneath lethally arched brows. Slender hoop earrings so large they touched her bare wrinkled shoulders completed her outfit.

This can't be my client. She had to be at least in her midseventies, but her outfit—and body—shouted twenty-four.

"Hi." Priya smiled warmly. "I'm looking for Guadalupe Carranza?"

"Whatever you're selling, dear," the woman said, adjusting her kimono, "I'm not interested."

"I'm not—"

"Yeah, yeah. Save the spiel. Not. Interested." The door reverberated on the hinges with a heavy slam that would've broken her nose if Priya hadn't jerked back in time. Collecting herself, Priya knocked again—firmly. "Mrs. Carranza, my name is Priyanka Seth. I'm from Marek, Nagao & Silver. I'm here about your suit against your property manager."

The door opened again, and she reappeared, arm braced on the jamb, gold bangles chiming loudly at her wrist. "You got a card with you?"

"Absolutely." Reaching into her purse, Priya offered one to the woman.

She gave it a thorough once-over, then scrutinized Priya equally before she widened the door to let her pass. "Come on in."

"Thank you, Mrs. Carranza."

"Inside this home I'm Genie."

"Genie," Priya amended, not bothered by the informality.

"Sorry for snapping at you. I don't get many people knocking at my door, and the ones I do are usually from Triton. You're not the type Crowley sends to harass me, but can't be too careful with that scummy bastard."

"I'm sorry I've shown up unannounced. Work has been busy, so it was difficult to carve out time to meet with you. I tried calling before heading over, but your number went straight to voice mail." Priya removed her shoes and followed Genie into a living room where a collection of brightly patterned couches sat draped in crocheted blankets. A bronze screen depicting geishas dancing by a waterfall divided the room.

The rest of the living space was stacked with boxes and

knotted black garbage bags. If Priya didn't know any better she'd swear Genie had either just moved in, or was on her way out. As for the home itself, everything inside was about as rough as the exterior of the unit. Like it'd endured a hurricane, a flood, and a tornado all in one.

Overhead, the ceiling bubbled under a large stain that went from rust to mustard and met crumbling plaster denoting serious water damage that bled down a wall covered in splotchy red handprints. An abstract design choice that evoked a gruesome crime scene.

"Sorry about that. I keep it disconnected these days and screen the recordings." Genie whisked her hand over the cushions of a printed couch that backed up against the window, scattering a cloud of crumbs and dust. After several hard sweeps, she gestured for Priya to sit down. "Do you want some tea? I have jasmine or chai."

"No, thank you."

"Water, then? I'm not one for coffee, I'm afraid." Removing her kimono, she draped it over the arm of the couch. "Not good for my blood pressure."

"I'm fine. Really. So, reading over the file I have a sense of what this case is about, but I'd like you to go through the specifics with you. I know that might seem a little redundant, and I apologize for the necessary inconvenience."

Genie waved a hand. "When you get to be my age there isn't much you consider inconvenient." Running her gnarled fingers through her hair, she gathered the bulk of her curls on top of her head in a pineapple that she cinched with a blue scrunchie.

"It all began when this parcel was purchased by Triton

about six years ago. Barely a month later, the incidents started. No water for weeks on end, no gas for significantly longer, and the pests started springing up—mice, roaches, and in one case, bedbugs. All harmless enough if you didn't factor in the muscled heavy who showed up every three weeks applying pressure." Genie muttered something indiscernible under her breath, her explosion of curls flouncing like a rabbit's tail. "Triton deliberately let our homes decay to drive us out."

Priya withdrew a lined pad from her satchel and began scribbling notes. "This is when you and the other tenants attempted to speak with Mr. Crowley, yes?"

"Damn straight. Tenants have a right to be seen and heard by their landlord." Genie crossed a leg with surprising agility. "But we were told by security at Crowley's office that we would not be admitted, and that the police had been contacted. Therefore if we did not vacate, we would be arrested for trespassing. Morale deflated rather quickly after that."

"And how many of the original tenants still reside here?" It would certainly be helpful to her case to get corroborating testimony.

"I'm the only one left standing." Genie lifted a shoulder, the wrinkled skin crinkling like old newspaper over arms wiry with muscle. "The churn and burn took a toll on those of us who tried to fight back. It's tough waiting weeks or months or *years* for assistance. Those with families were the first to toss in the towel—understandable, given the circumstances. But me? I've no one to worry about and I'm tough, it takes a great deal to scare me off. A great deal. I haven't come across it yet." Her eyes gleamed with a verve that belied her years. "When I first moved in, this neighborhood was ninety percent Black or Hispanic. Now? Maybe two percent, and falling rapidly. Crowley is a cancer, stripping away culture and heritage from this community for profit. I'm gonna put it to you straight: he wants people of color out so he can charge more." She pointed sharply to her left. "Two blocks over, a unit goes for five *thousand* a month now."

"How much are you currently paying in rent?"

"Four hundred and eighty-seven."

Priya choked on air. You couldn't rent a closet the size of a subway tile in Manhattan for that price. "What do you do for work?"

"Burlesque."

"As in . . . *dancing*?"

"Yes. At La Scandal." Genie waved her hands, mimicking the seductive flow of large, feathered fans flowing before her. "Been at it twenty years now. I became a bit of a neighborhood celebrity as its only mature dancer. That's where I got the stage name Genie."

Head lowered, Priya pressed her lips together to mask her smirk. "And what about your countersuit? Can you explain the circumstances surrounding the damages you're suing for?"

Genie sighed, a hard and heavy huff of breath. "All winter I'd hounded Triton about the radiator. Some days it boiled too hot, other days it wouldn't run at all. Damn near froze my ass off." She stamped an aggravated foot. "I had to buy space heaters and such to keep warm but on the very bad nights I'd go to a motel—sneaking the cats in with me, which wasn't easy, let me tell you."

Priya swung her gaze around the room. "You have pets?"

"*Had*—I got sick and went to the hospital with pneumonia.

I was gone for two days, and during that time the radiator flooded. I returned to find a glass cabinet shattered, wood shelves warped and collapsed, the plastic spray arm in the sink melted, an outlet popped out of the wall, the ceiling and walls bubbled. Worse still . . ." A watery gleam filled Genie's eyes but she set her narrow shoulders and stiffened her lips.

Something twisted hard in Priya's chest as she imagined the horror of walking through the front door to find the devastation that lay within. "How many did you have?"

"Eight." Genie's eyes misted and she pressed a hooked finger beneath her nose, gathering her composure. "I lost my husband and children in a drunk driving accident . . . so those cats." Her firm voice wavered. "They were my family, you see, and—"

"Mrs. Carranza, I hate to cut you off but emotion won't sway a judge. Facts will. So let's keep as tight to them as possible, okay?"

"Sure." Genie sat back, lips firming. "You're the pro, albeit a young one."

"I am young, but I'm very good and will get you the best outcome for this case."

"Then that's all I can ask for. Far as facts go, I've lived here for fifty-three years and never once have I been late or defaulted on my rent. Not once in five decades. Until now. After the incident, Crowley *claimed* no one entered the unit, but my neighbor said she saw some beefy bruiser leaving my place, and not long after steam was pouring through her walls. So I called the police to file a report—cops came out two days later to take a statement—wasn't an 'emergency.'" She wiggled her fingers with air quotes. "But coincidentally, my neighbor now had a different story. Saw nothing. Knew nothing, that sort of thing."

"You think they silenced her?"

"She was scared. A young mom of two, all on her own. Moved barely a month later. Triton accused me of negligence, so I stopped paying." Genie shook her head, hands looped over the knee of her crossed leg. "This home is all I have left, so I'll fight with my last breath to keep it. Can you help me?"

"Yes." Priya capped her pen and tucked it into the spiraled spine of her lined pad. "Yes, I will.

Chapter Twelve

When setting a trap for an ambush, the first thing you needed was to ascertain location. It would've been easier to call Triton offices and schedule a meeting, but Priya wanted Peter Crowley in the open—without the power of his corner suite, where he towered over Manhattan like a god. She wanted him in the streets, unprepared. And, thanks to Lorraine's administrative whisper network, Priya had the perfect place in mind.

Every Monday, Wednesday, and Friday from ten to ten thirty in the morning he frequented the same café hitched to the base of his towering corporate building. So Priya made sure to head down early that same Friday morning and secured a table near the patio doors, giving her a view of the entire venue while she awaited her prey.

It was just the sort of place she would have loved to come to for any other reason, all weathered wood paneled walls stamped with graffiti ink and bistro style chairs lining the paved brick patio. Certainly not the sort of place she would have pegged for the likes of Triton Property Management's COO.

Punctual to the minute, Peter Crowley swanned onto the patio, sat down at a small corner table for two, and opened the paper he'd brought with him to the financials. Crisp and dark blue, his suit was expertly tailored and probably cost more than what Priya's mother paid monthly for their apartment in Chelsea. Thick black hair, scattered with a hint of white, was swept back under a heavy layer of gel, and his skin was doused in tanner, evident in the faded line she caught beneath the edge of his jawline from a fresh trim of his goatee. Yet, despite the hooked nose and sunken cheeks, the brawler's granite jaw helped pull the eye and make it linger. This was a man who cared about appearances, leaned into it for power. Priya knew his type far too well.

"Is this seat taken?" Without waiting for a response, she dragged out the chair across from him and sat down.

Crowley arched a brow, but the appraising look in his eye told Priya he wasn't at all bothered by her bold approach. "While any other day I'd welcome the beautiful company, I'm expecting someone in fifteen minutes."

"Then I'll only take up ten."

A hint of cunning amusement sharpened in his gaze. "It's my wife, and she is a very jealous woman."

Which was part of the reason Priya had settled on this being her point of attack. The second important element of setting an ambush: pressure. "Sheila Marrone, yes? CEO of Triton. Married you five years ago, and six months later pulled you up the ladder from director of business development to chief operating officer with a cushy corner office and a seven-figure salary."

The gleam of interest vanished, turning his eyes as flat as stone beneath the hard line of lowered brows. "Who are you?"

"My name is Priyanka Seth." She presented him with a

business card, which he snatched from her fingers. "I'm here on behalf of my client, Genie Carranza."

"Ah, yes. The ever-gouging thorn in my side." He eased into his chair, finger rubbing pensively across his bottom lip. "Did she send you to finally make good on her back rent?"

"No."

"Well, that's unfortunate."

Priya crossed a leg. "I'd like to discuss the damages she's suing you for."

"Suing *me*?" His face split into a wide, disbelieving grin, revealing impossibly white teeth. "That's cute."

"You won't think so in a moment."

Now his attention dropped to the embossed lettering on her business card. "Marek, Nagao & Silver." He whistled sharply. "Tell me something." He flicked the edge of the card with his middle finger. "How did she manage to afford you if she can't afford her rent?"

"It's pro bono."

"Lucky break. Too bad it's not going to do her any good. I'm well within my rights to turf her out tomorrow. I've tried to be patient, but it's worn exceptionally thin." Clasping his hands, Peter leaned forward. "I'd hate to see her pushed out, but at this rate she's leaving me with little to no choice."

"Oh yes, you appear terribly choked up over it." Opening the file she'd brought with her, Priya set it down before him. "This is an itemized list of all damages sustained by the radiator bursting in her unit. China cabinet with antique crystal, wine collection, vintage artwork. And of course, her animals."

"This says ten *thousand* dollars."

"That's right. We're also requesting another five for emotional pain and suffering."

"That's obscene."

"What's obscene is walking into a house full of dead cats and destroyed valuables after enduring a frigid winter with no *heat*. I'd say fifteen grand is more than fair, under the circumstances."

"We called a technician as soon as we could, but unfortunately she wasn't cooperative about allowing him access to her unit. My company manages over two thousand properties spread across the city of New York." Crowley shrugged. "We do our best for our tenants, but if they won't cooperate, we can't be held liable."

"Genie says the man who showed up wasn't a service technician but a thug sent to intimidate her into breaking her lease. The same one who muscled out half your tenants during your first year of ownership."

"That's absurd."

"So it's just a coincidence that the only tenant preexisting your ownership of West 109th is Genie Carranza, and all the other units were put forward for significantly higher rent?"

"What are you insinuating?"

"That perhaps the only tenants you're interested in doing the best for are the ones who pull in more profit for your books. Perhaps I'm wrong." She mirrored his earlier shrug. "Why don't you provide me with the work order—it should have the date when the request was issued."

"No."

"How about the contract for the company you used?"

Crowley shook his head.

"How about a *name*?"

"Sorry, dollface, can't help you."

Priya flexed her fingers, cracking her knuckles. No, he wasn't going to help her, because nothing about this was about doing what was best for his tenants. This was about pushing an elderly woman out of her home by any means necessary, and he'd made the mistake of thinking Genie was cornered, too weak or frail to fight back. But now she had Priya in the corner with her, and Priya knew a thing or two about fighting with her back to the wall.

"Do I need to get a judge to order you to turn over these documents? Because I will."

"Do whatever will make your little heart happy, dollface." He waved a hand, shooing her aside. "But I'm done being charitable with my time."

Priya rose and gathered her file. "I came here as a courtesy, to give you an opportunity to act in good faith, but I'm glad you didn't make this easy." She threw him a lethal grin. The one she'd spent hours in the mirror perfecting throughout law school. "Because according to your company's recent press release, you've got several other projects in the works—big plans. Shiny new condo development. Very luxurious."

"So what?"

"The longer my client refuses to leave, the more money gets chewed up in delays. How are you going to explain that to your board when you convene next quarter when you could have easily and quietly settled right now? Instead, I get to haul your ass to housing court and believe me"—she leaned in, tapping a fingertip on the edge of the table—"I clerked for the DA's office for a year. I will eviscerate you."

Peter wiped his fingers with a napkin, before rolling it into a tight wad. "Fifteen. And I'll waive back rent, which is more than generous, but I want her out before the end of the month. Nonnegotiable."

"My client wants to stay."

"That's out of the question. The brownstones are coming down in September, so unless she wants to be buried in rubble . . ."

Priya rolled her tongue into the pocket of her cheek. "In that case, you're going to have to offer more than fifteen."

"Don't be coy, Ms. Seth, what's your number?"

"Thirty-five."

Peter Crowley narrowed shrew eyes. "Thirty. Not a penny more."

Priya schooled her face to calm neutrality, but inside she was bursting like a firecracker. She'd leveled him quickly, and now was her cue to get up and walk away. Though it likely would take a bit of persuasion to bring Genie around on the matter of leaving her home, thirty grand was a glorious outcome and would go a long way to securing her client a fresh start elsewhere. No one could have come away from the table with more under the circumstances.

The other associates at MNS were about to eat her dust and choke on it.

"You have my card." Priya swung her purse onto her shoulder. "Call me when the check is ready."

* * *

"I've got a bone to pick with you."

Isobel lifted her eyes from her laptop screen as Shayne hoisted herself on top of the desk. Haloed by the wash of burnt-orange sunset pushing in through the filmy windowpane, she looked like a warrior angel; all leather and tattoos, tousled indigo hair wreathed in fire.

It took Isobel a moment to shake off the impact of Shayne's stark, raw beauty—rivaled only by her older brother, Marco, the Golden Prince, as the tabloids dubbed him. "Huh?"

"I heard a rumor someone got a fancy new job?"

Heat rushed into Isobel's cheeks. "Oh. Yeah. Just had an interview of sorts two days ago. Totally random."

"And? Why the fuck am I only hearing about it now? How was it?" Shayne removed a sucker from her jacket pocket and shucked off the wrapper, listening intently as Isobel told her everything.

After showing Nneka out, Isobel had raced upstairs to her room and jumped onto her laptop to find her inbox was flooded with an overwhelming number of notifications. Tens of thousands of them. Comments, likes, shares, and even emails from people offering words of encouragement or reaching out to share their own harrowing tale of heartbreak.

Isobel had spent hours reading through them all, one after the other, until her back ached and her eyes burned. But for the first time in far too long, her heart hummed with so many rising emotions that reverberated against her ribs like a flock of frantic caged birds, but at the forefront was excitement. The initial spark of joy. And true healing. She'd actually started writing again! And had been just about to post a new entry to her blog when Shayne had bounded in.

"Bel, you gotta do this. It's perfect. Call her." Shayne slapped a hand across her desk, searching for Isobel's cell phone. "Do it. Right the fuck now."

"I can't."

"What?" Shayne stopped midsearch. "Why the fuck not?"

"Did you not hear me say they want me to *travel*?"

"Yeah." Shayne's eyes did a confused left-to-right shuffle. "Once a week."

"And what about my dad? How can I leave him alone for days at a time when he can't even manage more than a few hours at best? It was bad enough when I worked for *The Six*— but this will be too much." Isobel ran a strand of hair through her fingers, threading it with long fast strokes.

"So that's it?" Shayne's brows flattened; an irritated line drawn over electric golden eyes. "You're giving up?"

"What do you want me to say? Am I disappointed? Of course. The salary was great, and it's absolutely a project I'd love to be part of, but I can't figure out the logistics. I have responsibilities here." She hadn't spent a night away from home in nearly eight months, and before that it was the occasional stay at Kyle's—and she'd always slept horribly. Her mind sick with worry. Tears burned like acid but Isobel swallowed them down. "I'll find another job."

Shayne swirled the sucker in her mouth with a long twist before yanking it out with a decisive pop. "That's it, I'm staying."

"What?"

"The only reason you're backing off this is because Pops will be alone—so I'm staying. That's it. Problem solved."

"Shayne. You can't."

"Don't see an alternative. You have a chance to get your life back on track. You think I'll let you pass that up? Fuck no."

"But you've been gone from LA for over a week already. What about your training?"

Shayne jerked a thumb over her shoulder. "Last I checked there are plenty of gyms in Toronto."

"And work?"

"Clubs too."

"But—"

"But nothing." Shayne took Isobel by the shoulders, giving them a reassuring squeeze. "Look, I know I stepped on your toes at the travel agency." Isobel dropped her eyes. "And I'm not saying I'm moving in, but I can stretch out a couple of weeks to give you time to settle into the new job and sort things out."

"I don't know Shayne . . . this is too much too soon. I have to think this through."

"Are you kidding me? This is everything you'd dreamed of for yourself. Why are you sabotaging it?"

"I'm not sabotaging anything," Isobel grumbled, standing up. "I'm looking at the bigger picture. I'm being responsible."

"No, you're being an idiot." Shayne whirled around, blocking her retreat. "What's our code, Bel?"

"Shayne, enough, I've got laundry and dinner and—"

"The code." She crossed her arms. "What is it?"

"Sisters before all."

"The other one, smart-ass."

Isobel rolled her eyes with a gentle sigh. "Chase dreams. Not drama."

"Good. This is it—your dreams have come knocking. Chase them or give up—the choice is yours." Shayne backed out of the room, closing the door behind her.

Rummaging around on her desk, Isobel found her phone

tucked under her journal and weighed it in her hands while she paced in a looping, awkward circle. It was an incredible opportunity, one that might never have come to her without the attention of the viral scandal. And while this wasn't exactly Global or CTV, it was a connection with young minds she could help shape and mold with the variety of content she would bring to the roster. So why was she running away instead of galloping toward it?

Was Shayne right? Was she actually just finding excuses to self-sabotage because at the core it was failing that terrified her most? The fear of getting so close to her dreams just to see them ripped away—again?

Maybe.

So much had changed so quickly, and Isobel had never been good with change. New always terrified her.

Not like Shayne. Where everyone was expected to slot themselves into a box and stay there, Shayne lived her life round—her world vast and infinite and full. Apology or regret were two concepts she vehemently refused to adhere to, and from a young age she'd always possessed a clarity of self unlike anything Isobel had ever seen.

Leaving Spain, her family, and the shackles of monarchy— even a distant one that didn't live in a fishbowl like the British royals—required a strength of self, a boldness Isobel couldn't begin to fathom. To shed her identity at eighteen and forge one of her own.

A new name. A new country—a new life void of anything familiar. She'd certainly made it look far too easy, bending like a blade of grass in either a gentle breeze or a hurricane, and adapting with a smile. Maybe that was what Isobel needed to do. Live without fear. Seize opportunity without regret. Adapt.

If Shayne could so fearlessly remake herself, so could Isobel.

Time to be brave. Lowering herself to the edge of her bed, Isobel cradled the phone in her hands and gathered herself with a breath before dialing. Nneka answered in two brief rings.

"Nneka, I've made my decision. I'd like to accept the offer."

Chapter Thirteen

The settlement paperwork arrived in Priya's inbox bright and early on Sunday morning, without a single comma out of place.

"It was brilliant, totally had him by the balls." Priya smiled around a mouthful of yogurt and berries. "Not only did I smash this case out of the ballpark in less than fifteen minutes, my client is getting *double* what I'd banked on." She high-fived the air with her spoon. "Total annihilation."

Hadrian, dressed in a fitted T-shirt and sweats, smiled at her through the screen of her iPad as he smeared cream cheese onto a bagel. "Brilliant." He deposited both halves onto a plate. "You said that to him? Eviscerate?"

"He kept calling me *dollface*."

"Well, then a show of strength is definitely warranted under such circumstances. Why did you approach him without scheduling a meeting first?"

"I didn't want to give him time to prepare—or even worse dodge me all together—and from what I saw, he's an overdressed corporate bully, easily rattled."

"I'll take your word for it. I don't know much about him other than he's a philanthropist who frequently attends fundraisers and charity events. The most recent, I think, was the Tribeca Film Festival. Supposedly he's very generous with his time and even more so with his money."

"His *wife's* money," she said, her tone as dry as the stale granola she'd unearthed for her breakfast. "And likely only for the tax write-offs."

Hadrian chuckled. "Indeed. All that's left now is getting my client to sign on the dotted line."

"You may have a bit of an uphill battle on your hands, there. Can't imagine fifty years will be easy to walk away from. Not at her age." Hadrian's face closed in on the screen, all tousled hair and gilded green eyes as he licked something off his thumb.

Easy, whoremones. Dunking her spoon into her bowl, Priya stirred aimlessly. "Maybe. But that's part of the job, isn't it? Sometimes the outcome isn't what the client initially hoped for, but a win is a win." At best she'd expected to clear back rent and damages, but *this*? Whatever her score, Priya was going to shoot up to the top of the pack for sure, especially after escaping the War of the Senior Partners unscathed, and come Monday morning, Michael wasn't going to know what hit him.

"Then I guess congratulations are in order."

"Thank you." She gave a mock bow but a knock at the door interrupted her. "Must be the concierge. One sec, I promise we can discuss your case after this."

Hadrian lifted the half of his bagel and bit into it. "Take your time."

Priya raced to the door and opened it to find Caitlin, dressed in a sunny yellow blazer, leather harness bra, and ripped boyfriend jeans, on the other side.

"Why are you dressed like it's Tuesday?" She pulled

tortoiseshell glasses down the length of her slender nose, sneering at Priya's slacks and blouse. "Bitch, you forgot."

Brunch. Pathos. Dammit. "I did, I'm sorry, but it's not an issue." Priya waved her inside. "I just have to stop over to see my client. It's on the way."

"Client?"

"For my pro bono. You'll love her, promise."

"Okey dokey. I'll adjust our reservation. Free mimosas are available until one, so we can just order a dozen when we get there and pound them back like shots."

"Perfect." Priya stopped by the counter. "Hadrian, I'm so sorry, I need to go."

"Not a problem." His gaze flitted over her shoulder, and he smiled warmly at Caitlin. "I see you've got company."

"Yes. This is my sister, Cait."

Caitlin's mouth tumbled open in a slack-jawed grin. "Hello, handsome!"

Hadrian gave her a shy grin that somehow made him even more endearing. And devastating, if such a thing was possible. "Pleasure to meet you."

"Pleasure's all mine." Caitlin leaned companionly against the counter and propped a chin on her fist. "What's your sign? Aquarius? I bet it's Aquarius. You've got that free flowing intellectual, effortlessly magnetic vibe. Priya's a Leo, by the way. Highly compatible match. Fire and air."

"Hadrian, I better let you go before Cait starts dissecting your entire birth chart. I'll let you know how the client meet goes, and we'll circle back on your case later this afternoon."

"No worries. Enjoy yourself, and once again— congratulations, tiger."

The call ended and Caitlin spun around, swatting her with both hands, and squealed, "What the actual fuck, bro. Who was that?"

"Panty Thief."

"Shut up!" This time when her jaw unhinged, it struck the floor with a laugh. "How's the spark between you? Still blazing hot?"

"Yes, but as it turns out, he's also my co-worker."

"*Oooh*, the plot thickens." Caitlin wiggled lavender brows. "You going to let that stop you from jumping his bones?"

"I can't get involved with someone at the firm. It's tacky."

"Shame. And yet another reason why I'll never become a corporate grunt, slaving away for the Man when fashion is far more liberal." Caitlin raised her arms and twirled on her toes. "Endless travel. Free clothes, hot sex, what's not to love?"

Priya rolled her eyes. "Give me two seconds, and we can get going."

After an outfit change and a quick Uber ride, they were outside Genie's place in under fifteen minutes.

"Whoa." Sliding out of the backseat after Priya, Caitlin pushed her glasses atop her head. "This place is *gorgeous*."

"Are we looking at the same property?" Standing next to her, Priya angled her head. Squinted. "No, can't be. It's still a dump."

"That's because you lack imagination. I'm sorry, but it's true." Giggling, Caitlin took her by the shoulders and squared her with the front steps. "Forget the mess on the surface. Look at those bones. The lines. The character. Now imagine that front refaced, so the red *pops* like terra-cotta tiles fresh from the kiln. A new gate lacquered black to match the doors, and windows washed until they shone. Weeds rooted out from the front garden and new sod put down . . ."

Maybe it was Caitlin's ardent passion, her words weaving a glossy picture before Priya's very eyes, but there *was* something different about the way the light refracted off the dusty windows and glittered across the weathered stone.

"Well, if you want to see a gorgeous brownstone, walk through Harlem, the West Village, and the historic districts all over Manhattan. You'll find immaculate blocks of them," Priya said. And in those areas, it was almost like stepping back to the nineteenth century, when New York was on the rise. But these were just beaten down. Far from their former glory.

"This is an *actual* brownstone, not a cheap imitation or knockoff."

"How can you tell?"

"The seamless lines between townhouses, the uniformness of the exterior, and this." Caitlin slapped a hand to the carved newel post made of the same material as the rest of the structure. "It's not brick, it's sandstone that turns brown when weathered—hence the name. You know these were originally single and two-family layouts, but the majority have been chopped up and converted into modest-sized rental, condo, and co-op buildings."

"How do you know so much about architecture?"

Caitlin shrugged. "I admire beauty and creation in all their forms."

"All right, well, unless you want to continue admiring said beauty, we need to hurry or we'll miss out on free mimosas."

"Say less." Caitlin shot up the steps with Priya, laughing, close behind her. This time when she knocked and Genie answered, she was received with a grin instead of a scowl. Genie's white steel-wool hair was brushed out into a dense halo of curls reminiscent of a '70s Afro, and was accented by large gold hoop earrings.

"Priya. You're back quickly." Her eyes swished over to Caitlin. "Who's this adorable little minx?"

"Caitlin Choi-Emerson. My sister."

"Well, come on in."

They followed Genie into her home, and Caitlin's smile morphed in an agonized groan. "Oh, sweet mother of couture." Leaning against the wall, arms spread, she stroked it gently, as if it was a baby suffering from colic. "There, there. Priya is gonna make it all better, I promise."

Genie covered her mouth with bejeweled hands, barely containing the chortle glistening in her eyes. "Now, what's this good news?"

Priya withdrew the check from her purse and offered it to Genie. "Crowley agreed to a settlement."

The light in Genie's eyes immediately dulled with temper. "Settlement?"

"Yes, it's a pretty generous offer. Along with all back rent waived. Once you've caught your breath I can come by later, we can sign the paperwork, and—"

"I think we've had a misunderstanding." She crossed her arms. "I'm *not* leaving."

Here we go. But Priya was no pushover and her time clerking at the DA's had given her more than enough experience with de-escalating someone's expectations. "I know this isn't what we'd hoped for, and change isn't easy, but this is a fresh start for you."

"What makes you think I want a *fresh start*?" Genie tossed her hands, and a ring nearly flew off one slender finger. "I told you this is my home. I want to stay."

"I wish I could give you that, I truly do, but the reality is we can't always get exactly what we want. I understand this is a shock, so take the afternoon to review everything, and we can discuss further if you'd like, but we need to have this signed before end of day. Crowley needs you out by the end of next week."

"*He* needs me?" Galled, Genie shook her head, white curls swaying like wheatgrass in a stall summer wind. "Are you my lawyer, or his?"

"Yours. I'm on your side."

"Doesn't sound like it." The edges of her snarl stiffened with disappointment. "You knew what I wanted, the only thing that mattered to me was this. Did you even try?"

Priya opened her mouth to answer, then paused with a heavy breath. "I mentioned it."

"Mentioned," Genie echoed. "That's all?"

"Anything more would've been a wasted effort!" Why couldn't Genie see that? Why did she even have to explain?

"I see."

"Genie, when we sat down during our initial meeting, I promised to get you the best outcome for this case. This is it."

"No. I'm staying in my home!"

"A judge won't support that. Not when Triton is in negotiations with another developer to rip down these brownstones and erect a condo in their place. This whole block will be razed to the ground by end of summer."

Genie's eyes blazed. "Like hell they are!"

Clutching the check, Priya held it between them. "This is thirty grand. *Thirty.* If we go to court, I can't promise I'll get you what you want. In fact, I doubt we'll come away with an offer half as good as the one we have right now. Do you really want to risk that?"

"Thirty grand?" Genie accepted the check once again, tongue skimming the pocket of her cheek before she tore it in two. And then tore it again. And again. Aghast, Priya's mouth fell open and Genie flung the scraps of paper like confetti. "If I have to choose between my home or getting what I'm owed—" Her lips pursed in defiance. "Fuck money."

"Yeah!" Caitlin punched the air. "Fuck money!"

Priya spared Caitlin a *you're not helping* glare. "Please be reasonable. I don't think you appreciate what's at stake here."

Filmy eyes sparked like firing lasers, and shot Priya through. "I have more at stake in this gambit than you, kid. Far more. I'm fighting to hold on to what is *mine* and so, if you won't fight with me." She bared her teeth. "Then I'll find another lawyer who will."

No. This was not how this conversation was supposed to go. The only thing worse than coming out of this with a less promising win was losing her client all together. "All right, you win. We'll do it your way." Priya slapped an aggrieved hand to her thigh. "We'll fight. But if we're going to court, we can't have you standing before a judge in bad faith."

"Meaning?"

"We need to make good on what you owe."

"I'm not giving that slumlord a dime."

"You don't have to give it to him directly, just park the money in escrow."

Genie arched a brow and cocked her hip. "So if I lose, he gets it?"

"You wanted to roll the dice, this is it, Genie. This is our best move."

Genie rubbed a hand over her shoulder, kneading the muscle. "That's all I have left."

Priya didn't need her to finish. A woman of her age, without relatives or friends she could turn to for help or support, she'd be in a shelter, or worse—on the street. "You wanted to gamble." Priya shrugged. "But I won't let that happen."

"Okay, kid. I'll get my checkbook."

* * *

Pathos hummed with the sound of a dedicated brunch crowd packed onto the large rooftop patio atop a squat brick building. Tables flanked by a large cross section of exposed whitewashed brick wall were transformed into a gallery with whorls of spray paint and bold brushstrokes creating vivid portraits capturing the evocative nature of raw human emotion.

The style was bold. Edgy. Compelling. And struck you clean off your feet with unapologetic intensity. The longer she stared at those overlapping lines forming colorful distorted faces verging on the grotesque, Priya couldn't quite tell if they fascinated or repulsed her—but that was the beauty of art. It wasn't always meant to be beautiful or comfortable, or safe—it was meant to make your feel something. And these certainly did.

"Wow, I love this place." Caitlin spun full circle, and then shoved her face an inch from the wall. "This guy is a genius."

"He's talented." Priya mused, and dragged her seat from the table.

"Utterly brilliant." Seated beneath a slat of gilded sun, Caitlin dropped her purse, a handmade bronze piece decorated with studded detailing and semiprecious gems forming an intricate pattern, on the reclaimed wood table with a *thunk*. She'd bought it last year during a trip to Bali—and it had set off every alarm from there back to Manhattan inside her carry-on. "And speaking of brilliant, Genie's freaking adorable. Seventy-year-old burlesque dancer? I want to adopt her."

"Seventy-four. And she's a pain in my ass." Priya pushed the thick weight of her hair off her back, shaking out the strands with her fingers. Even though painfully overdue for a trim, after a childhood of terrible haircuts she'd learned to love its wild length. "I had everything tied up in a perfect little bow, now I have to unravel it."

"You heard her, Priya, it's not about cash."

"I know. I know. I just . . . I needed this done and behind me. That settlement was more than I could've ever hoped to have achieved on her behalf, and I did it like that." Priya snapped her fingers. "It was a win. A solid win—for both of us. Now I have to start over."

"Can you get her what she wants?"

"If I can find precedent, maybe—but it's a much harder battle without it."

"The Priyanka Victory Seth that I know doesn't back down when things get tough."

No, she didn't. She'd faced off against bigger bullies than

the likes of Peter Crowley. It was her favorite hobby, if she was honest, shattering the fragile male ego, and the bigger the challenge, the greater the payout when she triumphed.

Priyanka Seth didn't lose. She conquered.

Chapter Fourteen

"Stop pacing, you're making me dizzy." Genie crossed a leg, dressed like she was ready to go dancing on Saturday night instead of spending her afternoon in housing court in black skinny jeans, feathered heels, and gold-beaded bolero.

Priya had made a concerted effort to convince Genie into wearing something less . . . well, *less*, but had been met with unwavering resistance. Soon enough annoyance gave way to acceptance—what did it matter, anyway? Genie wasn't on trial for her wardrobe. Might as well let her wear what she wanted.

Priya, at least, had pulled out all the stops wearing the custom suit that hadn't made it to the interview. Squaring off with Genie, she set her hands on her hips. "We should go over things one more time."

"Kid, we've circled it backward, forward, and sideways. Enough." Genie scooped her hands around her crossed knee, her white curls stretched and combed out in Diana Ross glory. "I know I've pushed you into a fight you didn't intend to wage, but win, lose, or draw—thank you. At least if I go down, I do so in a blaze of glory."

After leaving Genie that day, Priya had devoted every spare minute she could carve out to hunt for precedent while also calling in a favor with a former colleague still at the DA's office. In lifting the proverbial rug to see what kind of dirt Peter Crowley had buried within the last six years at Triton, she'd been astounded to find there wasn't much. What little she had unearthed was circumstantial at best and would stick like an old bandage—holding for maybe a few seconds before falling off, no matter how hard she pressed.

Crowley covered his tracks well, but Priya had mopped the floor with far less under her belt.

"We're not going to go down." Determined, she took one of Genie's hands in hers. "Trust me."

"I wouldn't place any bets on that, just yet, Counselor."

Priya turned to face the brusque voice and the man who'd spoken. Her first impressions? Expensive; cultured but approachable. Dressed in a pristine blue suit so dark it was almost black, he had mottled brown skin covered with freckles, tight groomed curls, and a friendly smile that evoked ease and comfort. Familiarity.

He thrust out a hand, fingers short and thick, with a gold ring on his pinkie. "Emanuele Hayes."

She accepted, his grip firm but not bruising. "Priyanka Seth."

"You didn't flinch." He released her hand with a bemused tilt of his head. "I'm guessing you haven't heard of me."

"No, but even if I had, I don't impress easily."

"Then maybe you've heard of my firm. Carver & Price."

It took every ounce of restraint to school her features into placid neutrality. She'd banked on in-house counsel to represent Peter Crowley, but apparently, he had gotten spooked and called in bigger guns. Carver & Price was the only firm in New York big enough to swallow MNS whole and spit out nothing but bones. This time when he smiled, she saw the gleam of an aged and experienced predator shine beneath the mild-mannered expression.

"Now that you know who I am and who I represent, why don't I throw you a lifeline?" Emanuele pulled an envelope from his leather-bound dossier. "Here is our revised offer. Please keep in mind it expires the second the judge calls us to docket . . . which is soon."

Priya opened the envelope and withdrew the contents. A single sheet of folded paper. "Is this a joke?" She turned the page over. "It's blank."

"That's right. A blank slate. Not many get the opportunity. Take it and your client walks without issue, but if we stand before the judge not only will I ensure she's out before the end of next week, I'll have her footing the legal bill for this hearing along with monies already owed both in back rent as well as damages sustained to the unit as a result of her lack of cooperation." His smile spread, sharp as a freshly honed blade. "And I'm quite expensive."

"I have your client for negligence as well as harassment resulting in damaged property and the personal distress of a widowed senior citizen. The moment the judge hears what Peter Crowley put Mrs. Carranza through, you'll be lucky if we walk out with less than what your client initially offered."

"Well, he didn't have me present at the time, otherwise he'd never have offered a dime. This is the best your client can hope for."

"We'll see if the judge agrees."

Emanuele tucked the dossier under the fold of his arm and

inhaled deep, nostrils flaring. "All that blithe confidence, but you smell green as freshly cut grass. This is your first official hearing, is it not?"

"Yes."

"Then I hope you know what you've gotten yourself into, little girl, because I've personally overseen three hundred evictions for my firm—and won them all. So, I look forward to ripping you open and seeing what you're made of." He leaned in and winked. "And I won't be gentle."

Emanuele waltzed through the doors of the courtroom like he owned the place, and Priya took one more moment to gather herself before entering behind him. The courtroom was a dull square made of gray walls, with a high, glossy wooden bench at one end where the judge, a woman robed in black and white, sat beneath a large crest.

On the wall to her left the clock ticked loudly, and Priya could almost feel the vibration of each passing second behind her eyes, the left lightly twitching in harmony with every stroke. Litigation wasn't for the faint of heart, and Priya's third-year law professor had once proclaimed before the entire class that she had balls of solid titanium. So what if she was about to go against a more experienced lawyer from a massive firm?

Bring it, that daring voice inside of her echoed. *We were born for this.*

"Carranza v Triton Property Management." The bailiff wiggled his fingers, glasses perched on the end of his bulbous nose. "Come forward."

Priya swung open the partition and waited for Genie to pass ahead of her, then steered her client to their plaintiff's table while Emanuele and Crowley took the other.

"Good morning and welcome." The judge linked her hands together, leaning forward to speak clearly into her mic. "We're here to determine eviction due to withheld rent, is that correct?"

Emanuele swept a hand down the length of his tie. "Yes, Your Honor."

"And why hasn't your client paid, Counselor?" The judge turned her gaze on Priya, signaling that it was her turn.

"Your Honor, Mrs. Carranza was forced to live in a home without heat in the middle of one of the city's coldest winters on record, over the course of which she called dozens of times asking for assistance, until finally in May the radiator malfunctioned while Mrs. Carranza was in hospital for pneumonia, pumping out an alarming amount of steam before eventually bursting. Her home suffered major damages as a result, including the death of her beloved cats."

"Repairs *were* ordered on Mrs. Carranza's unit," Emanuele interjected, "but never completed because she barred access more than once, therefore the unit failing is not the fault of my client, but the tenant."

"If the bruiser who showed up on my doorstep was a repairman then I'm the fucking queen of England dressed as Santa Claus on Easter."

The judge banged her gavel. "Counselor, get a hold of your client, please."

"Genie." Priya leaned in with a hushed voice. "Let me handle this."

Lips pursed, Genie rolled an indolent shoulder but otherwise held her tongue.

"There we have it, Your Honor, admission straight from

the horse's mouth. What was the contractor supposed to do? *Expecto Patronum* his way inside?"

"It's *aparate*, for the record—maybe stick to what you know and leave the pithy pop culture references to me." Priya fluttered her lashes. "When I approached Mr. Crowley, asking for proof of service requests, he refused. I also have Department of Buildings records that show a slew of similar complaints made from three separate buildings owned by Triton within the past five years. The highest number of complaints were including, but not limited to—" Priya paused to read from the list in her file. "No hot water, no gas or electricity ranging for spans of a few days to several weeks. And bedbugs."

"Triton often purchases properties in a state of extreme disrepair. My client can hardly be faulted for inheriting the problems created by previous owners."

"Mrs. Carranza never filed a single complaint until ownership changed hands to Triton."

"Well, if she was so unhappy with their management, why didn't she move? Seems to me it would've been far simpler than withholding rent."

"My client is seventy-four and a widow earning a meager salary performing on weekends at a local club. There's no way she was ever going to find another rent-controlled apartment in the city. Your Honor, we respectfully ask that the court rule to not only allow Mrs. Carranza to stay in the home she's lived in for the last fifty-three years, but to also seek restitution for damages incurred as a result of Triton's negligence."

"Your Honor, this is an eviction hearing. All that is pertinent is whether or not rent has been paid, which it hasn't. For *four* months. Anyone else would've evicted Mrs. Carranza immediately, but Peter Crowley was lenient, given her long standing tenancy and age, offering her countless opportunities to make good on what was owed, and yet she refused."

"Rent may be withheld when habitability has been breached."

Emanuele arched a glare at Priya. "It's not uncommon for tenants to file bogus repair claims in order to skirt paying rent."

"I have phone records showing Mrs. Carranza called Crowley's office three times a week for four months straight."

"Those calls consisted of the plaintiff harassing my client."

"Begging your property manager to fix a broken radiator in the middle of winter hardly constitutes harassment. And if you check the dates of those calls, you'll see more than half correlate to when weather forecast records show the city's overnight temperatures plummeted well below twenty degrees Fahrenheit, forcing Mrs. Carranza to seek temporary refuge in a motel, receipts for which are also provided."

The judge waved a summoning hand. "I'd like to see these phone records and receipts. And pictures of damages sustained to the property, as well."

Priya handed them to the bailiff, heart pounding behind her ribs.

"Several voice messages Mrs. Carranza left on my client's answering machine threatened bodily harm and her refusal to pay her rent, but nothing is ever mentioned about issues with heating or damages sustained to her property." Emanuele raised a recorder. "I have provided the court with notarized transcripts, but I am happy to play the recordings."

"That's not necessary. The transcripts are . . . colorful enough. Mrs. Carranza, did you in fact threaten to"—the judge paused to read off the page—"'cut off your balls and shove them down your windpipe before I pay a single hairy nickel'?"

Genie bobbed once with a stiff nod. "Bet your tits, I did."

Fuzzknuckles. "Your Honor, my client's not a Mafia enforcer, she's an elderly woman who, under extreme circumstance was frustrated and angry—rightfully so—but I can assure the court that she has every intention of honoring her rent agreement, which is why, in good faith, she placed the entire overdue sum into escrow pending the final decision of this proceeding."

"I'd like to see the copies of those checks in escrow."

"Of course." Priya opened her file folder, and barely choked down her gasp. Instead of the printout of checks that she'd prepared for court first thing that morning there was a photocopied handprint, fingers curled and middle finger raised, flipping her off.

Michael.

"Counselor, I'm waiting."

"I . . . Your Honor, I . . . uh . . ." The room spun. Her knees threatened to buckle. *Don't pass out. Don't you dare pass out. Breathe. Breathe!*

"Do you have the checks or not?"

Priya slapped her file shut. "Not here, no, but I can easily call the bank to—"

"Save it, Ms. Seth. While I'm sympathetic to your circumstances, Mrs. Carranza, I have adequate proof in front of me of repair orders issued by Triton Property Management, along with records of your voice messages corroborating the defense's claims of your unwillingness to cooperate or pay your rent, I'm afraid the court has no choice but to uphold the eviction notice." The judge slammed the gavel. "You have thirty days to vacate."

"Your Honor, we'd like to request *immediate* removal from the property."

"Of a seventy plus woman who's lived in that home for five decades? Denied. Thirty days. And as for you, Ms. Seth—a parting bonus: you're fined three thousand dollars."

"Your Honor!"

"Oh, I'm sorry, is that a painful shock for you? Imagine how your client must feel right now after losing her *home*. You've been slapped on the wrist, Counselor, let it serve to teach you a valuable lesson: come to my courtroom prepared or don't come at all." She banged her gavel again. "Dismissed."

* * *

Dazed, Priya staggered out into the hall, Genie close at her side. *I lost. I lost?*

"Kid." Genie snapped her fingers before Priya's eyes. "You still breathing?"

Priya blinked, eyes burning and throat tight. "Genie . . . I'm so sorry."

"What happened in there?"

How the hell was she supposed to explain this? "When I told you a lot was at stake for me, I meant it." Priya sighed. "Long story short—I have a target on my back at my firm, and you got caught in the crossfire."

Genie's lips pursed for a long, bracing moment before they softened in understanding. "I see."

"How are you so calm? You just lost your home because of a personal vendetta. Why aren't you furious with me?"

"Kid, I'm a woman of color. I get it. If I had a nickel for every time I dealt with fragile toxic masculinity, I'd be richer than a dozen Peter Crowleys." She clapped a hand to Priya's shoulder. "Besides, I can tell by that look in your eyes that even if our ship's taking on water, we're far from sunk."

Far from it. They had thirty days to appeal. Miracles had been performed in less time. Gathering herself, Priya rubbed her hands against her thighs. "It won't be easy, but I will devote every minute I can. I'll find a way, I promise you."

"That's the spirit." Her eyes flickered over Priya's shoulder and sharpened with avid female appreciation. "Woof." Genie pressed a hand to her chest. "Who's the fox?"

Priya turned to see Hadrian, his eyes scanning the passing faces in the corridor when he caught sight of her and smiled. "Excuse me, Genie." She sped toward him. "What are you doing here?"

"Moral support." He tucked his hands into his pockets. "I made lunch reservations nearby. Figured you'd want to celebrate your win."

And dammit, that made her want to scream. Or punch something. "You shouldn't have come."

"Why? What's wrong? What happened?" His eyes narrowed. "You *did* win, right?"

"I would've. If not for this." She handed over her file folder, and shocked disbelief exploded across his face when he landed on the printed eff bomb that had literally blown up her case.

"This isn't good, tiger."

"Thank you, Captain Obvious." Priya snatched the

folder back from him and shoved it into her satchel. "I'm sorry, I didn't mean to snap at you. I need to head back to the office."

"Work can wait. Fresh air and food will clear your head, and the place I booked is close by." He jerked his head to the left of his shoulder. "A stone's throw, I promise."

"It's not a good time. I've got to fix this. Fast."

"You're not going to do that in the next hour."

"Maybe not, but I need every second I can steal."

"Then I'll ride back with you, and you can tell me more about what happened in there."

Priya sighed with a dramatic eye roll and though she feigned annoyance, in truth it might be nice to talk to someone who'd understand and appreciate the finer details without needing the minutia clarified. There was nothing worse than FaceTiming with her sisters and watching their eyes glaze with boredom. "Let me say good-bye to Genie and make sure she's able to get home."

"Looks like she's already taken off." Hadrian gestured, and sure enough Genie was no longer in sight.

As he turned to lead the way, her eyes were drawn to his strong legs, which supported a high, firm ass. And she wanted to grab it, squeeze it—*bite* it. *Classic, Priya.* Her brain diverting to sex to distract her from the mess of her imploding life.

Outside the courthouse Priya pulled on her sunglasses. The sun was warm on her skin but it did little to warm her foul mood.

"Was that Emanuele Hayes I saw leaving with Peter Crowley?" Hadrian asked, busy with his phone as he ordered an Uber.

"One and the same. Bastard tried to corner Genie before the hearing." A total breach of ethics, but as few lawyers were ever sanctioned, there wasn't exactly anything stopping them from pushing boundaries if it meant winning the case without setting foot in the courtroom. "Thankfully, even if she had been alone, that woman is not easily intimidated."

"What was their offer?" he asked as their vehicle arrived in less than a minute, and let her slide in ahead of him.

"An insult, not surprising." Priya drummed her hand against her thigh as their car sped off down the street. "Peter Crowley is just another high-powered executive exploiting an overburdened system, but he's not the only one, which is why housing court is always swamped. Over two hundred thousand lawsuits were filed against tenants last year with complaints ranging from failure to pay rent to other purported lease violations."

"I had no idea it was *that* saturated."

"Want to know how many of those Triton filed?" Priya scoffed. "Nearly two thousand in less than six years, and almost all of them were against rent regulated tenants. Of those who won in court, nearly sixty percent were promptly hauled back as many as five times. In one particular day, Triton sued thirty-eight tenants from eighteen different properties. More than half were served with eviction warrants, and what happened with the rest was a little fuzzy, but I smell shady."

Hadrian's features darkened. "Why hasn't anyone come after them for this? Surely a judge must've noticed this pattern."

"Because on average they sit through as many as ninety cases before lunch, so the odds of slipping through the cracks are *huge*. Crowley knows this and uses it to his advantage. The system creates an incentive to file as many cases as possible, regardless of merit. For a major company like Triton, filing en masse with a high-powered firm backing them, they can rope in *hundreds* of properties around the city, all in struggling, low-income neighborhoods that they later sweep clean of original tenants and gentrify. It's a money-making wheel." One far too big for Priya to stop on her own.

"So, what's your plan of action?" Hadrian rolled down his window an inch letting just enough summer breeze waft into the stifling vehicle without the risk of the funneling wind messing up Priya's hair.

"If I'm going to flip this around. I'll need to get creative." But *how* was the trick question. "The biggest issue I have right now is keeping my loss in court today from Dani. At least until I have a plan to recover from this tailspin."

Hadrian winced. "When do you next sit down?"

"Thursday." That left forty-eight hours for Priya to find a miracle and dig herself out of this grave. But first things first—Michael. This was more than workplace rivalry; he'd cost an innocent woman her home just to kick Priya down the ladder. He needed to be dealt with *immediately*. Though she'd never considered herself a vengeful person when it came to the pursuit of her goals, Michael was about to discover that Priyanka Seth wasn't a woman to mess with. She was a tiger, and tigers had claws.

It was time she used them.

Chapter Fifteen

Priya walked through the front doors of the small studio gym, dressed in brand new yoga gear, long hair wrapped in a tight bun, and face scrubbed clean of makeup. This wasn't her usual brand of facility, but she hadn't come for a workout.

She'd come for Michael Winship's head.

"Can I help you?" The guy manning the desk had biceps the size of tree trunks, and more tattoos than Shayne, if such a thing was possible. They crawled down from his neck, across his chest, arms, and from what she could see, all of his legs, vanishing into the hard line of white tube socks.

"I'm here for the MMA class." She shifted the weight of her gym bag on her shoulder. "There's a first-time drop-in special, right? First time is free?"

"Yeah, but we don't usually get chicks in here." His eyes scanned her from head to toe, equal parts appraising and judgmental. "Not for this class."

"Is there a rule against women joining?"

"No. But it's a rough group." He rubbed a hand over the back of his reddening neck. "You look a little . . . light."

"I can hold my own."

"Your funeral." He jerked a thumb. "They're near the ring getting gloved up."

"Thanks."

Crossing the gym, she didn't bother to look around, but she could feel the eyes on her and hear the breaks in the rhythm of harsh breathing or clanging weights as heads snapped in her direction. There wasn't a single other woman to be seen, and the air stank of sweat, ripe as moldy garlic.

The ring wasn't hard to find; its mesh screening and posts wrapped in dense red padding drew the eye like a target. The coach stood on the steps near the gate, his black T-shirt stretched taut across his chest and black hair winged back from a sharp angled face. He halted midsentence as she settled in behind the wall of men and dropped her bag.

"Excuse me, miss, but we don't run Pilates here." The group snickered.

"Good. I came for sparring."

"Got any experience?"

"Yes."

The coach angled a disbelieving look. "Well, get up here." He whistled sharply. "Pedro, you take this round."

"I want *him*." She shot out a finger, and all eyes turned to Michael.

"He's out of your weight class."

Priya shrugged. "I don't care."

"This a lover's quarrel?"

She cracked a smile, dazzling and fearless. "In his wildest dreams, and my darkest nightmares."

The men whistled and laughed, egging Michael up to the front with elbows and shoves. "Sorry, Cal." The word struggled its way out of his mouth like it was barbed with hooks and razor blades. "This is my colleague."

Not after tonight.

"You got any issues with this?" Cal jerked a thumb at Priya. Michael shook his head, cheeks pinkening. "Good. I'll give you three five-minute rounds. No gouging, hair pulling, or low blows." Cal switched his gaze to each of them. "Keep it clean. Stop when your opponent taps or you hear the whistle. Jojo, gear 'em up!"

Priya shot out an arm, gesturing toward the stairs. "Asshats first."

Inside the ring, the mat was firm under her bare feet. Priya shook out her arms and wiggled her shoulders as Jojo scuttled over on heavily muscled bowlegs, and handed her a padded helmet and mitts.

Michael snaked in at her side as she worked on the helmet. "What exactly are you doing?"

Priya fastened the straps under her chin. "What does it look like?"

"Like you're about to get your face pounded into the mat. I didn't think you were the type to enjoy humiliation."

"That's a terrifying talent. Making a comment both insulting *and* sexually creepy." Priya slipped on the gloves, flexing her fingers before winding the bandages around her wrists. "Why don't we up the stakes? If I beat you, then tomorrow you hand in your resignation at MNS."

"And if I beat you?"

"Same." Priya held out her wrapped fist. "Deal?"

Michael snorted and bounced his gloved fist against hers. "I'm going to enjoy this."

Priya moved to her corner of the ring and waited for Cal to

finish checking Michael's gear. When he was done, he held up his hands for Michael to fire a couple of test punches—which he did with far more intensity than necessary.

Cal crossed the mat and came over to her next and started his inspection of her headgear and gloves. "Clearly this ain't your first rodeo."

"Told you."

"All right. Up top. Give me two." Priya drilled into the heart of his palms but kept them light and butterfly soft.

Michael's laughter rippled to her from across the ring. "You got pudding for wrists?"

Priya smirked. *Good, underestimate me.* The gym fell silent as everyone gathered around to watch. She hadn't banked on an audience, but it was too late to worry about it now. Now she had to put her money where her mouth was.

The last time she'd fought anyone, it was Shayne. After Priya's third brush with stealing, her mother had decided that she needed an outlet for her anger and had hired a personal Krav Maga instructor who was also training Shayne. The girls had been paired one afternoon so they could have the opportunity to put their skills to the test.

Always a star student, Priya was good—clean and methodical, but Shayne? Pure technique matched with lethal instinct, she was born to fight. While Priya had held her own, Shayne dominated every single time. Even though Priya hadn't kept up with the classes beyond that summer, she'd remembered how to defend herself—but was it enough?

Cal exited the cage and closed the gate. Priya bounced her gloved fists together.

It would have to be.

* * *

Three taps in fifteen minutes—Priya walked out into the night with a victorious laugh. A cool breeze kissed her sweaty skin, and she pushed back her hair from her face. Michael had charged her like a freight train, thinking if he went in heavy, she'd balk under the force. Instead she'd danced and dodged, using his momentum to make him swing and miss.

It took twice as much energy to miss as it did to connect, and it wasn't long before the fatigue began to show. That's when she struck, taking him down to the mat. The second round went much quicker—his anger made him brash—while the need to save face in front of his fellow gym rats pushed the third a full minute longer. He'd nearly gotten the best of her in that one with a left jab that made her starry eyed and dizzy, but thankfully the exhaustion from earlier had taken enough of a toll to make him sloppy and inefficient.

Besides, no one hit as hard as Shayne, and no one fought harder than Priya when backed into a corner. It was kick Michael Winship's skinny ass or lose everything she'd worked for.

"Fuck you if you think I'm actually going to quit."

Michael's harsh voice stopped Priya in her tracks. The door to the gym snapped shut behind him, and Priya kept one hand high, gripped on the strap of her gym bag in case she needed to drop it fast to dodge or deflect a blow. "We had an agreement."

"Well, guess you came down here and got all sweaty for nothing—I'm not throwing away my career over some bullshit bet."

"Oh, sweetie, I already have everything I need to take you down, I just wanted to slap you around a little first."

"What are you talking about?"

"You tampered with my court documents ahead of my hearing." Priya squared up with him and this time she had the pleasure of seeing him inch back a step. Not so cocky now that he knew what her jab and cross felt like. "There are cameras all over the firm, did you really think one of them wouldn't catch you in the act?"

Michael's eyes narrowed for a moment, then slowly eased with understanding. "Andrew."

Priya notched her brow the barest increment in response.

"Whatever. I don't care what that pissant gave you, footage of me doing business as usual is circumstantial at best. I could have had any number of reasons to be in the copy room."

"I never said *where* you got caught." She wagged a finger. "If you have issues with me—come for me, bro. I've seen it, heard it, and faced it a hundred times before. It's not original. You don't intimidate me, you don't threaten me, you don't even rate in the top ten of the least of my concerns. But you made the mistake of screwing over an old woman who didn't deserve to lose her home. So now I am going to make sure you pay for it."

"Fuck her and fuck you. I'd do it again, except next time, book a seat front and center so I can watch." His smirk turned cold. "Although I hear you were drowning even before my little gift was uncovered, but I'm glad it was the final nail in your coffin. Either way, you've got nothing on me."

"There's always your admission of guilt." Priya removed the tape recorder from her pocket, holding it between them. And *tsked*. "Very stupid of you."

She'd gotten it from Andrew after stopping by his office to

hash out her plan. High grade, perfect for picking up a whisper from clear across a conference room with heavy construction mixed in for flavor. While the entire floor of MNS was in fact under surveillance, only the meeting rooms had audio recording, which meant their showdown in the corridor— even though it took place under the eyes of IT and security— was little more than a silent film that could be interpreted any number of ways.

So Priya had decided to get creative. Because at the end of the day, Michael was a bully, and all bullies loved the opportunity to gloat. She just needed to throw him off balance first, rouse his temper, then stand back and let him spew like a lanced boil.

It was so easy that it was almost pathetic.

"That's not admissible."

"In a courtroom, sure, but we're not going to trial. Resign, first thing tomorrow morning, or I'll see that a copy of this is waiting on Marai Nagao's desk along with a very detailed outline of the case and everything you did to sink it. I can almost see the memo headline." Priya splayed her hands as if etching the words into the air between them. "Misogynistic and racist junior associate fired for tampering with pro bono case, landing an elderly widow on the street."

"You're bluffing."

"Am I?" Priya edged in closer. "If you think I don't have what it takes to expose you for what you've done, think again. And I can guarantee the firm's partners would absolutely take swift and violent measures against *anyone* who interfered with a case thereby impacting their reputation."

Michael glared at the recorder, the seam of his throat

bobbing. "If you wanted me fired, you'd have gone straight to Marai. How much is this going to cost me?"

"Your pride. Your ego. While it would be satisfying to watch you being escorted out the front doors, I want *you* to quit so that all the other associates will know that not only can I take down anyone who messes with me—but I can make you do it of your own volition."

"You fucking bitch."

"No, you're the bitch who couldn't handle losing to a brown girl. Well, now I've got your balls in a vice, and with the barest flick of my wrist, I'll twist them off. Don't push me."

Michael huffed, nostrils flaring, hands clenching into fists. "I should punch your teeth into the back of your throat and make you swallow them."

He was mad enough to try it. Priya had taken him down on the mat, but that was in a controlled environment, now, with his rage and adrenaline, anything was possible, but she didn't so much as flinch. Instead, she stepped in closer. Daring him. Knowing if she backed down an inch, he'd charge.

"Go ahead. Streets are flooded with traffic and people. Plenty of witnesses for assault." She smiled, letting it sparkle in her eyes, but inside she was shaken. This was what it meant to be a woman, to smile in the face of sheer terror in the hopes that holding her ground would be enough. "Imagine trying to find another job with *that* stain on your record."

Michael dropped his fist but the fire still blazed in his eyes. Smoked in his voice. "One day. One day you'll pay for this. On my life. One day."

Priya tapped the mic at her chest. "Still recording, moron." And walked away.

* * *

The next morning, Priya arrived at work to find the air rife with scandal and suspicion. By the time she reached her workstation, a chorus of stunned gasps and stage whispers rose all around her, Michael Winship's name dripping from everyone's lips.

"Morning, tiger."

Priya jerked at the unexpected sound of Hadrian's voice. Growling, hand on her heart, she turned around and faced his teasing gaze. "Can you please stop sneaking up on me?"

"Sorry."

"No, you're not."

"You're right. I'm not. Apparently, Winship quit this morning. Effective immediately and without notice." Crossing his arms, he leaned casually against the paneled barrier of her cubicle. "What did you *do*?"

Glory punched through her chest but her face remained neutral. Barely. "Me? Nothing."

"I'm not buying it."

Priya shrugged, hoping for unaffected and disinterested. "Whatever the reason, he won't be missed by me, that's for sure." In hopes of dismissing Hadrian, she made a point of rooting around in her satchel, waiting for the soft footfall of his retreat, when a clapping of hands jarred her out of her chair.

Only Heather clapped like that, and if she was on the floor, then it meant something big was about to happen.

Pushing past Hadrian, Priya joined the gathering of associates. Heather stood at the front of the room, flanked by mobile whiteboards, one with each of the associates and a three-digit number alongside it. And Heather wasn't alone.

Marai stood, regal as ever, in an ivory pantsuit and red blouse. "Good morning." Her voice carried with little effort yet exuded complete authority.

Only Marai Nagao could make a whisper have the impact of a scream.

"I know everyone has a long and busy day to get to, so I will keep this brief. Every year, we host an annual partners' dinner, celebrating their achievements and dedication to this firm. All associates are expected to attend, and it's there we will announce my chosen mentee. Invitations will be sent out later this evening, I ask that you please ensure RSVPs are returned to Heather in a timely manner." Her gaze skimmed as she spoke, gentle as a hand gliding through water, meeting each of them but not holding long enough to make you squirm.

"Secondly, for those of you who haven't already heard, a promising associate elected to leave us today. Though we are sad to see him go, we wish him well in the next stage of his career, wherever that should prove to be."

A body settled behind Priya. She knew without turning around that it was Hadrian, and sensed that his attention was fixed on her rather than Ms. Nagao.

"For those of you who have remained, you'll find your names on the whiteboards behind me, with current scores determining your rank in our little contest, ranging from highest"—she gestured to her left—"to lowest."

To no real surprise, Priya found herself listed near to dead last.

She might have gotten rid of Michael, but she had a long, long mountain to scale if she was going to battle her way to the top, and it was never going to happen if she couldn't think of a way to win her case.

"Ahem . . . Priya." A hand tapped her shoulder as the crowd of associates broke, and Priya turned to face Xander. All six foot four inches of him tucked in a gorgeous buttery ivory suit and silver frames. "I'm sorry to chase you down, but Dani wants a word with you."

"Our meeting isn't until tomorrow afternoon."

Xander bridged the tips of his fingers and bounced them together. "She's moved it to now. Right now."

Michael. Clearly, the bastard had found a way to get one last dig in before departing. This was always going to happen, but she'd hoped to have an answer before it did. A way out of the hole she was currently in. All she could do now was face Daniella and get it over with.

When Priya entered her office, Daniella turned from her window, fuming, with hands on her hips and eyes blazing as bright as the yellow silk scarf wrapped atop her head. "Can you please explain to me *how* exactly you lost a simple rent dispute?"

"It's wasn't simple. I was shredded by a shark." Priya sat down in the chair facing Daniella's desk and crossed a leg. "Emanuele Hayes."

"Hayes?" Daniella jolted. "Did you say *Hayes*?"

"Yeah. You know him?"

"Emanuele isn't a shark, he's a megalodon. He wasn't supposed to be on this. Triton has their own in-house counsel."

"Yeah, well, I guess they decided to upgrade."

"Which means your case just got very sticky." Daniella paced, thumb and forefinger rubbing together in swift circles as she worked over whatever was racing through her mind.

"Here's what you're going to do: when you're back at your desk, pick up the phone, call Triton and find out what they'll offer for Genie Carranza to evacuate as quickly as possible."

"Why? I've got a month to file an appeal and *fight* this."

"No. You don't. Right now, your client has a narrow window of leverage but it won't hold for long. I'm thinking you can get them on board for two . . . maybe five."

"That's an insult."

"It's the best she's going to get."

"She doesn't want money."

"Under the circumstances, she doesn't have a choice, so I suggest you convince your client to see it that way, too, and close this case."

"I don't understand—why are you hamstringing me on this?"

Daniella's tongue skimmed the edge of her top lip before she settled on something with a shrug. "The firm is in a delicate position with George Silver retiring, along with the loss of a few key clients last quarter. We can't afford to expend resources to go up against a firm like Carver & Price for the sake of a pro bono. It's all risk, and no reward."

"So because we stand to gain no financial profit, we abandon Genie? She's my client, I'm obligated to give her the best legal defense possible."

"Your obligation, first and foremost, is to the firm." Daniella drilled a fingertip into her desk. "She's an anchor in a hurricane. Cut her loose unless you want to drown with her. You have one week. If she insists on fighting, ask Xander for the number to the Matheson Clinic. It's a small practice where we push the pro bonos we can't take on."

Priya stood up sharply and planted her hands to the edge of Daniella's desk. "A clinic will be flooded and have even fewer resources to face down Emanuele Hayes."

"I know." Daniella rose slowly and mirrored her pose. "Which is why you should do as I suggested and get your client some semblance of a settlement offer."

"It's her home, Dani."

"I admire your dedication and conviction, I really do, but the reality is we have responsibilities. Overhead. All of these things require money, and if we squander our resources for every bleeding-heart case, we'll never survive. Now get out there." She whisked a dismissive hand toward the door. "And get this done."

Priya opened her mouth to argue but a stony glare from Daniella stopped her cold. "Fine," she grumbled. But nothing about this was fine. Far from it. Once back at her desk, still fuming, Priya snatched up her phone and dialed the one person she could think of to help dig her out of the hole she'd been buried in. "Derek, it's Priya."

"Well, that was quick."

"I'm not calling for *that*." She rolled her eyes. "This is professional. I need a favor."

"Why would I do *you* a favor?"

Priya hooked her tongue over the edge of her teeth, sucked hard. "Remember that night in SoHo?"

The line hummed with pensive silence. "What do you need?"

"Triton Property Management. I'm going up against them for a case."

Derek chuckled. "Okay?"

"Have you heard anything about Peter Crowley in the investment circles?"

"I can't really *tell* you that."

"I'm not looking for an insider trading tip. I just want to know if there's anything in the pipeline that I can leverage for my case. Legally."

Derek sighed, the sound punctuated by the clicking of keys. "Well, according to Triton's latest press release, Peter Crowley is negotiating an offer on a parcel of brownstones with a major condo developer."

"I already know about that."

"Yeah, but this is huge, Priya. This is laying the foundation for a merger."

That popped her straight in her chair. "Merger?"

"My guess is they want to migrate from leasing rental properties into owning condominiums. Triton's share price was driven down in a competitive market, and the board wants to offload their problematic locations. He can't afford to have the buyers walk away from the table. Not with the way Triton's fiscal performance has struggled over the last three years."

Wonderful. If she had more time, and the firm's support—which she absolutely didn't—she could've blasted heat on Crowley's sketchy practices and stalled the transaction. But if she was going to sway Daniella to let her play her hand, she needed something bigger than a shot in the dark, Hail Mary move. "Anything else?"

"Uh . . ." A few more clicks met with dragging silence. "His wife has voting shares in the company and a seat on the board?"

"So, nothing." Not a damn thing. "Thanks, Derek. Appreciate

the effort." Priya ended the call with a groan and was about to drop her head to her desk in defeat when her cell phone chimed with a message from Isobel.

Hi—thanks again for letting me stay with you while I'm in New York for the night. My flight lands tomorrow, so I can cab from the airport and be at your place before five—can't wait to see you!

Fuzzknuckles. Isobel. She'd nearly forgotten in all the chaos, but a thought quickly sprang to mind. Excited, Priya dialed Genie's number and sighed at the answering beep of voice mail. "Genie, it's Priya." She looped the phone cord around her finger. "I've got an idea about our next move."

Chapter Sixteen

Isobel spun through her kitchen, a frazzled mess of anxiety, and yanked open the fridge door for the fourth time to take stock. Each shelf was brimming with fresh produce, an assortment of healthy snacks, and containers of pre-portioned meals that she'd prepped like a madwoman since accepting Nneka's job offer three days ago.

She could feed an army for over two weeks, but a voice still nagged it wasn't enough. God, she'd nearly called Nneka to quit half a dozen times this morning alone. *Maybe I should ask Mr. Nunes across the street if he wouldn't mind checking in.* And if she pulled out some clothes for the week, put them in easy reach so her father wouldn't have to bend or stoop—the doorbell rang, interrupting her busy thoughts.

"Are you expecting anyone?"

"Dunno." Declan, perched at the breakfast nook, disappeared behind the pages of his newspaper. "Maybe."

Isobel wiped her hands on her jeans and reached the door as the bell rang a second time. A portly woman, middle aged with dark hair threaded with white and wearing a dumpy jacket pulled over a pale-blue uniform, stood on the threshold with a heavy bag set at her white-sneakered feet.

"Good morning." Her glowing grin brightened the apples of cheeks scattered with dark freckles. "My name is Luz Sandoval. I'm the care provider from the Enriched Wellness Center."

Isobel widened the door, a little dazed. "I didn't—?"

"Ms. Priyanka Seth placed the call last night and set up a meeting for today. I understand you're looking for coverage starting this morning, yes? Until Thursday evening? We customarily do a home walk-through prior to introducing ourselves, discuss care needs, and review paperwork, but given a generous donation on the behalf of a Ms. Shayne, we've agreed to start immediately."

Isobel shook her head with a sigh. *Why am I not surprised?* "Of course, come on in." Leading Luz into the house, Isobel shot a glance into the kitchen and caught her father—apparently a co-conspirator—sneaking a guilty look over the folded edge of the paper he hid behind like a shield. "Dad. This is Mrs. Sandoval."

"Hello," Luz sang cheerfully, her cheeks reddening. "And how are you today, Mr. Morgan?"

Isobel forgot how often women used to blush at the sight of her dad—his strong chin beneath slate scruff, broad shoulders, strong arms, and dazzling smile had turned more than a few heads before the accident. It appeared even after it he hadn't lost his touch.

The paper crinkled as Declan folded it down on the counter, eyes shying away from Isobel's pointed glare. "Ah, em—fine, just fine. Lovely to meet you. I think I'll see myself to the garden."

Isobel's lips pulled into a thin line as her father made a

not-so-subtle escape through the patio doors. *Chicken.* "Will you be staying overnight?"

"The center thought it best," Luz answered, her hands gripping the leather straps of her bag. "Ms. Seth provided the center with detailed copies of your father's current health records and care needs. We're quite up to speed."

Of course she did. Isobel had sent her everything a few weeks ago along with all the settlement paperwork, and Priya had clearly decided to put it all to good use. God, with friends like hers the world didn't stand a chance—and right now she loved them for it. "Let me show you to the guest room, and we can walk through his routine."

It took about an hour to cover it all, from medication to stretches, and Isobel listened attentively as Luz explained the plan and policy paperwork. Thanks to her new job's benefits package, Isobel wouldn't have to worry about the expense eating a hole in their savings for at least three more house calls. It wasn't much, but it bought Isobel peace of mind, as well as freedom. Still, as she'd left Luz to get better acquainted with her father while she finished packing her bags for the trip, anxiety left Isobel speechless.

"Well, that's everything." Isobel stopped at the base of the stairs as Luz came to join her, drying her hands on a towel from the kitchen where she'd been washing dishes. "Is there anything else I should—?"

"I have the list on the fridge." Luz draped the towel over her shoulder. "And all of your contact details should I have any questions. We'll be fine."

Isobel nodded slowly, her heart rising higher in her throat. "Okay. Well, I'll say a quick bye to my dad before heading out." Swinging out the back door, she found her father seated beneath the heavy canopy of a stately maple tree crowned with deep burgundy leaves. Hearing her approach, he lifted his eyes and his smile spread, bright with triumph.

"So, you're off, then?"

"Yes." She sat down next to him, tucking away a lock of hair that the passing breeze had tugged free.

"Is there some reason you look like you're heading to a funeral instead of the job of your dreams?"

God, I really need to work on my poker face. Nneka had asked Isobel to do two things after accepting the offer. The first had been simple enough: She had to reactivate all her social media and pin down accounts for whatever she didn't currently have. Post stories and content to establish the foundation they were going to build off once she finally went live. As for the second, Isobel had to start brainstorming so she could come to the table with ideas. A vision. *You're our voice, Isobel, so you'll need to have one. A clear one.*

And that was where Isobel had hit a wall. Voice? It was one thing to write for herself—or even the threadbare, faceless audience she'd acquired over the last year. But something of this scale, being thrust so intensely into the public eye, shot her through with doubt and uncertainty.

What if everyone hated what she had to say? Hated *her*? What if her writing was flat, her voice derivative? What if they laughed her off-air and shamed her across Twitter? She'd witnessed many dreams end in a fraction of a second over one comment, one tweet, one stray whisper that sparked a wildfire that blazed someone's career to ash.

"I'm a bit nervous."

"Ah, Bells." Declan sighed. "You want my advice?" Isobel nodded. "Forget all this mess. Forget it all and step outside your comfort zone. Be free, for once. You have a rare opportunity to discover who are you are again. You. After eight years of *we*."

"It's only two days, Dad. Hardly enough to eat, pray, and whatever into Isobel Morgan 2.0." *Whoever that would be.*

Amusement shone like stardust in his eyes. "You might be surprised. Go. Off with you. And don't call every bleeding hour. I mean it." He wagged a finger. "This is the closest to a holiday you've had in a long time, and you'll have Priya for company. I expect she'll cram in a bit of fun so forget about responsibilities for a little while and enjoy yourself." Holding her face he pressed his lips to her forehead. "You've earned it."

* * *

It was a short flight over to NYC, and before Isobel could even gather her bearings, she was rolling through customs with her single suitcase in hand to find Priya waiting for her with a flurry of balloons, stuffed animals, flowers, and a bedazzled sign with Isobel's name.

They embraced with a squeal and bobbed in an endless, giddy bouncing hug punctuated by Priya chanting, "You're here, you're here, you're *finally* here!"

Flushed and breathless, Isobel pulled away, her cheeks burning from excessive smiling. "I know; I can hardly believe it." Anxiety tempered her joy as her fingers itched for her phone. "Do you think I should call him? I should call him."

Priya rolled her eyes, smiling as Isobel rooted around in her purse and shakily dialed her father's number. When he answered the tightness in her chest eased. He sounded cheerful, and more than a bit amused she'd made it all of thirty minutes after touching down. Apparently, he'd won the bet, and now had twenty bucks to show for it.

"So, Nurse Ratched hasn't killed him yet?"

"Go ahead and make fun of me. This is a big deal." Smiling, Isobel tucked her phone away and helped Priya gather her Welcome to NYC shrine, stuffing it all into bags.

"Why do you think I procured the help?" Priya snickered. "Have you seen Shayne in the kitchen? Epic disaster. Girl doesn't have a single domestic bone in her body."

"She basically grew up in a palace, why would she?"

"Hardly Windsor Castle or Buckingham," Priya tossed back. "And she left all that behind. Shayne's just lazy, but whatever, I'm so glad you're here!" She latched onto Isobel with another fierce hug. "Now, let's grab a taxi, and you can run it all by me again. The *Passivist Activist*—how they're transforming your blog into a *thing*?"

Pulling up the handle on her carry-on, Isobel dragged her small suitcase behind her, hurrying to keep up with Priya's fast stride. She never meandered or strolled—Priya flew, whether in sneakers or heels, she didn't waste a single second. "It's all live. No prerecordings, aside from the spot features we do ahead of time. But I handle my own scripts, decide the topics, and then it's all pitched out there via various forms of social media. TikTok, Twitter, Instagram—the works."

Pausing to hold open the door, Isobel let Priya sweep out of the airport first and trundled after her, the wheels of her carry-on catching on the tracks in the automatic doorway, pitching slightly before correcting themselves. "The idea is to connect with the younger demographic, to move them past this state of passivity and prompt them into real action, into immediacy, hopefully by engaging with me live, in the moment."

Priya lifted sunglasses from her eyes, pushing back dark waves of hair from her stunning face, bright with excitement. "Babe. I'm so proud of you. This is *major*."

They stopped at the curb where a line of people waited in line for cabs. It wasn't long before the attendant reached them and took hold of their bags, hauling them into the trunk of the canary-yellow vehicle. "Tomorrow I'm meeting with Nneka and the team."

"Are you nervous?"

"A bit. I've never been on camera before. Always behind it." Isobel slid into the backseat, Priya scooted in after her and shut the door, their conversation pausing long enough for Priya to give the driver the address of her mom's apartment in Chelsea.

"The hardest part will be trying to sort out what our first story to launch will be. Something with heart as well as impact. Nneka really loved that bit I did on the incident that happened in Toronto. Remember? Guy went berserk and mowed down that woman in his utility van because she said no to going on a date with him?"

"Hell hath no fury like an insecure cishet man spurned." Priya released a heavy breath, dark eyes blazing like embers. "If anyone hurt my sisters I'd tear the world apart and show the bastard the true meaning of eternal suffering."

Isobel didn't doubt that declaration for a moment. Few people were as terrifying as Priya when crossed. Even Shayne knew to tread carefully.

"When does your boss fly in?"

"Tomorrow morning. It was supposed to be this afternoon, but she had a last-minute conflict and bumped her flight." Which was annoying when Isobel could've made this into a day trip rather than overnight and had debated more than once about changing her flight. The only thing that had stopped her was knowing Shayne would've crucified her for it.

Priya's dazzling smile morphed into a villainous grin. "That means you're all mine."

"More or less."

"Good. Because if you want a story I've got something perfect in mind."

"Oh?" Surprised, Isobel sat a little straighter, and listened as Priya told her everything about her client, Genie Carranza. "Oh, honey, I'm so sorry." Standing on the curb outside Priya's building, Isobel waited for the driver to wrestle her suitcase from the trunk. "I can't believe your colleague did that to you."

"I knew I was going to have issues. Gender, race, being the daughter of a Nobel Prize–winning author—any combination of those puts a target on my back. I'm used to it. But this was ugly. I got rid of him, at least. Now I've got to fix the mess he made."

"By putting a spotlight on it and cranking up the heat."

"Precisely." Priya handed the driver a tip, then swung open the front door to the lobby of her building, and they both strode inside. Cool gray marble with gilded accents and bold, plush textiles. It was a gorgeous little building that melded artistic style with upscale polish—very Priya.

The security desk sat in the center of the space, sleek black glass with an elegantly dressed team of people who smiled politely, but Isobel could see the sharp look in their eyes, assessing and pinpointing Priya as a resident, and Isobel as her guest.

"I know this is a big ask," Priya said as she unlocked the door when they reached the apartment and pushed inside. "And I hate to do it to you, but you could have the reach to make a difference in this case."

"I'd love to help but I just got this job—this amazing opportunity—I don't know if this is . . . *big* enough?" Isobel tucked her suitcase in the corner of the foyer by a walnut side table topped with an arrangement of pale pink roses. "I think they want things that punch to the top of media headlines."

"Isobel, the entire world is talking about shootings and politics and climate change. Every channel, every platform. You want to stand apart? This is it. This is everything that you do. Everything you believe in. Gripping stories with heart."

"But won't you get in trouble with your boss for . . . I don't know . . . breach of ethics?"

"I might step on a few toes, but if Genie decides to share her story publicly, who am I to stop it? Ultimately, the only thing that matters is results. Once I win this case, this all becomes a forgotten issue."

"And if you lose?"

"I *won't* lose," Priya answered, eyes sparking with determined fury. "Genie needs our help, because Triton Property Management is only interested in profit and greed. And they're not alone in that mentality. Rent-regulated apartments are vanishing as gentrification surges through New York's boroughs, and those who aren't born with silver spoons are pushed out to Siberia, or end up sleeping over grates on the street—which is where Genie is headed in thirty days—if we don't rally support to stop them."

"Triton?" Isobel blinked dully. "They're one of the biggest clients for the company my father worked for."

"Then you know what I'm up against. You can give her story the focus and attention it needs. Please. She needs our help."

Isobel worried her hands, linking and flexing her fingers. Nneka had told her to come to the table with ideas. A voice. And now she had a personal connection to weave in and enhance the emotional blow. "Okay," she said at last. "Let's do it."

"Great. Because Genie's waiting for you on the terrace."

Isobel cast her a baleful stare. "And if I said no?"

Priya's answering smile was saccharine sweet. "I counted on my irresistible charm to sway you to the dark side. Come. Let me introduce you." Priya hooked her arm through Isobel's and guided her across the cozy and ruthlessly chic apartment— all whitewashed wood, soft textiles, and gleaming accents of gold—to the double doors leading out to a corner terrace nearly as big as Isobel's upper floor.

Genie turned from the glass parapet, beneath the wash of afternoon sun that shone down on her like a spotlight. Regal, was Isobel's first impression. Gold and turquoise earrings dangling from stretched lobes, and rioting white curls that haloed a heavily lined face brightened by vivid fuchsia lipstick while glittering purple shadowed eyes matched her flowing two-piece outfit made of filmy silk.

"Genie." Priya brought Isobel forward with a smile. "This is my sister, Isobel Morgan."

"I must say you have a dazzling array of sisters." Genie

smirked. "First the little pixie you brought with you last week, and now this remarkable beauty." She pushed up Isobel's chin with a crooked finger. "Such remarkable eyes you have, dear. A luscious shade of green—like bottle glass in sunlight."

Isobel blushed. "Thank you. They . . . my mom. They're hers."

"Truly breathtaking. You must thank her for sharing them with you."

Unsure how to answer that, Isobel's blush deepened. "I wish I'd brought my camera with me." She sighed. "Nneka is definitely going to want footage and I'm not prepared."

"We can use my phone. I have a selfie stand with a light ring. Will that do?"

"Yeah. Actually, that's perfect."

"Great. You two get situated, and I'll grab what we need."

"Come, darling." Genie gathered Isobel's hand and led her to the sectional tucked into the corner beneath an ivy-wrapped trellis dripping with flowers, and lowered herself into the corner cushion. "I appreciate you taking time to do this," Genie began, crossing a leg with a flash of bold red strappy heels and gold painted toes, vivid against her warm brown skin.

"Oh, it's my pleasure. Priya gave me a little background on your circumstances—anything we can do to help."

"There." Priya returned a few moments later and set out a trio of glasses and an uncorked bottle of white, along with the light-ring perched on a tripod. "What do you need me to do next?"

"Pour the wine, and I'll get this set up." Beyond them New York spread in towering buildings that glistened in the sunlight like the surface of water. The roar of the city adding wonderful texture and grit to contrast the softness of flowers blooming in wild abundance across a trellis roped with fairy lights that flanked the cobalt sectional and a concrete firepit topped. It was the perfect scene for two women having a casual conversation over wine in the late afternoon summer sun.

Finished with the fine tuning of the light ring, Isobel assessed the angles and activated the video recording feature on the phone before sitting down next to Genie. "Okay, now let's just have a conversation. Tell me about you, Genie. Anything you think I should know about who you are. The life you've lived. Try to forget about the camera. You talk, and I'll listen."

Genie looped her hands around her crossed knee and drew back her shoulders with a sassy wiggle. "I'm ready for my close-up, Mr. DeMille."

"Wait—I'm sorry." Priya waved her hands in apology. "But we need to draw focus to the case. Not her life story."

"People won't care about what's happening to her if they don't first care about her."

"Right. Okay." But Isobel could see Priya's apprehension.

Not everyone understood the flow of storytelling. Priya was brilliant with delivering facts for the sake of winning an argument, but this required something she was unfamiliar with—feeling. Luckily, exploring emotion and communicating it was Isobel's superpower.

"Priya told me you've been in your home for fifty years," Isobel began. "That's a long time to have lived in one place."

"You'd be surprised how quickly it can all go." Genie tipped her glass in salute. "The older you get—time just whizzes by . . .

like the beat of a hummingbird's wings." She snapped a bejeweled hand laden in turquoise, citrine, and amethyst. "Fleeting and frantic—and fragile."

"Fragile. That's an interesting choice of word."

"Loss has a way of making everything onward appear so delicate. Until then, you don't think of life ending. Why would you? We all know death is an absolute, but until you've sampled its icy breath—it's just a figment in the back of your mind."

Isobel's heart twisted with understanding. "Who did you lose?"

Genie took a moment to gather herself—her breath and her voice. "My husband had gone out of town with our two kids to visit relatives for Thanksgiving while I was in bed with the flu. Darling that he was, he didn't want me to feel left out, and rushed home after dinner, the kids asleep in the back with leftovers and gifts, when they were mowed down by a semi— the driver was . . . intoxicated. He got away with barely a scratch. But my entire world was obliterated. I was thirty-five . . ."

Isobel pressed a hand to her aching heart as Genie lifted a beaten photo album from her purse and touched a finger to the embossed leather cover before handing it to Isobel. She opened it to a picture of two figures huddled close and smiling outside of a brownstone. Genie was unmistakable with her thick, curling black hair falling down her back, and arms thrown around her husband's neck, towering at least a foot over him.

He had his head tossed back, wearing a gapping grin and floral shirt buttoned low. They were such an oddly matched pair and yet so blissfully happy it made the ache in Isobel's heart deepen to despair.

"We moved to Manhattan dirt poor, little more than a suitcase between us. Just a couple of newlyweds eager to start our lives away from our crazy families. This was the first place we came to see but we knew immediately it was home. A few years after we moved in, I had Rosa. One Sunday afternoon I was repainting the kitchen cabinets and after finishing the first coat, I took a nap on the couch while Rosa slept in her playpen. Not that it ever contained her for long. Jorge called her Houdini because she could escape from anything when she put her mind to it. Then I woke up to this!" Genie scooted in closer to flip through the pages to a photo of an interior wall, the bottom half covered in splotchy red blobs stamped by hands.

Tiny, little hands.

"I was so mad—for all of a second—until I saw her luminescent face. Her joy. Three years old and just so damn proud of herself. So I decided fuck it. Let's make it into something *really special*. And instead of covering it up, we added to it with handprints of our own. This is me. This is Jorge. And a year later, we added Jorgecito's. Called it my *field of roses*." Genie smiled down at that image, her chin wobbling.

"When they died, I sat there for days. Weeks, even, just staring at those prints. I'd press my hand to the wall and talk about my day, share my dreams, my hopes and fears. When I touch them it's like they're here with me. This is all I have left. Echoes of so much love trapped in paint and plaster. You see now? Why I can't leave?"

"Yes." Isobel blinked back tears. "Yes, I do."

Fifteen minutes later, twisting around, Isobel turned off her phone and scrubbed a hand over her heart. "I think we've got everything we need. I'll get started on writing the piece while it's fresh and see where it takes me."

"Well, this was lovely. Thank you for the wine and the little chat." Genie rose to embrace Isobel and placed a couple of airy kisses over her cheeks. "How long are you in New York?"

"Just tonight. I fly home tomorrow."

"Pity. Your next trip you must come visit me at the club. I perform from Thursday to Sunday. I'll make sure to reserve our best table with all the champagne and oysters your heart desires. On the house, of course."

"Deal."

"Thanks, Bel. Come on, Genie." Priya set a hand at her back, "I'll walk you out."

While Priya led Genie away, Isobel opened her laptop and set to work, pouring emotions into words like water into a cup. It flowed and ran with such graceful ease she barely noticed time had slipped away until Priya returned to sit with her as the sun hung low on the horizon, its light rapidly fading from a burning sky.

"How's it going?"

Isobel attached the document to an email and hit Send. "It's done."

Priya poured out a fresh glass of wine from the nearly finished bottle. "Thank you, Bel, for doing this."

"No, thank *you*. You were right, this story is remarkable." Ordinarily, she'd have to guide someone through the paces, help them find the flow, but Genie had been a natural with the gilded way in which she spoke, giving so much poetry and sentiment to her words. So much raw truth.

"I knew you'd think so." Priya set down her glass on the edge of the fire pit. "Man, I feel like such a jerk, though."

"What?" Isobel stopped halfway through zipping her laptop case and sat next to Priya. "Why would you say that?"

"When I first met Genie, I saw this flamboyant old woman, her home in shambles—mainly because of the damage it had sustained. But she tried to tell me what it all meant to her . . . and I just dismissed it as unimportant. I didn't care. I didn't *want* to care."

It wasn't often that Isobel witnessed Priya struggle through emotions or get overwhelmed by them, but here she was, softening before her eyes, and Isobel ached to hug her. To soothe away that pain. But it was clear she needed this. Not just for the story, but for herself.

"I even begged the senior partner at my firm for a new case. Nearly had my head chewed off for it." She sighed. "Genie Carranza could've given up and instead chose to not only survive, but thrive. She's funny and sharp and proud. I've never met anyone like her. Cait's literally obsessed. Wouldn't surprise me if she's filing adoption papers as we speak."

Isobel set a hand over Priya's. "What matters now is you're fighting for her in every way you possibly can."

"Do you think your team will go for it? This story?"

"I honestly don't know, but I think this is the best thing I've ever written. I hope it's enough."

"It's something. If this doesn't work out, I've got a couple of weeks on the clock." Priya shrugged. "And nothing motivates me like extreme pressure."

"Speaking of pressure." Isobel waved her phone, her boss's

name on the screen. Taking a deep breath to brace herself, she answered. "Hi, Nneka."

"I don't know what side of the bed you woke up on, but this is *brilliant*."

"Really?"

"Really. It's got heart. Grit. And that added personal touch you wove in with your father . . ." Nneka's words dropped with a heavy sigh. "It's the perfect aperitif. An amuse-bouche of what's to come."

"I'm so glad you loved it." Isobel looked at Priya, mouth falling open in a silent squeal.

"I want to follow up on this story with a sit-down conversation—you and me together with the mayor of New York. Think Jada Pinkett Smith's *Red Table Talk*. He's staked much of his platform on alleviating the affordable housing crisis and rise in homelessness. Let's confront this issue of powerful landlords abusing the court systems for profit."

"Sounds great."

"I do have a few minor notes on the written piece, which I've emailed back to you, but provided you don't have any issues with the changes, feel free to update and post. We need a slogan—something catchy."

"Slogan?" Isobel looked to Priya. "Like something we could use in a hashtag?"

"Exactly. Off my head, how about #IStandWithGenie?"

"Too ableist, I think." Not everyone could stand.

"Right. #FreeGenie?"

"That makes her sound like she's in prison awaiting execution for a crime she didn't commit." Priya snatched up a pen and scribbled quickly on her palm then waved it at Isobel. "How about #GenieFromTheBlock?"

The line bubbled with Nneka's laughter. "Yes! There it is. Brilliant. Let me know once you post the story and I'll flag the team to signal boost and give this the leg up it needs. And Isobel? This is exactly what I wanted to see from you. Well done!"

Priya sat next to her, hands pressed anxiously to her mouth, frantically waiting for Isobel to end the call. "Well?"

Dazed, Isobel stared at her phone. "We're going live. It's going live. I'm going live!"

Throwing up her hands, Priya whooped with joy. "Yes, bitch! We're going out. Dresses and drinks! Tonight, we celebrate, because tomorrow—the work, and our dreams, begin!"

Chapter Seventeen

Clearing the line, the hostess showed them to a curved velvet booth tucked off the dance floor, across from the DJ. Inside, the venue swelled with people, the air humming with the thrill of energy and music. Rich dark wood and bold paint met neon signs emblazoning every corner with social media worthy quotes.

Aside from when the Sisterhood had come to Toronto to wrestle her out of her grief, Isobel couldn't recall the last time she'd dressed up for a night out. She certainly hadn't packed for it, so Priya loaned her a strapless black dress with a high slit on the right side that cut up near to her hip. It hugged her slender figure, giving the illusion of real curves.

You're like a swan, Caitlin once said. *All graceful lines.* As the consummate ugly duckling in her youth, Isobel hadn't felt like a swan, but she'd eventually grown into her white feathers. And neck.

"Damn." Priya pouted. "Cait can't make it. She's stuck at the studio. Apparently the designer decided he hates his entire collection and wants them redoing every stitch and seam ahead of his upcoming runway show next week."

"Oh, that's too bad."

"She says she can try to see us tomorrow after you finish your meeting." Priya tucked her phone into an azure studded clutch that matched her stunning sheath dress. "Are you excited?"

"Oh . . . yes, absolutely." The story had gone up nearly an hour ago, but Isobel had turned off her phone, unable to stem the anxiety. *What if it falls flat? What if everyone hates it?* No likes. No comments or shares. No views. What if she'd thrown away her dream before it even truly began?

"Stop it."

"What?"

"That defeatist internal self-talk you do oh so well." Priya spun a finger in Isobel's face. "I can almost see the insecurity emanating from your pores."

"I'm sorry, but it's hard."

"It wouldn't be if you'd allow me to confirm what we both already know—you're killing it. People are devouring your words and begging for more."

"What makes you so sure?"

"Because you're brilliant, Bel, and now the world will know it too." Tucking away her phone, Priya planted her elbows to the table and bridged fingers. "So, how does it feel?"

"What?"

Priya batted her lashes. "Freedom."

Isobel's cheeks warmed through to the bone. "Good." God that was hard to admit. The weight of being away from home had settled on her chest like an anvil the moment she walked out her front door, but it had lifted substantially. And now it was almost featherlight. She hadn't felt the compelling need to check her phone for the last three hours. Knowing her father was in capable hands, with Shayne nearby to offer a second set if needed, really gave her so much peace.

"Shall we start with martinis? Or champagne?"

"Why not both?"

"*Ooooh.*" Priya pursed her smiling lips. "Double fisting. I like this new and improved Isobel." After a quick pursual of the menu, Priya settled on a bottle of Moët along with a couple of ginger hibiscus martinis, which arrived at the table in less than ten minutes.

Isobel started with her martini. The first sip was both sweet and spicy, with subtle floral notes that teased her palette and senses. "Oh wow." She pressed a hand to her tingling lips. "That's incredible."

"Everything here is. To the start of a new and dazzling future." Priya clinked her glass to Isobel's. "Chase dreams!"

"Not drama," Isobel finished, and sipped again. This time long and deep. God! There really was so much to celebrate. The *Passivist Activist* was going *live*. And even though the last time she'd been to New York was with Kyle, memories that echoed with every twist and turn through the city's chaotic streets, Isobel intended to scrub them all out. Starting with tonight. No more living in the past. It was time to forge a new future. And the future was looking bright.

That was when it struck her, a velvet wave . . . slow and rippling across her skin. Intangible and visceral all at once. Isobel leaned into the sensation, her gaze following the pull and connecting with the source, seated across the dance floor, at the bar. Handsome and refined, but casually put together. Dark hair winged down over his brow and brushed the black frames of his glasses, while his sculpted face was cool and aristocratic in its shape, and his skin was golden from both sun and lineage.

His presence sent a shock of electricity across her skin, as direct as a bolt of lightning that struck in places she never expected to feel again. Straight through the center of her chest. Reviving a dead heart and forgotten urges . . .

"You all right?" Priya asked, when Isobel nearly fumbled her drink.

Isobel wiped droplets off her hand. "Oh . . . yes. I'm fine."

Priya launched back into the conversation, but Isobel's eyes drifted away once again, searching for the presence that even now was coiling deep inside her body and filling her with heat. So much heat.

He'd transitioned from the bar to a table with his friends, and sat on the corner edge, blazer undone, forearms planted in front of him, the neckline of his shirt open to reveal the hard caps of his muscular chest. Smooth. Strong. And decorated with dark, curving lines of tattoos that were somehow natural instead of forced, but *oh* did they make him look sexy.

And dangerous.

His gaze found her and a jolt snapped through Isobel, fast and bright. Not even the framed glasses could detract from the intensity of his dark eyes, though she saw gentleness there to soften their dizzying power.

"Hey." Priya's fingers snapped in front of her face. Breaking the connection. The spell.

God, that single, searing second had felt like an hour had stretched between them. Strong and tenuous. Every inch of Isobel tingled and hummed, begging for more like a junkie craving another hit.

"You totally spaced out on me. *Again*."

"No, I didn't."

Priya crossed her arms. "What was I talking about?"

Crap. Isobel sipped at what was left of her martini, stalling for a few precious seconds as the gears of her memory churned with fierce effort to rewind the last few minutes. "Something about a tiger . . ."

"I knew it." Priya shook a bemused head before pressing the back of her hand to Isobel's brow. "My baby girl is in heat."

"What?" Isobel swatted her away. "No! I'm not."

"Yes, you absolutely are. Let's see, which one's got you all hot and bothered?" Smirking devilishly, Priya's gaze swept out across the busy establishment. "Is it the bronzed god in Tom Ford?"

Galled, Isobel nearly dropped her glass. "How did you know?"

"Because he's checking you out—*hard*."

She didn't need to look to confirm Priya's statement, and the exhilarating rush sent little licks of excitement to twine with nerves, leaving her giddy and a little breathless.

"*Oooooh*, you're blushing. And bravo, sister. Bra-effing-vo. He's *delicious*."

He was. Like warm caramel on a spoon.

"If I didn't know any better, I'd say you were in the mood for a random hookup."

"Maybe I am."

Priya laughed, but that laughter quickly sobered into surprise. "Why do I get the impression you're not joking?"

Isobel toyed with the stacked rings on her fingers—thin, delicate gold bands. Perhaps it was the alcohol, or being in

New York, or even Priya's light mocking, but suddenly, and for once, Isobel wanted to break free of her skin and do something reckless. Part of her marveled at the surge of awareness inside of her. She'd heard her sisters speak of it often—Shayne and Priya especially—but had never experienced anything like it herself. This jolt of instant attraction and lust and something altogether unnamable. A kind of primitive and sudden spark that burned away the lingering vestiges of pain and hurt of her broken heart, giving her courage. Clarity.

Step outside your comfort zone. Be free, for once . . .

Isobel scooted closer to Priya. "Tell me how to do this."

"Are you sure you're ready? Emotionally, I mean."

"You do it all the time."

"I'm not the one healing from heartbreak."

"You didn't wait after Bhavin?" Isobel pointed out.

"That was different. I wasn't in love with Bhavin, which is *why* I dumped him."

A week shy of their one-year anniversary—the longest relationship Priya had ever had. Isobel's heart had broken for the poor guy, but it hadn't come as a shock to any of the sisters. Priya had never seemed especially connected to him, or anyone else, before or since. She loved men. Love their company and attention, but they never got close to the core of her. "I'm sorry, I didn't mean to bring it up if it's awkward."

"No, it's not," Priya assured her with a sincere smile. "Bhavin was like you. He wanted a future and a family, and I wasn't willing to give up my dreams just to give birth to his. I'm not ready for all that. I don't know if I'll ever be. I like simple and easy and uncomplicated, but I don't know that it will suit you."

"If it's so easy and uncomplicated, then why not?" She

could certainly use something easy and uncomplicated right about now.

"Because you have a big heart that feels everything. It's what I adore most about you—you have no walls. No armor. You're love, through and through. Casual intimacy requires the opposite."

Defeated, Isobel frowned. "Does it really make that much of a difference?"

"Honestly? I don't know. I haven't really fallen in love before."

"Maybe you're right. But I won't know unless I try." Isobel twirled the stem of her glass between her fingers and watched the spinning dance of refracting light. "I refuse to continue to think about what happened as a loss; I can't lose someone who didn't want to be a part of my life," she said. "And you know what? Not everyone *deserves* to be. He didn't deserve to be." Dragging her eyes up to Priya's, Isobel set her shoulders.

Resolute.

"I know what I want, and I think I am actually *ready*. Not for complicated, but I'm ready to start putting myself out there. For intimacy. Sex." *Oh God, I actually said it.* "Which kind of scares me, but I am."

"Babe, it doesn't have to be tonight."

"Yes, it does. Once I'm home I'll be so wrapped up in responsibilities, and I don't want Kyle's to be the last hands that touch me. I need to move on. I need to see if it's even possible. Help me, Priya. Please?"

Priya sank her teeth into her bottom lip, a gleam in her eyes that was pleased and more than a little proud. "Then let's start by getting his attention." Stealthily, she gave a toss of her long dark hair and cast an assessing glance over to his table. "You're going to buy him a drink."

Isobel blinked. "*Now*?"

"Sweetie, that man isn't going to be unattended for much longer."

"But this is our girl's night, I don't want to spoil it so early . . ."

"Are you kidding?" Priya's hands closed over hers atop the table, squeezed. "I can't tell you how happy I am to know you're recognizing your needs as a woman and are finally *owning* them. And after that, no more booze," she added, gesturing to what remained of Isobel's flute of champagne. "If you're potentially getting your groove on, I want you sober, babe. Sober and *sure*."

"Won't it be weird if he's the only one drinking?" she asked as Priya polished off her drink.

"Order a Perrier on ice; pretend it's a G&T. I do it all the time. When they come over to thank you, I'll take care of his friends so you two can talk alone. Feel him out."

"But he's got two with him." Isobel leaned in to whisper, "Can you handle *two*?"

"Oh, my sweet summer Isobel." Priya tipped her a bemused gaze and smiled. "Watch and learn."

It took twenty minutes and three attempts before they succeeded in attracting one of the servers; a brunet wearing a fitted red dress that exploited every inch of her killer body, and with a face contoured to Kardashian perfection. Isobel ordered a mezcal martini for Priya, sparkling water for herself, as suggested, and a round of whatever her mystery man and his friends were drinking to be put on their tab.

As the server walked away, a sliver of hesitancy and self-doubt wormed through the rush of adrenaline. *What the hell am I doing?* She'd seen her sisters in action many times, but this would be her first conquest. Her first foray into the unchartered waters of the casual one-night stand.

Can I actually do this? Isobel already knew she *wanted* to, but flirting—seduction—was so far beyond her scope of understanding, a vital set of skills she'd never really had to learn after eight years with one man. What little she knew was tangled up in Kyle, and hadn't she just watched this gorgeous specimen swat down a flock of stunning women?

Maybe he's married or in a relationship. Because no way a guy that attractive could possibly be single. What if she made a complete idiot of herself?

"*Oooooh*, good they're getting their drinks," Priya squealed. "And the waitress pointed you out. *Niiice.*"

"Oh God," she squeaked, all of her earlier bravado evaporating in panic. "What do I do? What do I say?"

"Start with easy conversation and if the connection is there the rest will fall into place, trust me." She covered Isobel's trembling hand with a reassuring grip. "Chemistry can't be forced. You'll know as soon as he sits down, and if it's there, get close. Give lots of eye contact. Proximity turns up the heat. Like this." Priya eased in, the liquid amber pools of her eyes intensifying with a primal allure Isobel had witnessed her turn on to draw in countless men but was now aimed directly at her.

Her gaze magnetic, compelling and the gentle stroke of Priya's fingers across the back of her hand made Isobel's heart dance wildly in her chest.

"God . . . you're *good*."

"I know, darling. I know." Priya pulled away, breaking the spell, and tossed her length of glorious hair with a wicked chuckle. "Now, if, for whatever reason, you're not feeling the vibe, excuse yourself to the ladies' room; I'll make sure he's gone before you get back."

Isobel's heart kicked down a notch from sheer panic to mild terror. "Sounds . . . efficient."

"The sisters always have an exit strategy." She winked. "But if everything does go well, don't leave without telling me exactly where you're going, and if you're not back at my place by sunrise, I will hunt him down with my baseball bat— swinging first and asking questions later. Got it?"

A smile tugged at Isobel's lips. "Okay."

"Good. Now take a deep breath," Priya added with a hushed whisper. "He's almost here."

"What?" Isobel barely croaked out that single panicked syllable when a voice, deep and sooty as burnt velvet robbed her of breath.

"Evening, ladies."

A little lightheaded, Isobel slowly swiveled around in the booth. He stood over her, tall and broad shouldered. God, those eyes were more powerful up close. His smile flashed, warm, full, and everything inside of her burned hotter.

Brighter.

"Sorry to disturb you both, but I understand I have you to thank for this?" He raised his glass of what she guessed was scotch while his two friends saluted her as well.

"No disruption, whatsoever. I was just telling my sister how I *love* this song, but she doesn't seem to want to dance."

Priya turned dark, glittering eyes on her targets with a dazzling smile that could bring a man to his knees—and often did. "How about you boys escort a lady to the floor and show me your moves?" Sliding out of the booth, Priya held out a hand for each of the friends and, arm in arm, lured them out into the swelling crowd. They never stood a chance.

He watched them for a moment, amusement flashing across his face before pinning his intense gaze on Isobel again and gesturing to the booth. "May I?"

A thousand words clamored within her, and Isobel struggled to pick through the possibilities of what to say—from simple to witty to eloquently aloof—and tumbled headfirst into analysis paralysis. No, tonight she was going to be fearless. Daring, for *once*.

"Yes. Please." Her voice came through sure and steady. A good start.

Setting his drink down on the table, he slid in behind the table and came close enough for the solid weight of his thigh to press against hers. Rough denim against soft skin. "I was hoping for an excuse to come over and introduce myself. So I'm thankful you gave me one." A blush warmed his cheeks, a boyish glimmer lit his eyes, and seeing it relaxed her.

She wasn't the only one who was nervous and out of her depth.

"My name is Hideo."

"Isobel," she said, running damp palms along her thighs, causing the material of her dress to move and shift around her legs. "That's a wonderful name. Japanese?"

He nodded. "After my great-grandfather."

"Your accent, though . . . it's not Spanish. Portuguese, maybe?"

"You have a keen ear. I was born in São Paulo, and lived there until I was twelve. Been all over the world, since, but never really lost it." Hideo dragged his glasses from his face, Superman slipping out of the guise of Clark Kent, and tucked them into the inner breast pocket of his jacket. "I never believed in miracles, but tonight proved me wrong. An intriguing young woman who is beautiful, generous, *and* intelligent. Please tell me you're single or else you'll break my heart."

Isobel's cheeks burned as she smiled, laughed. Her head dipped and a wing of brown hair swept forward before she tucked it away behind her ear. "Yes. I'm single. Though I was supposed to be married. This September, in fact." Pain bloomed in her still mending heart, and she barely resisted the urge to press a hand there and rub away the ache.

"What happened?" Concern mingled with interest in his voice. He wasn't asking only to be polite; he genuinely wanted to know, and that calmed her.

Anchored her.

"I guess you're not big on mainstream news or social media."

"No. Not so much." Hideo lifted his shoulders, let them fall. "I travel often and work long hours, so when I have a spare moment for myself, I prefer to read."

Relief cooled the burn of humiliation. "Well, then, I won't bore you with the details. We were together for eight years, and now we're not."

"What went wrong?"

What had gone wrong? She'd asked herself the question

a thousand times over the last few weeks, but the answer came easily now. Clear as the blast of a foghorn rolling across Harbourfront, where as a kid she'd fed ducks and swans with her dad. "I wasn't enough for him because he wouldn't let me be." There it was. Simply put, but no less impactful than the knife of betrayal Kyle had lodged between the delicate bones of her ribs.

Except now she felt that blade slip free and each breath was lighter. Easier. After a lingering moment of silence, she looked up and into Hideo's quiet, careful gaze. One long finger pressed against his lips.

"Aren't you going to say the perfunctory 'I'm sorry'?"

"Do you want me to?"

Isobel sighed. "Not really, no."

"Good." Hideo shifted in the booth so he could face her more directly. "Experiences, even the horrible ones, are necessary. Important. Each obstacle presents a series of choices and it's our choices that determine not only who we are but who we will become. What you endured held the power to either break you or strengthen you; you chose strength. That's something that should be celebrated, Isobel. Not apologized for."

Isobel sipped her water, quelling the urge to appease her curiosity. However poignant, she sensed that there was a more painful truth buried underneath his statement, and though her instinct was to pry for the answer, she clamped down hard to repress the urge. "Where I come from, we apologize for everything. Even if we're not at fault."

"Where's that?"

"Toronto."

His smile returned, bright and swift. "Ah, so you're Canadian."

"Born and raised. I'm here for work, and staying with my sister, Priya." She nodded in the direction of the dance floor where she caught the sway of Priya's arms in the crowd. Music swelled and lights spun, forcing them closer if they wanted to be heard. It was a little intoxicating, being this close to him and yet not quite touching.

"You don't appear related."

"We're not, but we're still family." Isobel smiled. "Where's home for you?"

"Vancouver." He lifted his glass in toast, from one Canadian to another. "But back-to-back contracts have me bouncing between New York, Germany, and Hong Kong. Sometimes Spain."

"Sounds exhausting." *And exhilarating.*

"It can be." His smile dimmed a fraction. "I'm in and out for weeks at a time. My clients set me up in furnished apartments for longer stays, but otherwise it's a lot of airports and living out of suitcases. I enjoyed it once, the rootless, nomadic existence, the freedom of not being tethered so I could roam and explore, but it's become challenging."

"I have the exact opposite problem. I never travel anywhere."

"What's holding you back?"

"My dad. He had an on-the-job accident three years ago. I've been tied to home ever since, not that I'm complaining, I love my father. He's all I have in the way of family, aside from my best friends—my sisters—but it's been impossible to get away for long." *Or do much of anything.* A single, depressing thought, and one more reason that tonight was about departure as much as it was about escape. From herself. From her fears.

Isobel flicked the edge of her tongue across her bottom lip.

What would Priya or Shayne do now? Even Caitlin was known to charm the pants off anyone she set her eyes on. Perhaps the only other sister in the group who was equally out of her depths in the dating pool was Eshe, but with her runway legs and stunning bone structure, Eshe merely had to enter a room and attention flowed to her, whether she wanted it or not.

Proximity. Eye contact. Priya's words returned to her. *Turn up the heat.*

Isobel set her hand on his thigh, just above the knee. "I want to tell you something."

He slid closer, his hand resting along the curved back of the booth. "Okay."

"It's crazy, and I'm going to make a complete idiot out of myself because I don't know how to do this. How to say *this* any other way but as directly as possible."

"You have my complete attention." He came closer still and the air between them sizzled. The room around them faded away. All sound. All movement and time.

"I'd like to sleep with you." His humor-filled eyes widened in shock, and embarrassment kicked her hard in the teeth. "Oh my God." Isobel buried her face behind her hands. "Oh my God, I'm sorry, I didn't mean to—I shouldn't . . . I knew I was going to make a complete idiot out of myself. I don't know how to do this. Oh my God!"

"Please don't." He tugged her hands away and crooked an elegant finger under her chin, angling her gaze up to his. Those eyes weren't shocked anymore. They burned with arousal. "I admire honesty and respect courage. You have both." His hand dropped to link with hers in her lap, and the strong sweep of his thumb across her skin calmed her anxiety as Hideo's gaze skimmed over her face, searching. "Why me?"

Isobel held in a single breath then released it. She'd already humiliated herself, might as well keep going. "For weeks I've been a ghost, dragging around chains of grief. I'm tired of being in pain." And, God, she was. "I want to feel again."

"What's stopping you from feeling?"

"Fear. My ex was my first, and . . . there hasn't been anyone else and what terrifies me is not knowing if I'll ever experience anything close to what I felt with him again, if I'll ever want to. But for some reason when you walked in . . . I felt you. I *feel* you. Beneath my skin." She slid her palm over her arm. "It's like electricity and velvet. I can't explain it."

"Then you honor me." The curiosity in his gaze gave way to understanding. "And you don't have to explain. I feel it too."

He was close. So close she could feel the press of heat from the wall of his body, and his sharp, clean scent filled her lungs with each shallow breath. Priya was right. Chemistry couldn't be forced. A connection couldn't be faked, but there was something there. Definitely something.

"I'm a passionate guy and not easily affected," he continued, "but you affect me, Isobel. I find you fascinating. Shy, but receptive. Eager, but uncertain. So, let's make you certain." A whisper of his thumb over the curve of her cheek; her lips parted and his descended.

First a gentle press, an easy glide, and when her tongue slipped out to meet him, Hideo sank in deep. Long, slow, and thorough. Until a quiver seized her belly, skidded up the notches of her spine, and snapped back down, creating waves of pleasure.

Endless ripples that stole her breath.

Eyes were on them, and she didn't care. Nothing mattered beyond that staggering connection of mouths and his hand at her neck, giving a delicate squeeze. She was helpless to contain the soft moan that escaped when their lips parted.

"That was only a hint," he whispered. "There's more. So much more. Let me show you." The statement hung between them, open ended. Waiting for her to decide to act on her desires or to turn away from them. Whatever her doubts, her worries, and hesitations, one thing was definite—she'd never felt anything like *this* before.

The wild and reckless pull of lust. On top of being attractive and attentive, he was temporary, and temporary was what she needed most of all. Someone who would respect her body and her feelings without getting lost in emotional attachment, and who would be gone from her life without leaving the stain of regret in his wake.

"Okay," Isobel whispered. "Show me."

Chapter Eighteen

Priya cast a quick smile as the hostess returned with another hibiscus and ginger infused mezcal martini and climbed up the narrow steps to a wraparound upper level that overlooked the dance floor. Music thumped in a firm, steady beat, throbbing like a pulse between the exposed brick walls. Vivid neon lighting bounced off polished wood floors and sculpted tin ceiling; it was the kind of venue that was coolly dignified without trying too hard to impress.

It had required some stellar wing woman moves to lure the two friends away, and after twenty minutes of dancing, followed by a classic bait and switch at the bar, Priya had passed off the duo to a small group of young girls eager for attention. The handover had been flawless, and now Isobel had plenty of privacy without the risk of interruption.

Pleased with herself, Priya sipped her drink, ginger warming her throat, hibiscus cooling her tongue, and watched Isobel, deep in conversation with the delicious hottie. Even from this distance, she could see obvious sparks of attraction flying off them. Bright and powerful. This was one hell of a matchup. No wonder Isobel hadn't been able to hold her focus for more than a few straggling seconds before getting sucked back under.

Not that Priya could fault her. The guy was gorgeous, and she knew a thing or two about drowning in the alluring waters of potent attraction. What she experienced with Hadrian was no small thing; despite all her efforts to pretend otherwise, she was drawn to him in a way she couldn't explain. He was a distraction she couldn't allow to cloud her focus, but knowing that didn't stop the whoremones. All he had to do was walk into a room and it washed over her. Shocking her senses, awakening them so every part of her went hot, jittery—humming with an interest she avidly tried to squash, but nothing she did cooled the need for him.

"Hello, tiger."

Think of the devil . . . Priya swallowed as a flurry of wicked chills raced down her spine as she turned around to face the manifestation of her wickedest fantasies. "Guess I shouldn't be surprised to find you at the hottest new lounge in Manhattan." Pathos was developing a fierce reputation for bringing out the best of the best in the city; of course *he'd* be here.

"I had a date," Hadrian confessed. "Just across the street, but it didn't go so well. Was terrible so I came here to escape. You?"

"Girl's night with my sister, but now I'm playing wing woman," she said, easing back a step when he got close enough for her to catch the musk of his cologne. "The brunet in the second booth from the left."

Hadrian's eyes scanned the room, then popped wide when he found his mark. "Ah, I see. Looks like she's certainly enjoying the company."

Priya laughed. They weren't kissing anymore, but it was obvious the two were lost in each other. "I'd have to agree."

"Sister?" Hadrian arched a brow.

"By choice."

"I have a few of those in my life." Turning away from the dance floor, Hadrian leaned against the glass panel. "I must say, tiger, you've got some nice moves." He flashed his phone screen for her to see the headline of a featured article quoting Isobel's segment on Genie Carranza.

Plucking the device from his hands, Priya scrolled through and barely resisted the urge to hug the phone to her chest. They'd released the story a little over an hour ago and already it was blowing up with #GenieFromTheBlock going viral across every major platform.

"I knew you'd find a way to turn this around, but must admit, this wasn't what I'd expected."

"It's a start." The pressure of many voices rising together was powerful. Inescapable. Now the heat was on—high—and there was no way Daniella could shove her off the case, but it would fade if she didn't keep the temperature cranked. She needed more. Something to tip the scales just that final bit into victory. But what? She'd called in every favor owed to her and they'd all come back dry.

"Do you think you could put me in touch with an investigator your dad used?" Priya asked, handing back his iPhone. When you were a lawyer that high up the ladder, you found yourself a guy who knew how to skirt the boundaries of the law to get you things, and which were often the difference between winning or losing a major case.

"I should be able to dig up his contact."

"How much do you think he can get in twenty-four hours?"

"Seventy-two would be better."

"I won't have that long."

"What's the urgency?"

"Dani found out I lost in housing court and told me to drop the case." Priya crossed her arms. "Because pro bonos don't bring in money, they take it, and she doesn't want the firm on the hook given name partnership is at stake."

"So, you went over her head?" Concern slid over his face like water over sand. "You're playing with fire, tiger."

"Michael put me in this mess." Priya shrugged. "I know at first I was self-focused, but I'm not anymore. I promised Genie I'd keep fighting, and that's what I'm going to do, whether Dani likes it or not."

The look in Hadrian's eyes changed, and it was a shift of expression that Priya wasn't entirely prepared for. Warmth. Respect, and a hint of attraction simmering underneath it all, stoking something within her. And not all of it was sexual.

Priya had hoped by now that she would have grown accustomed to the way her body reacted to his stare—flashing with alternating waves of heat and spikes of cold. Thrilling little rushes that heralded vibrant chemistry and attraction, but each time it stole her breath all the same.

No. There was no getting *used* to a man like Aurelio Hadrian Marek. He was a *tempest*. Beautiful to look at, compelling and breathtaking, but dangerous if you got too close. A veritable force of nature against which there was no fortification. He came, he saw, and he conquered.

Priya didn't stand a chance. All she could do was hold on to some vestige of self-control and pray she didn't get swept away. Even if everything inside of her wanted to yield to the wanton urge to sample the dark, wicked flavor of his mouth and feel the hard, unrelenting demand of his hands . . .

"Okay, tiger, you win. I'll get you the contact on one condition."

"What?"

"Tell me what happened with Michael?"

Priya rolled her eyes. "Seriously?"

"Curiosity is killing me." His eyes gleamed darkly. "I've got a table and some food coming, join me. It's just over there." He gestured to an empty table with a clear sightline overlooking the rest of the venue. If she sat on the left, and craned her neck, she'd be able to still keep tabs on Isobel without too much issue.

Priya ran her tongue along the edge of her teeth. "All right. I'll text Isobel and let her know where I am, in case she needs to be extracted."

"Oh, I doubt it."

Priya followed his gaze and watched as Isobel leaned into a rather passionate lip-lock. "Kids." She sighed, dashing away a not entirely imaginary tear. "They grow up so fast."

"Come on." Hadrian took her hand and led Priya to the table where a fresh bottle of Chianti had been left to breathe. Priya slid into the left side of the booth, and Hadrian claimed the right, the space between them just enough for her knees to brush against his thigh. He poured out the wine, offering her the first glass, and listened intently as she told him everything that had happened at the gym.

Comfortably reclined with his nearly finished glass of wine in hand, he smiled at her. "You dazzle me."

"That's not the response I'd expected." Or prepared for. "I

thought you'd call me reckless and act like some white knight who would've ridden in to fight my battle for me."

Hadrian sipped his wine thoughtfully before setting down his glass. "My cousin Maria disabused me of the notion that girls are weaker than boys. Who am I to tell you what to do or what you should've done when clearly you know what you're capable of? But I *definitely* would've loved to watch." Straightening in his seat, he paused to top up her wine before refilling his, draining the bottle. "I was worried about you, though. The way he got to you. You seemed pretty distressed that first day."

Priya sighed. "It doesn't happen often, my skin's usually very thick, so when someone manages to get underneath it, they tend to go pretty deep."

"Can I ask you about it? I don't mean to pry. It's just . . ." Hadrian swirled the rich burgundy wine in his glass, his eyes lifting to hers, inquisitive and unsure. "I want to know how you feel about the whole thing. What it was like for you, growing up?"

Any other night she might've shut his curiosity down cold. The truth about her parentage wasn't a subject she easily broached with just anyone, but whether it was the alcohol or the high of impending victory, Priya found herself inclined to answer.

"My mom was thirty-two when she decided she wanted to have a child, and with no desirable prospects on the horizon, she was never the type to kick back and *wait* for anything, much less a man." Priya set her arms on the table and stroked her hands over her exposed arms. "It was weird," she mused, "not knowing the other half of my origins. My smile and love of classical music obviously came from my mother, along with my feminist ideals, but there are parts of me that are a complete mystery I stopped trying to solve."

"Were you ever angry about it?"

"Oh yeah. I found out accidentally when I was thirteen, after years of her playing the *I can't talk about this right now* game that aggravated me to no end. So yeah, I was pretty angry to be born into this situation, with its limitations and confusion, ignorant of my biological roots. To realize I would *never* know who he was, never have those questions answered almost pushed me and mother apart."

As Hadrian speared the last of the grilled calamari topped in a rich, spicy sauce, Priya helped herself to one of the chorizo sliders. The air around them was thick with summer heat but softened by the strong brush of breeze pushed through the opened wall of windows. A truly gorgeous evening to spend with incredible food and great company.

"I couldn't stay mad at her for long," she continued, licking grease off her thumb. "All my life she was my hero, my everything. So as a coping mechanism, I thought of him as dead. That made it easier. But I was still angry, you know? No one understood or could relate. Not even my sisters." She nodded to where Isobel sat still ensconced in deep conversation in her booth. "Isobel and I were both raised in a single parent home. Her mother took off when she was seven and she didn't talk about her much, but I was so jealous. She at least knew her mother's face, her voice, and had memories. All the things I wouldn't. And in some ways, it made me angrier."

Hadrian's expression melted into regret. "I'm sorry; we don't have to talk about this anymore if it's upsetting you."

"No, it's okay." And for reasons she couldn't understand, she had to talk about this. Needed to. "Eventually, I channeled my anger into school, and worked myself to the bone. The more I excelled, and the higher I soared, the less of that anger and pain remained. I discovered that if I was best at everything, nothing and no one could touch me. My entire life's self-worth became wrapped up in being top of my class. Highest grades. Most potential. I didn't realize until much later that it wasn't so much anger I had felt as a kid, but fear. Fear of the unknown. And never knowing who I was. My mother always referred to him as a donor rather than a person, and I don't think she did it consciously, but that made me feel like I wasn't real somehow too. That I was *less*. It took a long time to see past that, to see myself in the mirror and not become overwhelmed with fear and loathing."

He watched her as she spoke, spilling her deepest insecurities into the space between them, and it was hard for her to meet his thoughtful, penetrating gaze without losing herself in it. She wanted to bask in it for hours.

"I'm surprised you were so hard on yourself. People do IVF all the time."

"Couples, sure, but a single woman with donor sperm?"

"Again—common, I'd expect."

"How many do you know? Personally?" Hadrian sat back in thought, but as the silence stretched, she smiled, having made her point. "Insemination boomed in the nineties and, yes, there's more of us kicking around than you could imagine, but back then? No one openly discussed it. I was a sideshow freak. The girl born in a Petri dish. Kids were . . . cruel." *Very cruel*. But they'd made her strong. Thick skinned. Resilient and determined. Her childhood tears had watered the determined seeds of future success, and now she stood on the cusp of achieving her dreams.

"I made peace with it after a while. My mother married her long-term boyfriend when I was eighteen and having Hernan in our lives mended a hole in my heart I'd never truly known was there until he filled it. I think my mom could have raised me alone and done a brilliant job of it, but it feels complete with him."

Hadrian nodded. "We assume that the people who share our genes will love us unconditionally, but that isn't always the case. It's completely possible to be a biological father and not a dad, as many people know, but it's just as possible to be a dad and not a biological father."

"Exactly." Priya smiled. "He's the one who asked about my day, no matter how busy he was, went to all my school events, took us on holidays every year, and bought me all the birthday or Christmas presents I could ever want. He taught me to appreciate the ballet, told me the candid truth about boys, and cried when he dropped me off for my first term at Harvard."

"Did you always want to be a lawyer?"

"I actually dreamed of being an artist when I was little. Painting."

"Why didn't you?"

Priya shrugged. "I have the soul of an artist, but not the talent."

"Talent is subjective."

"Not as Lakshmi Seth's daughter," No. She couldn't afford to be anything less than perfect. Glorious.

"I think you're being hard on yourself, but I get it. Our

parents cast long shadows for us to climb out from under. What brought you to law?"

"Shoplifting. I got arrested, again, and was down at the station waiting for my mom to get me when in walked Marai Nagao wearing a leather jacket and that side fade she became famous for, and I watched her shred a detective over the way they booked her client. She was like a superhero. It was incredible, and I realized I wanted that too. That power. That respect."

"You know I looked you up, after we bumped into each other after our interviews. The mock trial championships you won two years ago." Hadrian settled his forearms on the table and leaned in closer. "You were breathtaking. You really are born for this, Priya."

A simple declaration, boldly stated, it made her heart stutter and blood warm. "All right. Enough about me. Your turn to start sharing."

"Fair enough." Hadrian grinned, a dazzling flash of white teeth against stubble and buttery bronze skin. "I have a tattoo."

"Oh, that's deep." Priya snorted. "What is it?"

"A dolphin. I'll have you know they are nature's most majestic and noble animal," he added when she burst into laughter. "One even saved my life."

"Get out."

He paused for a moment before scooting deeper into the booth, bringing them closer together, and dragged his right leg up between them, cuffing his pants to the knee to reveal a length of tanned skin streaked with puckered scars.

Priya sucked in a breath, her belly knotting with a mixture of shock and sympathy. The injury, and whatever had caused it, would've been horrific to account for such damage. "What happened?"

Satisfied she'd got a long, hard look at it, he rolled the denim back down, hiding his savaged limb. "I'd gone out to the coast of Oahu with some mates to celebrate graduating our senior year." He folded his hands together and set them in his lap. "Like a bunch of morons, a few of us went out for a bit of night surfing, when a shark got a hold of me just above the knee and dragged me down."

To be entombed in black waters with nothing but fear and blinding pain, the sting of salt in his eyes, searing down his throat as he screamed and choked on bloody water . . . Priya's chest tightened, imaging his terror.

"I would've died, but a pod was passing through and chased the bastard off. I can't say how I got back to shore." His voice darkened with the strain of memories. "I remember looking down at my hands in too much shock to feel pain. But the blood I'll never forget. It shines black in the moonlight. Black as ink."

Hand over her mouth, she listened as he spoke of the airlift to the hospital, nearly dying twice, once en route and again during a six-hour surgery.

"Eighty-four stitches to close the gash. Destroyed my knee, and my femur is sandwiched between two titanium plates, effectively killing my chances of pro sports. That's why I limp a bit, though I hide it as best I can. They found this tooth embedded in my cracked kneecap," he said, leaning forward to show her the one he wore around his neck.

All this time she'd thought it was some pretentious hipster thing, but the truth was far more meaningful.

"My dad flew up to stay with me in the hospital for the six weeks of recovery and we did nothing but talk, play video games . . . work didn't come up once. It was great to have my dad like that. We'd never been so close, and I learned things about him in that hospital room that I'd never known before. He told me stories and jokes; we laughed and cried." A soft smile full of emotion crossed his face. "Then I got the all clear, and Dad went back to the hotel to pack up ahead of our flight. I was going to move in with him, start law school in the fall, but he never made it past the hotel lobby. Heart attack dropped him like a stone and that was it. He was gone."

"I'm so sorry."

"You ask anyone they'll tell you my dad was a hard man to love." His eyes met hers, dark with grief. "We didn't agree on much, and he didn't know the first thing about being a family man, but he tried in his own way. I see that now. So now I wear this to remember that time we shared together." He stroked a hand over the shark tooth again, fingers circling the shard of bone that had almost cost him his life. "To remember what I survived, how fleeting life is, and to always—always—be fearless. To take chances. To live."

Pausing long enough for Hadrian to pay the bill, Priya gathered herself and her emotions. Life was full of brutal experiences, but this touched her more deeply than she knew how to process. Maybe because it shamed her to realize that everything she'd thought about him—assumed about him—was so wrong.

"Your father would be proud of you," she said as they exited the booth.

Tucking away his wallet, Hadrian's eyes slid down to her. "You think so?"

"Definitely. Without question." She stroked a hand up his arm and over his shoulder, a gesture meant to soothe as words escaped her. His gaze shifted from friendly to feral.

Hadrian took her by the hand and, with a quick jerk and spin, dragged her around behind him into the curtained area of the empty and unattended coat check. The curtain floated shut behind him, a heavy drape of blood-red velvet, muting the light. Her back met a wall and he placed his hands on either side of her, caging her. Instinctively, hers shot out to brace against him, but she was torn. Push or pull?

"You might not remember the night we met, but I do. And I can't stop thinking about it."

"Hadrian—" Lust spiked hard from her belly, a delicious, dark tremor that rippled through her from the seductive glide of his lips against her neck, and when his teeth followed, there was no holding back the hungry groan. "This is a really bad idea."

"Kiss me." His thumb scored across her bottom lip, silencing her. "Prove me a liar and that everything I remember was only a fluke. Aren't you even a little bit curious?"

Oh, she was more than curious. She was ravenous. On the verge of desperate.

His mouth was right there. A single, punctuated breath was all that separated her from rationality and desire. Desire won. Hands sliding around his neck, she dragged him down. Took him fast. So fast. Quick lips, warring tongues. All of her was starved. Wild. And yet for as much as she took, she gave and gave and gave.

Trapped between a hard wall and a harder man, she moaned, then sighed as his lips broke from hers to blaze a scorching trail down her throat as his hands wandered and seized—discovered, but with an edge of familiarity that said he'd explored her before and remembered exactly how and where to drive her wild.

"You told me once to make myself clearer next time. Consider this me being clear. Come home with me," he whispered, sliding in for another kiss, this one slower but no less staggering. "Forget the rules. Forget common sense. One night. Just one. My home. My bed. My rules." He breathed through a wicked chuckle, soft and dangerous as velvet and lightning. "I want you in a hundred different ways, Priya. From now until sunrise. Let me."

His heart hammered against her hands, vibrating through his chest in a bone rattling beat that shook straight into her like an earthquake. Splitting her foundations. Cracking her wide open. Hands still fisted in his hair, she sucked hard on the fullness of his bottom lip, pulled with a needy bite. Hunger coiled in her belly. Excitement rippled in her chest. Priya wanted to eat him alive, but even if she wanted him fiercely, sense doused her like cold water over burning coals.

"I can't. We can't." Needing space, she nudged him back and without hesitation Hadrian let her go.

"Right. The rules." Sliding his hands into his pockets, probably to keep from reaching for her again, and it thrilled her to know she could affect him so much yet he'd listened and obeyed when not many would, under similar circumstances.

"The rules," Priya echoed. Weak and more than a little breathless, all it would take was the barest push and she'd cave like a house built on sand. But she had to remain strong, because at some point they were going to have to square off, and the last thing she needed was lust and whoremones impeding her from going for the jugular.

"We should get going before someone finds us in here."

"Yeah. Right. Just one more thing." His hands encircled her hips and whipped her around so her back was flush against him.

"What are you doing?" she asked as he slipped something out of his inner jacket pocket, and laughed when he flicked the cap off a pen.

"You'll see." His breath whispered over her skin and a playful nip of teeth followed, putting that firm resolve of hers to the test as he dragged her hair over her shoulder, exposing the length of her neck. She shivered as the pen pressed against her skin with demanding lines, and her fingers curled, nails scraping the wall, as he blew a cool breath over his handiwork, drying the ink. "There." He swept her hair over her shoulder. "Our little secret."

"What is it?" Priya turned around slowly and braced the wall with one hand, not yet trusting her legs to hold her steady on their own. "And how am I supposed to see it back there?"

"Get creative." Hadrian reached for the curtain. "Think about me tonight." He eased into the corridor, laughter dancing in his wicked eyes. "Think about me wanting you. Suffering."

And let the curtain fall.

⁕ ⁕ ⁕

"There you are." Priya found Isobel outside the front doors and looped her arm around her sister's waist.

"Sorry, I was trying to find you." Isobel's green eyes were bright with the sparkle of excitement. It warmed her cheeks, giving her already beautiful face a captivating glow.

"So. What's his name?"

"Hideo Ogaki," Isobel said, voice hushed for discretion.

"Good. Text me when you know where you're going." Priya hugged her tight. "And have fun. Lots and lots of *fun*."

"I can't believe I'm doing this." Isobel giggled, her soft blush deepening. "Should I do this? Oh God, is this a horrible idea? It's horrible, right? I have work tomorrow!"

"Don't overthink it. You deserve this, but I'm a phone call away if you need me." Priya gave her a final squeeze as a silver Mercedes pulled up to the curb and a valet slipped out to open the passenger door. Like a consummate gentleman, Hideo helped Isobel in, and it became instantly obvious there was so much more than his handsome face tugging on Isobel.

"Do you need a ride?" he asked. "I'm happy to drop you home."

"No, thank you. I'm not far and an Uber is on the way." Reaching up, Priya pulled him into a friendly hug. "Keep in mind I've seen your face, know your name, and if *anything* happens to her under your watch, I'll hold you personally accountable. She's your responsibility until she crosses my threshold." She drilled a pointed finger into the center of his chest. "Got it?

Hideo blinked three times in rapid succession. "Of course."

"And don't mistake Isobel for something she's not," Priya added, not caring if she stepped on his toes. This was her last chance to vet him and, if necessary, abort what was about to happen. "She's a gem and if you can't see that, you don't deserve to have her."

"She must be truly remarkable to inspire such dedication," he said, without a hint of irony or annoyance.

"She's the best. The last of a dying breed. Be good to her."

"I will. I promise." Spoken with utter warmth and sincerity. A gentleman through and through.

And the final vestiges of her doubt eased with a smile. "I believe you." Priya watched as the Mercedes rolled out into the street and took off, a bit like an emotional mom, stressed with worry but also proud. All she could do was help Isobel cast off her training wheels as she set out on her own path, and be there to help her back up if she toppled over. Getting hurt was always a possibility, but that was the price of *living*.

A second later Priya's phone chimed, and as requested, there was a message from Isobel with Hideo's address. As Priya sent a quick reply, the wind teased her hair, each brush and stroke of shifting strands reminding her of Hadrian—which was exactly what he'd wanted.

Curiosity burned through her as she raced home, and stopped by the hallway mirror, full length and framed in bronze. Drawing her hair back, she turned and assessed the length of her neck and there, etched in dark blue ink was a small leaping dolphin.

Think about me tonight. Think about me wanting you. Suffering.

Well, it worked. She was thinking about him. A lot.

Chapter Nineteen

Hideo swept an arm around Isobel's waist and steered her into a stunning living room. His apartment was a lushly furnished three-bedroom space in one of the most expensive condominiums in Manhattan, with elegant wainscoting, high ceilings, and large windows.

Isobel's eyes danced over the cream-colored upholstered couch and Aubusson rug. She'd worked for a couple of years after high school as an assistant to an interior designer in Toronto who had her own reality TV show, and knew how to recognize quality. An apartment like this would have cost well over a half a million in décor alone. Whomever he worked for, to say they were generous was putting it mildly.

Hideo flicked on a side-table lamp that cast just enough light to give warmth while still allowing for the private intimacy of shadows. She felt more confident in the dark, where the heat of her blush and the glimmer of nerves would go unseen.

Shucking off his blazer, Hideo tossed it over the arm of the couch and reached for her. Even in heels, the top of her head only brushed his angular chin. Her eyes fixated on the fullness of his lips and a rush of need spun thicker in her blood. *Kiss me.* Every fine hair on her arms begged for that mouth to descend. To claim.

"How can I feel like this when I don't even know you?"

"We know what we need to know. Everything else is just facts, which are irrelevant to chemistry. Instinct." He rolled his bottom lip between his teeth. "But there's so much about the biological that extends beyond binary. It's . . . essence and endless. It's magic." As if to prove his point, he let his hand glide along her neck, still not quite touching, and when his fingers circled around, the pads finally connected along the delicate points of her skin—the shock of thrill, bright and fast as electricity racing through a live wire.

Raising her hand, Hideo kissed the sensitive curve of her wrist before setting it on his chest. Inches above his heart. "I'll go as far as you need me to. As slow as you want me to."

Beneath her palm the steady rhythm rose to greet her in soothing, calming pulses. "Shouldn't it be the other way around?"

"No. No, I think you need this, and that scares you. Needing something for yourself, something as simple and honest as physical connection."

Isobel breathed in slow, panting breaths that made her head hazy and light. "And you think I shouldn't be scared?"

"No. Not of this." His hands stroked up her arms. Slow. Easy. "Not of me."

With the light spilling over her shoulder, his face came in clear and honest. Hand still resting over his heart, she held his gaze, searched it, and saw only truth. No games or pretenses. No thinly veiled lies. The beat of his heart remained steady, strong, and consistent, and whatever her hesitation, Isobel could see he stood by every word. Every syllable. She knew, down to the deepest corners of intuition, she could trust him.

Doubt yielded to desire. "Okay."

His smile broke, swift and bright, with a kind of joy that transformed him beyond handsome into something truly breathtaking. His lips descended, and he drank in her gasp of surprise, her moan of surrender. Firm, demanding, but without urgency. This was the controlled seduction of a man who preferred to sip and savor. Not gulp. The hand around her neck urged her closer with the slightest application of pressure guiding her to him, and with each new point of contact her body sparked to life, like lightning striking the ground in a storm.

Dazzling. Terrifying. Powerful.

Her fingers curled in his shirt before her hands moved of their own volition, sliding over the capped muscles of his chest, around wide shoulders, squeezing over strong biceps as his mouth worked miracles.

God, his mouth. His touch.

Head spinning, she clung to him, and a smile crept in around the edges of his kiss as she surrendered. A nip of teeth and glide of tongue. She could kiss him, just like this, for hours. Lost in endless waves of pleasure, each stroke and glide left her a little more dazed and breathless, as if he wove a sensual spell with lips and tongue. A siren, calling her deeper.

And deeper she went until she drowned. *Willingly.*

Easing him back and onto the couch, Isobel sank with him, straddling his lap, and drove her hands into his hair. Her fingers found anchor as she pushed him a little faster, a little deeper, until his own hands knotted in the fabric around her waist, dragging her against him where desire swelled hard and hot between them. Teeth joined lips and tongue as a shock rippled through his body, peeling away the first layer of control to show the barest hint of primitive desire beneath. The animal within the man.

His hands slid up from hips to waist to the sensitive underside of her breasts, the heat of his palms searing through silk, fusing to skin. And that first wanton touch unraveled what remained of her barriers as he squeezed, kneaded—a hard brush of thumbs over taut nipples shielded behind too many hindering layers. She wanted skin. Skin and heat and nothing else.

"More," she breathed into him. Moaned. "I need more."

Strong arms stole around her, answering her demand, as his hard body levered up and out of the couch with surprising control and grace, her weight secured against him. Hideo crossed from couch to bedroom in a series of long strides. Her heart kicked with excitement. His body vibrated with restraint, both of them lost to anticipation and pure, unadulterated desire.

Such was his power. And *hers*.

"Open your eyes," he said, shutting the bedroom door with a sweep of his foot. Isobel did as he asked, her feet landing on the floor as he set her down on weakened legs. Thank God his arms were still around her, otherwise she might have slid into a puddle at his feet. Hideo lowered Isobel to the edge of the bed, kissing her firmly before straightening to stand.

"Get back. All the way," he said, nodding toward the center where pillows were laid out, white against gray bedding. Doing as she was told, Isobel slid back until she felt the padded backing of the tufted headboard—distressed, dark leather studded with bronze nails.

A wicked gleam glowed in his dark-brown eyes as his fingers worked over his shirt. Carefully, he peeled it off one sleeve at a time, leaving his torso and chest bare to her appreciative gaze. His fingers dropped to his belt next, pulled the buckle open, dragged down the zipper, denim sliding to the carpeted floor, leaving strong legs encased in black, fitted boxers that didn't leave a whole lot to the imagination.

He stalked forward, his movements languid and prowling, muscles rippling, and Isobel's mouth went dry as he circled around and set a knee to the edge.

"I like this," he said, brushing a finger down the side of her face. "That look you get as you watch me." Holding that same finger between them, he crooked it beckoningly. Turning her body to fall in line with his, gripping her ankles, he guided her legs on either side of him, and his body folded on top of her but leaving a sweltering space of needy heat between them. Hideo claimed her with a hot mouth and hotter hands. "I want to watch you."

Isobel moaned, arching against him as her dress and whatever else she had on seemingly melted away. With every inch his hands uncovered, his lips followed. Over breasts, belly, and below where he teased and tormented her beyond reason.

Beyond breath.

"Let me . . ." he whispered against her thigh, fingers filling and stirring deep. "Let me watch you."

Helpless, she could do nothing except surrender as pleasure took over. But underneath it, a thought sliced through, dulling the delicious tremors coiling where she so desperately needed release.

This wasn't Kyle's body. This wasn't his mouth or his hands or even his bed. She was naked with a stranger. Making love with a stranger. A small, dark part of her screamed from the deepest corner of her heart, which still yearned for what had been so recently stripped away, rallying in resentful defiance of her newfound freedom. In the fog of doubt, she heard a drawer shut, the crinkle of plastic, the glide of latex.

"Only me," he whispered hot against her mouth and slid into another drugging kiss that stripped her mind bare. And silenced all doubt.

Overcome, overwhelmed she clutched at him, blind to anything else but those eyes. That mouth. That body, as something harder and hotter filled her, stretched her.

"That's it. Forget, Isobel." He drank in her gasps and sighs. "Feel. Feel me. Only me. Only us."

Mouth to mouth, they moved, hips rising and rolling. Sinuous. Lost, lost to feeling, lost to the potent climb of pleasure, the wild spin. Their moans twined, their bodies moved, and her hands slid over his back, gripped his hips, her thighs locking tighter. Urging for more. For all he had. For all she could take. And he answered, teeth, lips, and breath at war.

Gathering her hands, Hideo pinned them over her head and levered up, sliding deep and hard where she was overcome with the most exquisite agony. Pressure, so much delicious pressure. Rocking back, he dragged her against him, guiding her arms around his neck and her legs on either side of his hips as his mouth dipped, sucking hard and fast on her breast, tongue gliding over her nipple and his teeth. God, his teeth.

And she came! A hard peak followed by a quiver, a tremble, and a delicious glide. She floated back into her body with a silken sigh and opened dazed eyes to gaze into his smiling ones as he stroked harder, faster, and tumbled headlong into his own release.

* * *

Isobel returned to Priya's apartment as the rising sun hung low on the horizon, pushing pale tendrils of gold through the blue shroud of predawn. A delicate spiderweb of sunlight. She slumped against the wall with a sigh, toeing off her heels before climbing the polished wood stairs, leveled to perfection without a single creak or groan. Unlike at home, where every floorboard complained like an arthritic old woman.

Priya's dark head popped up as Isobel nudged open the door to her room, hair a messy tumble around her sleepy face. "Morning." She yawned into a stretch, T-shirt falling off one brown shoulder. "How was it?"

"Perfect." Too perfect. Until it wasn't.

She'd lain curled up against his warmth in the quiet dark, sleep calling with drugging allure, but Isobel couldn't succumb. After the third round she'd stopped counting, stopped caring, but once it was over, and the heat of passion had cooled, there was nothing to stop the strange sort of chill that crept into her. Slow at first, starting with her feet, but it rose, steady and incremental in its approach, up her calves, her thighs, spilling into her belly and rising farther still. Her doubts and demons, cutting their teeth into all the parts that ached so miserably, drawing fresh blood.

"I should go," she'd said, and gave in to the momentary temptation of brushing her fingers through his hair. Soft, wispy strands. So different and unfamiliar. Just like his body. Kyle, though fit, was lithe and slim, but Hideo was corded with muscle. Powerfully built. The contrasts clashed in her head. Battering against each other from opposing sides of the field.

He'd dragged her closer by the waist, his face nuzzling between her neck and shoulder. "And if I wanted you to stay?" he asked, voice husky with fatigue.

"I shouldn't."

His face lifted a notch and even in the dark she could see his eyes; the glimmering facets that had struck her speechless earlier that night still dazzled. He regarded her in careful, scrutinizing silence, as if seeing beyond her to the chasm of emotional turmoil she kept buried deep within before he leaned in with a slow, lingering press of lips that made her insides ache as much as it soothed.

"You can do whatever is in your heart to do, Isobel," he said gently. "Stay. Leave. You know where I fall on the subject."

Stay. Every part of her had screamed *stay*, but that was precisely why she had to go. *I'm not ready to feel something like this just yet. Not again.* Isobel drew in a breath. "I'm sorry."

The shadows that fell across his face had nothing to do with the dark as he nodded. "I understand." His voice kind, patient.

Isobel had dressed quickly without stopping to look back at him once, wondering what to say or do next, but fell short. What could you say when walking away from perfection? "Thank you," she offered weakly.

Hideo had rolled onto his back but otherwise hadn't made a move to rise and come to her though she'd sensed he grappled with the urge to do just that and more. "Take care of yourself, Isobel Morgan."

I could love someone like you. And it would be so easy. So beautiful, if she wasn't already damaged, broken, and still healing.

Great guy.

Horrible timing.

Crossing Priya's room, she sat down on the edge of the bed and hooked a leg underneath her. Shoulders heavy, a needling pain blistering behind her eyes. "He was sweet and seemed to know exactly what I needed. Tenderness. Patience. Very, *very* thorough. I couldn't have asked for a better lover. So why am I crying?"

Priya rested a hand over Isobel's, squeezing gently. "I think you didn't want to like it as much as you did, and that part of you hoped it would be terrible to justify that Kyle was the one."

God, she's right. Distant corners that she hadn't known were still intact suddenly broke anew and each jagged crack and fracture split through her in fresh waves of agony. Pain. So much pain, and God, she was so tired of hurting. *Does it ever stop?*

"I hate this. Why do I still love him?" Isobel swiped at her face, pressed the heels of her palms to her eyes to stem the flood. "I gave him everything. Everything he could want or need—I did it because I loved him. Completely. With every fiber of my being, I was his. So why wasn't it enough?"

Priya's expression eased with understanding. "It's never enough for the wrong guy. But one day, someone truly worthy will see you for the remarkable treasure that you are, and will protect your heart *fiercely*. I promise this will pass. It will get better."

God, she wanted to believe that. Needed to. But right now, the pain was too vivid, too searing, for her to see clearly beyond this blistering moment. Hand to her heart, Isobel massaged against the ache. "I dream of him sometimes." A whispered confession, so low she could scarcely hear herself. "And it's like it never happened or we've fixed it. We're together and happy. Then I wake up . . ." And for a moment suspended in that soft, cotton candy haze between awake and asleep it still felt real—before it wasn't. Then her heart broke all over again with the truth.

Every day. Every single day.

"Letting go feels like dying. I know that's melodramatic, but there's no other way to describe this agony." The passing of eternity within a moment where everything inside of her clawed back, fighting to breathe. To feel. To exist. Every desiccated organ. Every raw nerve. Every opened vein.

All of her—from breath to bone—fought to hold on to the remnants of what once made her feel so alive. So whole and vital. Fought to rebel against an unnatural force wrenching her into a darkness she didn't want to explore, but was thrust into all the same. And there she drowned. Over and over. Waging battle after battle because healing was pain, and it demanded to be confronted, endured before it could then be released. The problem was Isobel didn't know how much more she had left in her to keep fighting. *I'm doing the work. I'm fighting to let go.* To heal. So why wasn't it getting any easier? Why was she still drowning?

"You know what hurts most?" Isobel's features twisted against the pull of grief and fresh tears. "I don't have to just kill the love I have for him—this bright, abundant, and beautiful thing I've let grow inside me for all these years—I have to kill all the memories too. Every precious moment. Every treasured experience. I have to lose them *all*." Just like she had with her mother. Ripping them out like weeds to be burned and the ashes discarded to a strong wind. A process that had hollowed Isobel out as a child and had left her shockingly numb for what felt like an eternity, until the Sisterhood breathed life back into her soul.

Her hand closed around the pendant weighing over her heart. Losing someone you loved to disease or circumstance was brutal, but to lose someone you loved by choice? *Their* choice? It was a miracle she'd managed to pull all the pieces of her heart and soul together again. To do so a second time? Was it even possible?

"You don't have to lose the memories, Bel." Priya stroked her fingers over Isobel's cheeks, cleaning away tears, but more rolled down. Relentless. "You just can't live in them."

Supportive arms gathered Isobel close and held her as her tears turned to sobs and sobs became wet, heaving breaths. Priya held her until she was spent, and there, in pale gold light of dawn, they clung to one another in sleep. In dreams, where Isobel found nothing but shadows and ghosts of what might've been.

Chapter Twenty

Priya woke to a city on fire for Genie Carranza. Isobel's online post had reached near a million views in a matter of hours, and by morning it shot through the sound barrier of viral. It was more than Priya could've hoped for, and with Hadrian's private investigator digging into Peter Crowley, soon she'd bring the weight of this crashing down with the force of an atomic bomb.

Arriving at work with that single thought occupying her focus, Priya skidded to a halt barely in time to avoid a collision with a blond blur and the hot slosh of coffee that would've otherwise destroyed her ivory slacks and rose-dust blouse. Shaking dark beads of brew off her burning hand, she swallowed an equally scalding curse. "Watch it!"

"There you are." Heather seized Priya's bicep, holding tight with an elegant manicure that dug into her like talons latching onto their prey. "Keep up." Without another word, she blazed a scorching path to Marai's office.

Inside, Daniella paced by the wall of windows while Marai stood by her desk, arms crossed, as still as flawlessly honed marble.

"Thank you, Heather." Marai turned on strong legs and

lacquered heels, her pointed chin rising a degree higher. "Please leave us." Heather retreated without a word, and once back at her desk, she activated the frosted glass for added privacy. "Please take a seat, Priya."

Marai gestured to the chair facing her desk, and Priya's gaze landed on the collection of swords mounted on the wall behind it. Four of them, all forged in the mountains of Japan by the hands of her great-grandfather, a renowned master. Not a single one had a trace of dust, and each was probably sharp enough to cleave a body in two with a single stroke.

"I have a meeting that I'm already late for, so I will keep this brief." She dropped her arms but her posture was no less severe or intimidating. "Tell me why I woke up to media outlets salivating over headlines about a junior associate going up against a real estate giant?"

"Apparently, Genie was inspired to share her story with the public. If she elected to do so—without my knowledge or counsel—that's her prerogative."

"Are you seriously denying involvement in this fiasco?" Daniella demanded.

"I did not give any direct quotes nor was I formally interviewed regarding this case."

"And the fact that the person reporting it is a childhood friend of yours is what, exactly?"

It shouldn't have shocked her that Marai and her team had connected the dots so quickly, but Priya's masked it with a breezy shrug. "A happy coincidence."

"Bullshit!" Daniella bellowed. "I told you to settle this quickly and quietly. Instead, you turned it into a David versus Goliath circus to spite me!"

"Damn right I did." Priya hitched her chin up, unapologetic. "I didn't agree with you but you backed me into a corner because you only care about making the short list for name partner, so I did what was best for my client. But none of this would've happened in the first place if the associates hadn't been pit against each other like gladiators in the ring."

"Yes, I know all about your little quarrel with Michael Winship," Marai said with a dismissive flick of her fingers, "and the events that led to his departure from the firm."

Priya blinked, surprised at Marai's calm response. "How?"

"When you returned the equipment you *borrowed* to our IT department, the recording was cataloged and brought to my attention."

No, that wasn't possible. "I deleted the file." Andrew had confirmed it with a giddy high five when she'd returned the recorder to him the next morning.

"On the device, yes, but all recordings are automatically synced with our firm's servers and then reviewed by our team within seventy-two hours of entry."

Priya swallowed hard. "Well, since you know everything, then surely you can see I had no choice; Genie didn't deserve any of this."

"While I'm inclined to agree with you, as you chose not to come to us with that vital detail, and instead took matters in your own hands not once, but twice, this is the consequence for your hubris. My firm has a long-standing reputation for success that I will not see you further taint with your inexperience and arrogance, which is why you're going to pass this case over to Daniella."

"*What*? Why?"

"Because you baited a lion; now they're coming for our throats," Daniella answered. "You pushed out a story slandering them, now they're suing us to the sum of two *million* dollars."

"Perfect. It means they're afraid." Priya rose from her chair, inspired. "Don't you see? The entire city is talking, and more people are going to come forward. Slander? They'll be lucky if we don't hit them with a class action when this is over. I'm sorry I didn't discuss this with you first, but I knew you wouldn't believe that I'm well in control of this case, and Genie's defense strategy."

"You don't have a strategy! You have a prayer!"

"Better than not having a conscience," Priya retorted, and the muscles in Daniella's shoulders tensed like those of a lioness about to pounce, straining against the urge to vault over the desk and strangle Priya with her bare hands.

"Does your arrogance know no bounds?" Daniella snapped, a Brooklyn edge creeping into the vowels of her words and the sway of her head. "You're lucky I don't kick your skinny little all-knowing butt right now."

"Enough!" Priya and Daniella flinched at the whip-crack of Marai's tone. "This isn't up for further discussion. Thanks to your theatrics, time is a luxury we don't have. They're hauling us into court the day after tomorrow." Marai curled one hand into a fist and scored her thumb across her knuckles. "You're off the case. Daniella will take over and negotiate them down to a reasonable sum while getting your client to concede to vacating as quickly as possible. In the interim, I will also need to issue a statement of apology on behalf of the firm for the slander, and if we're lucky, that'll be the end of it."

Priya rocked back, horrified. "No. That's not acceptable. I

promised Genie I would fight for her home. I won't break my word."

Marai angled her head, her dark curtain of hair rippling like a wave threatening to crest into a tsunami. "I think you've forgotten your place, so let me remind you that *I* am the managing partner of this firm, and *you* are a junior associate who has severely overstepped."

"And thanks to you the senior partners are about to lose a lot of money." Daniella arched a brow, arms crossed with a dry smirk. "You can *definitely* kiss the mentorship good-bye."

"I don't care about the mentorship anymore," Priya snapped back. A shocking declaration that stunned everyone into silence, including herself, for a solid three seconds. "Did you even read the article? Listen to her story?"

Daniella and Marai exchanged glances. "It was a poignant piece," Marai answered. "But it doesn't change circumstances."

"I can't believe you. I've idolized you for fifteen years . . . you were everything I aspired to be." She swept a disgusted hand at Marai. "How can you be such a coward?"

Daniella's jaw unhinged and struck carpet. Despite the bright glare of morning sun pushing through the wall of windows, coldness seeped into the room as Marai's expression darkened like a wakening storm poised to break and swallow Priya whole.

"As Lakshmi Seth's daughter," Marai spoke soft as a whisper but each syllable resonated with absolute ferocity, "I thought I'd extend you the grace of a second chance to learn from your mistakes rather than snuff out a budding career. Mistakes happen, especially when you're too young and stupid to know better. True wisdom is gained from experience, but apparently you're determined to do this the hard way." She scored her tongue over her upper teeth and bounced a fist off her thigh.

"You're fired."

Chapter Twenty-One

Shame clung to Isobel like a greasy blanket, too thick and filmy to scrub away, though she ardently tried. Slipping out of bed she disappeared into the shower to weep. She'd been foolish to think eight years of feeling would evaporate in the span of a single night in the arms of a stranger. Stupidly naïve. And instead, what was meant to have liberated her had plucked up painful emotions, like errant fingers picking at a healing scab, but she couldn't stop herself. Or the bleeding that followed.

Call him, her heart wheezed with the desperation of the dying. *No*, her head pushed back—though the tone had lost its warrior edge and become almost a pitiful whisper.

Isobel's fingers fluttered to her neck, to the delicate gold chain and the simple little pendant that dangled there. Old and cherished. Memories, so many memories connected them, each a delicate thread, but infinitely looped until they were strong as steel. She was so entwined with Kyle, how could she ever hope to successfully separate herself without losing all that she was in the process?

"Enough," Isobel whispered to herself. Last night had been amazing. Hideo was amazing, and Isobel refused to let anything taint the memory of that experience or make her feel guilty for something she deserved. It was wonderful. Powerful. And even though the urge to fall back into the familiar was strong, Isobel was determined to be stronger.

"Am I late?" she asked when she arrived to find Nneka waiting for her in the lobby, pacing beneath a glowing neon sign: THE FUTURE IS FEMALE.

"No, you're right on time. The team's all assembled—you'll get a proper tour after. Promise." Swooping in, she hooked an arm through Isobel's and led her into the back end of the newsroom studio, where the team was already gathered and waiting.

As soon as they strolled inside, the clamor of voices dropped away, like gossiping students the second the teacher returned to the classroom. Papers were scattered around the length of the oval surface, along with various bottles of water and half-finished cups of coffee dotted in between and an open box of gourmet donuts that were almost too pretty to eat.

"Hello, boys and girls." Nneka claimed the available seat at the end of the table, off to the left. "This is Isobel Morgan, for those of you who have been living under a rock."

Laughter circled the table, and Isobel's cheeks flamed with nerves as she took the only free seat left open, at Nneka's side.

"You'll have plenty of time to get better acquainted as we'll be working rather closely should the *Passivist Activist* program take off, as I expect it to, so let's do a round of quick and dirty introductions, starting from the left."

Isobel's gaze slid around the table as Nneka fired off each name. Eight in total, a mix of young and old, men and women, all watching her with varying degrees of interest.

"Now that we have the particulars behind us, let's dive

in, shall we?" Nneka set her elbows on the table and leaned in. "I think it's safe to say we've had a productive morning with overwhelming response to Isobel's inaugural story, GenieFromTheBlock."

"It was such a great piece!" Stacy Wu chimed in. Large, hopeful brown eyes shone beneath the blunt edge of the bangs of a rounded bob. "The coverage has been major!"

"Right?" Ingrid Reid tossed her goddess locks, the ends faded to a pale gold that matched the arresting hue of her eyes. Though she was white passing, like Isobel, she'd embraced her roots unapologetically, balancing corporate without compromising her Blackness. "We've received coverage from all major media platforms and networks—with dozens of celebrity boosts, including JLo, herself. The response has been huge, and it's not slowing down."

Applause echoed around the table, and Isobel's flush deepened.

"Do we have a preliminary on numbers?" Nneka looked at Alejandra Villarreal, an amazon with waist-length red hair and a body that must've demanded an eternity in the gym.

Alejandra swiped across the screen of her iPad and sent the stats to the large flat screen facing the table, all splayed out in eye-popping charts and graphs. "As you can see, numbers are soaring beyond what I had expected to see so far."

Beneath the table, Isobel tried to resist the urge to cross and recross her legs as Alejandra played clips she'd found on YouTube and hoped no one could see that she was really a nervous wreck wrapped in the guise of poised confidence.

"That's what I like to hear. All in all"—Nneka set a hand on Isobel's thigh, stilling the restless bounce—"I think you can agree that *Passivist Activist* has debuted to a roaring success."

"Here, here." William Cruz, an older Filipino gentleman, raised his hands in delicate applause. Florescent light gleamed off the smooth dome of his shaved head and the polished citrine that clung to his left pinkie. "Nneka told us you were going to be the voice of a generation, and you delivered. Bravo," he said with such a degree of sincerity Isobel felt the flash of heat in her cheeks and knew she was about as red as Nneka's cherry-colored tailored slacks.

"It's given us the foothold we needed, now we need to find the right story to build off that momentum." Nneka spread her hands, red nails flashing. "Any ideas?"

"I've actually got something that's going to blow everyone out of their seats." Ingrid reached across the table to take the iPad from Alejandra. "Out in Miami there's a story that's really racking up interest about a young woman who caught her boyfriend cheating. After kicking him out, she took the various text messages that she'd uncovered on his phone and transformed them into revenge art. But it's not vicious or dragging. The piece is meant to convey strength, survival, and growth."

"Ooooh," Stacy cooed, pushing her glasses up her nose. "I heard about this! Hashtag don't get mad, get inspired. Turning Pain(t) into power, yes?"

"Yes! The videos she's posted are skyrocketing. Here, take a look."

The screen changed to play a collection of clipped videos spliced with music showing a young woman's artistic journey of rendering her pain into a large-scale piece of art.

A woman's face emerged from almost a frenetic array

of color and texture. Surrounding it, she'd written a bold message that wrapped around the exterior of the canvas—but the true impact came when she flashed UV light across the surface, illuminating all his torrid messages in glowing ink. The truth buried among the lies. It was evocative. Confrontational. And heartbreaking.

> Queen, the surface message read, *battles have been fought, and wars have been won.*
> *Honor the warrior you have become.*

The piece was abstract and confrontational; Isobel's heart ached with joy as well as empathy as she watched the artist's process of discovery and healing.

"The project isn't complete but the concept is breathtaking. She's posting short videos as she creates, spilling the tea along the way. I reached out to her by DM and told her about the *Passivist Activist* initiative," Ingrid continued. "Naturally, she'd heard of Isobel and the whole viral cheating thing—which I think connects beautifully—and she's superstoked to meet with her."

"Amazing. Isobel." Nneka looked at her. "What do you think?"

"I love it," Isobel agreed. "She's done something remarkable. Admirable, even. We often hear stories about the jilted ex slashing tires, destroying property . . . going for blood. But what she's created is evocative. She's reclaimed her power and worth by creating something to inspire strength and remind her of what not to tolerate ever again." Isobel's eyes returned to that painting, to the surface message written with a defiant strength she admired and envied. "It's stunning."

"Excellent. That's what I like to hear. When does she think she'll have it complete?"

"She's having a gallery showing two weeks from now."

"Based on that timeline, that pushes us out a bit more than I'd like, but I do think this is a solid follow-up from Genie, and the segue into your own story gives us a strong foothold. Stacy, why don't you pull flights and hotels for Isobel and see what's available in the next two weeks. I want Isobel there for the final reveal."

"I—*Miami*?" Isobel blinked, stunned. "Can't I interview her remotely over Zoom or something?"

"Nah," Ingrid interjected. "I think this is one we need to allocate our travel budget to, for sure. The visuals alone will be worth it."

"I'm inclined to agree." Nneka nodded. "After that, I want us back in studio for Monday to reconnect with Genie for our round-table chat. She's such a bold character and will make for fabulous airtime. After that we can sit down with the network producers and—"

"Can we push that a week or two?" Isobel interrupted. "I'll be in Greece."

"Oh! Right, your girls' trip!" Nneka smacked a palm to her brow. "Totally blanked on your email. Of course. Okay, send your travel dates to Stacy and she can work the schedule around it, give you a day or two to catch your breath."

"Noted!" Stacy commented, scribbling on her pad.

"We also need to schedule time for a sit-down with producers and start filming. I think we'll need to get at least four segments lined up ahead of our live-to-air round-table talks. I'm thinking Monday to Wednesday each week for filming and Thursdays for team meetings."

"This sounds like a lot . . ." More than they'd discussed when Nneka had shown up at her home dangling her dreams like a golden carrot. Far more.

"It's just for the interim until we secure our foothold with the network and audience. It'll taper down after the first quarter, I promise."

"Sure. Okay. I think I can manage." *Somehow.*

"Can you imagine the impact of getting them both together?" Alejandra planted her hands on the table with an excited gasp. "What if we have Isobel not only as the interviewer but the subject of her next *Paint Into Power* piece? Imagine what she could create from Isobel's story!"

"That's actually brilliant!" Nneka pointed at Alejandra. "Love the ingenuity there."

"Oh, I . . . I don't know." Swallowing her nerves, Isobel dug down for her voice, for her confidence. "I told you I didn't want to talk about Kyle."

Nneka angled herself so she was facing Isobel directly, manicured nails bouncing atop her notes. "Part of what made Genie's story so impactful was the connection you drew to your own experience. To your father. You gave it heart and we'll need more of that if *Passivist Activist* is going to take off. This is your project now. Your face. Your voice. Your brand." Her lips curved in a sympathetic pull to the left. "Think about it, all right? Ultimately, it's your call."

Isobel dropped her chin. God, she could only imagine what they were all thinking. Who was this idiot girl to complain when she'd been handed a job any one of them would have yanked out their front teeth to have? "Okay. I'll consider it."

"Excellent." Nneka clapped her hands. "Now that we have something to chew on, let's get this ball rolling. Stacy, I want those travel itineraries for approval within an hour. Nico, reach out to our new subject and let her know we're going ahead with the interview. Well done, Isobel." Nneka gripped her arm, gave it a firm squeeze. "This is just the beginning."

By the time the meeting ended, Isobel was buzzing. Energy crackled through her veins, firing across every nerve until she was humming with so much joy that she could've grand jeté'd across New York to Toronto.

At the airport waiting for her flight, Isobel dug out her phone to FaceTime her dad. He answered on the second ring, face filling the screen.

"Hello, love, you look to be in a fine mood." In the last couple of weeks he'd started putting on weight—the right kind of weight—and it warmed her heart to see his cheeks glowing with restored health.

"Oh, I am." Isobel sang as she parked her suitcase by the row of seating outside her gate. "Have you seen the news? My story is getting so much coverage, and the team has so many amazing ideas. So many directions we're going to go."

"Wonderful, love." He eyed her over the edge of wire frames balanced on the wide tip of his nose, head haloed by an array of pillows. "Didn't doubt you for a moment."

"It's going to mean a bit more travel." Isobel flexed her fingers and shook out her anxious hand. "They want me in Miami this weekend, then back to New York to film." Bringing her down to the wire for the Sisterhood trip to Mykonos. "I called the clinic, but they didn't have anyone available to send out before Sunday, which means you'll be alone with Shayne while I'm gone."

"I think we can manage for two bleeding days."

"Where is Shayne?"

"At the gym, I expect."

"And Luz?"

"Left about an hour ago."

Isobel worried her bottom lip between her teeth. "Are you sure everything was fine while I was gone?"

"Yes, love." Declan rolled his eyes with a dramatic grumble. "Stop worrying your pretty little head."

"Don't I always?" But his response made her smile all the same. She wasn't going to have a spare moment to breathe—and she honestly couldn't wait. If she could get a part-time nurse to stop by a couple of hours a day for three days a week, it wasn't an ideal solution, but it certainly wasn't terrible either. Her father would have more independence, and Isobel would have more freedom to stretch her wings.

God, she hadn't realized how much she'd missed this until taking this first meaty bite of freedom here in New York, now the juices were rolling down her chin, and she was salivating for so much more.

"All right, Daddy, looks like they're calling passengers to board. I'll see you soon." Blowing him a kiss, she hung up and gathered her suitcase with one hand, phone still gripped in the other as she rushed to near the front of the line.

"Boarding pass and passport, please."

As she handed over both to the flight attendant, Isobel's phone vibrated incessantly in her hand with incoming messages. A quick glance down at the screen made her heart seize before rupturing inside her chest, obliterating in all thought and reason in a single, whooshing breath. She didn't know *how* to think. React. Move. Breathe.

Tinkerbell . . .

We really have to talk.

I need you.

Chapter Twenty-Two

I don't care about the mentorship.

I don't care about the mentorship?

What on earth had possessed her to think something so categorically stupid, let alone say it aloud to Marai Nagao's face?

Shell-shocked, it took every ounce of strength Priya had left in her to walk back to the bullpen, eyes raised and stride steady, but she could feel everyone's gaze on her. Impossible. No one could know, but the sting of it seemed to vibrate in the air like a rogue electrical current that burned her exposed nerves.

Her last few steps were uneven as she fumbled for her satchel, her phone, and coat. Priya wasn't allowed to pack her desk—she'd been advised that everything would be collected and shipped to her home. Not that there was much to worry about. She hadn't been there long enough to garner a collection of framed pictures or personal trinkets. Just the photo of her and her sisters from when they had sworn their vows of sisterhood in her mom's closet.

Camera perched on a shelf, Shayne had set the timer before racing to join the group, and had collided bodily with Eshe, tumbling them into a heaping pile of laughter, limbs, and flying slices of pizza. A chaotic, blurred mess that carried so much love and joy. Priya had made a copy for each of them and carried it wherever she went. Her talisman for luck. Tears stung her throat like she'd swallowed a horde of wasps.

Not here.

Not here.

Not here.

Tucking the picture into her pocket, she made a quick exit for the elevator bank, and finally exhaled, knees shaking and fingers clenched so tight around her arms they'd started to go numb. Everything felt tight and hot and confined. She wanted to pull the pins out of her hair and let it tumble free, to pop open the buttons on her blouse, and heave a chair out the nearest window so she could gulp in air. Or throw herself out of it.

"Damn, tiger. It's barely nine in the morning. Where's the fire?"

"Leave me alone, Hadrian. I can't do sassy with you right now."

"Sorry, I was only pulling your leg. You all right?"

No. No, I'm not all right. I'm drowning and now I've tied a thousand-pound anchor around my ankles. I don't know what to do. I'm lost.

"Hey!" His arm slipped around her waist when her knees buckled, holding her steady. "Tiger, what the hell?"

Priya wanted to shove him away but she was limp. Boneless. "It's over. It's all over. I don't know how I'm going to tell Genie."

"You're not making any sense."

"I was fired."

"Tiger . . ." His face softened but his arms remained strong. "What can I do?"

"Nothing. It's okay." She gave him a tight smile. "I'll be okay." An obvious, useless lie, and not one that he believed for a moment if the tightening of his jaw was any indication, but she had to believe it, that there was light at the end of this impossibly dark tunnel, because the alternative was crippling, soul crushing failure that would render her entire life obsolete.

All the years of work, dedication, and planning wasted . . . gone. Priya shoved the darkness and bile down, stuffing it into a box, and yanked on an ill-fitting lid. It didn't need to hold for long, just long enough for her to get the hell out of there in one piece.

Extracting herself from his grasp, she thrust out a hand between them. "Congratulations, Hadrian."

His eyes dropped to her hand but he refused to take it. "We can still fix this, tiger."

"No." She forced a smile. "We can't."

The elevator arrived with a cheerful *ping* and she rushed onto it, punching the button for the ground floor, unable to look at him as the doors whispered shut. Every step from the office was a blur. Nothing could penetrate the fog in her mind until she was safe at home.

Hands shaking, heart racing, Priya shut herself inside her bathroom and let the mask drop. The surprising ache of tears blistered and stung as they burst from her in a relentless, gushing flood she couldn't control, only purge, until her arms shook and her legs buckled.

She shuffled on weak knees to the sink and braced herself against the marble countertop, gazing at her splotched, tear-soaked reflection. Thankfully, she'd had the foresight to wear waterproof mascara. She could deal with blotchy cheeks and a red nose but raccoon eyes? Hell no. Turning on the water, she dipped her hands into the cold stream and pressed wet hands to her warm face.

"Priya?" A knock brushed from the other side of the bathroom door. "Is that you, darling?"

"Mom?" Confused, Priya turned from the mirror, swiped hastily at her cheeks. "What are you doing home?"

Her mother breezed into the bathroom, dark hair sleek and brown skin glowing. Glorious and radiant. "I flew in for a meeting with my agent and screenwriter regarding the adaptation of my recent collection of essays. I suppose I could've conference called but I wanted an excuse to surprise my darling girl." Dark brows arched over liquid amber eyes. "But shouldn't you be at the office?"

Priya burst into fresh sobs and ran into her mother's arms. "I screwed up. I screwed up so big."

"Oh sweetheart. Listen, why don't you take a nice hot bath and have a good cry while you're at it? I'll order us some food, open some wine to breathe, and when you're ready you can tell me all about it, okay?"

"It's morning."

"This is an emergency." She cupped Priya's face. "And emergencies demand wine, regardless of the hour."

Priya nodded around a wet sniffle. "Okay. Okay."

Kissing her brow, Lakshmi released Priya. "Go on, I'll set this up for you."

Priya lumbered into her bedroom, stripping out of her work clothes with lethargic movements and more tears, and by the time she returned to the bathroom in a robe, she found her mother sitting on the edge of the freestanding tub, testing the warm, bubbling water.

Candles were lit, and she'd set out a stack of fluffy towels from the built-in linen closet, as well as a tray of luxurious soaps and lotions.

"There. All ready for you." Drying off her hands, she rose to hug Priya again with affirming strength. Warm as the cozy flame of the candles, and much like wax, Priya felt her broken pieces slowly melding back together into a single goopy mess. "Soak as long as you need to, then come find me in the living room."

Removing the robe, Priya slipped into the steaming warmth and reclined against the porcelain, tucked beneath a blanket of bubbles thick and soft against her skin. It might as well have been ice on a lake—nothing penetrated the numbness that cloaked her body like a shroud.

This is what Isobel must've felt like, she realized. The shock of a broken heart, and broken dreams, was staggering, and for the first time in her life, Priya didn't know what to do about it. She'd never failed at anything. Once she set her mind to a task, she saw it all the way through and conquered.

Wonder Woman.

Queen.

She'd worn those monikers with pride, but now her crown had fallen, and her armor had been stripped away, leaving a terrified little girl huddled in a corner wondering where she belonged in the world. Accomplishment gave her purpose, and she derived her identity from conquest. But that was the thing about winning—you had to keep winning.

The mentorship was gone and no reputable law firm would dare hire her after a debacle like this. Barely twenty-five and she was going to have to start all over.

Priya refilled the bath twice and sat until the water was tepid and her fingers pruny before climbing out to dry off, forsaking the lotions. Sweet flowery scents were too happy. Even the plush towels grated on her skin like sandpaper. Once in the living room, dressed in a pair of old fluffy pajamas, Priya sank into the couch with a sigh.

"Well, that was quite the soak." Lakshmi dog-eared the page of her book before putting it down between them. She'd showered from her flight and changed into slim black leggings and a matching shirt that fell elegantly off one shoulder. Her curtain of raven hair hung loose in a long, pin-straight, glossy curtain. Her mother had a way of making all black appear regal rather than cold. "It's been four hours."

"Didn't feel that long."

"Grief has a way of manipulating time." Reaching for the decanted wine on the coffee table, her mother poured out two glasses and handed one to Priya. "This is one of the best Pinots from Hernan's latest harvest. Have a sip. It's glorious, you'll see."

It tasted like battery acid, tainted by despair and failure. "It's great."

Pleased, Lakshmi settled into the cushions of the sectional and the mountain of throw pillows scattered across it, bare feet tucked under her. "Now, let's start with the news, as I suspect that has some bearing on why you are a miserable mope."

Her mother listened as Priya worked through every detail, never once interrupting. Exhausted by the end of it, Priya swiped at her nose, frowning at her still untouched glass while her mother topped up her second.

"So, you asked Isobel for help to force the firm's hand. And it backfired."

"Big time." Priya sniffled. "But what other choice did I have?"

"You could've talked to Marai directly, or even Daniella, beforehand."

"They'd have never listened to me."

Lakshmi pursed her lips, the length of her aquiline nose wrinkling in thought. "Perhaps not. Or perhaps yes, if you'd come back to the table with further evidence to support you."

"Mom, please. I really don't need this right now."

"Oh, I'm sorry, I didn't realize you were only looking for sympathy, not sincerity."

"Okay. You're right. Is that what you want to hear?"

"Priya, I'm not trying to make you feel bad."

"Well, you are." Tears welled. "I know I screwed up. I know. Michael got under my skin, and I let him throw me off balance."

"I'm glad you see that now." Lakshmi stared down at her wine, sighed. "Does it truly bother you that much? My decision?"

"I made peace with it a long time ago, at least I thought I did." Priya worked her bottom lip between her teeth. "But he used it to make me feel small. Insubstantial. Like I wasn't a real person because I wasn't made from love. I was manufactured."

"Priya. . ." Lakshmi took away Priya's untouched glass of wine then gathered both of her hands. "You were absolutely a product of love. *My* love. My desire to be a mother, knowing that I didn't want to risk losing that dream waiting for some guy to show up, or rushing in with the wrong one just because of a ticking clock. You are the greatest wish I've ever had for myself come true. It hurts to know you feel that way about yourself. But I suppose that's my fault."

"Mom! No . . ."

Lakshmi silenced her with a gentle lift of her hand. "I was blessed to know my heritage. My roots and who I came from, but with you I decided to be more flexible and allow you to create your own identity. I thought that was the best approach, but perhaps I was wrong." Straightening in her seat, she assessed Priya carefully. Decidedly. "Your biological father was little more than a collection of medical history, a heavily redacted résumé, and regrettably British." Lakshmi snorted. "A detail I made certain never to share with my father. But he also included a breathtaking personal letter that made me cry, and if the sexual orientation had been listed as hetero, I would've hunted him down and proposed on the spot. That letter showed me he had a beautiful soul, and while he knew he didn't want children of his own, he recognized perhaps there was a couple who would need help. Or a single mom, like me, who may want a family without the burden of a man or marriage. I knew this was someone I could create an even more beautiful child with, and the instant you were born, I knew I was right. You are everything I hoped and dreamed for. You are my miracle. As for that obsequious little turd . . ." Her eyes flared with the wrath of a mother scorned. "What he did was cruel and unfair, but you gave away your power by letting his opinion of you matter more than your own."

"I know." Michael may have complicated things but in the end, Priya had stupidly bit off more than she could chew and had choked. The worst part was knowing that not only had she broken her promise to Genie, but she'd dragged Isobel into the fray. Because if Triton was suing the firm, it stood to good reason Isobel was next in their line of fire. Unable to meet her mother's gaze, Priya's eyes dropped to her lap. "I've made such a mess. I don't know what to do, Mom."

Why was that so hard to admit? So terrifying?

Because I'm Priyanka Victory Seth. I always know what to do. Everyone turned to her for answers, for inspiration, for motivation. She was the girl who had it all together, and now in less than two months, she'd fallen so epically flat on her face it was a wonder she hadn't broken all her teeth on impact.

"If you made a mess, Priya, then you fix it by cleaning it up. My father, rest his soul, gave me exceptional advice while teaching me how to drive. He said: 'Whenever behind the wheel, behave as if everyone around you is an absolute moron, because they are, and you will be prepared for anything thrown your way.' He may have been talking about idiots on the road, but it's equally applicable to all facets of life too. We can't control what is thrown at us—only how we react to it. That's all you were trying to do. Be prepared for everything."

"I wish I'd had a chance to know him better."

"So do I, sweetheart, but for the short time he was on this earth, I'd never seen him happier than when he held you in his arms the moment you were born. You have his smile, you know. And his stubbornness. If he were here now, he'd tell you that life demands more than just book smarts, Priyanka. It demands patience, resilience, perseverance, awareness, and above all a thick skin that can only be gained from experience in moments like this." Leaning in, she kissed Priya's cheek. Her lips were warm, soft, and firm. "Adversity breeds strength. I know it feels impossible now, but you'll get through it. And be better for it."

"Maybe if I was you."

A shocked laugh teased the back of her mother's throat. "Why would you say that?"

"Because you've never failed at anything. You're just . . ." Priya waved a hand at her mother with a disgusted grunt. "Annoyingly perfect."

Now her mother did laugh, and tossed her head back as a rich, full-bodied wave of it burst out of her, so hard and loud it was almost *ugly*. And Lakshmi was never, a single day in her life, anything less than spectacular.

"Oh." She dabbed at the corner of her eyes, capturing tears with one hand, the other pressed to the plane of her belly. "Oh, that's rich. Oh my, I can't remember when I last laughed that hard. I think I have abs."

"I wasn't trying to be funny."

"Well, then you're a natural comedian. Priya?" She shook a bemused head, eyes sparkling like a thousand stars. "I have failed more times in life than there are grains of sand on a beach in Dubai, and that's perfectly normal. In fact, it's the only way to truly succeed. You fail, and then you fail again, and again, and again, and each time you learn a bit more. About life. About yourself. About what it is you truly want. All of it. It's necessary. It's unavoidable. Sweetheart? Did you truly think you'd be the first person in history to never hit rock bottom?"

Priya squirmed among the cushions. "It's just . . . people call me Wonder Woman. They say I'm confident and beautiful and capable and smart, but truth is I've just been faking it when you really *are* all those things. You make it look so easy. So effortless. I've frantically tried to keep up with following in your footsteps but I'm stumbling all the way. And when I fall, I get up quick so no one sees, but now my knees are skinned and my hands are raw. There's no hiding the truth—I'm a fraud. A cheap imitation of you."

"You are not faking anything. You *are* accomplished and motivated and certainly beautiful." Lakshmi tossed her length of silken black hair with a siren's smile. "But you should never ever aspire to be me any more than it is possible for me to be you. My parents didn't always agree with my decisions—my father most especially—but they respected them. I was raised to follow my truth, which is all I've wanted for you. To live your truth, Priya. You are exactly who you are meant to be, and I couldn't be prouder of the woman you are becoming."

A knock interrupted the moment, and Lakshmi popped up from the couch. "That must be the Uber Eats delivery." Rushing from the living room, she returned a few minutes later, but it wasn't with takeout.

Hadrian walked in behind her, devastatingly handsome as ever with disheveled curls. Priya, on the other hand, hair in a wet topknot and decade-old fuzzy pajamas, was a tragic mess, and would've given her eyeteeth to sink into the cushions and disappear.

"Well, now, there she is." Lakshmi winked at Priya. "I'll leave you two to talk."

Cheeks flaming, Priya rose from the couch. "What are you doing here?"

Breathless and a little sweaty, he waved a USB key. "You're going to want to see this."

Priya's eyes rolled into the back of her skull. "Go back to work, okay. I'm exhausted. It's over." Weaving past him to get to the kitchen, she made it all of three steps before he caught her by the arm.

"Seriously, Priya." Hadrian dropped the USB key into her hand. "Just do it."

She blinked up at him, a little startled. She'd never seen him so serious, and until this moment he'd never used her name before. Hearing it made her pause long enough to concede. Exhaling with a huff, wisps of stray hair fluttering from the gush of breath, Priya hunted for her laptop to plug it in and download the file. Opening it, after a stunned thirty second pause, she screamed.

"How!" Priya shook her laptop like a snow globe. "How did you get this?"

Hadrian bit down on his proud grin. "I got in touch with the investigator who used to work with my dad, like you asked." His shoulders bunched up in a slight shrug. "And that's what he dug up."

"Oh my God." In all the chaos, she'd completely forgotten.

"Now you can take this to Marai and get your job back."

This would do more than just get her rehired . . . this was a fully loaded AK-47 that would blow Crowley, and the other associates at MNS, out of the water. "I don't understand. You won, Hadrian. You *won*."

"To hell with that. We're allies, remember? And the way I see it, as the son of the founding partner and you, the daughter of a veritable genius, if we can't convince Marai Nagao to see the profound advantage of mentoring two accomplished and capable associates, then neither of us truly deserves to win."

Hadrian slipped his hands into his pockets and jerked a shoulder. "We make a pretty solid team. I don't see why that has to change."

Priya swallowed thickly, her blood humming with adrenaline and too much feeling.

Pleased he'd rendered her speechless, Hadrian winked. "Now go get 'em, tiger."

✶ ✶ ✶

It took thirty minutes for Priya to get ready and a covert phone call to Lorraine to track down her quarry. She jumped out of her Uber just as Marai Nagao exited the lobby of MNS and headed her off at the base of the stairs. Marai took one look at Priya and, without a word or a whisper in her direction, kept walking.

Sighing, Priya trotted after her. "Please, I just need a moment of your time."

"I don't have a moment. I have a client meeting I'm late for. Go home, Priyanka."

"Then give me ten seconds." Cutting her off, Priya splayed her arms. "I made a mess of things, I get that, but I found a way to salvage this. We can beat Crowley. We can win."

Marai lifted her chin and sighed, a combination that either meant Priya had secured her full attention or was a breath away from getting laid out cold. "How?"

Reaching into her satchel, Priya held out a file of documents and images she'd printed out while dressing, and waited with anxious anticipation as Marai carefully, and with slow precision, turned the pages.

About a third of the way through, Maria snapped it shut. "All of this is inadmissible. We can't use this in court."

"Not in court." Priya's eyes gleamed. "But we can with his *wife.*"

Marai worked her tongue across the edge of her teeth before she pulled out her phone. "Heather, I need you to call Patrick's office and extend my deepest apologies. Something has come up. Reschedule for whenever is convenient on his end. And Heather,"—her eyes locked on Priya—"get me the number for Sheila Marrone."

Chapter Twenty-Three

Three hours later, Priya and Marai walked into the offices at Triton, where Crowley's assistant waited for them at the reception foyer.

"Everyone is gathered in the conference room. If you'll follow me."

Marai inclined her head. "Lead the way."

As they wove down the corridor, Priya could see into the room where Crowley waited along with his team of attorneys she didn't recognize, and Emanuele.

Marai breezed into the conference room with as much poise and confidence as an empress ascending her throne. "Emanuele. Thank you for agreeing to see us on such short notice."

"It's been a long time since we faced off against one another."

"Indeed." She stopped by the table and gazed along the line of faces. "I wasn't expecting such a gathering."

"It's not every day one gets to witness the infamous Marai Nagao falling on her sword."

To Priya's surprise, Marai's cool facade didn't waver as she dragged out a chair and sat down. "I hate to disappoint, but I believe my young associate promised an evisceration. I've merely come for the show."

"Then I guess we should get down to it." Amused, Emanuele set his clasped hands atop the glossy table. "What's your offer?"

"Here it is." Still standing, Priya whipped out a sheet of paper and set it down before him. "The same offer you so graciously gave me at our first meeting. The chance to walk away clean with your tail tucked between your legs. Now I'm returning the favor."

Emanuele laughed. "That's adorable. Very well. Since you want to play games—instead of suing you for two million, now it's five, and if you persist in taking us to trial, I'll bump it up to seven and bury you in paperwork for the next ten years, after which your client will likely be dead, and so will your firm."

"Miss Seth may be a bit green around the gills." Marai crossed a leg. "But I'm far from a novice no-name solo practitioner operating out of a mall kiosk. I'm the head of a global firm with four international offices and eight hundred of the best goddamn attorneys under my belt, and believe me when I say I'll devote every single one of them to shredding you to the bone for as long as it takes."

"Oh please." Emanuele swatted her volley with a backhanded wave. "My firm is twice your size. You're outgunned and we have all the leverage."

"If this were yesterday," Priya interjected, "that might've been true, but since then, new information has come to light."

"And what's that?"

"This." Enjoying herself far too much, Priya slapped down the folder and pushed it across the table. "We've got at least twenty pages of correspondence between Peter Crowley and an ex-cop he hired to intimidate former tenants not only at West 109th, but also Danbury Hills, Spanish Villas, and

Pembrooke Estates, to name a few. This man was empowered to use any means necessary to empty out units for development so they could be flipped at a higher profit margin. We also have surveillance footage from a stoplight camera across the street of the same man leaving Genie Carranza's unit moments before it flooded."

"Illegally obtained, no doubt." Emanuele arched a glare, but it had lost its lethal edge. The blade of his confidence was beginning to dull.

"Much like your client's love nest on Fifth," Marai chimed in. "The one he bankrolled three years ago for his mistress under his deceased mother's name." Her head tilted. "And if you keep going, you'll get to the pictures we have of them together in the Maldives from last November when Peter was supposed to be on a business trip."

Crowley hooked a finger into the collar of his shirt, dragged it across. "You think you can embarrass me into settling?"

"I know I can." Priya smiled. "And while we could drag this through court, effectively killing your company's share price, an extended trial doesn't serve the best interests of our client. So, here's what we propose. Transfer ownership of the brownstone into Genie Carranza's name, along with payment for renovation and repairs, all wrapped up with a nice punitive sum for pain and suffering."

Crowley sputtered but Emanuele stilled his tirade with a single raised finger. "How much are we talking?"

"Oh." Priya dragged in a long breath through her nose. "Something with quite a few zeros affixed to the end."

"This is extortion. I'm not paying that woman shit."

"Yes, you are. You see, before coming here tonight, I paid

a visit to your wife and to describe her as irate about the revelation of your indiscretions is an understatement." Marai leaned on the table and rolled her shoulders. "In the interests of protecting her company, if you agree to the terms of our settlement offer then you will be allowed a graceful and quiet resignation, but if you don't, then she will take the damning information that I brought to her this evening to your board of directors, who will vote you out of the company, leaving you to face the wolves alone." Marai cast him a predatory grin. "And by wolves, I mean *me*."

"Emanuele—"

"Represents Triton Property Management." Priya interrupted. "And as a former employee, you would no longer fall under his protection."

Crowley's cheeks paled with shock. "My wife would never agree to that."

"You told me yourself, she's a jealous woman." Priya crossed her arms. "But I can call her to join this discussion, if you'd prefer."

"You conniving little—"

Emanuele pressed a hand to Crowley's forearm. "Stop talking, Peter."

"I'd listen to your counsel while you still have one," Marai said with a cautionary lift of her finger. "My firm will also be representing Sheila in your divorce, so rather than go to war, let's put this matter to bed, which should be easy for your client." She inclined her head at Emanuele. "He seems to like it there."

* * *

Marai stopped next to her chauffeured town car, a glossy black sedan. Her dark eyes narrowed with approval. "You did good."

"Thank you. I'm just relieved we were able to get Genie what she deserved."

"Hm." Marai nodded, lips pursed, before turning to open her door. "Do you require a ride home?"

"No. I think I'll walk a bit." Not when she was so ready to explode with excitement. She was a bomb set to go off.

"Hm." Marai slid one leg into the sedan. "Priya." She paused, casting a sincere smile over her shoulder. "I expect to see you at your desk tomorrow." Then vanished the rest of the way, disappearing inside the car.

Only once she was far enough down the street, did Priya launch into squealing fist punching glee, whooping loud enough to make a few evening pedestrians stop and stare. Hands shaking, eyes blurred with tears, Priya wrestled her phone from her purse and, to her shock, it wasn't her sisters she called. Or her mother.

But Hadrian.

"Hey." He answered after the first ring, sounding surprised, but pleasantly so. "How'd it go?"

A laugh burst out of her that wavered in a single bright, weepy note. "We did it." Priya pressed her hand to her mouth and smiled. "We *slayed*." Faced tipped back, she smoothed her hand over hair. "You should've seen it. Crowley rolled into the meeting with three lawyers, including Emanuele."

"The others were clearly for show."

"Totally. But Crowley collapsed like a Styrofoam cup beneath a boulder in less than twenty minutes." She'd never forget the expression on his face when he had. Or how Marai had stood with her, shoulder to shoulder. They'd been a team. A unit. "Not only will Genie become the new owner of her brownstone, we've secured an additional five hundred thousand in punitive damages." And tomorrow it would be full steam ahead to get everything drafted and finalized before end of day when she would get to tell Genie the amazing news and present her with the check, as well as the ownership papers.

"It's crazy. It's so crazy, I can still hardly breathe. It's like . . . everything before this moment—it was important and meaningful, but different. As a student, I felt like there was always this barrier between me and the cases. A force field. Everything was happening but nothing really touched me, you know?" She was babbling like a moron but Priya didn't care.

"It was safe. There was always an opportunity to start over, to reset the tally, but every move we make from this point onward is carved in stone and will follow us everywhere."

"Exactly." Priya smiled as she dabbed at her cheeks and under her eyes with the pads of her fingers, clearing away fresh tears. "I didn't think I'd feel like this. So emotional." Maybe because this had moved so quickly, and what should've taken months had blitzed to the finish line in weeks.

"And what about you?"

Of course he'd ask. "I'm officially rehired."

"Then congratulations are definitely in order." He laughed, too, a gentle sound that made her shiver. "I can get us a table at Pura Vida. Meet you there in thirty?"

Priya's stomach rumbled at the mention of food, and more so at the thought of spending time with him. "I don't think I'm fit to be seen in public right now. Everything is just . . . too vibrant. You know?" It was like a thousand threads of electricity were connected to her skin, pulling her in every direction, begging her to burst into an explosion of light.

And she knew exactly what she wanted to do with it all.

"How about I come over there?"

Tension snapped across the silence. "I'll send you my address."

"Okay," she said. "See you soon."

Fifteen minutes later, Hadrian met her in the lobby of his condo and led her to the elevator bank. Once inside, he punched the button for his floor.

"No. There. Stay right there," he said when the doors slid shut, sealing them inside four walls of polished steel and pristine mirrors. "We've done this dance before. The night we met." A wry smile tugged across his lips, and the fire in his eyes underscored his voice. "This time we're making it *inside* before I get my hands on you."

She laughed as understanding registered, and moved into the far corner as instructed. Arms at her side, she slid her hands behind the small of her back and crossed her legs at the ankle. "Are you sure you want to wait?"

Muttering a curse, Hadrian spun to face the panel of buttons as the elevator whisked higher in a silent, never-ending climb to the penthouse. Hands shaking, he worked each of his fingers, knuckles kneading in his palms like a man frantically recalling game stats to keep his mind off temptation.

Not that she was fairing any better. Priya prided herself on patience, but right now her patience was eroded down to a raw, aching nub. Two minutes stretched to the point of absurdity before the doors opened. Hadrian reached for Priya's hand and pulled her along behind him.

"Wow," she said when they were inside. "This is a hell of a place." Warm wood and slate tile with pops of steel and gold, the apartment was masculine and powerful yet inviting.

Hadrian slipped off his shoes. "Couldn't bring myself to sell it after my dad passed away, but I've added a thing or two since then."

Priya set her purse on the glass-topped side table. Turning to face him, she saw that the flicker of heat in his eyes mirrored the scorching fire blazing in her, and before she could blink his mouth was on hers. Hot, hard, but holding there, waiting for her to yield. To accept. And she did. For a single, wanton instant, she slid into that possessive glide of lips and greedily took before he pulled back. Breath short and golden-green eyes blazing, he pressed his brow to hers. His chest vibrated against her palms with bone rattling beats that shook straight into her like an earthquake. Splitting her foundations. Cracking her wide open.

"Last chance, Priya."

"For what?"

"To stop. Decide right now." His hands, like molten iron on her waist, melded to her curves, but with just enough slack for her to pull away if that was what she truly wanted. "We're co-workers, again. That means the rules still apply."

She angled her head, hair sliding across her shoulder. "Not until tomorrow." Rooted, Hadrian sucked in a deep breath, nostrils flaring as her hands unfastened the row of buttons from neck to navel before peeling off her blouse, revealing the wispy silk of her bra, and let it fall.

He lunged and she was in his arms before the silk pooled on polished marble tiles. Her hands tangled in his hair, legs locked around his waist and her mouth—hot, wild, and desperate, she sucked him in until she felt his body vibrate with barely leashed restraint.

"Bed," he panted, and together they staggered down the corridor into his bedroom and tumbled onto the king-sized mattress. Priya gasped as he folded over her and his hands claimed, controlled, conquered. Stripping and peeling, wrestling with the remaining layers between them until hot skin met hotter need.

For all his intensity, she matched him with equal fervor, but the sharp bite of his teeth and score of his nails down her back pushed the red of her vision to blistering white. If he didn't get inside her soon, she was bound to go insane.

"Hold up." He snapped his fingers in front of her face. Startled, she blinked up at him through the fog of arousal. "How many fingers do you see?"

Laughter rippled through her chest. "Two broken ones if you don't shut up."

"Easy, tiger. I'm only making sure you're coherent and won't pass out on me again, but that's okay, be a smart-ass—let's see if you're still laughing when I'm finished with you."

The rest of her laughter bled into a gasping moan as his mouth latched onto her breast, trailing across the landscape of her body with a nip of teeth and glide of tongue. Lower, parting her thighs, Hadrian settled between them and claimed.

Priya's body seized with a gasp, and bowed against him. Her hand stroked over his head, fingers curling in his hair, the arch of her back and the rock of her hips all urging him to take and take more as she sobbed his name.

Almost there.

He pushed her harder, ruthlessly, to that blinding peak. To that glorious edge—and over into a hard, rocketing fall. She came with a violence that punched through her soul, left her dazed and breathless to the point of incoherence. Spent, Priya struggled to regain her breath, her focus, and had a vague awareness of Hadrian reaching for the top drawer of the nightstand.

"Wait," she panted, her hand stopping him short from ripping through the square packet with his teeth.

"Priya . . ." Her name was a strangled whisper. Braced on his knees, her body spread across his bed like a banquet, control was a thin, elusive strand, but she watched as he grasped it with both hands, battling to rein himself in like a beast that had to be caged.

He thinks I want to stop, she realized. But he would if she said so, and knew he'd do it without casting guilt or blame or anger. A simple but staggering truth that touched her deeply.

Thankfully, she had other ideas.

Priya reached between them, circled her fingers around his hardened length. "My turn."

By the time he was on his back and her nails skimmed across his thighs, understanding dawned in his gaze as her mouth sank over him. Eyes locked, he watched her a moment longer, breathless and awestruck, before losing himself in the wet, sensual pull of her lips and the commanding stroke of her hands.

Hadrian's fist shot to his mouth and he bit down hard on his knuckles as sounds poured out of him—delicious and primal as his hips rose with shallow pulses—pushing a little deeper into her talented mouth. And she took him all.

"*Jesus*—" With a groan, Hadrian popped her off him to devour her in a kiss that was all brutal, passionate need—possession—and scored a path down from throat to breasts. "Now," he commanded as he dragged her onto his lap as his hand slid between them, rolling the condom in place. "No more teasing. I need you now."

"Now," she agreed, deepening the kiss as their bodies merged in a single, deep thrust. Her hands locked around his neck, her mouth fastened to his, and her soft moans spilled into him, filled him as her hips rocked and circled in a slow, deep, yearning dance.

Take me, his body seemed to say, rising to meet her, arching to claim her. Their bodies moving in unison, each attuned to the other in ways that overrode logic, transcended the physical. *Take all of me. I'm yours . . .*

Head falling back, Priya gasped. Eyes shut and lips parted, that first shock dazzled her—lost and blind to anything else but this moment, this feeling, it sliced deep into the cavern of her chest where there was so much light she couldn't contain it all.

"Again." Hadrian's arms tightened around her, drawing her closer so that they were joined in every way possible. Higher. He took her higher with commanding strokes. Helpless to do anything else, she opened to him, and held on as it built in the rise of her chest and the cry of her voice. He pushed her higher still.

And this time, as the world shattered, he fell with her.

Chapter Twenty-Four

Loose and warm, Priya sighed as the heavy beat of her heart shook her back into focus. Into awareness. Arms stole around her, and Hadrian's face nuzzled against her throat as tender emotions swept through him and *into* her. Heavy, lapping waves over the glistening sands of the shore, but each wave sucked bits of sand, drawing it deep into the black depths. She was the beach and he was the tide, stripping her bare. Leaving her raw and exposed with feelings too big for her to process or handle.

"You all right?"

"Yeah." Was she?

"I'm going to get some water. Want some?"

"Sure." His lips pressed to her brow before his warmth lifted away and he padded from the bedroom. Grateful for the moment alone, Priya sat up and kneaded a hand over her heart. What was this? What was happening? *Get a grip, Priya. It was just sex.* But it wasn't. That had been the furthest thing from just sex she'd ever experienced, and that was the problem. Something had cracked open inside of her, and now she was drowning in feeling.

Priya's never been cracked.

Heart of granite and steel. Impenetrable as Fort Knox.

Ha! If Shayne could see her now, she'd die of shock. Priyanka Seth. In love. The sticky, saccharine taste of it coated her tongue and she wanted to claw it away. No. No. No. She couldn't fall in love. Not now. Not with him. Not with anyone.

It wasn't part of the *plan*.

Her phone chimed, and Priya reached for it. Blinking at the notification on the screen, she opened it to an email from Andrew forwarding a thread from the firm's HR department discussing an amendment to an internal memo regarding the announcement of Marai Nagao's mentee: Hadrian Marek.

Chilled, Priya jerked upright and pushed matted hair from her face. *Hadrian?* Heart hammering and palms sweating, fresh spots of panic danced in the periphery of her vision as the words washed over her like a bucket of ice water over her head. *No. No. Not after everything. This can't be happening.*

"Here we go." Hadrian returned to the bedroom with a glass in hand. "It's cold but if you want ice I can—"

"What is this?" She turned her phone to Hadrian and waited as he sat down on the edge of the bed. As his eyes skimmed across the text of the email she dissected every trace of emotion that flickered in his gaze as it shifted from confusion to understanding.

"How did you get this?"

"It's true?"

"Priya."

"The first thread of this conversation was dated nearly eight weeks ago. Eight!" Before they ever set foot in the boardroom. Before the contest had formally begun. The hand holding her phone shook. "Did you know?"

His chin lowered, confirming her worst fears. "Yes. It was always in the pipeline, but to avoid any backlash Marai opted to continue with the illusion of a fair contest for the sake of appearances."

Galled, Priya leaped out of bed. "I knew it!" she seethed. "I fucking knew it." *Don't look at him. Just go. Get out quickly. Leave.* Those were the only thoughts circling through her head as she whirled from the bedroom to the foyer like a tornado, hunting for her clothes.

"Priya, stop. Wait. I can explain."

"Can you?" Already half in her shirt, she battled into her pants. "Good. Go ahead. Explain. Explain it to me."

"The firm is struggling. The last few years have been hard on the books, and things never really recovered after my father—" Hadrian dropped his hand with a sigh. "Now with George retiring, clients were getting even more skittish. The senior partners felt that me stepping in as Marai's mentee would restore faith in the legacy and stem the hemorrhaging."

"All this time," Priya whispered, tears searing her voice like raindrops splattering on a forest fire, creating billows of steam but doing nothing to stop the blaze. "You had the nerve to talk about allyship, and honesty, and us being a team, when you knew this all along and said nothing."

"I wanted to tell you."

"But you didn't. You stupidly let me believe that you cared, and that I could trust you." All that posturing in the boardroom about collaboration and teamwork, right down to his gallant arrival at her apartment with the file to obliterate Crowley in her hour of need, none of it had been sincere. It had all been one big lie.

"I meant it when I said we'd make a good team, Priya. I can convince Marai to work with us both. This doesn't have to change things between us."

"It changes everything." She shoved at him, and he absorbed the blow without resistance, which only made her even more furious. "I trusted you." She shoved him again as tears burst from her with a sob. "I trusted you!"

"It's my father's firm. It's all that's left of him." Defeated, Hadrian released a weary breath. "I can't let it die too."

"I have to go." Grateful for the dim lighting that at least hid most of the tears on her cheeks, Priya snatched up her shoes and purse and shot out into the hall.

And didn't stop running until she was home.

∗ ∗ ∗

Priya hadn't slept a single minute since leaving Hadrian's place. The next morning, blood boiling, she blazed to Marai's lush corner office and burst in. Marai sat on her couch reading from her tablet and at the sound of Priya's abrupt entry, her stark gaze lifted with a purse of burgundy lips, but she otherwise didn't even blink at the sudden invasion of her inner sanctum.

"How dare you." Priya shook her head as if it would somehow clear away the truth like the passing of an eraser across a whiteboard. "I did everything you asked of me, and brought in a major win for this firm that yielded a powerful new client who will bring in a substantial amount of money for you and the senior partners. You can't choose him! It's not fair!"

"Is it not?" Marai lowered the tablet to her side with slow, graceful ease, eyes gleaming like freshly forged steel. "He's a talented young associate, and I worked with his father long enough to know exactly where that file you presented to me truly came from."

"I had all the pieces already in play." Priya clenched her teeth, flexed the muscles in her jaw. "Hadrian just helped me get to them quicker."

"I'm curious as to why he helped you at all?" Priya snapped her mouth shut and Marai's smirk deepened. "He's Aurelio's son. On that technicality alone, he outshines you."

"If you choose him, everyone will know it's because of nepotism instead of merit." Priya pressed. "And if they don't, then I'll make sure of it. Just like I did with Genie."

Marai angled her head, the wing of dark hair skimming over the line of her shoulder. "You'd go that far?"

"For my dreams? Yes."

"Good."

"I'm not—" Priya's brain ground to a screaming halt. "Good?"

"Close the door, Priya. Sit." Marai gestured to the matching settee. Legs somewhere between rubber and lead, Priya sat down as Marai folded her hands in her lap. "The purpose of the pro bono challenge was to test your limits. We purposely plucked cases that were lackluster to teach you humility, but I also wanted to see if you could take a losing case on paper and dig deep for creativity. Ingenuity. We only want the best minds working for this firm, who aren't afraid to think outside of the box; you've shown me that, and should be proud of yourself. I don't say those words lightly."

Priya tried to find her tongue, her voice, but it was hard to manage when every wire in her brain was short-circuiting.

"Truth is," Marai continued, "I am under immense pressure by the senior partners, who think it should be Hadrian. For publicity. Aurelio Marek was a brilliant lawyer and built a powerful legacy, which is why his name remains on our walls, but I never cared for the man."

Tension worked up the back of Priya's thighs and she fought against the urge to squirm. "But . . . he was your mentor. He made you named partner."

"Yes. Like any good lawyer, Aurelio knew how to recognize an opportunity and manipulate it to his advantage. I don't think I have to explain to you the challenges of ascending the ladder," Marai added after a brief pause. "At the time, having women, especially women of color, in positions of power was a rising, hot button issue. And as the firm was expanding, he needed a lieutenant at his side while checking all the boxes in his favor. I was to be a face. A marketing tool, and he did everything he could to keep me in a powerless chokehold." Battle glinted in the dark depths of her eyes, a glimmer of the warrior spirit that had earned Marai Nagao her fierce reputation. And Priya's adoration. "This firm has had its fair share of Mareks, and I'm not interested in giving a hand up to the next generation."

Priya pressed her lips together, swallowing her surprise.

"Despite my sentiments on the matter, I was willing to assuage the senior partners given certain discord with George Silver's retirement, but you've come in here threatening to pull the trigger on a very big gun, and put me in an awkward position."

"London."

Marai angled her head. "Excuse me?"

It came to her quickly. A solution to everyone's problem.

"Ship Hadrian to the London office under the guise of returning the prodigal son home for George Silver to groom ahead of his retirement. This way you can still weave the legacy tale for your clients and calm the nerves of the senior partners. It's a win for all."

"It has merit." Marai pursed careful lips. "Are you prepared to turn a powerful friend into an even more powerful enemy?" Her eyes narrowed. "It's more than apparent that you two are . . . close, and I won't have dissent in my firm, Priya. I cannot afford a civil war between you."

"It won't be a problem."

"Hm." Marai's gaze scrutinized her for a moment longer and her hands came around to settle in her lap. "Then you need to tell him before the announcement is made, and get him on board."

"What?" Priya gasped. "Why me?"

"You want this?" Marai picked up her tablet, signaling an end to the discussion. "Show me you have the balls to see it through."

Chapter Twenty-Five

Box tucked under her arm, Priya knocked briskly and waited for Genie to answer.

"Hello, there. Isn't this a lovely surprise?"

If it was, Priya was hard pressed to believe it when Genie looked about as miserable as Priya felt. "I have something for you," she said, adjusting her hold on the box. "Can I come in?" Genie pulled the door back and allowed her to enter, before locking it behind her. Inside, everything was boxed and bagged, but by far the cleanest Priya had ever seen the space. "You've been busy."

"Down to the last ten days, kid, it's going to evaporate in a blink. I'm viciously purging." Hands on her hips, Genie assessed Priya. "What brings you to my neck of the woods?" Setting the box down on the couch, Priya raised the lid, and two kittens shook out their ears and mewled loudly, large blue eyes in fuzzy black faces. Genie's face melted from curious interest into a mopey, love-struck mess. "Oh . . . oh . . ." Hand to her heart, she sat down slowly and lifted the two little black fuzz balls onto her lap.

"A woman was handing them out on the corner. These were the last two she was struggling to get rid of."

Tears rolled down Genie's cheeks, and she blinked up at Priya. "Why did you do this?"

"Because they needed a home, and I think you'll give them an excellent one."

"I won't have one to give them." Genie swallowed hard, her voice hoarse with too much emotion. "Not for much longer."

"Yes, you do." Priya removed a thick envelope from her purse. "I'm sorry, but I wanted it all signed and sealed before I brought it to you. Congratulations, Genie Carranza."

Accepting the envelope, Genie tore it open with a sweep of her thumbnail and then unfolded the document inside. After a few breathless moments, she nearly dropped the kittens. "Oh my God . . . I own—this is mine?"

"Yes." Priya laughed, following up the ownership papers with a check. "Peter Crowley has resigned from Triton. His wife has taken over his accounts and worked out a new plan with the developer to restore this parcel, rather than tear it down. And this is a little something extra to make sure you can bring this place back to its former glory."

Genie's jaw fell into her lap at the string of zeros, and to Priya's surprise, her dentures didn't follow. "I don't know what to say."

"Don't say anything." Priya handed her a pen. "Sign, and it's done."

Genie accepted the pen, twisting it between her fingers. "What's eating you, kid? You've handed me my hopes and dreams but look like the weight of the world is on your shoulders."

"It's nothing, just a long week at work."

"Stop." Genie tapped the couch with her hand, nudging the box aside. "Sit. Tell me what's wrong?"

Priya sank next to her, heavy as lead. "Where do I start?"

Genie pursed wrinkled lips, coral lipstick faded in the center. "The beginning's often best."

Priya nodded and proceeded to tell Genie what had happened.

After her meeting with Marai, the weight of the passing hours had slipped around her shoulders, each one weighing heavier and heavier. Though she'd felt Hadrian watching her, she'd given him a wide berth and struggled to keep her calm while the whispers spread. Everyone knew they'd lost the war; all that remained was the announcement to follow at the partner's dinner. But before that happened, Priya had to woman up and face the rest of the music—face Hadrian.

Lying to him would've been easier, but Priya, a slave to brutal honesty, could only bend the truth as far as facts would allow. To outright lie? The kind that demanded bits of your soul in sacrifice? That was a talent she'd never acquired the skill, or the taste, for. An interesting handicap for a lawyer, but the nerves made her sharper, more careful, more ruthless and organized in figuring out how to turn an argument on its head.

So, in an effort to rip off the bandage, she'd texted him to join her for lunch, but his face when he arrived told Priya that her carefully rehearsed speech wasn't necessary.

He dragged out the chair with a heavy hand. The metal legs scored loudly over patio stone, a noise that felt like it was grating against her teeth.

"I want to apologize," she said once he was comfortably seated.

"For what?"

So he was really going to make her say it. Perfect. Throat

dry, Priya longed to down her glass of water but knew if she didn't choke it all out now, she never would. "I went to Marai Nagao this morning."

Hadrian nodded slowly, his finger poised against lips shadowed by a ghost of a smile. "I figured as much."

"It's been decided that you are going to work out of the London office, as George Silver's personal associate."

His brows winged up, alarmed. "Am I?"

"Don't look at me like that." Priya clasped her hands to mask their trembling. "You stabbed me in the back first, Hadrian. Let's not pretend otherwise."

"I'm sorry you see it that way." Hadrian worked his tongue in the pocket of his cheek. "So what is all this, then? Why meet with me at all?"

Priya shifted uncomfortably in her seat. "Because I wanted to sit down with you to clear the air between us. If we're going to work together."

"We're not."

"Not what?"

"Going to work together," he answered.

"Don't be dramatic." Priya rolled her eyes. "We're still part of the same firm. Just different offices."

"You're not hearing me." Hadrian sighed. "I've resigned from MNS and accepted an offer with another firm. Or will be, soon as I get back to the office. Last week I sent out a few applications to test the waters. Sure enough, I received some compelling offers here in Manhattan."

Long before she stabbed him in the back, almost like he'd known she would. His words should have been music to her ears, a balm to the vicious ache of guilt in her soul; instead, they rang out like the screeching cry of a train veering off the tracks, and only made her ache all the more. "Why?"

"Because I knew it was the only way. You want the mentorship, fine, it's yours. You've more than earned it. I'll walk away and trust you to keep my father's legacy alive. I'll do it for us, Priya." Reaching between them, he took her hand, linking fingers and palm. "When I said we'd make a good team I meant it. Give this a chance. Give us a chance."

Understanding flashed warm to clash with the chill of panic, a warring of sensations and emotions that disoriented her thoughts, and made her heart ache like a bad tooth.

Love made women stupid, blinding them with thoughts of marriage and babies, of building a future that required that all of their dreams, hopes, and aspirations be set on the back burner while he was free to live without the burden of change or judgment.

She was entering the preliminary stages of a demanding career that wouldn't settle for second place in the list of her priorities, and a relationship needed dedication and time to flourish; both were luxuries she couldn't afford. And what happened when Hadrian decided she wasn't enough, or worse, selfish for her ambition? Resented her for it? She'd witnessed the detrimental aftermath of broken relationships with her sisters enough to know love would ruin everything.

You have a plan, Priya. A carefully mapped out life plan. Stick to it.

Priya extracted her hands from his grip. "I can't . . ."

Eyes hardening, the warmth and emotion were sealed away behind a thick, impenetrable wall. "Well, then, to the victor go the spoils." Hadrian's hand stroked over his chest, as if wiping the slate—and his heart—clean. Rising, he tucked in the chair and took one firm step before he stopped. Sighed. "I know why you really ran away that night, and why you were prepared to put an ocean between us just now," he whispered, his words soft in tone but heavy with a weight she didn't want them to carry. "Something happened between us. Something I don't have an answer for yet, either, but when you decide you're brave enough to want to figure it out, you know where to find me."

The kittens scampered around Genie's feet, and one clawed its way up her leg like it was a scratching post. "Love is a scary thing," she said when Priya was finished, wrangling the furball into her lap and letting it chew on her fingers with tiny milk-white teeth. "It's beautiful. Wonderful. And absolutely terrifying too," she continued. "My husband is the only man who ever breached my high walls. He was relentless, but he saw me, you know? Right to the core. And touched me just as deep. Scared me out of my wits."

"What did you do?"

"Blew up the damn boat. Tried to sink it as many times as I could, but he never gave up on me. Just bailed water, patched holes, until one day he sat me down and said enough was enough. I had to decide what was more important, my pride or him. So I did the scariest thing in my entire life. I chose him."

"I don't think I'm ready for what he wants."

"And you don't have to be right now. You're young, still figuring it all out, and if walking away is what's best for you then that's what you need to do, but do it the right way, you catch my drift?"

"It's too late for that."

"It's never too late to apologize." Genie patted her knee. "Trust me, kid. You know what you got to do—just do it."

Chapter Twenty-Six

I need you.

Those three small words fired through Isobel's brain like bullets. Over and over.

I need you.

Need you.

I. Need. You. What did that mean? Why did she even care? Exhausted after hours of sitting behind her laptop, Isobel glared at a blank screen, unable to shake those harrowing words from her thoughts. While in Miami, his text messages had ballooned into missed calls and voice mails, a final barrage begging her to come to the condo or call him back.

Caitlin had called it a classic narcissist maneuver, and Eshe bet that him ambushing Isobel at home was in her near future. Shayne had threatened literal castration if he tried.

On the verge of tears, Isobel pressed her hands to her face, a dam to stem the flood as those three words resounded inside her like a struck bell. Goddamn him for disrupting her life, her progress and healing. Selfish jerk. She'd been doing so well, and was so excited about life and all the upcoming challenges she had to look forward to; now it was all swept aside in a hurricane of emotions she didn't want to get swallowed up in again.

Take a break. Reset. Isobel made her way downstairs, deciding to step away from the screen to give her eyes and tormented mind a rest.

"There's my girl," Declan called from across the living room. "How's the writing going?"

"It's . . . fine."

"You don't sound fine."

Isobel opened her mouth but promptly snapped it shut. No, he'd just worry and the stress would only exacerbate his condition. "I'm just tired," she said instead. A white lie and a necessary evil. Lately, Isobel had found herself treading morally gray waters, but it was for the best. "All right, that's enough idle chitchat. I have to make dinner."

"Dare I ask what's on the menu?"

"Spaghetti with eggplant meatballs." One of the few dishes that her dad didn't prod sullenly with a fork like an errant child.

"Goody." Declan snorted. "I best go wash up, then."

In the kitchen, Isobel whirled from fridge to pantry, gathering and collecting spices, bread crumbs, and a carton of silken tofu, eager to lose herself in the comfort of making an early dinner. Cooking soothed her nerves, was a balm to her soul, and then afterward she'd return to carving out words for her article. Nneka was expecting the draft before Isobel flew out to Greece, and Isobel wasn't going to let her past derail her future.

Finished with the prep, Isobel had just slid the chopped onions and garlic into a skillet to soften when the house phone rang. Turning down the heat under the skillet, she caught it on the final ring. "Isobel, speaking."

"Hello, I'm looking to speak with Mr. Declan Morgan."

Oh God, what now? Isobel had scarcely a moment to breathe, let alone think for days. The last thing she wanted or needed was any more surprises. "May I ask who is calling?"

"My name is Cynthia Ortega, from the Enriched Wellness Center. I wanted to confirm his pickup on Thursday morning to bring him to our center in Montreal. Does ten thirty suit him?"

"Pickup?"

"Yes, for his residency program."

"I'm sorry, there must be some kind of mistake." Head spinning, Isobel adjusted her grip on the phone with trembling hands. "My father isn't going anywhere."

"Are you sure? Because we have his term of care paid for in full for the next six months, with a possible extension for another three, depending on the success of his treatment."

"Treatment?" Isobel startled as her father reached for the phone and took it from her limp grasp.

"Hello, yes, this is Declan," he muttered into the receiver, eyes dipped from hers. "Yes, next Thursday. I'll be ready. Thank you." What was left of Isobel's world bottomed out from beneath her feet. Declan returned the phone to the cradle before wrapping his arm around her shoulders. "Come, let's take a seat. We have a few things to discuss."

Isobel followed numbly as he prodded her into the soft corner of the worn couch. The only other time she'd seen her father this serious was the night he'd sat her down at the kitchen table to tell Isobel her mother was never coming home again. Isobel had cried herself to sleep for weeks on end, waking each day red faced and puffy eyed, her throat seared raw with grief.

Then Isobel had locked it all way, stuffing away the pain of loss deep in her bones. Now that poison erupted, spilling through her like oil. Coating every nerve. Drowning her in inky black.

"Who was that woman on the phone?"

"I wanted to wait until after your trip to tell you." Declan spun the recliner on the swivel base to face her and pinned his elbows to his thighs. "There was an opening for their short-term patient rehabilitation program."

"Rehabilitation?" Head spinning, Isobel gripped the armrest, holding it like an anchor to keep her from drowning. "You're leaving?"

"Only for a spell, love."

"She said six months! In Montreal!"

"It's for the best."

"I don't understand. You're getting better. Stronger."

"No, sweetheart. I'm not." Declan scraped a calloused palm over the rasp of hair at his nape. "That Genie story opened my eyes to how selfish I've been, relying on you all these years."

"I wasn't trying to make you feel bad, Daddy."

"I know." He sighed. "But the truth is I need help. *Professional* help. And you deserve to live your life not burdened with this. Not anymore. Not again." His eyes locked on hers, and in them she saw no room for negotiation. "I haven't been able to do much for my little girl, but I can do this."

"So that's it? I have no say?" Furious, Isobel jumped to her feet, shaking with the strain of sobs. "You're just going to abandon me like *Mom*?" The proud line of his shoulders lost their strength and with that one blow she'd broken his armor, a point on the scoreboard for her, but it felt like another loss. "Where did you even get the money, Dad? Because we can't afford this."

"I'm aware of that."

"Then ho—?" Understanding was a hard, brutal slap, and she recoiled from it. Dazed. "Shayne?"

Declan lifted watery eyes strained with grief. "Don't be angry with her."

Angry? Isobel wasn't angry. She was livid. Furious. On the brink of committing first-degree murder. But more than that—deeper than that—she was hurt. Devastated.

Just then the front door opened and Shayne spilled through the entryway with Eshe and Caitlin in tow, trundling luggage and laughter behind them.

Declan cleared his throat. "Hello, girls. You're all here?"

"Minus Priya." Eshe deposited the luggage in a corner and pushed down the retractable handles. "Apparently she needs to fix some mess with a bloke at work."

"Priya and Panty Thief." Caitlin pressed her hands to her chest, fingers shaped in a heart. "So cute."

"No. Not cute." Shayne scowled. "Don't understand why it couldn't wait until after our trip." Entering the living room, her eyes tracked to Isobel, then over to her father. "Who died?"

"Ah . . ." Declan rubbed the back of his neck. "Well—"

"Dad, can you leave us, please? I want to speak to Shayne. Alone."

Her father cleared his throat again. Nodded. "Right. Okay, love." Eshe's and Caitlin's smiles fell away as her father shuffled from the room, head hung and shoulders bowed.

"Everything all right, yeah?" Eshe asked gently, the first to break the harsh silence.

"Ask Shayne. Since she's so intent on making all my decisions for me maybe she should start speaking for me too."

Shayne ran her teeth over her bottom lip, sucked hard. "Pops told you?"

"He did." Isobel planted trembling hands to her hips. "*After* I got a call from the clinic confirming his admission for next week."

Sighing heavily, Shayne pinched the bridge of her nose. "Look . . . Pops didn't want you overreacting, like you are right now. Like you always do whenever he so much as stubs a toe." She tossed a hand at Isobel. "If he told you he needed help he knew you'd do something stupid, like quit your job. So I got him set up in a premium facility with world class care and treatment. It's not that big a deal."

"It is to me!" Isobel shouted back as the dam inside her cracked, splitting wide open so all the bitter rage she'd held back now seeped through. Putrid and raw. "You had no right to do this without speaking to me." She pressed a hand to her chest. "Involving me."

Caitlin slowly raised a finger, like a student afraid to interrupt the class. "Shayne meant well. And Quebec's not that far."

"Yes it—" *Oh God.* She hadn't said where he was going. "You knew?" Caitlin and Eshe exchanged guilty glances, and Isobel released a brittle laugh. Of course they knew. Everyone knew everything except her. Like always. Hands shaking, adrenaline surged, so bright, so fast, she was dizzy with it. "I can't be here. I can't even look at you right now."

"Fuck this." Shayne shot clear across the room before Isobel managed more than a few hurried steps and cut her off at the threshold, yanking her back into the heart of the living room.

"Let me go, Shayne."

"No." Shayne closed in on Isobel the way she did an opponent in the ring. Cornering her. "You're not running away like you always do. You're dealing with this. Right here. Right now. Let's go." She waved her hands, summoning her to step up and fight back.

"Stop it. Stop telling me what to do."

"Maybe I wouldn't have to if you weren't such a fucking doormat."

"Whoa . . ." Eshe whispered.

"All right." Caitlin wedged herself between them like a referee and smoothed a hand over Isobel's trembling shoulder. "Let's take a deep breath before we say things we can't take back, shall we?"

But Isobel was far too incensed to calm down. The poison was spreading, and something malevolent arose in its wake. She shucked Caitlin's hand from her, then rounded back on Shayne. "Doormat? Is that what you really think of me?"

"I love you, but yeah. You'd fight a war for any of us, but not for yourself. Never. Not with your douche bag boss. The travel agent. Or Kyle. Forget walking down the aisle, you were determined to sprint down it because you're too fucking afraid to be alone than admit to yourself that he was a cheating piece of shit and you deserved better." Shayne drove each word into her like a staggering blow to face and body. Brutal, punishing, and direct; Isobel didn't have time to brace against the onslaught.

"How can you say that to me?" she whispered. "You were my maid of honor."

"And I've done my job trying to *protect* your honor!" Shayne bellowed. "I swore a vow. Sisters before all else, and I've lived by those words every day since we swore them. So fuck you for trying to make me into the villain. I won't apologize for saving you from yourself, and for helping Pops." She pushed back her shoulders. "I did what I had to for family."

"He's not your family!" Isobel roared back. "He's *mine*, and he's all I have left. How dare you take him from me too."

Regret struck as fast as lightning and with the devastation of a bomb. Isobel had never said anything so vicious or so cruel in her life and could hardly believe she'd spoken the words at all, but the pain in her chest quickly obliterated any shame or guilt. Right now, all she wanted was for Shayne to bleed as she was bleeding, and Isobel had struck her bone deep.

The four of them stood in a fragmented circle, all disjointed and disconnected. Sharp edges and broken lines. Wrong. Frozen in that shattered silence, emotions swelled, hot and huge, a violent storm of all that was said and couldn't be taken back—it gathered. Loomed. Threatening to destroy their very foundation. They'd never had a fight like this before. Every rule broken. Every promise shattered.

There was no coming back from this.

Under any other circumstance, if it was anyone else standing before her, Shayne would have laid them out cold, but as it was Isobel, her hands remained in trembling fists at her side.

"If that's how you feel—cool. I'm done." Shayne's lip curled with a sneer but her eyes shone with the anguish of heartbreak. "You're on your own."

Chapter Twenty-Seven

Isobel slammed the front door, and it cracked behind her, sharp as a gunshot. She could hardly keep her thoughts straight and emotions centered when every inch of her was rigid with anger and emotion. How could he leave her like this? How could he leave, period? And Shayne, shoving her nose in the middle of it like always.

I can't do this again. I can't do this again.

A fraction of a second later the door opened again, and Caitlin sauntered out. "Careful. Your neighbors may think that was an earthquake and not you in a snit." She eased it shut in demonstration, and wiggled lilac brows. "See, that's how you close a door."

"What are you doing?"

"I'm here to talk you off a ledge, what else does it look like?" Caitlin jangled car keys. "Come on, let's go for a drive. Clear your head."

"I'm sorry, I'm really sorry, but I can't be around anyone right now," Isobel answered. She needed to move. To run. To breathe. "Go after Shayne, see if she needs you."

"I would but Eshe and I rock paper scissored for it—one round, I lost."

"Funny."

"I thought so." Caitlin lowered herself to the porch step, tapped the open space at her side. "Sit. Talk."

"What's left to say?" Exasperated, Isobel shoved her hands through her hair, itching to rip it out by the root. God, she was so angry she was vibrating. "You were there. You heard her." She'd hoped she was wrong—about Shayne, about everything—only to discover it was so much worse.

"Yes. I also heard you." Caitlin propped her chin on her fist. Attentive as a fashion editor scrutinizing an affluent designer's spring line sashaying down the runway. "I get that you're mad, but you didn't need to hit quite so below the belt."

"Just leave me alone." Blazing down the walkway, Isobel pushed through the gate and barely made it a few steps before her legs wobbled. Everything was moving too quickly. Her breathing. Her heart. She dropped to the curb; hand pressed to her chest.

"Slow down. Easy breaths," Caitlin urged, and sat next to her. "That's it."

Isobel pressed her face into her hands, and the sound that tore from her throat was equal parts sob and snarl. Her dad was leaving home and there was nothing she could do to stop it, but worse than that, she hated that she wanted to.

A rehabilitation clinic *was* the best thing for him, but it was the process of events that hurt her the most. Once again, a major decision had been made that would affect her life, and she'd been pushed out of it . . . this time by Shayne and her dad. The two of them in cahoots while she remained in the dark. How the hell was she supposed to process this kind of betrayal?

"You're not angry with your dad. Or Shayne. Not

completely," Caitlin answered as if she'd heard Isobel's warring thoughts.

A stunned laugh seeped out of her. "Then who am I angry with?"

"Your mother." That stopped her cold. "Hear me out." Dragging a knee up, Caitlin swiveled around to face her more directly. "For as long as I've known you, you've always wanted the picture-perfect family. That's what Kyle was. A pretty picture."

"Lots of people want that."

"Yeah, but I think what you've really wanted was to fix your own childhood—not to say that you had a bad one, your dad is pretty freaking awesome, but he was kinda clueless about how to raise a girl, you know? Or how to take care of a house. Which meant you picked up the slack very young. It's no surprise you developed a Cinderella complex." Caitlin smoothed a hand over Isobel's thigh when she bristled. "All I'm saying is I get it. Fear of change. Losing family. Abandonment. Your mom chose to walk away—but what's happening with your dad isn't the same thing."

"You don't know what you're talking about. You've never lost anyone."

"Haven't I?"

Isobel sobered. Caitlin's adoption was a well-known fact among the sisters, but they'd never explored beyond the surface or dug any deeper. It seemed pointless to do so when she had her parents—a loving, complete unit. But that didn't change the simple truth that Caitlin had lost plenty, long ago.

"I'm sorry." The chill of shame cooled the heat in Isobel's cheeks and voice. "I didn't mean to undermine . . ."

"You know the first thing people used to say to me when they learned I was adopted?" Caitlin interrupted gently. "*You're so lucky*. I hated hearing it. I'm not lucky. No child is *lucky* to be cast aside or orphaned, but I am blessed to have parents who love and understand me. Support me." Caitlin's fingers played with the metallic fringe of her wrap. "I love my family. I truly do. I've never felt displaced or lost. Maybe because I know that the answers to whatever questions I may have will be there for me one day, when I'm ready."

"Closure." Something Isobel never had with her mother, or Kyle. Isobel wriggled her toes against the grit of concrete flecked with broken glass and bits of stone. Water gurgled in the drains running beneath asphalt that sloped like the weather-beaten houses lining the street. She'd lived in this neighborhood her entire life. All of her memories, her hopes, and dreams captured within four square blocks. She'd connected so deeply to Genie's story for that reason, and like her, she'd fought to valiantly hold on to the remnants of her past. Unable to let go, because letting go was terrifying.

Letting go was . . . final.

Even if she'd tried to tell herself she'd pushed out all thoughts or feelings about her mother, the truth was she missed her deeply. And still loved her. The pain of loss clung to Isobel like a shadow she'd been unable to run away from, but she had to learn to move on from it, otherwise it would haunt her for the rest of her life. This fear of abandonment and of change.

"My mom was an artist," Isobel whispered. "She loved color. Painted the door that sunny yellow about a week before she took off. I remember how dull it suddenly appeared when she was gone. She brought color into our home, and my dad brought warmth." Tears spilled, hot and fast down her cheeks. "How cold and empty will it be when he's gone too?"

Without the sound of his voice and laughter? The warmth of his smile or the familiar sight of him curled up in his armchair in front of the TV with his sudoku puzzles, or pulling a face in the kitchen as she urged him to eat more vegetables? Even now, the thought of spending a night alone without his snores drifting down the hall terrified her.

"Have you thought about looking for her?"

Isobel shook her head. A slight, almost imperceptible gesture. Not since she was a little girl, crying into her pillow at night, confused by the changes of her body and envious of her friends whose mothers loved them enough to want to stay.

To share in all these bright, confusing, and incredible moments of adolescence.

"I was born in Jinhae. Apparently famous for its cherry blossoms," Caitlin mused, a secret kind of smile in her voice. "Maybe I'll go there one day."

"Why? Why now?"

Caitlin brushed tears away from the trembling curve of Isobel's chin. "I think you need someone to be brave enough to take the first step in their own journey so you can find the courage to do the same. But you won't have to go through it alone because I'll be there with you. Each step. Each hurdle. We'll uncover our truth and face it together."

Isobel drew in a shaky breath and held it. This was the love of the Sisterhood. Warm and soothing as a blanket, enveloping all the parts of her that were raw and bleeding. God, she was so tired. Now that the fire of her emotions had been lanced, fatigue hung from her joints with leaden weights of exhaustion. "What would I do without you?"

"We're sisters. You're never going to have to find out." Caitlin gathered Isobel into a hug and kissed her damp cheek. "Come on, let's go back upstairs. Hug it out with Shayne."

"No. Not yet. I have to do something first."

"What?"

Isobel weighed the phone in her hand. Kyle's last text to her that morning searing into her brain.

> Please come over tonight. Eight-thirty, Tink. I need you. I really need you.

"Closure."

* * *

Some conversations had to happen face to face, and as terrifying as the prospect was, she owed it to herself. It was time. Isobel lifted her chin and straightened her shoulders— and knocked twice. The door swung open barely a moment later, and Kyle stood before her, a smile on his face and surprise in his eyes.

"Tink." He swooped in and kissed her, and she was too stunned to dodge it. "You're actually here."

"I did text," she cleared her throat, "to confirm I was dropping by."

"Yeah, but normally you're like an hour early and it's after eight. Kinda thought maybe you were gonna ghost."

She'd wanted to. Oh, how she'd wanted to, but Isobel wasn't running from her problems anymore, or burying her head in the sand. She'd come for closure and wasn't going to leave until she got it.

"Come in." He pulled her into the heart of the condo, the space updated since she'd last been there, with a fireplace installed on the focal wall connecting to the dining room.

Two large sectional couches spread in a honeycomb pattern and a stunning woman with mile-long legs sat on the armrest of one of them, speaking briskly into her headphones. Just beyond her, a team of people swarmed about, staging lights and reflectors by the windows overlooking the core of downtown Toronto.

Isobel blinked at the flurry of movement. The chaos. But she'd worked long enough in media to piece together this was a production crew. "What is all this?"

"A surprise." Kyle squeezed her hand, drawing her attention back to the woman on the couch. "Tink, this is Phoebe Tanaka, my publicist."

"The Victoria's Secret model?"

"Former." Phoebe uncrossed one long, glorious leg and rose with a Cheshire Cat grin. "I moved over to managing talent three years ago, and you two are going to be my Sistine Chapel." She snapped a finger above her shoulder. "Let's get the lights over here, and some powder to cancel out the shine on Isobel's cheeks before we go live."

"Live?"

Phoebe looked at Kyle. "I thought you spoke to her about this?"

"She was hard to reach."

"We're streaming in *ten* minutes."

"Then give me five."

"Five. But just so we're clear, we don't have a show without her." Phoebe nodded toward Isobel. "So get her on board."

"You won't believe it, Tink." Kyle swooped in front of her, gathering both of her hands. "But Phoebe's network wants us for a new reality show slated to launch in the fall."

"A reality show about what, exactly?"

"Think *Real Housewives* meets *Ballers*." Phoebe splayed her hands with Vanna White flare. "Kyle pitched it to me last year during a press event in New York. It had potential, but it needed grit to find traction in the media."

"What is she saying?" Isobel swiveled on the spot, but Phoebe was already off speaking with a member of the crew who was adjusting a sound boom.

"Long story short? I'm getting into the music biz, Tink."

"Music?"

"Yeah."

"*Music*," Isobel repeated, drawing out each syllable, because no way in hell had she heard him correctly.

"Yeah."

Stunned, Isobel swiped at the air. "I'm sorry, none of this is making any sense. Where is this all coming from, Kyle?"

"I'm a pro baller, Tink, but for a Canadian team. We don't do so well on this side of the border. Maybe I'll get lucky and get traded to an American or a European club, but I've got seven—maybe ten—good years in me before I wash out, and that's if I don't get injured, again. I'm lucky I didn't need surgery on my ACL this time, but the next will likely take me out. Even then, there are a thousand young bucks coming up right behind me every step of the way. If I want to build a legacy I need to act now. Hence the show." His smile stretched across his face, broad and dazzling to match the eager gleam of excitement wakening in his eyes. "We're looking to build the hype, y'know? Figure after a season or two, we flip the script over to me launching into the music industry. From there—skies the limit. And with you by my side," he reached for her hand, squeezed it, "we could totally be the next Bey and Jay."

"We?"

"You've got killer vocals, Tink. Don't play, I've heard you."

"That's in the shower." Isobel pressed a sweaty palm to her brow, afraid her head was going to spin off her shoulders in shock. "I can't even do karaoke without having a panic attack. What you're talking about is big. Huge." Concerts, events, worldwide tours, not to mention thousands of hours in a studio.

"C'mon," Kyle scoffed, "you even told me how you wanted to be a singer."

"When I was *seven*!" A dream she'd abandoned after her mother had left. A dream she'd long forgotten, along with so many things. "Besides, this isn't about me, Kyle—you *can't* sing, or rap. You don't write lyrics. You don't play an instrument. You've never performed a day in your life."

Kyle shrugged an absent shoulder. "So? Half the people on radio today can't either. But I've got the looks and the charisma, the rest can be hashed out in a studio. Hire writers. Producers to tweak vocals. There's all kinds of shit they can do to make me sound good."

"You don't have those kinds of connections."

"I do, now."

The weight of silence stretched. Settled. *Teri Mauve.*

"Miami." Isobel's stomach plummeted to her knees. "You released the video? On *purpose*?"

Kyle nodded. "It was Phoebe's idea."

"Nothing sells like sex, a total cliché, I know." Phoebe sighed. "But it's worked for so many others, the Kardashians being a prime example. The true shocker in all this, though, is how strongly the market has responded to you, Isobel. You are our crown jewel." She clapped her hands. "And because of that, the network has decided to spotlight you and Kyle as our lead couple for the series."

"Oh my God." Isobel's heart sank with a final thud. She'd come for closure, and here it was. The truth laid bare. He hadn't reached out for her but for himself, as always. God, this was like a kick high and deep into her solar plexus, but she managed to quickly pull herself together and fortify the crumbling walls of her resolve. Isobel extracted herself from his hold. "How could you do this?"

"It was coming out anyway, so why not get ahead of it and make it work for me rather than against me? To build an empire sometimes you gotta burn down the forest, y'know?"

And she was the forest he so happily razed if it meant getting his fifteen minutes of fame. He'd let her walk into that—the humiliation and shame—without any warning, and for weeks after he'd still kept her in the dark. The only thing that had changed his mind was the fact she was getting more screen time now than he would ever be capable of alone. Everyone was talking about Isobel Morgan. No one apparently cared anywhere near as much about Kyle Peterson.

He didn't miss her. He didn't love her. It was right there in the text. Need.

"C'mon, Tink! Think about how great this will be for us. For your dad! You can take care of him the way you always wanted. Every door you can imagine is open to us now. We can build an empire, together. You and me. And the wedding— totally covered by the network, we wouldn't have to pay for a thing. What do you think?"

"I think it's fucking pathetic." Isobel swiveled at the sound of Shayne's voice as she swaggered into the room. "Coulda just opened an OnlyFans, bro."

More commotion erupted as Caitlin burst into the room, a little windswept, with Eshe hot on her heels. "Fab." Caitlin ruffled her fingers through her lavender faux hawk. "We're not too late."

"Classic Shayne, always in the middle of our fucking business." Kyle laughed darkly. "Isn't there a carpet somewhere you can munch on? Or have you finally tapped the world dry?"

"Don't dick measure with me, Kyle, we both know you're pulling more figures than you are inches."

"Fuck you."

"You wish." Plunking down on the sectional, Shayne removed her nearly finished sucker from her mouth, lips stained candy-apple red. "But don't worry, I just came to watch Isobel hand you your ass." She inclined her head to Isobel with a *you got this* nod.

And she did. She really did, but having Shayne there in that moment, knowing she had her back, but for once was going to let Isobel take control of the situation herself, pushed steel into her spine and power into her voice. *I got this.*

"I do love a good show." Eshe sat down next to Shayne.

"Me three!" Caitlin scooted around the ottoman to join her

sisters and clapped her hands at the stunned production crew. "Anyone have popcorn? Pretzels?"

"We should totally FaceTime Priya. She's going to be sorry to miss *this*."

"Already tried." Shayne crunched into her sucker. "She's on DND."

"Oh for fuck—" Kyle tossed an aggrieved hand. "Get out— all of you—before I have you thrown out."

"No." Isobel stopped him with the flat of her hand on his chest. "We're doing this with an audience. Just like you wanted. That's the point of all this, right? You made this public. You brought the entire world into our lives."

Kyle dragged his hand down his face with a heavy, petulant sigh. "How many times do I have to apologize?"

"You haven't actually apologized. Ever. At all. Not once in the history of our relationship, in fact."

"Can't you just get over it?"

"Oh no he didn't," Caitlin stage-whispered.

Eshe swayed into her with a giggle. "I love this song."

"*Get over it?*" Isobel scoffed, ignoring her friends. "Like what? A bad headache or a cold or my period? Just some mild inconvenience to be waited out?" *God, what an idiot I was to ever have loved this man.*

"Kyle?" Phoebe twisted anxious fingers. "I think we should postpone—"

"No!" Kyle snapped. "This is happening. Give me a minute. Just a fucking minute." But Phoebe was already clearing the room of cameras and crew, corralling them from the condo. Not that Isobel cared, she had her sisters and that was all she needed right now.

"Jesus fucking Christ. You see what you've done? You're ruining everything, Tink."

"I ruin—" Isobel shook with barely leashed rage. "You betrayed me, Kyle. In the worst possible way. You broke us. Everything that we were and could've been is gone because of what *you* did."

"You're being too emotional. As always."

"You mean weak."

"Yeah."

"Why? Because I feel deeply? Because I can experience depths you can't even fathom? I'm not weak." Isobel plowed on when Kyle opened his mouth to interrupt. He would not talk over her, working her into submission with his smooth voice and soft eyes. Gone was the pliant, meek Isobel. Gone was the little girl with dazzling dreams of a happy home and loving marriage to the perfect guy. She was wide awake, and for the first time she was seeing him as clearly as she now saw herself. "I am extraordinary," she continued. "I showed you what it was to be loved. Truly loved. You can't say the same."

"C'mon, Tink. No one will ever love you like I do. You know that." Kyle's smile was slick with charm as he skimmed a finger from Isobel's cheek down the line of her neck to the slender chain of gold draped there. "You can't let me go. You can never let me go." He freed the pendant from her neckline, dangling it from the tip of his finger.

The small, thin figure of Tinker Bell. His first gift to her when he'd asked her to be his girlfriend. A gift she'd cherished for the entirety of their relationship and had continued to thoughtlessly wear because on some small level, he was right: she had held on to him.

Not anymore.

"Oh no?" Isobel looped her fingers around the necklace and with a swift jerk snapped the delicate gold chain. "Watch me." Marching to the bathroom near the entryway, she tossed it in the porcelain bowl of the toilet and pressed the lever, flushing it all away. Kyle. Their memories. And all the bitter fragments that remained.

And suddenly, everything in her became lighter, as if she'd freed more than the weight of gold from around her neck, but the burden of memories along with it.

God, it felt good.

"The fuck did you do?" His hand closed around her arm, hellfire blazing in his eyes as the water in the bowl swirled empty.

"Let go of me, Kyle."

"Or what?" He shook her hard, fingers scoring into bone. "What are you going to do, huh? Hit me?"

"No, but I will." Shayne swung in between him and Isobel, and caught him with a quick, clean jab—straight on. His head kicked up with a satisfying snap a second before his knees buckled and he dropped on his ass.

"You all right?" Eshe looped an arm around Isobel, Cailin closing in on her other side.

"Yeah." Isobel nodded. "I'm fine." She rubbed away the phantom ache of his grip quickly turning into a bruise.

"Go ahead." Kyle swiped at his lips; blood glistened on his fingertips. "Walk away," he roared as the four of them turned to leave, staggering to his feet, his gray eyes watery with angry tears. "You'll regret it. And when you do, I won't be here."

Shayne stiffened, and Isobel stopped her with a gentle

touch before coming face to face with him one last time. "You know what the last few weeks have taught me? I lost nothing by losing you. Nothing. But I gain everything by letting you go." The potential of who he could've been had blinded her to the truth of who he actually was, but she saw it now, and the boy she'd once loved so much was now a pale shadow in the man who stood before her today. "You're not my missing half, Kyle. No one is. Because I am already whole, and the next man who comes into my life will be a welcome addition. Not my completion."

Slipping a green-apple lollipop from the breast pocket of her jacket, Shayne shucked the wrapper and winked at Kyle as she slid it in her mouth. "Now *that's* what you call entertainment."

Chapter Twenty-Eight

"Son of a fuckwad." Shayne shook out her hand. "When did Kyle get titanium plates for cheekbones?"

"Here, let me." Taking her hand, Isobel flexed the fingers gently. "I don't think anything is broken."

"I'll make an ice run. There's a Mickey D's up the street. Esh?" Caitlin elbowed her with a not so discreet brow wiggle.

"Ice. Right. Don't kill one another while we're gone, yeah?"

As the pair of them scampered down the sidewalk, heels clicking, Isobel shook away the urge to smile. "This was Caitlin's idea, wasn't it? Coming after me?"

"Maybe," Shayne grumbled, holding her abused hand against her chest. Isobel flung herself into Shayne's arms and when she latched on just as tightly, a tremor of relief poured through her. "I'm sorry, Bel. I'm so sorry."

Isobel hugged tighter. "Don't apologize."

"No." Prying free, Shayne swiped angrily at tears but more spilled. "I have to." Isobel waited, quiet and patient as Shayne pulled herself together, eyes closed and breathing determined. Balancing herself on the razor's edge of emotional sanity. "Pops—your dad," she corrected softly, "he begged me. *Begged.* How could I say no?"

"I get that." Isobel cupped Shayne's face in her hands, cleaning away tears with strokes of her thumbs. "You still should've come to me first and allowed me to be part of this decision."

"Would you have let him go? Honestly, Bel. Would you?"

"Not right away," Isobel admitted. "But I'd like to think in time . . ." She rubbed a hand across her brow, working away the stiffness there. "You can't always protect me, Shayne. I'm not that little girl in Starbucks who needed saving from the bullies. I need to save myself, and I need you to let me fail at it from time to time, if that's what it takes for me to learn. It's my life, my choice."

Because that's what it boiled down to: choice and the loss of it.

Too much had happened, in the last few weeks especially, that had stripped her of control, leaving her trapped and pressured and unsure as she was dragged toward an uncertain future. Her body lurching forward against her will when every facet of her being wanted to resist rather than embrace that change.

"Well, you fucking slayed douche bro, up there." Shayne pursed her lips in the direction of the building they'd exited. "I always knew you had strength in you. I'm sorry if I ever made you feel like I didn't. You were made to love, Bel, I've always known that about you, but you're built for war too. And I am so fucking proud to see you come into that power."

"Thank you." And God, that nearly brought her to joyful and humbled tears. "You weren't entirely wrong, though," she confessed, dropping her hand back to her side. "Part of me was lapsing. The past is familiar. It's safe. Nothing will ever be the same again and that scares me."

"I'm scared too." Shayne pressed her lips into a hard line, as if she didn't want to let the words out, to give breath to the deepest, darkest fragments of truth most wouldn't dare let themselves explore or say aloud. "I'm protective and I take it too far, I know, but it's because you guys are all I have. You're the only family who truly accepted me as I am. Not my parents— especially not my grandmother, and yeah, my brother's trying in his way, but it's not the same. I can't lose you."

"Why would you think that you'd lose us?"

"Because like you said, everything's changing. It's happening so fast, and it's pulling us apart. You, furthest of all." Shayne shook her head as tears splashed onto the sharp bones of her cheeks. "Marriage. Babies. I have no place in all of that."

"Shayne . . . no matter what happens you're my family. You will always be my family." Cupping her chin, Isobel angled her gaze so there was no escaping what she was about to say. "I should never have said what I did. I love you. Okay? I love you fiercely. Like Sheldon loves his spot."

"Love you too." Shayne's lips quirked into a murky smile. "Like Kanye loves Kanye."

"Awww, yay!" Rattling a McDonalds cup of ice, Cailin leaped against Isobel and Shayne, wrapping them into a group hug. "We're the Sisterhood again!"

Eshe melded into them as well, creating a web of arms, and Isobel sighed into the warmth of their solid embrace. "Thank you for coming. For not letting me do that alone, even if I deserved to be."

"We'd never leave you alone," Eshe sighed. "Ever."

"Sisters before everything!" Caitlin chimed in.

"I wish Priya was here with us. Can't believe she missed that epic throw-down!" Eshe grumbled, chin bouncing against the top of Isobel's head. "Would've served the prat right if the whole mess had been broadcast live. Given him a taste of his own bloody medicine."

"Well . . ." Caitlin stepped back with a smirk. "I might've been sneak recording on my phone."

"Shut up!" Shayne laughed. "When? How much did you get?"

"All of it."

Eshe thrust up her arms. "Cait for the win!"

"That's all I do, baby." Cailin looped her arms around Shayne's and Isobel's waists and bumped them both with a hip wiggle. "Now, ladies, shall we head back to Chez Morgan? I think there's a suitcase with Isobel's name on it in dire need of packing."

"Sounds like a plan." Shayne hooked an arm around Isobel's shoulder and kissed her brow. "But first I gotta see the replay of Isobel Morgan kicking Kyle's ass back to never-neverland."

Chapter Twenty-Nine

Heyy, we're all here

Bubbles are on ice

Move your gorgeous ass, bitch!

Smiling at Shayne's string of messages, Priya tucked the phone away in her clutch. Jet-lagged on the back of a twelve-hour connecting flight, exhaustion was a bitch that wouldn't quit, but Priya refused to set foot in Mykonos without changing first, especially when she had a party to get to. Ducking into the airport bathroom, she traded her travel clothes for a pale-yellow chiffon dress cut short to her thighs, Converse sneakers for lipstick-red heels, and emerged from the airport fabulous, but late.

"Good evening," the concierge said, his voice butter smooth and carrying all the charm of his heritage as he helped Priya from the backseat of the hotel shuttle. "May I help you with your luggage?"

"That would be wonderful. I'm here for the Shayne De Melo reservation."

The concierge's blue eyes brightened as he hefted her

suitcases onto a polished brass trolley. "We've been expecting you. They are on the rooftop. I will have your bags brought to your suite."

She thanked him as he pulled the door open, more polished brass, and Priya sashayed into the lobby, all white stone and marble. A quick elevator ride to the top and she swung out onto the terrace and was struck by the glorious view.

Mykonos spread like a white carpet toward a wall of sky and sea fused by a sun that set like a bleeding heart on its horizon. It was enough to bring tears to the eye, but the ringing of laughter pulled her around the corner where the Sisterhood stood all gathered. They made a gorgeous picture, surrounded by plush settees with sparkling lights draped overhead like a net of stars behind a thin layer of gossamer. Each of them matching in short chiffon dresses and Isobel at the center of it all in her vintage wedding dress. Even Shayne, who almost always preferred the comfort of pants, somehow managed to still look badass in cotton-candy pink, her midnight-blue hair swept up in a sassy do that was rocker chic.

The first to see Priya, Shayne thrust up her arms, a bottle of champagne in each hand. "Bitch!"

"Finally!" Caitlyn vaulted into Priya's arms. A five-foot missile of joy, and thankfully easy enough to catch. Her short lavender hair the perfect complement to her soft purple dress.

Hastily, Isobel mopped her face as Priya walked over to her, hand in hand with Caitlin, and scooped her into a hard, fast hug. "I didn't think you were going to make it in time."

"No way I'd miss the Sisterversary."

Eshe, a vision in mint, kissed her firmly on the lips. "You look fabulous, as always."

"It's the shoes." Priya kicked up a heel of her spiked red Louboutins. "So, what did I miss?"

"So far just these videos Caitlin found of your client. They're epic." Pulling out her phone, Shayne opened the app to a video of Genie dressed in full burlesque plumage wiggling to music.

"Oh no. Genie's found TikTok." Priya pinched the bridge of her nose like the bereft parent of a sprouting teen. "I can't."

"Hey, leave my adopted grandmother alone." Caitlin swatted Priya's arm. "She's precious—and those transitions were fire."

"Her username is GenieFromTheBlock." Eshe giggled. "She even did a duet video with JLo!"

"Ah," Shayne pressed a hand to her heart, "my second wife."

"Who's your first?"

"Priya's mom." Shayne wiggled her brows at Caitlin. "If she ever decides to divorce her husband I'll swoop in and make an honest woman of her."

Isobel touched the pendant dangling from a gold chain around Priya's throat. "This is new. I don't think I've ever seen you wear jewelry."

Priya's cheeks warmed. "It was a gift."

"Anything to do with the bloke you stayed back in New York for?" Eshe arched a knowing brow.

"Not bloke, Panty Thief," Caitlyn corrected. "And if you saw the guy, you'd let him steal your knickers too. Throw them at him, even."

"Yeah, well, you can stop shipping us, Cait. He's gone. I pushed him away because it was easier than trusting him. I was such a coward."

"Don't say that." Isobel gasped. "You're literally the *strongest* of us."

"Hey!" Shayne feigned disgust and flexed her biceps. "I disagree, respectfully."

"Respectfully, I think Isobel earned that title." Priya winked. "The video Caitlin sent me of the showdown with Kyle more than proves that."

"Well, I had you all to thank for making me realize how naïve I was." Isobel sighed into Shayne's embrace and squeezed Priya's offered hand. "All I could see was Kyle's potential. I thought if I loved him hard enough, deep enough, that he would do the same. That he would protect my heart the way I protected his."

"There's no guarantee in love. Good guy or fuckboy, doesn't matter—both will destroy you if they're the wrong one for you. That's it."

Eshe toasted Caitlin. "Well said."

"I thought so."

"So, what happened?" Isobel swept a hand over Priya's back. "Did you fix it?"

"I tried."

Just do it. Genie's words had hounded Priya like a skipped record and, after making it nearly to the airport, she'd ordered the cab to swing back around to Hadrian's apartment and pounded the door. Nearly smashed her fist into Hadrian's face when it opened.

He stood there for a beat, stock still. Blinking at her like she was an apparition before she launched into his arms. All mouth and purpose.

"I'm sorry," she whispered against his lips. "I'm so sorry."

His body stiffened with shock, softened with acceptance, and then his mouth gave back—oh, did it give back. She'd almost wept with relief.

"Hey." He stroked his thumb against her cheek, taking her in. "Aren't you supposed to be halfway to Mykonos by now?"

"I changed my flight. I leave in the morning."

His brow furrowed. "Why?"

"Let's just say I had a wake-up call." She sighed. "I was stupid." Priya eased back so she could meet his gaze. "I was a coward. You were right when you said I felt something I wasn't ready to explore, and I let it freak me out. If you hate me . . ."

"Jesus, Priya, for someone so brilliant you can be infuriatingly dense." Hadrian dragged a hand over his face with a resigned laugh. "I could never hate you. Yes, I was hurt, mostly my pride, but once my head cooled, I was relieved."

"Relieved?" she echoed.

"Yeah. You were right. My father's gone, and I can't keep living in his shadow or memory." Shutting the door behind her, Hadrian brushed a hand over the back of his neck. "So I've decided to take Marai's offer and go back to London. It's the UK. Not Mars," he added when he caught her disappointed wince.

"But it's so far."

His grin flashed. "Aren't your sisters scattered all over the globe?"

Now she smiled too. Damn him. "It's not too late, you know." Her fingers curled into his shirt, drawing him closer. "I can talk to Marai. I can fix this so you can stay."

"No. I need to carve out my own truth, whatever that may be, and this allows me the opportunity to forge my own path."

He cupped her cheek, releasing a heavy breath. "And you need time to figure out what's really in your heart without me nipping at your heels like a lovesick puppy."

She wanted to argue with him, to disagree, but something in her lifted. Eased. He wasn't wrong. As infuriating as it was to admit, Hadrian rarely was, and the truth was she wasn't ready. Not really. Not with the whole of her heart, and he deserved nothing less than complete certainty.

"I'm glad you came by, though. I have something for you. I was going to leave it at the office for you but . . . wait here." Hadrian left her standing in the foyer and returned a few moments later holding a small leather box trimmed in gold.

Priya accepted it with stiff fingers. "What's this?"

"You'll have to open it to find out."

Tears blistered the back of her throat and eyes. "I don't deserve this."

"It's a gift, not an engagement ring," he said, amusement gilding his voice. This was the Hadrian she'd always known. Handsome as sin and brimming with playful mischief. "Open it, Priya."

Bottom lip wedged between her teeth, she cracked open the top of the box and her breath caught in both grief and fascination. Nestled inside was a small golden arrow strung on a slender chain. It was simple, honest, and perfect.

"The night we first met, you told me that life is about risk and chance, without it there can be no reward," he said as the pendant settled against her fingers and the gold caught the light. "Let this stand as a reminder of those words, and of me. Be the arrow, shot from the bow, swift and powerful. Be bold. Be fearless, Priya. Always be fearless."

Her eyes fluttered shut, tears catching in the web of her lashes and pooling there as his hand cupped her chin, angling her face toward him so he could press a kiss to her lips, but didn't linger.

They'd parted ways without tears or bitterness at least, but Priya's heart was still a long way from steady. Maybe it would never be the same again now that Hadrian had touched it. Feeling for him scored deep like a brand that ached inside of her, but in a beautiful way.

"Oh, Priya." Isobel sighed. "I fell out of love, and you fell into it. Who would've thought?"

"Certainly not me." Priya laughed. "It was not part of the plan, that's for sure."

"Well, it might not be what we expected, or planned for, but I think we're definitely where we're meant to be." Isobel squeezed her hand. "It's a new start for both of us."

"Speaking of new starts, another reason why I'm late." Fumbling through her clutch, Priya withdrew an envelope. "It's a check. When I told Marai what you'd done to help my case, she decided to intercede on your father's settlement. Free of charge."

Isobel's eyes rounded in awe and went weepy at the sight of all the zeros. It wasn't enough for her to quit her job, but it would be enough to let her breathe with relief. "I don't know how to thank you."

"Yes! Now we can finally get this party started." Shayne poured out the champagne and handed a bubbling flute to each of them.

"To my sisters." Isobel raised her glass, voice wavering with emotion. "Here's to success, to sisterhood, and to whatever else the future may hold. Ten years of friendship has shown us we're strongest together. We've always been stronger together, and as long as I have you guys, I know I can do anything."

"Damn straight," Caitlin whispered, her own eyes shining. "Because we're more than friends by chance, we're sisters by choice."

"Here, here." Shayne thrust up a near empty bottle, then chugged down the rest.

"In the words of the brilliant Laurel Thatcher Ulrich," Priya toasted, "if well-behaved women seldom make history, I think it's time we start misbehaving."

Eshe tapped her glass to Priya's. "I'll drink again to that."

"I think we all should," Isobel agreed, resting her head on Priya's shoulder.

Shayne hooked her arm around Isobel's waist, and together they gazed out at the dazzling horizon of sea and sun. Drawing upon each other for love, strength, and sisterhood.

If this summer had taught Priya anything, it was that life didn't always go according to plan, but no matter what happened, whatever hurdles and obstacles were thrown their way, Priya was not afraid because she wasn't alone.

They had each other. Always.

THE END

Acknowledgments

This book was the one that nearly broke me.

Rewriting an entire novel after a devastating heartbreak, during the stress of a global pandemic while working seventy-five-hour weeks, while also trying and feeling like I was utterly failing at being a single parent, had me questioning my capabilities and sanity a hundred times over.

Suffice it to say, if it takes a village to raise a child, then it certainly takes a Sisterhood to birth a novel, especially amidst such chaos. And I would not be where I am today without the many talented, fierce, supportive women I am so blessed to call not only friends but family.

First, my Wattpad4 ladies, Leah Crichton, Rebecca Sky, Monica Sanz, Erin Latimer, and Lindsey Summers—where do I begin? You ladies plucked me out of the Wattpad trenches, dusted me off, and gave me so much support, community, guidance, and love. From Leah's selfless support as I pushed onward in So You Think You Can Write to Rebecca offering endless words of wisdom as I navigated the publishing wheel and struggled not to rip my hair out. I would be utterly lost without each of you.

The rest of my Wattpad family: Angelina Lopez, Kimberly Vale, Isabelle Ronin, Ellie Pindiola, Tammy Oja,

Jordan Lynde, Kristi McManus, to name a few, as well as the OG Wattpad HQ team: Caitlyn, I-Yana, Ashleigh, Aron, and of course Zoe (who found me on Twitter at RWA and changed the entire trajectory of my career over a glass of wine). Kevin Fanning: I remember sitting down with you for my first panel for FanExpo and being so starstruck by you, thinking, *How the heck am I even worthy to sit next to someone like him?* You're literally the reason why I'm obsessed with emojis and a secret Kim K fangirl LOL. You have my entire heart and I am so blessed to call you a dear friend who has always spoken wonders about me in every room you've set foot in.

The literal embodiment of Sisterhood, Anna Todd, I am forever floored by your generosity of self and spirit. Words cannot express how grateful I was that you took the time to share guidance, wisdom, and even offered connections within the industry to help bring my dream to fruition when I was literally the smallest fish in a vast sea. You are and forever will be someone I admire and respect with my whole heart. You absolutely deserve the world.

My Toronto and Twitter writing crew: June Hur, Elora, Maggie, Liselle Sambury, Deborah F. Savoy, Kelly Powell, Sasha and Serena Nanua, Kay Costales, Joanna Hathaway, Claribel Ortega, Tina Chan, Farah Heron, Ayana Gray, J. Elle, Ciannon Smart, Molly Chang, Wendy Heard, Akure Phoenix. My Dragon Hatchlings: Briston Brooks, Tiffany Elmer, Zabe Ellor, and anyone else I may be regretfully forgetting to name, you are all the very best CPs and writer friends I could ever ask for and so breathtakingly talented.

I am inspired by each of you.

Meredith Ireland: Thank you for being my strength when

I truly didn't think I could crawl another inch toward my deadline, and for allowing me a safe space to pour out my heart without judgment or criticism while also pushing me to pick myself up and get back to the grind. In true *Stiletto Sisterhood* fashion, even though I wanted to give up, many, many times, you refused to let me fail.

Of course, I cannot forget Saadia Naseer, for being the first person I ever felt safe enough with to share my work. You were my first devoted fan and pushed me to write for more than myself and gave me the hope that one day I could be an author. Nor can I forget my rockstar agent, Jim McCarthy. Even though we haven't worked on this book together, we've gone through the gamut together on others and I cannot tell you how much it means to me to have you as my champion as I forge through this journey. Thank you for your unwavering belief in me and my books. I can't wait to see what accomplishments lie ahead for us in the future.

And, saving the best for last, my real-life Sisterhood: Jenelle DeGuzman, Gaby and Daniella Menjivar, Juanita and Dariana, Jacqueline, Dana, Elizabeth Benitez, Caylin, and Moena—I am blessed to be surrounded by such remarkable, empowering, confident, accomplished, and inspiring women. Each of you has seen me through various stages of my life as I've grown, matured, and evolved into who I am today, but what I've grown into and accomplished would not be possible without each and every single one of you. Thank you for showing me the true meaning of friendship and family.

Finally, behind all strong women are the men who, for good or ill, forged her:

To Yunier, for showing me everything love is not supposed

to be, and shattering my heart. Your careless arrogance became the brutal catalyst for my greatest evolution. How could I not be thankful to be free of you?

To my "Hideo" (who shall remain a mystery lol)—thank you for the escape of memories and moments that opened my heart and healed my soul. For being everything I needed at a time when I needed it most, even if you didn't know it. You were the fire that forged me anew when I feared I would linger forever broken in a ruin of ash.

To Gary Reid, for being the one who truly believed I was a force to reckon with and whose unwavering assurance gave me the confidence for my inner Wonder Woman to emerge. Who never stopped believing in me even to this day. Because of you, I found the confidence to set out to conquer the world, to pursue my greatest dreams. Time will tell if I live up to your estimation of my capabilities.

Endlessly grateful for you.

About the Author

Fallon DeMornay is a YA fantasy and adult contemporary author known for writing powerful girls smashing the patriarchy. Through Wattpad, Fallon has worked with H&M, Pandora, and Warner Bros. She was a top ten finalist in Harlequin's So You Think You Can Write contest and has been featured in *Cosmopolitan*'s online magazine. Affectionately referred to as Wonder Woman by her own real-life Sisterhood, she can be found tearing up the dance floor to salsa or bachata when she's not writing. Fallon lives in Toronto, Ontario.

Turn the page to read a preview of

Available June 2022
wherever books are sold

1

A burst of adrenaline pulsed through Jada's veins, the sensation familiar but unwelcome. She exhaled shakily, secretly resenting that no matter how many auditions she'd been on, her nerves kicked in every time. Five years into her career, she had perfected her routine: 1) practice relentlessly beforehand, 2) arrive early and flawlessly dressed, and 3) jam out hard core to "Lose Yourself" by Eminem for some kickass motivation while she waited for her turn. Yet, Slim Shady's rapid lyricism could only do so much. Once Jada left the relative comfort of the waiting area to step into the casting room, she always froze up.

Now, as she faced the stern casting director, a lump formed in her throat. Alongside the casting director, the showrunner for *Deadly Intentions* also stared at Jada, although her expression was friendlier. The whole reason why Jada had been excited to audition for this production was because the creator, Jackie Fox, had a history of putting rising stars on the map. Snagging an audition to play the lead on her newest show had been a dream come true—one that Jada was about to royally mess up. Forcing herself to snap out of her BS, Jada flashed them a confident smile.

"Hello, how are you guys? My name is Jada Berklee. I'm twenty-four. I'm really happy to be auditioning for the role of Monica today."

The team returned her greetings and ended with the typical ready when you are spiel. Arriving at the moment of truth, Jada put aside her anxiety and allowed herself to get lost in the character: her motivations, emotional conflicts, everything that played into the makeup of the street-smart detective. After they asked her to try a few more run-throughs, Jada's optimism returned. Everyone knows you don't ask for seconds unless you like what's being served on the table.

"Thank you, Jada. That was lovely," Jackie acknowledged after several takes. However, her razor-sharp eyes flicked over Jada's appearance. Based on her rule to always be flawlessly dressed, Jada assumed she was taking stock of what Jada might look like in character.

"One last question, dear. Do you usually wear your hair this short?"

Reflexively, Jada lifted her fingers, tracing the short edges of her red curls.

"Oh, well, I currently have a supporting role in Ren Kurosawa's latest film, *Love Locket*. It's a rom-com. They had a particular look they wanted for my character."

"I see. How long does it typically take for your hair to grow out?" Jackie asked innocently enough, but Jada saw the writing on the wall.

Unless she could get her curly locks bone straight and as long as Gabrielle Union's, she could kiss this role good-bye. She fought back the urge to explain the intricacies of growing out Black hair, replying with a vague "Not that long."

"Ah, I see." Jackie's courteous smile remained cemented in place, more like a bad FaceTime freeze-frame than sincere understanding. Of course Jada's answer hadn't made the cut. With an offhand "We'll let you know," they escorted her ass out the door.

Refusing to give in to the brush off, Jada kept her head held high as she exited the building and made her way to her car. But once she slipped into the driver's seat, she rested her head on the steering wheel, a sense of defeat washing over her. To be fair, she could be overanalyzing. Yet she knew those backhanded comments and questions too well. The last time someone had made that kind of remark, the role that had been advertised for a woman of color had gone to a white woman.

"Whatever. There will be other roles, other jobs," Jada said, determined to give herself a pep talk in her rearview mirror. "Perk up, Berklee!"

Before said perking up could kick in, Jada's phone buzzed in her pocket. Her cousin, Mikayla, had sent her a text through the group chat with their other BFF, Alia. Jada had grown up next door to Mikayla back in Chicago and had met Alia when she got her first big acting job in LA. Back then, Jada had a supporting role on the popular fantasy show *Fallen Creatures*—with vampires and werewolves *galore!*—and Alia had been one of the staff writers. Alia became a close friend who even helped Jada and Mikayla find the apartment they currently lived in—right across the hall from Alia. The trio had become tight knit and their group chat was a daily texting must.

Mikayla: Hope the audition went well! <3

Alia: Ohhh, same. Sending well wishes from set.

Where we are currently drowning in demon blood
by the way

Picturing the poised Alia covered in sticky, fake blood
definitely led to a much-needed chuckle. Alia's star had continued
to skyrocket after *Fallen Creatures* ended. She was now the
showrunner of her own supernatural series, *Unbound*.

It was good. Fingers crossed! Jada typed back, deciding not
to bore them with the racial microaggressions she'd experienced.

Mikayla: In that case . . . I thought you might want a
heads-up on this . . .

Along with the ominous text, Mikayla sent a link to Jada's
least favorite site. *Sip That Tea* had gone from a small, superficial
blog to a digital kingpin of celeb gossip. The site's founders, social
media influencers and fraternal twins Tegan and Tammy Downton,
came from old-school, old-Hollywood money, which apparently
meant they could spend all their free time and connections
hounding and exposing everyone in the entertainment industry.
Luckily, Jada wasn't high enough on the A-list to make it into
their headlines often. Her ex-boyfriend, however, had his face
plastered on the front page.

DANIEL KANE SPOTTED WITH
YOUNG SONGSTRESS

Sip this, Tea Fam! If you were wondering what
our resident *Fallen* hottie has been up to, here's the
scoop. The luscious Daniel Kane has just gotten back
from filming a period drama in Germany. Aside from
learning the country's mother tongue, he's also been
snogging their hottest idol, Tilly Becker.

The German singer recently turned nineteen, but

the six-year age gap can't stop young love! After being spotted all around Munich, Daniel brought the European beauty with him on his return flight. We're looking forward to seeing more of these two! What about you? Will they crash and burn like Daniel's past conquests or stay #relationshipgoals?

As she finished the article, a sour feeling hit Jada's stomach. Reading it brought back awful memories, but seeing Daniel's smug smirk and the redhead clinging shrink-wrap tight to his arm made it worse. The young singer was staring up at him with complete, oblivious adoration. Jada had been like that once—a lovestruck fool—until Daniel's true nature had revealed itself. Because the one thing *Sip That Tea* had gotten right was that *all* of Daniel's "past conquests" *had* ended up burned. Jada was no exception.

Alia's incoming response snapped Jada out of her sullen reverie. Her bestie had the perfect comeback to the news.

Alia: Way to kill the mood, Mikayla :(

Mikayla: I just thought she should know!

Jada: Thanks, but all this means is I need a serious chocolate overload when I get home

Mikayla: Making brownies NOW to go with our rocky road supply!

Alia: SAVE ME SOME. I get off at eight

With the promise of brownie sundaes, Jada shook off her crappy day and headed home. Even if she didn't have a starring role or a trustworthy boyfriend, she had her girls and a reliable sugar rush waiting for her.

***

The drive from her audition in Burbank to her Culver City apartment stretched by at its usual traffic-jammed pace. But when she stepped through the front door, the rich smell of double fudge brownies made up for it. Like a bloodhound, Jada picked up the scent and made her way to the kitchen. Thanks to Mikayla's artistic flair, their apartment was decked out in vibrant colors and way too much pop-culture memorabilia. Of particular note were Mikayla's beloved superhero Funko POP bobbleheads on the mantel and the Dr. Frank-N-Furter cutout Mikayla insisted on keeping in the entryway. In her own words, *Anyone who can't handle Tim Curry being iconic doesn't belong in this house.* Either way, the eclectic style paired with the more sophisticated hardwood floors and marble fixtures all screamed home to Jada.

Pausing in the kitchen's doorway, Jada took in Mikayla standing at the stove, her Gordon Ramsay apron splattered with chocolate batter. Her colorful purple braids had been pulled back in a bun to keep them out of the way of her baking frenzy, and the end product looked deliciously unscathed.

"Perfect timing." Mikayla beamed at her. Even with her fashionable hair and glowing mahogany skin, Mikayla's smile was still her best feature. Her cousin's exuberance lit up the room, immediately easing some of Jada's tension.

"Damn straight," Jada said, sinking into the high-backed stool at the kitchen island. She tapped one of the ceramic bowls Mikayla had laid out. "Sundae me. Stat."

Mikayla gave her an admonishing look as she pulled the rocky road ice-cream carton from the freezer. "I knew the audition didn't go as well as you claimed."

"Unless you're psychic, I don't see how." Jada avoided her

cousin's eyes as she cut a sizable brownie to dump in the bottom of her bowl. Truthfully, she shouldn't have been surprised by the astute observation. When you'd grown up joined at the hip like they had, it was hard to hide anything. Mikayla was more like a nosy little sister than her cousin. The kind who would dig around in your room looking to borrow your clothes but then ended up reading your diary.

"While I am highly spiritually attuned, it's not that. You may be an awesome actress, Jada, but you have a shitty poker face. Even your text persona radiates sweaty guilt when you tell a white lie."

"Texts don't sweat." Jada corrected her as she dug into the ice cream. "And whatever. There will be other auditions. I should be focusing on *Love Locket* anyway. How's that been going?"

While Jackie Fox may not have been a fan of Jada's hairstyle for her upcoming role, it did epitomize her character, Lana, the quirky best friend and budding scientist. Filming didn't start for her character for a few more days, but Mikayla had managed to snag a costume production assistant job on the film. Well, with Jada's help. Ren had been open to hiring Mikayla since they needed someone on short notice. But at Mikayla's own conflicted expression, Jada's stomach dropped.

"What happened?" she demanded.

"Nothing! Nothing that bad. It's just . . . I don't think Ren likes me very much. I feel like he watches me like a hawk. More than Val, my actual boss. He caught me talking during a take yesterday."

"Mikayla!"

"It's not a big deal! He corrected me, and now it's over. I didn't bring it up because I knew you were focused on your own stuff."

"Still, you need to get along with everyone on set. This whole industry is about building connections."

Jada frequently wavered between being impressed by Mikayla's fearlessness and being horrified by her cousin's *c'est la vie* attitude. It was one thing to switch from graduating from the Pratt Institute with an art degree to trying her hand at costume design (a move in line with Mikayla's standard risk taking). It was another situation entirely to blow your first big job because of unprofessionalism, a.k.a. the scary, short-sighted side Jada could do without.

"Seriously, it turned out okay," Mikayla went on. "Tristan stood up for me, actually."

Jada shook her head at Mikayla's adoring smile. Tristan Maxwell was the star of the movie, alongside his leading lady, Angela Collins. While he was a great actor, who got his start as a teenager on the popular family comedy *Garcia Central*, Jada doubted he was as chivalrous as Mikayla's retellings of him. Like Daniel, Tristan had been the subject of several *Sip That Tea* articles regarding his infamous dating exploits. The twenty-six-year-old Colombian heartthrob picked up and dropped different women like he changed socks. Models, heiresses, even a real-life duchess, it didn't matter. They were all expendable. With his stunning blue eyes, tousled black hair and broad shoulders, Jada could see how so many women fell into the trap of his charm and good looks. She only hoped his dating habits were the extent of the man's downsides. She'd hate to work with the guy and find out he was secretly a cannibal or a cult leader. Honestly, the dark side of Hollywood was scary as fuck sometimes.

There were only two more days until she'd start her new role and meet the allegedly heroic Tristan Maxwell up close. She couldn't wait to discover if he was as talented as everyone claimed or just lucky due to growing up as one of Hollywood's beloved childhood stars. Not that she would ever admit that to Mikayla. Giving her cousin a coy smile, Jada kept the small flurry of nervous excitement to herself.

"I guess I'll see for myself soon.